WANTON ANGEL

Pulling her flush against him, Kit ran one hand up Angel's back, his fingers tunneling through the heavy mass of her hair. "I want to make it good for you," he said, his tongue tracing the outline of her lips. "I want you to tell me what pleases you." He pulled her bottom lip into his mouth, nibbling and suckling until she squirmed against him.

Lifting his head, he stared down into her flushed face. "Did you like that?"

Dazed, she managed a small nod.

"Then you must tell me when I do other things you like," he said, lowering his head to her throat. He kissed his way over the soft skin, up to her ear, then across her cheek.

"Kiss me," she whispered in a raspy voice. "I like it when you kiss me."

"Now you're getting the hang of it," Kit whispered, settling his mouth over Angel's in a fierce kiss.

* * *

Advance praise for DANCER'S ANGEL:

"A delightful western romance."

—*Affaire de Coeur*

"A heart-stopping tale with loads of sensuality and a cast of riveting characters that radiate emotion from start to finish."

—*Rendezvous*

HOLLY HARTE

DANGER'S ANGEL

ZEBRA BOOKS
KENSINGTON PUBLISHING CORP.

ZEBRA BOOKS are published by

Kensington Publishing Corp.
850 Third Avenue
New York, NY 10022

Zebra and the Z logo Reg. U.S. Pat. & TM Off. The
Lovegram logo is a trademark of Kensington Publishing
Corp.

First Printing: September, 1996
10 9 8 7 6 5 4 3 2 1

Printed in the United States of America

Dedicated to three very important men in my life.
To Evan and John, thanks for believing in me.
And as always, to Vern, with all my love.

Chapter One

"Company in the parlor, girls." The husky voice of Ruby, the stout, bewigged madame who sported a fake beauty mark next to her painted mouth, drifted up the stairway to where Angelina Coleman stood on the second-floor landing.

Angelina sucked in a deep breath, hoping to ease her trepidation. This was the moment she'd been waiting for, the moment she'd tried to prepare for over the past week . . . the moment she dreaded. Could she really do this? Would she be able to go ahead with what she'd told James Murray, owner of the brothel he called the Murray House? Thank goodness neither he nor Ruby knew the truth. If they found out their newest girl wasn't as experienced as she'd allowed them to believe. . . . She shuddered. The idea of being auctioned off like a prize bull made her skin crawl.

Pushing those unsettling thoughts aside, Angelina rubbed her damp palms along the skirt of the dress she'd selected for the evening ahead.

Fashioned of rose-colored silk, the dress had a fitted waist, short sleeves, and a narrow skirt. Her only concession to the nature of the business at hand was a neckline dipping much lower than she would have preferred. Glancing down at how the gown revealed the upper swell of her breasts, she realized worrying about her exposed flesh was a waste of time. Her reputation had undoubtedly suffered one crippling blow as it was—and was about to endure a more damaging whack—so the cut of her dress didn't matter.

Releasing her held breath in a long sigh, Angelina wondered again at the unfortunate string of events leading up to her working in the Murray House.

She didn't regret her father's decision to leave Georgia. To help his ailing wife, Douglas Coleman had sold their home in January of '85 and a month later moved his family west. Sarah's physician suggested the warm, dry climate of southwest Texas might be beneficial to her failing health. It had been a real disappointment to arrive at the ranch Douglas had purchased sight unseen and find the buildings in sad need of repair, the land long neglected. But Angelina had never shied away from hard work. Raised in a household with a mother ill with consumption and a sister lame from a childhood fall, she'd never known a time when she hadn't worked. When she should have been out having fun with young people her own age, she was home cooking, sewing, or waxing furniture. She'd missed many of the social events while growing up in Savannah, but she wasn't bitter. She'd gladly worked to help her family, and had done so again on the run-down ranch, laboring next to her father while her sister Chloe looked after their mother.

Then six weeks after their arrival, a freak accident took Douglas Coleman's life, leaving Angelina solely in charge of her family. She might have been able to handle the added duties thrust upon her if the vice president of the El Paso Bank hadn't paid the Coleman ranch a visit just one day after her father had been laid to rest. If not for Elliot Wentworth, the mortgage papers bearing her father's signature, and Wentworth's suggestion on how the debt could be paid, Angelina would not be standing on the second floor of a Utah Street brothel about to—

"Are you all right?" Jenna whispered, pulling her from her musings.

Angelina shifted her gaze to the woman with hair the color of toffee, one of the two close friends she'd made since coming to the Murray House. Jenna's full bust swelled above the deep décolletage of her dress, the rest of her well-rounded figure filling out the dark lavender silk equally well. Seeing compassion reflected in her friend's hazel eyes, Angelina swallowed the sudden lump in her throat. "I don't rightly know. I thought I was, but now . . ." Unable to voice her fears, she turned to watch the rest of the brothel's stable of painted ladies move to the head of the stairway.

The first in line, Penny, a tall, leggy redhead who used Garnet as her *nom d'amour*, started down the stairs, moving in a slow, deliberate rhythm, each step accompanied by the exaggerated swinging of her hips. Though Garnet disappeared from view, Angelina could picture what was happening downstairs, having witnessed the arrival of the house prostitutes many times from her former place at the piano on the other side of the parlor.

Each *femme de joie* would descend the stairs, strutting and wiggling, every move carefully choreographed to make the men in the parlor crazy to pay for their time. At the foot of the staircase, each woman paused until Ruby announced her, then moved to mingle with the gentlemen clientele.

After Garnet was announced, Inez moved into position. A *chola*—mixed Spanish and Indian blood—with a tawny complexion and jet-black hair and eyes, Inez was known to her customers as Lucinda. Next was Sadie, working under the name Coral, a plump blonde with leaf-green eyes, deep dimples, and a full mouth.

Angelina knew a moment of panic. She thought she had prepared herself for what lay ahead. But now that her turn was fast approaching . . . a shiver racked her shoulders.

"You don't have to do this, Angelina."

Her gaze moved from the stairway back to Jenna's face. The heavy application of face powder, rouge, and lip paint on the young woman she had come to care about always took Angelina by surprise. The makeup made Jenna look older than her eighteen years, hiding the sprinkling of freckles across her nose and cheeks, camouflaging the youthful glow of her skin. Though Jenna was four years younger than her, Angelina was amazed at Jenna's maturity, at how much she knew about life.

Staring at her friend, Angelina managed a wistful smile. "I wish I could agree, but I can't. I have to do this. Mama and Chloe need me. You agreed if I continued working as the piano player, it would be years before I could pay off my contract. I had to find a faster way to pay Mr. Murray. I had to find a way to get out of here, so I can move back to the ranch." She drew a deep, shuddering breath. "You know that's why I made the decision I did, Jenna. There was no other choice."

Jenna stared at her for a long moment, then said, "I really wish you would reconsider. Though I've told you everything I can, I'm still not sure you're ready."

Angelina squeezed her eyes closed. What would happen later that evening couldn't be worse than the awful pawing, leering, and crude suggestions she'd endured during the past few months as the brothel piano player. Could it? Forcing herself not to dwell on the answer, she opened her eyes, then said, "Waiting will only postpone the inevitable."

"I suppose." Jenna started toward the stairs, then turned back. "Don't forget about the La Clydes."

Angelina felt the heat of a blush creep up her cheeks. She shouldn't be embarrassed after Jenna's lengthy instructions regarding the use of the white petrolatum, something she was told was an absolute necessity in a brothel. Yet she still found such subjects much too private to discuss as nonchalantly as one would discuss the weather. Realizing Jenna was waiting for a response, she finally said, "No, I won't. You'd best get downstairs. Ruby will be fit to be tied if she has to come up here after y'all." Before Jenna could turn around, Angelina impulsively gave her a hug. "Thanks for your help."

Returning the hug, Jenna dropped her arms, then took a step back. "As soon as I start down that stairway, I become Topaz. Remember?"

"Yes, I remember." *And I'll be Angel.* Angelina shivered at the name the men in the brothel parlor had given her. She definitely didn't feel like an angel—not with what she was about to do. But as she'd just told Jenna, she had no choice. She had taken on the responsibility of paying off Papa's debt on the ranch, staunchly refusing to let her mother and sister lose their home. She would do what had to be done.

Squaring her shoulders and lifting her chin, she moved to the head of the stairs. She heard Ruby shout, "Gentlemen, for your pleasure, please greet the lovely Topaz," then the hoots and hollers of the men in the parlor. After whispering a quick prayer for the strength to get through the evening, Angelina summoned the cold veneer she wore while downstairs, then lowered one high-heeled foot onto the first step.

Kit Dancer shifted in his chair near the bottom of the staircase, his body taut with anticipation. Not long after his return to El Paso four months earlier, he'd started hearing the stories being circulated about the woman who would soon be making her entrance into the parlor of the Murray House.

At first Kit hadn't paid much attention to talk of the piano player at Murray's called the Ice Angel. He already had a woman on his mind—another employee of a house of ill-repute, a prostitute he called Red. As soon as he returned to El Paso, he'd headed for the brothel where he'd last enjoyed Red's company. Turned out he made the long trip from Galveston for nothing. Red had been moved to another city on the circuit of French-owned *maisons de joie* soon after he'd left town. Her moving on was probably just as well. He'd never intended to spend more than a couple of nights in her bed anyway.

The voice of the madame shouting for quiet jerked Kit back to the present. As each of the painted and perfumed doves wiggled her way between the tables, greeting the customers with a smile or a wink, he watched impassively. Once again he wondered why he remained in El Paso. He had no ties to the town, no reason to stay. Hell, he even knew Red would probably never return. Still he stayed, occasionally taking a job helping the city marshal collect taxes so he wouldn't have to use the money he'd salted away. For the first time in his thirty years, his life was at loose ends. He'd given up bounty hunting after the fiasco of his last job, and he sure as hell had no desire to pin a badge on his chest again. So, there he was in El Paso, sitting in the parlor of a brothel—one much more lavishly appointed than he was used to—with no definite plans for his future.

A hush fell over the crowded parlor. Whispers of "Here comes Angel" drew Kit's gaze back to the stairs. He straightened in his chair, his pulse increasing at the prospect of seeing the woman who'd caused such a stir: the former piano player whose rare smiles and cold-as-ice appearance had prompted the men in town to call her the Ice Angel. Talk about the woman hadn't piqued his interest until he heard she had reverted to her former profession, trading her piano stool for a bed in the brothel. Now that she was his kind of woman—no commitments, no words of love, just a plain and simple business deal for uncomplicated, mutually enjoyable sex—he'd decided he should see this Ice Angel for himself.

Forcing himself to relax, he eased back in his chair, watching the woman descend the stairs, his eyes shadowed by the brim of his hat. Though she was slimmer than the others, the rumors of Angel's beauty hadn't been exaggerated. Flawless skin, the color of rich cream, large heavily lashed eyes outlined with kohl, a full pouty mouth painted a dark red, and deep brown hair parted in the center and pulled into a simple, yet elegant knot at her nape combined to make her the epitome of every man's dream. Yet most notable to Kit was the lack of emotion on her lovely features. No happiness. No anger. Nothing.

She reached the floor of the parlor, then paused, hands clasped in front of her, eyes downcast. Ruby waited several seconds, letting the anticipation build before she said in a booming voice, "Gentlemen, may I present the final Murray House lovely. Angel."

When Angel remained at the foot of the staircase, Kit's brow furrowed at her stiff posture, the tightness of her clenched hands. Then a brief word from the madame brought her head up with a snap. As Angel started past his table, she turned to look in his direction. For a moment he looked directly into eyes the color of a fine aged whiskey. What he saw came as a shock.

What appeared to be resignation coupled with a deep-as-the-bone sadness filled her eyes. His fascination increased. Staring deeper into her gaze, he detected something else. A fire burned deep within this beauty, a fire held at bay by some unknown force, a fire he instinctively knew would burn hotter than any he had ever experienced. Just thinking about being the one to ignite that blaze sent a sizzling stab of desire to his groin.

This woman displaying an unemotional, controlled coolness, whose eyes spoke not only of incredible sadness but of extraordinary fire as well, intrigued him far more than any woman he'd ever known. For a reason he didn't understand, a reason that went beyond physical desire, he had the overwhelming need to find out what went on behind those sad, golden-brown eyes.

Kit exhaled slowly, willing his heart rate to slow to normal. He pushed his chair away from the table, then got to his feet. Approaching the crowd of men vying for Angel's attention, he elbowed his way to the front, ignoring the curses and howls of protest. Finally, the vision in rose silk stood before him, her spine ramrod-stiff, her gaze moving warily over her admirers.

"Evenin', Angel. Can I buy you a drink?"

Angelina started at the soft, masculine voice. She shifted her gaze from the horde of disgruntled men stubbornly holding their ground to the man standing beside her. Noting how the well-defined muscles of his chest, arms, and legs filled out his black attire, she held her breath while lifting her gaze. Unable to make out his features beneath the shadow of his hat brim, she felt a momentary stab of disappointment.

She exhaled, then said, "I don't imbibe." Realizing her words had sounded rude when the man dressed entirely in black had done nothing to deserve such behavior, she added, "Just because I don't partake of spirits doesn't mean y'all can't enjoy a glass of your favorite libation. I'd be happy to keep you company, Mistuh . . . ?"

Her soft southern drawl washed over him, sending his pulse into another fast cadence. Clearing his throat, he replied, "Dancer. Kittridge Dancer. But please call me Kit."

After a moment, she said, "All right, Kit."

Glancing over his shoulder, he said, "Okay, fellas, the lady's with me. Better luck next time."

The men gave a collective sigh of defeat, then moved off to find another form of entertainment.

Kit grasped Angel's elbow, then escorted her to the shadowed end of the small bar across the room. He asked for a whiskey, then turned to his companion. "That's definitely not a Texas drawl. Where are you from?"

He watched a small flicker of pain flash across her features before she said, "I'm originally from Savannah."

"Savannah. That's a long ways from west Texas. You been working the circuit of brothels?"

Her back stiffened. Forcing herself to swallow the retort on the tip of her tongue, she said, "No, I have not."

"So what brought you to El Paso?"

"It's a long story," she said in a low voice.

"I got plenty of time," Kit replied, surprised he hadn't given up his notion of finding out what went on beneath the icy facade and hustled her upstairs to ease the intense ache in his groin. Though he was strongly attracted to Angel physically, for the first time in a very long while, he looked forward to sharing a conversation with a woman. There would be time enough later for sharing pleasures of the flesh.

Angelina stared up at the man's shadowed face, wishing she could see more than the deeply tanned skin of his square jaw. He seemed sincere, yet she knew men who frequented the Murray House did so for only one reason: to relieve their physical urges. So what was she supposed to do now? How could she pay off her contract if all this man wanted to do was talk? Still, talk would be infinitely preferable to . . . . She repressed a shudder. But could she tell this man how she'd ended up working in an El Paso brothel?

The touch of his hand on her forearm jarred Angelina from her thoughts. As his long, blunt-tipped fingers trailed up her arm, she shivered. An unfamiliar warmth swept through her body, settling low in her belly. Swallowing hard, she said, "I'm afraid y'all might find the story of my life on the boring side."

"I wouldn't be bored, Angel. Nothin' about you could ever—"

A loud crash behind them cut off Kit's words. Turning toward the sound, he saw one of the tables had been overturned. The men responsible were squared off, knees bent, feet spread, clenched fists raised. Several more of the customers jumped to their feet, eager to join the fray.

"Damn," Kit muttered under his breath. He managed to pull Angel to the side of the room before all hell broke loose in the parlor. More tables were overturned, chairs went flying, followed by a body catapulted by a vicious blow from an angry fist.

Ruby shouted for the fighting to stop, but if the men heard, they paid her no heed. Her painted mouth pinched with annoyance, she skirted the room, then shoved through the front door. Lifting the police whistle—identical to the one each brothel madame had been issued—she drew a deep breath, then blew with all her might.

A shrill sound rent the air. Still the combatants did not slow their punches. When Ruby came back inside, she motioned for each of her girls to move the kerosene lamps. Fire was a constant threat in a town as hot and dry as El Paso, and making sure anything that could start a blaze was kept out of harm's way was always a priority.

Angel reached for the lamp nearest her and quickly turned down the wick. A thin trail of smoke swirled up the glass chimney, then drifted into the room in a tiny black cloud.

"You'd better get upstairs, Angel," Kit said, leaning close to her ear, "before you get hurt. Ruby's whistle will bring the law in no time."

Shifting her wide-eyed gaze from the lantern she held, she nodded. He stared down into her golden-brown eyes, expecting to find fear or disappointment reflected in their depths. Instead he saw what looked like relief. Surely she wasn't relieved her evening had ended without—The arrival of a half-dozen El Paso lawmen halted his musings.

As he was ushered out of the Murray House with the rest of

the patrons, Kit was already looking forward to the following night. Now that he'd seen the Ice Angel for himself, he was intrigued. He also knew she had been given an incorrect nickname. Though an Angel she might be, he knew without question she was definitely not made of ice. Angel needed a man to ease the sadness in her eyes, to break through the icy facade she insisted on presenting. Most of all, she needed someone to set her inner fire ablaze.

Kit figured he was just the man for the job.

Chapter Two

Kit brushed the dust off his black trousers, then adjusted the silk bandana tied at his throat. He couldn't remember ever having been this nervous at the prospect of seeing a woman. The day had dragged by, but it was finally time for the businesses on Utah Street to open their doors. One business in particular was of interest to Kit: the Murray House.

He waited for a few minutes, not wanting to appear too eager, then finally crossed the street and entered the adobe and wood building. The parlor looked much the same as when he'd arrived the night before, not like when he'd been ushered out after the police broke up the fight, with tables and chairs tipped over and shattered glass littering the floor. The only evidence of the previous night's excitement was the rearranged furniture, shifted to camouflage the removal of the damaged pieces. Nothing else in the elegant parlor looked like it had withstood a brawl.

Though other houses of ill-repute in El Paso were elegantly furnished, the Murray House went beyond sumptuous, bordering on the ostentatious. The parlor's Brussels carpet, velvet draperies, ornate crystal chandeliers, gilt-framed pictures, and marble-topped bar were much too showy for Kit's taste. The elaborate furnishings were a sharp contrast to his plain clothes, making him feel painfully out of place.

But he had a reason for visiting the fancy brothel again . . .

Angel. He'd been able to think of little else since meeting her the night before.

He selected the same table near the foot of the staircase and pulled out a chair. Just as he started to sit down, his attention was drawn across the room. A woman came through the door at the rear of the parlor, a large tray balanced against one hip. The corners of his mouth lifting, he straightened. As his gaze dropped to the woman's clothes, his smile vanished. The simple, high-necked calico dress and soiled apron had no place in a brothel parlor. He scowled. What the hell was going on?

His gaze glued to the knot of brown hair at the woman's nape, he made his way to the other side of the room.

"What are you doing, Angel?"

Angelina started, instantly recognizing the soft voice. She looked up from the tray she held, her brow crinkling at the harsh line of his mouth. "Lin-Shee, the cook, took sick this afternoon. Someone had to fix supper and make the hors d'oeuvres for tonight's customers. So, when Ruby couldn't find a replacement on such short notice, I volunteered."

Kit's eyebrows shot up. "She's letting a whore take over in the kitchen?"

Being called a whore, especially by a man who wasn't like the other brothel customers—at least Angelina had hoped he wasn't—hurt a great deal. She bit her lip against the pain, but didn't correct him. After all, wasn't that her plan? If not for the brawl last night and Lin-Shee's illness today, she would have already joined the ranks of the other soiled doves at the Murray House. Still, she couldn't ignore his comment completely. "For your information, Mr. Dancer, I'm a mighty fine cook."

Wondering at the pain in her eyes, he forced his voice into a lighter tone. "I like it better when you call me Kit." Reaching for the tray, he added, "Here, let me help you with that."

Grateful for his help, Angelina murmured her thanks, then relinquished the tray. When his fingers brushed over hers, her breath caught in her throat. Heart pounding against her ribs, cheeks warm with a flush, she looked up at Kit Dancer, wishing again she could see his face. Though a gentleman was supposed to remove his hat in the presence of a lady, he refused to follow the custom. Realizing his reason, she dropped her gaze. Not being considered a lady hurt more than she wanted to admit.

The lighthearted moment shattered, she turned toward the door. "Just put the tray on the bar, please. Y'all will have to excuse me. I have work to do." Lifting the hem of her skirt, she nearly ran from the parlor.

"Hey, wait a minute. Angel?" Kit stood there, tray still clutched in his hands, staring at an empty doorway. *Damnit, Angel, what are you afraid of?* In spite of the prospect of another evening without a female to ease the ache of desire, his spirits were surprisingly light. Though he wouldn't get a chance to sample what she had to offer, her working in the kitchen did have one satisfactory consolation: She would not be accessible to the other men patronizing the Murray House. Before he met Angel, he'd never given a second thought to sharing prostitutes with the other customers. Now the idea filled him with disgust.

Setting the tray on the bar, he turned toward the front door. No point in staying as long as Angel wasn't available. Leaving the Murray House, Kit wandered down Utah Street. He passed a number of other parlor houses, and although he considered going into one to find a replacement for Angel, he didn't.

He wanted only one woman, and he was willing to wait to have her.

As soon as Kit entered the bordello the next night he made some inquiries. He was pleased to learn the cook had recovered and was back at her job, and more importantly, Angel would be among those working as Murray House lovelies that evening.

When Angel came down the stairway, this time in a gown of peach satin and lace, Kit had to call on every bit of his willpower not to jump up and grab her. But as soon as she stepped away from the foot of the stairs, he shoved out of his chair and strode toward her, pushing aside anyone who tried to cut in front of him.

The other men's groans of protest only served to intensify Kit's purpose. Ignoring their pointed glares and hostile complaints, he reached his destination.

"You're looking mighty fine tonight, Angel," he murmured near her ear.

Though the bright smile she flashed up at him was definitely artificial and didn't begin to erase the sadness in her eyes, Kit still felt certain she was happy to see him.

"Why thank you, kind suh," she drawled, laying a hand on his forearm.

Kit sucked in a sharp breath at the lightning bolt of desire her touch sent racing through his body. He longed to pull her against his chest and taste her sweet mouth. Instead, he cupped her elbow with one hand and escorted her to the bar, leaving a half-dozen disappointed Angel enthusiasts in their wake. As he moved past the grumbling men, he heard one of them say, "Damnit, man, hurry up. We want a crack at her, too."

The irritation he felt at the man's words caught Kit off guard. He wasn't sure why an offhanded comment about a prostitute should bother him, but it did.

Forcing his mind away from any introspection, he said, "I need a drink before we—" He ran a fingertip down Angel's right cheek. "—move on to other things. Will you keep me company while I wet my whistle?"

Angelina swallowed, then nodded. Though she still dreaded what would happen to her that night, her anxiety was lessened by the possibility of the man standing next to her being her first customer. Of course, he didn't know she would be paying a much higher price than he for bedding her, and she certainly had no intention of telling him. He would find out soon enough.

"Something wrong, Angel?" His voice jerked her from her musings.

"No, I . . . um . . . I was just . . . . Never mind."

Kit eyed her for a minute, wondering at her distraction. Finally, he said, "Would you like something to drink? Maybe a sarsaparilla?"

"Yes, I believe I would."

Kit turned to the man behind the bar. "Barkeep, I'll take a whiskey and a sarsaparilla for my companion."

After getting their drinks, Kit led Angel to a table in the corner of the parlor. He pulled out a chair for her, then sat down in the one to her right.

Once they were settled, he said, "How do you like Texas?"

"It's hot and dusty."

Kit chuckled. "Ain't that the truth. I imagine it's pretty hot in Savannah."

"Yes, but there's always a breeze blowing in off the ocean. I reckon that makes the heat less noticeable."

"Reckon so," he replied, absently twirling his glass on the marble tabletop. Watching her lift her drink to her painted mouth, seeing the way her tongue peeked out to lick the moisture from her upper lip, a stab of red-hot lust sizzled through him. He shifted in his chair, trying to ease the sudden tightness beneath the fly of his trousers. Lifting his glass, he downed the last of the whiskey in one gulp. "Drink up, Angel, so I can see about taking you up to your room."

Angelina's gaze snapped to his shadowed face. Seeing the hard set to his jaw, the way his hands gripped the arms of the chair, she knew there was no point in trying to stall. She reached for her drink, praying her hand didn't shake. Just as she lifted the glass off the table, a loud popping noise stilled her hand in midair.

Her eyes wide, she said, "What was that?"

"Sounded like something upstairs exploded." Kit pushed his chair away from the table. "Don't move, I'll be—"

"Fire! Fire!" The shouts came from the second floor, followed by a partially clad Garnet racing down the stairs. "The lantern in my room exploded. The man with me, he was right next to the lamp when—" She drew a deep shuddering breath. "The kerosene sprayed all over him."

For a moment no one reacted. Then all at once, pandemonium broke loose. Women screeched in fright and scurried outside, chairs were shoved back and overturned as their occupants bolted from the parlor. Several customers, in various

states of undress, rushed downstairs and headed straight for the
door, followed by their scantily clad companions.

Over the din, Ruby yelled for someone to notify the fire department, then turned to the men still in the parlor. "Any of
you boys willing to try and get that man out of Garnet's room?"

A man across the room stepped forward. "Yeah, I'm willin'."

Kit rose from his chair. "Me, too."

"No!" Angel slammed her glass on the table, then jumped
to her feet. "Kit, you can't go up there." She grabbed his arm.
"Please, don't do it."

He smiled down at her, then peeled her fingers from his
shirtsleeve. "I'll be fine, Angel. Don't worry. The fire can't
have spread far." He loosened the knot of his bandana, pulled
it up over his mouth and nose, then retied it behind his head.
Handing his hat to Angel, he said, "Hang on to this for me.
Now, go outside with the others. I'll be along directly."

Gulping down her terror, she nodded. Kit's hat clutched
against her breasts, she followed the last of the employees out
the front door.

Kit and the other man who'd volunteered took the stairs two
at a time, following the smoke to the room where the fire
started. A man lay face-down in the doorway, his clothing
charred and smoldering.

Kneeling beside the man, Kit looked into the room. The
draperies, one entire wall, and the bed were fully engulfed in
flames. "We need something to wrap him in," he shouted over
the roar of the fire.

The second man nodded, then headed for one of the other
rooms. When he returned with a quilt, Kit had hauled the un-
conscious man out into the hall.

From the street, Angelina watched the yellowish-red glow
flickering behind the window of Garnet's room, her heart in her
throat. The wood and adobe of the house were bone-dry, perfect fuel for a hungry fire, an all-too-common occurrence in
town. Why would Kit risk his life to save a man who surely was
beyond help? Would he suffer the same fate, being swallowed

alive by the flames? She squeezed her eyes closed, unable to watch the fire envelop more of the building.

"Hey, here comes somebody!"

"It's a miracle anyone got out alive."

The shouts of two of the men gathered in the street to watch the fire brought Angelina's head up with a snap. Her gaze immediately sought the front door. A male form appeared in the doorway, but his small stature told her the man wasn't Kit. Swallowing hard to dislodge the lump of disappointment in her throat, she never took her gaze from the front of the Murray House. Finally another shape filled the doorway. This time it was Kit who stepped across the threshold and into the street, a bundle wrapped in what looked like a quilt slung over one shoulder.

Easing his burden onto the ground, Kit said, "He's alive. Barely." He coughed, trying to clear the smoke from his lungs. "Someone better get a doctor," he added in a raspy whisper.

"He's on his way," one of the men replied.

The hose carts of the fire department came rumbling down the street. The firemen hooked up the hoses and began pumping water onto the second story of the building. Kit watched through eyes blurred by smoke, his lungs still burning.

When he could breathe normally, he turned and moved through the crowd, searching every face. He finally spotted the one he sought and started toward her. Angel stood transfixed, one fist pressed against her mouth, the other curled around the brim of his hat.

He pulled the bandana off his face with one hand while reaching for his hat with the other. "Are you all right?" he asked in a gentle voice, prying her fingers from his hat brim.

For just a moment, Angelina got her first glimpse of his face. Illuminated by the fading glow of the fire, the heavy eyebrows, high cheekbones, and long narrow nose were visible for only an instant. Just before his features returned to the shadow cast by his hat brim, she was sure she'd also seen a scar on the right side of his face.

Compassion welled in her chest. What could have caused

such a scar, and was that why he always kept his hat pulled low
over his face? Did it still pain him? Was he—

"Angel?"

Jerked from her musings, she swallowed the questions she
wanted to ask, then said, "I'm fine. Now. I was so frightened
when you went up that staircase. But now that you're safe . . ."
She turned away, unable to finish the rest of her admission.

Kit wrapped one arm around her shoulders and pulled her
close. She shivered against him, not from a chill but from his
potent male scent—still detectable over the smell of smoke—
and being pressed against his muscular body. She longed to
wrap her arms around his waist and hold him tight, but she resisted the urge.

In less than fifteen minutes the El Paso fire department had
extinguished the blaze. Staring at the blackened walls of the
Murray House with the gaping hole where the fire started, Angelina wondered what would happen now.

She was unaware she had spoken her thoughts aloud, until
Kit said, "Do you need a place to stay? I have a room at a
boardinghouse across town. It isn't much, but you're welcome
to it."

"Thanks, that's mighty kind of y'all. But only a couple of the
Murray House employees live there. Lin-Shee lives in China-
town, and the rest of us have rooms in the building next-door."
She motioned toward a two-story clapboard house sitting farther back from the street just south of the brothel.

"Good thing the firemen stopped the fire before it spread,
otherwise you might be out of more than a place to work."

Angelina nodded against his chest. But what about working
to pay off her contract? Would she be forced to work in one of
the other businesses James Murray owned?

Someone calling her name roused her from her thoughts.
Angelina pushed herself out of Kit's embrace to find Jenna approaching them.

"Angel, Mr. Murray is here," Jenna said, pointing down the
street. "He wants to talk to all of us."

Realizing her questions were about to be answered, another shiver racked Angelina's shoulders.

"Do you want me to go with you?" Kit asked, rubbing a hand up and down her arm.

Lifting her chin, she stared up at him. His offer touched her deeply, but she knew she had to do this on her own. She shook her head, then started to pull away.

Kit tightened his grip. "Wait. Can I see you tomorrow?"

"Tomorrow? I . . . I don't know. With the fire and all, I don't know what—"

"How about in the morning? You'll be free then, won't you? We could take a walk down by the river."

"Well . . . Yes, I guess I could."

Angelina could see the white flash of teeth in his shadowed face.

"I'll pick you up at, say nine?"

"Fine. I'll meet you in the downstairs parlor. Now, please release me."

In spite of her snappish tone, Kit couldn't wipe the smile from his face. Bowing his head in acquiescence, he dropped his hand from her arm. Before she moved away, he bent to whisper, "Until tomorrow, my sweet Angel."

His softly spoken words sent a dusting of gooseflesh over her arms. Her throat so tight she was unable to speak, she nodded. Turning from the man who made her body react in the most disturbing ways, she headed to where the Murray House employees had gathered.

Kit watched her walk across the street, each gentle sway of her hips increasing the now-familiar ache in his groin, heating his blood even more. He drew a deep breath, then exhaled slowly.

Soon he would ease the ache and cool the fire in his veins. Soon he would kiss Angel's sweet mouth, caress her lovely breasts, sink into her welcoming body. Soon he would slake his lust while bringing them both incredible pleasure. He felt himself harden even more.

Being so obsessed with a woman was not familiar to Kit, and

something he was not comfortable with. So how did he go about putting an end to such an obsession?

Surely several healthy romps in Angel's bed would rid him of the fascination she held. A few times of tasting her charms and he would grow tired of her. But until that eventuality came, she would be his.

His smile broadened. Until then she would be Dancer's Angel.

Chapter Three

The following morning Kit rose before dawn. Since he'd bathed the night before to remove the stench of smoke and soot from the fire, he wiped a wet cloth over his face and upper body, then carefully shaved. Standing in front of the mirror which hung above the wash stand in his room, he stared at his reflection. He lifted one hand and ran a fingertip over the right side of his face.

The corners of his mouth turned down. Though the scar had faded with time, Kit still saw it much the same as the first time he'd seen the result of his wound . . . raw, repulsive, certainly nothing a woman would want to lay her gaze upon.

Dropping his hand, he reached for a clean bandana. As he wrapped the black silk around his neck and tied the ends in a square knot, he kept his eyes focused on his throat, away from the line of slightly puckered skin. Even after five years, the memory of how he'd received the scar remained fresh.

His jaw clenched with the gut-wrenching fury the memory always stirred. How could he have been so stupid? How could he have ignored the threat of a criminal known for his skill with a knife? If only he'd taken the man into custody earlier, he could have saved himself a month-long chase. If only he'd arrested the man, he could have prevented the fight which left him scarred for life. More importantly, he could have saved his family.

Kit closed his eyes, willing his boiling anger to cool. After a moment, he exhaled in a long sigh then opened his eyes. At least he could take some small measure of solace from his fight with the knife-wielding madman. The bastard would never cut anyone else ever again—no county sheriffs . . . or helpless women and children. He'd made damn sure of that.

He drew in another deep breath, remembering how his days of tracking the killer ended, feeling again the sharp bite of the knife blade slashing across his face. He recalled the exact moment he had wrested the man's knife away from him, then plunged the blade into the bastard's black heart. And just as on that day, the same conflicting emotions engulfed him: the exhilaration of the kill, followed by the nausea of having taken a life.

Kit hated himself for killing. He'd been working as a sheriff, sworn to uphold the law. But no one deserved to die more than the scum who'd robbed him of everything he held dear.

Blinking several times, he finally chased the memories from his mind. Life went on, such as it was. And for the first time in a long while, he had something to look forward to. His spirits lifting at the thought of seeing Angel, he grabbed his hat, then crossed the room and reached for the doorknob.

Angelina smoothed the skirt of her mauve walking dress, then left her room on the second floor of the house where she and the other girls who worked for James Murray had rooms. She shouldn't have agreed to see Kit Dancer. Jenna had warned her about getting too close to her customers. But Kit wasn't one of her customers—not yet anyway. As much as she dreaded the night when she'd be forced to take a man into her bed, she wanted a familiar face, someone she'd known for longer than the time it took for money to change hands in the brothel parlor. For reasons that befuddled her, she wanted that man to be Kit.

Making her way down the stairs, she recalled James Murray's words after the fire. Since the Murray House would be closed for an indefinite amount of time while repairs were made, he said he would try to find work for all his employees in his other businesses. Angelina had foolishly hoped last night's fire would keep her out of work for a while, thereby delaying her entrance into prostitution. But Mr. Murray had squashed her wishful thinking.

Maybe she would be given a position as a piano player, or even a waiter girl. She frowned. At best, the possibility was remote. Mr. Murray all but told her she would be joining the *ladies* at another of his brothels. She had resolved herself to doing whatever was necessary to pay off her contract. But as her decision met with one delay after another, her nervousness increased. Only one thing eased her apprehension. Kit Dancer.

She stepped into the small parlor at the front of the house and found the man of her thoughts standing by the fireplace. Wearing his usual black, he stood with his weight on his right leg, left boot crossed over the opposite ankle, one arm casually resting on the mantel.

As she approached him, the strange warmth she'd experienced the night before, the intense swirling of heat in the pit of her stomach, returned. Her voice came out as a low rasp when she said, "Good morning, Kit."

Her soft greeting sent a ripple of pleasure up Kit's spine. Pushing away from the mantel, he touched his fingers to the brim of his hat. "Mornin', Angel. Ready for our walk?"

Cheeks warm from the intimacy she heard in his voice, she nodded, then wrapped her hand through his proffered arm.

The early October morning was pleasant, with a deep, clear blue sky and a gentle breeze stirring what leaves remained on the trees, as Kit led Angel along Utah Street toward the river.

After a long silence, he looked down at the shiny brown hair gathered into the familiar knot at the base of her neck, at the way her breasts pushed against the bodice of her dress. Once again his body told him the woman on his arm was the most desirable creature he'd ever met.

Tamping down the urge to find a deserted alley, or even a shadowed doorway where he could taste her sweet mouth, he said, "I've been meaning to ask if Angel is really your name."

Other men at the Murray House had asked her the same question; apparently it was common knowledge that prostitutes used a different name when working. But never once had she told anyone her name was anything other than Angel. Glancing up at Kit, she surprised herself by saying, "My given name is Angelina. I only use Angel while I'm working."

"Angelina." Kit liked the sound of it. "That's a beautiful name. Like you."

Feeling another blush creep up her cheeks, she ducked her head. "You're too kind."

"I'm not bein' kind, Angelina. Just honest." Her chin came up. Her wide-eyed gaze briefly searched his face, then skittered away.

For a moment, he thought he'd managed to coax a genuine smile from her. He frowned. *Guess not.* His gaze traced her delicate nose, thick lashes, and full lips. Why didn't she smile more? Smiling could do nothing but improve her looks, making her even more beautiful. Just as the lack of face paint enhanced her beauty. Kit halted that line of thinking. Smiling or not, wearing makeup or not, she was a prostitute, meant to give him pleasure. Nothing more.

When they arrived at the end of Utah Street, they crossed a patch of grass to the banks of the Rio Grande, stopping beneath a large tree. Angelina dropped her hand from Kit's arm, then moved away from his side. Being so close, the heat of his big body soaking into her skin, the scent of his bay cologne tickling her nose, made her feel flushed all over, her breathing slightly irregular.

From a few feet away, she surreptitiously watched him. Legs widespread, hands braced on narrow hips, hat pulled low over his face, long black hair ruffling in the breeze off the river. He was without a doubt the finest looking male she had ever seen.

"Why do you wear only black?"

He glanced toward her, then shrugged. "I prefer it. Black seems . . . appropriate."

"Appropriate? Do you mean, like for mourning? Is that—?" The sudden tightening of his jaw halted her questions. After a moment, she said, "Well, black certainly becomes y'all. It complements your hair and complexion."

She watched the stiffness leave his shoulders. Then to her amazement, a deep dimple appeared in his left cheek.

He turned to face her. "Thanks. I think you'd look good in just about anything." He lowered his voice to add, "But I'd especially like to see you wearin' nothing but a great big smile."

Her light mood evaporated. Shifting her gaze to the Stanton Street Bridge downriver, she swallowed hard. For a moment she'd forgotten Kit thought she was a soiled dove. She'd forgotten that for all but the final act, she was what he believed her to be. "I'd like to go back now."

Peering down at her through narrowed eyes, he wondered what had brought about the coolness he heard in her voice. "Why?"

"I . . . I just remembered, the girls from the Murray House aren't supposed to leave the tenderloin unless we go with Ruby. She warned us about it often enough, how the people in town don't take kindly to having us anywhere near decent folk. But I forgot."

Confused by the bitterness of her reply, Kit said, "No one is going to know you work in the tenderloin." When she didn't reply, he added, "Are you sure you want to go back?"

She lifted her chin to give him a pointed glare. "If you don't want to accompany me, I can find the way on my own."

"Don't be ridiculous," he replied, offering her his arm. As he escorted her the several blocks back up Utah Street, he tried to draw her out of the shell where she'd withdrawn. His efforts failed.

When they reached her rooming house, he insisted on taking her inside. Noises drifted to them from upstairs and the back of the house, but the entry was deserted.

She murmured a good-bye, then turned toward the staircase. Grabbing her arm before she could move out of his reach, Kit swung her around to face him. "Wait a minute, Angel." When she didn't protest, he wrapped his arms around her and pulled her close. Holding her snugly against his chest, he lowered his face.

He gently rubbed his lips over hers before deepening the kiss. He groaned deep in his chest, the soft silk of her mouth setting his body afire. Teasing the seam of her lips with his tongue, he tried to gain entrance into her mouth but she refused to comply. She stood stock-still, allowing him to kiss her, yet not participating.

Frustrated with her lack of response, Kit lifted his head. She stared up at him with dilated eyes, her cheeks flushed a deep coral. In spite of her lack of a reaction, he felt certain she hadn't been totally unaffected by his kiss.

After an awkward moment, he said, "I . . . uh . . . enjoyed our walk."

Clearing her throat, she managed to say, "So did I." She tried to free herself of his embrace, and was glad he didn't try to keep her pressed against him. When he dropped his arms to his sides, she took a step toward the stairs.

"Wait." He grabbed her wrist. "Can I see you tomorrow?"

"Tomorrow is Sunday."

"Yeah, I know. So?"

"Even if the fire hadn't closed the Murray House, I don't work on Sundays."

"Then let me take you to dinner."

"I can't. I have other plans."

A muscle ticked in Kit's jaw. "Plans? What plans?"

Angelina stiffened her spine. "What I do on Sunday is none of your concern. Please release my arm. I want to go to my room."

Unsure exactly why news of Angel's having plans for Sunday irritated him, Kit loosened his fingers on her wrist. "Fine. Go."

Her fine eyebrows pulled together, she gave him a questioning look, then lifted the hem of her skirt and started up the stairs. He knew he'd sounded overly gruff and longed to call back his words, but he kept his lips pressed together.

Leaving the rooming house, he wondered what was wrong

with him. He was behaving like a besotted fool, and over a prostitute for God's sake! What did he care if she had plans for Sunday?

By the time he arrived at his own boardinghouse, Kit had not only been unable to shake Angel from his thoughts, but he'd also decided on his own plans for Sunday.

Kit drew back on the reins of Sid, his piebald gelding, then eased the big horse from their hiding place. In the past, remaining unobtrusive had been part of working as a bounty hunter, so he'd always ridden horses of nondescript color and markings. But after making the decision to get into another line of work, he'd spotted Sid at an auction and figured what the hell, it no longer mattered what color horse he rode. But after deciding to follow Angel, he regretted buying a horse whose coloring was as noticeable as a new saloon in a church district.

He'd followed her at a discreet distance from her rooming house to a stable, then watched her ride out on a dun-colored mare. Again he followed her as she directed the horse to the northern edge of town. When she kicked the dun into a lope, he pulled up. As he waited for her to get a head start before following her trail, he dismounted to check the hoof prints her horse left in the sand. There wasn't much cover in the surrounding countryside, so he couldn't risk sticking too close and having her spot the beacon of his gelding's distinctive black and white hide.

As he remounted, then touched his heels to Sid's sides, he wondered again why he was going to so much trouble over a woman.

Maybe the knife wound he'd suffered in Galveston had become infected, leaving him with a brain fever. He probed his shoulder for soreness. Though still tender, he experienced no pain. Since the wound had completely healed, a fever didn't seem likely. Even so, he couldn't deny—regardless of the reasons—his fascination with the Ice Angel.

The corners of his mouth lifted. When he watched her leave

the rooming house and head down Utah Street, she'd looked nothing like the Murray House lovely. Wearing a split riding skirt and boots, her long hair tied with a ribbon at her nape, she bore little resemblance to the Ice Angel. Nor did she resemble the smartly dressed, carefully coiffed Angelina he'd escorted to the river the morning before.

Recalling their walk, his thoughts drifted to her reason for declining his dinner invitation. Surely her plans for the day weren't just for a ride. No, he knew when someone wasn't riding for the enjoyment of the scenery. He'd followed enough people to know Angelina had a definite destination in mind. So where was she headed? And what was in the pair of large sacks tied behind her saddle?

As he pondered those questions, he kept his gaze on the dirt road. Her trail had stayed in a northerly direction for close to ten miles, then turned east toward the foothills of the Franklin Mountains. Keeping his horse to a slow walk, Kit took the same path off the main road, his senses alert for any sign of trouble. The narrow road wound its way through the hills to a deep crescent-shaped canyon. After another mile, he spotted the chimney of a building and pulled Sid to a halt. Reining his horse off the path, he found cover for Sid, then dismounted and moved closer on foot.

From his vantage point, crouched in a thicket of mesquite, Kit could see where a stand of cottonwood trees had been cleared at the rear of the canyon. In the center of the clearing were a house and barn. Angelina's horse stood in front of the house, tied to the porch railing, the pair of sacks no longer behind the saddle. He frowned. The horse deserved a place in the shade after riding hard for more than ten miles.

He'd no more than thought of the dun's well-being when the front door swung open and Angelina stepped onto the porch. She glanced around the dirt yard, then untied the mare's reins and led the horse to the barn. A few minutes later, she returned to the house.

Staring at the single-story house of crumbling adobe and weathered wood siding sadly in need of paint, with its sagging porch and poorly patched roof, Kit's brows pulled together. The barn and small corral were in the same sorry state. *What's she doing here? Looks like the place has been neglected for a heck of a long time. Hell, a stout wind could blow down the house.*

When she hadn't left the house again after half an hour, Kit made his way back to where he'd picketed his horse. After loosening the cinch and making sure the gelding had sufficient cover, he grabbed his canteen and a packet of jerky, then returned to his hiding spot near the edge of the clearing.

A while later, he noticed movement on one side of the house. Carrying a bucket, Angelina crossed the clearing to the stream running close to the base of the hills. After making several trips to the house with the bucket filled with water, she made two more trips outside, each time to fetch an armload of wood.

Chewing a piece of jerky, Kit tried to come up with a reason for Angelina's riding out to this run-down ranch. Perhaps she was visiting one of her clients from the Murray House. As painful as the notion was, Kit forced himself to roll the idea over in his mind. If that were the case, toting water and firewood weren't the kind of services she'd be paid to perform. No, whoever lived on this sad excuse for a ranch wasn't paying for her to warm his bed.

Maybe the man wasn't paying her. Or maybe she wasn't charging the man because she cared for him. Maybe—With a growl of disgust, he shoved such unpleasant thoughts aside.

The last of the day's light was nearly gone when Angelina emerged from the house. Rubbing the small of her back, she walked to the barn, her steps slow and deliberate. A few minutes later, she led the dun mare outside, then closed the barn door behind them. By the time she mounted and touched her heels to the horse's sides, Kit was on his way to where his horse stood dozing beneath a small tree. He tightened the saddle's cinch, then placed a hand over Sid's muzzle to keep the gelding silent. After Angelina rode past his hiding place, he waited a few minutes more before sticking his foot into a stirrup and swinging into the saddle.

Though certain Angelina was returning to El Paso, he decided to risk discovery and follow her at a closer distance. Since darkness would descend before she got back to her rooming house, he wanted to make sure she arrived without incident. His concern for her safety not sitting well, he pressed his lips together in irritation.

Against his will Angelina was becoming more and more fascinating. Like wild mustangs catching the scent of water in the desert, instinctively drawn to where they could quench their thirst, so, too, was Kit drawn to what he thirsted for—the Ice Angel. Though he tried, he was helpless to stop the force pulling him.

Chapter Four

Bright morning sunlight filtering through the window in her room, Angelina rolled over in bed, then stretched. Every muscle protested the movement, making her grimace. She'd nearly worked herself to a frazzle the day before.

Thinking about the time she'd spent at the ranch, she swung her legs to the floor, then sat up. She was terribly worried about her mother. Since her visit the previous Sunday, Sarah Coleman seemed much weaker, her coloring not at all good. Maybe she should have Dr. Irvin ride out to the ranch. Rising to her feet, she discarded the idea. She was already paying the doctor to stop by the ranch on a regular basis, and unless it was an emergency, she just couldn't afford to pay for any additional visits. Her salary simply wouldn't stretch that far. After paying her room and board and making the payment toward her contract, there was barely enough left to keep food in her family's pantry. Besides, Chloe had promised she would monitor their mother's deteriorating health more closely.

Her sister was good in so many ways, yet she still lacked the skills to run a household. That's why Angelina's entire body ached that morning. She'd arrived at the ranch to find the furniture dusty, the floors dirty, dishes piled everywhere in the kitchen. When she'd confronted Chloe, she got the usual reply. One of Chloe's animals had taken sick, and when she wasn't with their mother, the rest of her time was spent nursing the critter back to health.

Angelina smiled at her sister's devotion to animals. Chloe had a real calling. Too bad their parents hadn't been able to afford furthering her sister's education. But in spite of Chloe's lack of formal training, she was better than most college-taught animal doctors, though no one around El Paso had yet learned of her skill.

Thinking of her futile attempt to teach her sister how to bake bread, Angelina's smile faded. *If I could just get her to do a few of the household chores, I'd have more time to spend sitting with Mama instead of cleaning and cooking the whole time I'm there.*

While she gave herself a quick sponge bath then dressed, she wished again for a faster way to pay off what she owed Mr. Murray so she could move back to the ranch. Every time she rode out there, it broke her heart to see how pitiful the place looked. Though neither her mother nor Chloe complained, she still hated for them to have to live in a house needing so many repairs. *Oh, Papa, why did you have to die and leave us in this mess?*

Straightening her shoulders, Angelina shrugged off her melancholy. So far she hadn't buckled under the weight thrust upon her shoulders, and she didn't intend to do so now. She had to be strong. Her mother and sister depended on her, and she couldn't—she wouldn't fail them.

After securing her hair in a customary knot, she left her room and headed downstairs. Though it was earlier than the other girls usually crawled from their beds, she knew Jenna was an early riser and would likely be drinking coffee in the kitchen. Maybe Jenna had learned something regarding the future of the Murray House employees.

Several hours later, Angelina went back upstairs, her heart heavy with what she had learned. She and Jenna were to start work that evening just up the street at the other brothel James Murray owned, the Shamrock.

Her gaze downcast, she opened the door to her room, then stepped inside. The sudden prickling of the hair on her nape jerked her from her musings. Slowly lifting her head, her gaze landed on a pair of black boots, crossed at the ankle on the foot of her bed. Her breath catching in her throat, she forced her gaze past the boots, up the black trousers hugging a pair of muscular thighs, past the black silk shirt pulled taut across an equally muscular chest. The dark hat, canted at its usual angle, revealed only the lower third of the man's face.

Seeing the flash of teeth as a smile curved the familiar lips, she scowled. "You! What are you doing here?"

His smile broadened at her indignant tone. "Mornin', Angel. Is that any way to greet your guest?"

"Guest! Only the girls who live in this house are supposed to be in these rooms. We aren't allowed to have guests. How did you find my room?"

"An experienced bounty hunter has no trouble finding out where someone lives . . . or which room belongs to a particular woman."

She took a step backward, pressing her back against the closed door. "Bounty hunter? You're a—"

Kit silently cursed his loose tongue. "Used to be. Not any more."

She forced herself to push away from the door, then said, "Well, regardless of how you found my room, I think you'd better leave." Keeping her gaze on the man lounging on her bed, she reached behind her for the doorknob.

In one easy motion, Kit swung his legs off the bed and rose to his feet. In two strides he crossed the small room. Wrapping one hand around her elbow, he said, "I'm not leaving, Angel. Not yet anyway." He moved back to the bed with her in tow where he gave her a gentle shove. Her bottom hit the mattress with a soft bounce. She did not protest, but remained seated on the edge of the bed. Pulling the chair out from under her dressing table, he straddled the seat and folded his arms across the back.

"I'm only here to get some answers. Once I have them, I'll leave, but not before. Understood?"

Angelina's breath escaped in a long sigh of relief. For a moment, she'd feared he was there to finish the transaction he'd started the night of the fire. Thankful her fears were unfounded, she finally nodded. "What do you want to know?"

"I wanna hear more about you. The other night you told me you're from Savannah. So my first question is, why did you come to El Paso?"

Taking a moment to gather her thoughts, she began speaking. "My mother has been ill for just about as long as I can remember. Consumption. The doctor in Savannah said a change in climate might help Mama. Since El Paso's warm, dry air is touted back East as a paradise for the pulmonary invalid, Papa decided to move west. He sold our house, packed up our belongings, then loaded my mother, my sister, and me onto a westbound train."

Though certain he already knew the answer, Kit said, "Where did you live when you got here?"

"About ten miles north of town. Papa contacted a real estate man here in El Paso before we left Savannah and arranged to buy a ranch. Though Papa spent his entire life working in the shipping industry and didn't know the first thing about ranching, he thought living away from the city would be best for Mama. He wanted so much to do whatever he could to help her, but unfortunately, he was too trusting and didn't . . ." She twisted her hands in her lap, memories of her first view of what would be their new home vivid in her mind.

"He didn't what?"

"He didn't check into the condition of the ranch. If he had, he never would have bought a place in such a sad state of repair. When we arrived at the ranch and he saw where his money had gone, he was devastated. But Mama, bless her heart, told him not to be so sour-faced. She said living there would surely be an adventure."

"Was it?"

"For a while. Mama's health did seem to improve at first, and though Papa wasn't very handy with a hammer, he was game to fix up the place. When I wasn't busy keeping house or tending Mama, I tried to help him. But no matter how much we did, there was always an endless string of things needing fixing."

She drew in a deep breath, then exhaled a long sigh. "Then Papa was killed in a fall from the barn loft, and the adventure Mama predicted turned into a nightmare." Angelina caught her bottom lip between her teeth, the painful memory of the days immediately after her father's death washing over her.

"Is that when you came to work at the Murray House?"

Lifting her face, she stared at him with sad eyes, the corners of her mouth turned down. "No, not right away. As bleak as the future looked without Papa, I was still willing to put every ounce of my strength into turning the ranch into a decent home for my mother and sister. Then the day after Papa's funeral, my mother was paid a visit by Elliot Wentworth, vice president of the El Paso Bank, who put a halt to my plans. Mr. Wentworth told her Papa had borrowed money from his bank not long after our arrival, money he claimed Papa wanted for improvements on the ranch. And according to the terms of the note, Papa's death made the loan due in full."

"You didn't know about the loan?"

She shook her head. "Mama, Chloe, and I couldn't believe our ears. Papa had paid for the ranch with the money from the sale of our home in Savannah. Most of what was left paid for our tickets to Texas. He told us he'd opened an account at the El Paso Bank soon after we arrived and had the small balance in his Savannah bank account transferred by wire."

"Makes sense a man would borrow money from the bank where he has an account."

Angelina pulled her brows together in a frown. "I suppose. But he never said anything about borrowing money, and he certainly never used the money to make repairs around the ranch. When we told Mr. Wentworth we knew nothing about his claim, he expressed his dismay over a man keeping something as important as a sizeable loan from his family, but assured us Papa had done exactly that. And when I told him I still didn't believe him, he pulled out the mortgage papers."

"You're convinced your father signed the note?"

"We weren't at first. Even though Papa had a very distinctive hand, and the signature on the bank papers bore a strong

resemblance to his, we wanted to be absolutely certain. I went
to town and talked to the man who'd signed as witness on the
mortgage. He insisted Papa's signature was genuine. Even so,
I went to see an attorney. After reading the papers, he told me
everything seemed to be in order and unless we could prove
Papa didn't sign the mortgage, there was nothing he could do.
We finally had no choice but to agree the debt was valid, though
we told Mr. Wentworth we had no means to repay the money."

"How did he react?"

"He seemed . . . I guess you'd say, undisturbed by the news.
In fact, now that I think about it, he actually smiled, an . . . oily
kind of smile, if you know what I mean. Anyway, before he left,
he said he would be contacting us again regarding payment."

"What about the money your father borrowed? If he didn't
use it to fix up the ranch, doesn't it make sense the money had
to be around somewhere?"

Angelina nodded. "That's exactly what we thought. Chloe
and I searched the house, the barn, every place we could think
of. But we didn't find anything. We'll probably never know
what Papa did with the money."

Kit stared at her for a long spell, thinking over what she'd
told him. Something just didn't sit right about the whole thing,
but he couldn't put his finger on exactly what bothered him.
Finally he said, "So, I take it your father's loan has something
to do with your workin' in a bawdy house?"

Swallowing hard, Angelina cleared her throat. Staring at
the floor, she took up the story again. "Mr. Wentworth came
back to the ranch a week later, again looking to be paid. When
my mother again told him we didn't have the money and had
no way of getting it, he said we'd better come up with something within a month or he'd have no choice except to foreclose.
I knew there was no way we could raise the kind of money we
needed and trying to get a loan from another bank to pay off
Mr. Wentworth would be a waste of time. No bank would even
consider lending an invalid woman and her two daughters that
much money, especially since we didn't have sufficient collat-

eral or the means to make the ranch productive enough to repay a loan.

"By the time Mr. Wentworth paid us another visit, I was in a real frenzy. I asked to speak to him in private and begged for more time. I told him I couldn't just stand by and watch my mother and sister get thrown out of their home. He patted my hand and told me not to worry. He said he had friends in El Paso who would be willing to help, and he'd work something out. For the first time since Papa's death, I felt a glimmer of hope that everything would be okay." She took a deep shuddering breath. "The next time I talked with Mr. Wentworth, my hope died."

As Kit realized the direction of Angelina's story, a muscle ticked in his jaw. Clamping his mouth shut, he waited for her to continue.

"He said he'd found a man who would pay off the note to the bank in exchange for my going to work at one of the man's businesses in El Paso." She paused a moment, remembering the reproach she felt toward Wentworth for making such a suggestion, and the humiliation she experienced at knowing she had no choice except to agree to the terms he offered. At last she said, "That man was James Murray."

In spite of Kit's initial suspicion, hearing her confirming words still came as a shock. "You became a prostitute because Wentworth sold your note to a man who owns a whorehouse?"

The harshness of his voice brought her chin up. Glaring at his shadowed face, she said, "No. While it's true I had no other option as far as paying off Papa's debts, I did have a choice in what I did for Mr. Murray. I have always been very musically inclined, so I chose to play piano in the main parlor."

"But you were working as a prostitute the night I met you."

"Yes, that's true. I had asked Mr. Murray if I could be one of the . . . um . . . girls, and he was happy to oblige me." She saw no point in explaining why she'd asked for the change in positions, the personal sacrifice she was willing to make, or how difficult making the decision had been. To Kit Dancer, she

was already a fallen woman, and nothing she could say would
alter his opinion.

"So, you never worked in a parlor house before you moved
to Texas?"

Her chin tilted higher. "No."

"Surely your mother and sister must have objected to what
you're doing?"

"I told them I worked evenings playing the piano, but I could
never make myself tell them where I worked or that I had asked
to change jobs. With Mama's health being so frail, I thought it
better not to upset her."

He nodded his understanding, then after a moment he said,
"Becoming a prostitute didn't bother you?"

Hearing the underlying reproach in his voice, Angelina swallowed hard. "Of course, it bothered me." She wanted to add
how much it still bothered her, but instead, she said, "I did what
I had to do."

Clenching his hands into fists, Kit pressed his lips into a thin
line. The possibility that Angel had deliberately sacrificed her
virginity and sullied her reputation by turning to prostitution,
even to save her family's home, was too appalling to abide.

But then, perhaps she hadn't been an innocent when she
came to the Murray House. Perhaps she had already lost her
maidenhead to an overzealous swain back in Georgia. He ran
a hand across his stubbled jaw. Yes, that made more sense.
There had to be some indiscretion in her past to account for
Angel's willingness to join the ranks of the prostitute.

Still, in spite of her lack of innocence, the circumstances
which prompted her to make that decision fired his temper.
Anger, hot and savage, surged through his body. He couldn't
believe her father could have been so stupid as to take out a loan
he apparently had no means to repay. That Angel had been
placed in the position of being responsible for keeping her family in their home was equally enraging.

But the true target of his anger was the man named Wentworth. That the banker would even suggest she work in a
brothel—regardless of her virtue, or lack of it—to pay off the

debt was beyond belief, and worse, completely unconscionable.

Kit closed his eyes, willing his anger to cool. He took a long, deep breath, then exhaled slowly. When the last of his outrage slipped away, he opened his eyes to find Angel staring at him. The wariness in her eyes, mixed with the usual sadness, clutched at his heart. Shaking off his unfamiliar and unwanted reaction, he rose from the chair.

"I have to be going. There's something I have to do." Taking a step closer, he gave in to temptation and reached down to run the fingers of one hand over her cheek. "How about supper?"

Angelina repressed the urge to shiver from his touch. "I . . . I can't. I have to work tonight."

"Work! Where?"

"I'm starting at the Shamrock this evening. It's just up the——"

"I know where the hell it is," Kit snapped through clenched teeth.

For a reason which eluded him, the idea of her working at another of El Paso's brothels was not something he wanted to contemplate. Realizing he couldn't let her in on the plan that had just begun formulating in his mind, he forced himself to say, "Well, maybe I'll see you there."

After pressing a brief, hard kiss on her mouth, he turned and left her room.

As the echo of his boots on the stairs faded away, Angelina wondered if she'd ever see the mysterious man in black again. The idea that he had just walked out of her life was much too painful to consider.

Chapter Five

Kit walked the several blocks from the house where Angelina lived on Utah over to El Paso Street, wondering about his sanity. Was he seriously considering actually going through with his plan?

He tugged on his hat brim, pulling it lower on his forehead. *Christ, Dancer, whatever sense you had must've skedaddled as soon as Angel spilled her story.* He scowled. He wasn't used to feeling sympathy when someone told him a tale of woe. If he'd empathized with every criminal he'd chased down, he wouldn't have made a cent as a bounty hunter. And he sure as hell never figured a hard luck story would prompt him to take the drastic action he had in mind.

But the truth was, he had no plans for the money he'd accumulated during his five years as a successful bounty hunter, though after giving up that line of work, he'd given some thought to settling down somewhere permanently. For reasons he wasn't comfortable with and didn't fully understand, helping Angel had become his first priority. He couldn't wait to see the expression on her face. Maybe his news would coax a real smile to her mouth, or maybe she'd throw herself into his arms . . . . Realizing his overactive imagination had jumped the gun, he forced himself to concentrate on the present.

Outside the bat-wing doors of the White Horse Saloon, Kit stopped to think his plan through one more time. Though he still thought he must have lost his mind, he also hadn't been able to come up with an acceptable reason to change his plans. Intent on his purpose, he pushed through the doors and entered the saloon. After telling the bartender he wanted to see the owner, he was directed to the second floor.

Kit found the office at the end of the hallway, then knocked on the door. When he heard a muffled call to enter, he stepped into the room and closed the door behind him.

James Murray looked up from the pile of papers on his massive desk. "Can I help you with something, Mr. . . . ?"

"Dancer. And, yeah, I have some business I'd like to conduct with you."

"Okay, Mr. Dancer. Why don't you have a seat? Give me a couple of minutes to finish this letter, then you can tell me what this is about."

Kit nodded, then eased down into one of the leather chairs in front of the desk. As he waited for Murray, he studied Angel's boss.

The man looked to be in his mid-forties, perhaps a little older, his dark blond hair slicked back with a layer of pomade. He sported a long, reddish-gold moustache, the ends shaped into elaborate curls by a heavy application of wax, and a thick, neatly trimmed beard over a firm jawline.

When Murray finished, he laid his pen on the desk, then leaned back in his chair and smiled. "Now, what can I do for you, Mr. Dancer?"

Though the smile appeared genuine enough, Kit noted how it didn't reach the man's dark brown eyes. Seeing one eyebrow lift in anticipation, he cleared his throat, then said, "I'm here regarding the contract you have with one of your employees. I'd like to see about paying off whatever is owed."

Murray's brows rose sharply, then lowered over squinted eyes. "Really? And who might this employee be?"

Resisting the urge to vent his outrage at Murray's business practices, Kit forced himself to remain calm. "Angel, actually Angelina Coleman, from the Murray House."

If Murray was shocked by his answer, the man's expression revealed nothing. Raising one hand from his desk, he fiddled with one side of his moustache. "Have you any idea how much she owes me?"

"I have a pretty fair idea."

"Do you? I take it you and Angel have discussed what you're proposing?"

"No. She doesn't know I'm here."

"Ah, so you haven't read her contract?"

"No, I haven't read it, but that—"

Murray held up one hand, then rose from his chair and moved to the safe sitting in the corner of his office. He opened the safe's door, rummaged through the inside, and finally withdrew an envelope. After closing the safe, he returned to his desk and tossed the envelope down in front of Kit.

"I suggest you read the contract, Mr. Dancer," he sat back down in his chair, "then we'll talk."

Kit's gaze moved from Murray's face to the buff-colored envelope. Angel's name had been scrawled across the front. He picked up the envelope, broke the seal, and withdrew the contents. Unfolding the several-page document, he turned his attention to reading the contract. Everything was as he expected until he got to one particular clause. After rereading the surprising addition to the agreement, he read the rest of the contract, then laid it back on the desk.

"Anything in there you don't understand, Mr. Dancer?"

"No."

"You read the clause outlining the conditions for ending Miss Coleman's employment prior to the scheduled termination of the contract?"

"Yeah, I read the conditions."

"Good. Then I suppose you're no longer interested in continuing this conversation. Can't say as I blame you since—"

"No," Kit said with more force than he'd intended, bringing Murray's surprised gaze to meet his. "I'm still interested."

"Really? Well, all right. As long as you're sure you can meet the terms, I'd be happy to oblige your request."

"I have the money to pay off Angel's debt, if that's what you're gettin' at."

"Well, that's certainly a good start. But what about the other condition? It doesn't bother you that the only way she can get out of her contract early is by marriage?"

Kit stared at the man sitting across from him for several moments. He had to hand it to Murray. Putting such a stipulation in Angelina's contract had been a clever ploy. How many women working in a brothel found a man who was willing to not only pay off her debt but marry her, as well? Damn few, he'd wager. Yet, there he sat actually talking about doing exactly that.

Though Kit had never planned to marry again, the sadness in Angel's eyes, the pain in her voice were too hard to forget. Besides, if he were to marry again, he couldn't make a better choice than Angel. He sure as hell wanted no part of a virtuous female, the kind he avoided at all cost. So, the way he had it figured, he and Angel were perfect for each other: a guilt-ridden man who wasn't worthy of an innocent woman, and a sullied beauty who'd turned to prostitution to keep her family together.

Aside from that rationalization, he couldn't ignore the other, more powerful force prompting him to take Angel as his wife. His attraction to her. He'd never experienced anything even close to the pull he felt toward Angel. Though he had desired his first wife and thought she was the only woman he'd ever want, he now knew he'd been wrong. One sad-eyed young woman with a cool facade had changed all that.

A craving to break through Angelina's coolness constantly gnawed at his insides. He longed to spark the fire of passion he knew lay hidden beneath the protective layer of ice. Each time he saw her, his eagerness to melt her icy reserve and stoke the heat beyond increased tenfold.

Kit shifted in his chair, the leather creaking with the movement. Finally, he said, "I'm willing to marry her."

The smirk on Murray's face faded. "Really?" His eyebrows pulled together. "Well, she is attractive enough," he mused. " 'Specially if you like a woman on the skinny side."

Kit wanted to say Angel wasn't skinny, she only appeared so

next to the other girls at the brothel who ranged from full-figured to downright plump. Instead he said, "I reckon you won't have to worry about her looks for much longer. I'll wire for the money as soon as I leave here. And as for the other, I'll also look into findin' someone to marry us."

The fingers of Murray's right hand once again twisting one side of his moustache, he said, "There are a number of churches in town. I expect you can find a minister who's willing to perform the ceremony on such short notice."

Kit gave him a long, cool stare, then said, "I'm sure I can. I'll be back this afternoon to settle up with you."

Murray smiled, another curving of his lips that didn't go beyond his mouth. "Fine. Fine. I'll be expecting you, say at three?"

"Shouldn't be a problem," he replied, getting to his feet.

Though Kit wanted to get away from Murray as quickly as possible, he took the time to offer his hand before making his exit.

Back on the street, Kit realized his spirits were much lighter than he would have imagined, given what he'd just agreed to do. He headed for the telegraph office, anxious to finish there so he could tell Angel what he'd arranged.

A knock on her door startled Angelina from her musings while sitting at her dressing table. Staring at her reflection, void of the paint she would soon apply, she said, "Come on in, Jenna."

The door swung inward, then closed softly. Turning around on her chair, Angelina opened her mouth to speak, then sucked in a surprised breath. "Kit! I was expecting . . ." She pulled her eyebrows together in a frown. "I declare! How do y'all keep getting in here without someone stopping you?"

He chuckled. "Someone did try to stop me this time, one of the other gals, the one called Coral. When I told her I had something real important to tell you, she let me come upstairs."

The creases on her forehead deepened. "And just what's this *something* that's so all-fired important?"

"I paid a visit to James Murray today," he said, pausing to build the anticipation. "I paid off your contract. You no longer work for the man."

Her mouth fell open. Blinking several times, she finally snapped her mouth closed. After giving her head a little shake, she said, "I must have heard you wrong. Would y'all mind repeating that?"

Smiling, Kit said, "I said, I paid off your contract."

"I don't understand. I told you I couldn't afford to pay off Papa's loan. That's how I ended up working for Mr. Murray in the first place. So surely, you must know there's no way I can repay you."

"I didn't do this because I want or expect to be repaid, Angel."

"Then, what did possess y'all to do such a thing?"

Kit moved to the bed, then took a seat opposite her. "I didn't like how that banker, Wentworth, coerced you into signing a contract with Murray. So, I decided to pay off what you owe. Except for one detail, you're a free woman."

One hand pressed to her bosom, her voice was breathless when she spoke. "What do you mean, 'except for one detail?' "

"I assume you read your contract before you signed it." When she nodded, he said, "Do you recall a clause about gettin' out of the contract early?"

She gasped, the confusion in her eyes suddenly clearing. "I have to get married. Surely, you're not suggesting you and I . . ."

"Would that be so bad, Angel? We get along well, and unless I'm mistaken, you desire me as much as I do you. I've seen plenty of marriages based on a whole lot less."

The heat of a blush spreading across her cheeks, she dropped her gaze to where she held her hands clasped in her lap. So that's what this was about. By paying off her contract, he'd bought her. Though they would be husband and wife, the amount of money he'd paid would make him expect her to be at his beck and call, taking what he wanted whenever he chose. Tears stung the backs of her eyes. If she agreed, she would be trading one form of prostitution for another.

She squeezed her eyes closed at the thought. What would he say if she told him the truth? Would he believe her? She drew a deep quivering breath. No, he'd probably accuse her of making up stories to get him to change his mind. She opened her eyes, then lifted her face and looked at him. Now that she knew his motive, what was she going to do about it?

Kit saw the emotions flicker across her face, recognizing her struggle to accept the turn of events. Figuring she was trying to get used to the idea of having a husband in her bed night after night, he pushed himself off the mattress and hunkered down in front of her chair.

"Listen, Angel, I know this must be quite a shock. But I think I understand at least part of what you're feeling."

Angelina frowned, thinking he couldn't possibly know what she felt. Rather than speaking her thoughts aloud, she remained silent.

"I want you to know I won't put any pressure on you to make our marriage a real one." Seeing her frown deepen, the confusion in her gaze, he added, "I'm sayin', I promise not to make us man and wife, in the . . . uh . . . physical sense until you say you're ready. Fair enough?"

Though another fiery blush heated her face at his frank declaration, Angelina nearly collapsed with relief. In spite of not knowing Kit Dancer very long, she didn't believe him to be a liar. She already knew him to be well-mannered, tender, and considerate. He'd never pawed her or made lewd suggestions like some of the other brothel customers. And being honest with herself, she wasn't opposed to their relationship eventually becoming intimate—actually she found the idea very appealing. But was that enough on which to base a marriage?

Considering the alternative, such concern about how much she knew about her future husband struck her as being both ridiculous and insignificant. Something else about her reflections struck Angelina, as well. Since she already thought of Kit as her soon-to-be husband, her decision had been made.

Looking into his shadowed face, she said, "Though I have no right to ask anything of you, in light of what you're doing for me, I have several conditions I'd like you to agree to before we're married." Not giving him time to object, she rushed on, "I don't want my mother or my sister to ever learn where I've been working, or the circumstances of our marriage."

"Where do they think you've been working?"

"I told them I was playing piano in the theatre room of one of the saloons. Mama was upset enough. I couldn't tell her I was really working in a bawdy house." She stared up at him with beseeching eyes. "If they ever hear the truth, I want to be the one to tell them. Will you agree to that?"

Kit thought about her request for a moment before answering. "Yes, I agree." When she remained silent, he said, "You said you had several conditions?"

She bobbed her head, swallowing hard. "The other is, I don't want you to feel beholden to remain my husband. Whenever you feel you've gotten your—" She'd almost said "money's worth," but managed to halt the words. "Whenever you feel like moving on, I won't try to . . . that is, you'll be free to leave."

"Your contract says we have to stay married for a minimum of twelve months or there's a breach in the terms."

"Yes, I know. But just so there are no misunderstandings, I want to make something clear from the start. When the year is up, I don't want you to feel obligated to stay one day longer than you think necessary, even if . . . even if there's a child. Then after . . ." her fingers plucked at the fabric of her dress ". . . after you've been gone a few months, I'll find an attorney, say you deserted me, and file for a divorce."

Kit rose from his crouched position. Staring down at her, a muscle worked in his jaw. He couldn't believe she was planning their divorce before they'd taken their wedding vows. Knowing how difficult saying the words must have been, his spurt of pique faded. How could he be annoyed with her for voicing an issue he'd already spent time considering? Though in his plans *he* had been the one seeking a divorce, but not until after he'd made damn sure the ranch was on its feet and capable of supporting the Coleman women.

Forcing his facial muscles to relax, he blew out a resigned

breath. "Okay, agreed. If I want to leave after twelve months, you won't stop me. As for the issue of a child, you probably know more ways to prevent that possibility than I. So rest assured, between the two of us, we'll take care not to get you with child. Now, is there anything else?"

Shocked speechless by his blunt statements, she shook her head.

"Good. Since we've covered your conditions, there is . . . uh . . . one thing I need to take care of before we go any further. I have to show you something, then if you want to change your mind about marrying me, I'll understand."

Her curiosity aroused, she watched him raise a surprisingly unsteady hand, grab the crown of his hat, then slowly lift it from his head. Clutching the hat against one thigh, he turned so the light from the window fell across the right side of his face.

At her first view of Kit's eyes, Angelina blinked, her breathing erratic. She'd never seen such beautiful eyes. Deep-set beneath thick black brows, their color was a mesmerizing pale blue. Trying to control the wild pounding of her pulse, she studied the scar she'd only glimpsed before. Her gaze traced the slightly puckered red line from where it began over his right eyebrow, around his eye, down the side of his face then curved back to end just beneath his right cheekbone. Frowning, her heart contracted with concern over the pain such a wound must have caused. Her throat clogged with emotion, she swallowed hard.

Seeing her throat muscles work, the knot in Kit's gut tightened. She obviously found his looks so revolting speech was impossible. "You don't have to say it. I'll say it for you. You want to call off our deal. No problem. I—"

"What are you talking about?"

"I saw how you reacted to my scar. I can't expect you to marry a man who turns your stomach." He started to put his hat back on, but she jumped to her feet and knocked his hand aside.

"You don't make me ill. In fact, I think you're an extremely handsome man now that I've finally seen all of your face."

"You don't have to try to pacify me with false words, Angel. I know what—"

"Pacify you? Kittridge Dancer, how dare you say such a thing! I wasn't using false words. You *are* a handsome man. And as for the scar, if you saw me react at all, it was because I was thinking of how much pain it must have caused you. It doesn't repulse me in the least." To prove her point she lifted one hand and traced the crescent-shaped line with one finger. "In fact, I think without it, you would be much too handsome for your own good. At least the scar keeps y'all from getting a swelled head about your looks."

He inhaled sharply. "A swelled head? Why you—" He halted his heated reply, trying to soothe his irritation. After a few moments, his lips twitched with amusement. In a much softer voice, he said, "You little minx." He pulled her hand from his face and placed a kiss on her palm. Looking down into her upturned face, he saw she had spoken the truth. There was no revulsion, no pity reflected on her lovely features.

As he continued to stare at her, he watched her lips curve into a smile. The beauty of the first real smile she'd ever given him struck him like a physical blow. His stomach muscles tightening in reaction, he jerked, releasing her hand.

"Are you looking for an excuse to get out of our bargain?" she said, her smile slipping. "Is that why you were trying to put words in my mouth?"

Desire ignited and charged through his veins. He bit back a groan. At that moment he regretted promising not to consummate their marriage until she was ready. The suggestion that he take back his word wiggled its way into his brain, only to be dismissed with lightning speed. No, he was a man of his word. He would keep his promise to Angelina regardless of how much it pained him.

"No, I wasn't looking for an excuse to get out of our bargain," he whispered. "And as for your mouth . . ." He lowered his head, the rest of his words muffled by his kiss.

After kissing her thoroughly, Kit pulled her close and held her pressed against his chest. He closed his eyes, willing his heart to slow to a normal rhythm. Though desire still sang a thunderous melody in his blood, he was aware of another stirring deep inside—one that rocked him more than his physical reaction to Angel. He barely knew the woman in his embrace, and yet he recognized the signs—signs of feelings he'd never thought to experience again.

He could care for Angel. He could care one helluva lot.

Chapter Six

After Kit left to make the final arrangements for the wedding and their move to the ranch, a dazed Angelina went looking for Jenna. Her friend wasn't going to believe what had just happened—heavens, she hardly believed it herself! Finding Jenna in the kitchen talking to the Murray House cook, Lin-Shee, Angelina pulled out a chair, then plopped down on the seat.

"Howdy, Angel," Jenna said, flashing a smile. "Lin-Shee was just telling me about when she arrived in El Paso back in '81. She came here with her husband when he was hired with hundreds of other Chinese workers to build the railroad. The town was pretty wild back then and—Angel, are you okay? You're lookin' a mite poorly."

"Yes, Missy An-ge-rina, not look good," Lin-Shee said, bobbing her dark head, her single, thick braid swaying with the motion.

The way Lin-Shee pronounced her name always tickled Angelina, but that day she couldn't muster even a smile. "I . . . I'm fine. I just . . ." She shook her head, then took a deep breath. "I'm getting married."

"Married!" Jenna and Lin-Shee exclaimed in unison.

"When's the wedding? Who is he?" Jenna said, her eyes wide with anticipation. Before Angelina could respond, she answered her own question. "I bet he's that fella who's been hanging around here lately." She shifted her gaze to the young Chinese woman. "You know, the one I was telling you about,

Lin-Shee. That well-built devil who dresses all in black. He's real mannerly, but kinda mysterious."

She turned back to Angelina, waving one hand back and forth in front of her face. "Lord-a-mercy, my heart's a-racin' just thinking about that tall parcel of pure man." Leaning across the table, she lowered her voice to a whisper. "I've never seen him without his hat. Is he good-looking, Angel? Ooh, I bet he is." She dropped her voice to a conspiratorial whisper. "And, I bet he'll know all kinds of ways to please a woman. Don't you agree?"

The heat of a blush spreading across her face, Angelina couldn't meet Jenna's gaze. "First of all, y'all are correct about the man I'm to marry. His name is Kittridge Dancer, and yes, he's very handsome. But, as to the other, I don't think we should be discussing my future husband's . . . um . . . prowess."

Jenna sat back in her chair with a sigh. "You're right. Sorry, Angelina. Guess my mouth kinda got ahead of my brain."

"When you get married?" Lin-Shee said.

Angelina glanced at the smooth, round face of the tiny woman who was only a few years older than her own twenty-two. Her friends were certain to find her answer strange, but there was no way to change the facts. "We're to be at the minister's house at six. Kit said he'd be by to pick me up at quarter till."

"Six? You mean today?" Jenna's voice rose sharply. "My goodness, he sure didn't waste any time. He must've fallen for you hard."

Her face ablaze with another blush, Angelina cleared her throat, then said, "It isn't exactly what you think."

Jenna's eyes narrowed. "What are you trying to say?" When Angelina remained silent, she said, "Are you telling me you two aren't head over heels in love?"

Staring at the table, Angelina shook her head.

"But you like each other, right?"

Angelina lifted one shoulder in a shrug, then said, "I . . . I like him well enough, considering I've only known him a few days. But, I really don't know what he feels for me."

"Why you marry man who not love you?" Lin-Shee poured a glass of lemonade and pushed it across the table to Angelina. "In China, many couple marry who not know each other, but here love always most important."

Needing the distraction so she could think, Angelina lifted the glass of lemonade to her lips. She couldn't admit her misgivings about her marriage to Kit, especially about his motives, even to her best friends. Still, since they were the only ones who knew how she'd ended up working for James Murray, they should know at least part of the truth about her marriage.

After a few moments, she set the glass back on the table and said, "Kit wanted to know how I came to work at the Murray House. When I told him, he got very angry. I thought his anger was directed at me, but later I found out his fury was aimed at Mr. Wentworth for suggesting I work for Mr. Murray. That's when Kit decided to pay off my contract. He didn't find out about the marriage clause until he went to Mr. Murray's office."

Jenna accepted a glass of lemonade from Lin-Shee, then took a long drink. "I wish I could find a man willing to marry me and take me away from this place."

"I thought Austin said he wants to marry you."

"Yeah, that's what he always says when he's hot to take me upstairs," Jenna replied, thinking about the man who'd been a regular customer for several months. "But I finally figured out he doesn't really mean it. Him saying he wants to marry me is nothing more than lust-crazed talk. Once he gets what he wants, he sings a different tune."

Lin-Shee chuckled. "That true. Men not think like women. Their brain in different place, much lower, between legs."

Jenna laughed, her hazel eyes twinkling. "You've got that right." Sobering, she turned to Angelina. "You're lucky, Angelina. You met a man who meant what he said."

"Then you don't think I was foolish to agree to marry Kit? You don't think he's . . ." She swallowed. ". . . he's just being a good Samaritan?"

" 'Course I don't think you're foolish, Angelina. And as for him being a good Samaritan, I reckon you could call him that, but only 'cause he cares for you. I don't know this Kit fellow, but I've got a real strong notion about him. He'd never marry a woman he didn't have some feelings for. I'd stake my last dollar on it."

Angelina blinked with surprise. Was it possible Kit had more than humanitarian motives, that he felt more than desire for her? Her hopes lifted at the thought, then immediately sank. Kit thought she was a prostitute. That he could forget her past, especially one more sordid than it really was, and come to love her were just fanciful musings, like in a fairy tale, not a plausible development in their marriage.

"I'd like to believe you, Jenna. But I'm not as confident as you are about Kit's feelings for me."

"Look, Angelina, if you don't marry Kit and get out of your contract, you know what the alternative is."

Angelina slouched against the back of her chair. Jenna was right. If she didn't take the opportunity presented to her, she'd have to go back to her plan to pay off her contract by submitting to every man who paid for her time. The notion sent an icy shiver up her spine. That settled it; marrying Kit was the right choice.

Pushing away from the table, she rose. "I'd best get upstairs. It's nearly five, and I still have to figure out what I'm going to wear, then pack my things."

"I'll help you," Jenna said, shoving her chair back from the table.

Angelina nodded, then started to turn toward the dining room door.

"You come say good-bye before you leave, Missy An-ge-rina?"

"Of course I will, Lin-Shee. It won't take me long to pack. I'll be back in a few minutes."

Kit stood in the downstairs hallway of the house on Utah Street, one arm draped over the newel post, Angelina's two small bags at his feet. The wagon and team of horses he'd

bought waited in front of the house. Originally he'd planned
on renting a buggy to make the trip to the Coleman ranch, but
changed his mind when he saw the matched set of chestnut Belgians. The ranch could use a pair of work horses and a sturdy
wagon, so he'd decided buying would be wiser than renting.

He could hear muffled voices from the back of the house
where the woman he would soon marry was saying the last of
her good-byes. Waiting for Angel to return so they could keep
their appointment with the minister, Kit's thoughts drifted to
his second conversation with James Murray earlier that afternoon.

Once he'd exchanged the bank draft for Angel's contract, Kit
took the opportunity to ask some questions—questions which
had nagged at him since he'd heard how Angel had ended up
in Murray's brothel.

Though he tried to keep the questions innocuous, they cen-
tered around the man's practice of requiring his employees to
sign contracts, and more specifically, his business dealings with
Elliot Wentworth. Though Murray seemed surprised by the
line of questioning, he hesitated only briefly before making
short, brusque responses. At least he hadn't refused to answer
as Kit had feared.

When he left the White Horse Saloon a few minutes later,
Kit was certain James Murray hadn't been totally honest. As
he'd made his way to his rooming house to collect his belongings, his instincts told him the business relationship between
Murray and Wentworth bore looking into.

Though Kit wanted to do just that, he knew he wouldn't be
able to do any investigating right away. His first priority had
to be turning the Coleman ranch into a productive operation,
so that once the required twelve months had passed, he could
move on knowing Angelina and her family could take care of
themselves. Devoting time to anything else would have to wait.

His thoughts were interrupted by Angel's entrance into the
hallway. The pale yellow dress she wore was faded and slightly
worn, yet still most fetching with her dark complexion and
deep brown eyes. Though the dress was plain in design and of-

fered him no glimpse of bare skin other than her arms, Kit experienced another stirring of desire from just looking at her, from inhaling her sweet scent.

Jerking his mind away from the tantalizing thought of what lay hidden beneath her demure dress, he dropped his arm from the newel post and straightened.

"Ready?" he said, studying her face.

Angelina dabbed one last time at her eyes, then lifted her chin to stare up at him. Her voice was firm, revealing no trace of tears when she replied, "Yes."

Kit picked up her bags in one hand, then offered her his other arm. "The wagon's right out front."

The Reverend Morton was a tall, thin man with a hawkish nose and an unruly ruff of gray hair circling his bald pate. Kit hadn't felt particularly comfortable with the man during their earlier conversation, but he was willing to overlook his discomfort since the reverend had agreed to perform the wedding.

The front door of the parsonage swung open and Reverend Morton stood in the doorway, smiling broadly. "Mr. Dancer, right on time." He shook Kit's hand as he stepped inside. "And this must be your intended."

The smile on the minister's face disappeared. His graying eyebrows pulled together in a fierce scowl. Angelina stared up at the man, her stomach dropping to her toes. When Kit told her the name of the man who was to marry them, she'd been relieved that he hadn't contacted the minister who'd started visiting the Coleman ranch soon after her family moved in. She couldn't imagine how she would have faced the pastor who'd shown such kindness to her mother.

But now, standing in front of Reverend Morton, being the object of his scrutiny through a gaze so piercing it seemed to probe into her very soul, she wished she could just close her eyes and disappear. Of all the other preachers in town, why did Kit have to pick this one? Though she'd never heard the minister's name, she had seen him before. At the Murray House where he'd come to preach the gospel. And from the sour look on his face, he remembered seeing her there, as well.

Seeing the reverend's expression change and Angel's stiff posture, Kit's brow furrowed. "Is there is problem?"

Angelina started at Kit's voice. Turning her gaze to meet his, she shook her head.

"Reverend?"

After clearing his throat, Reverend Morton said, "No. There's no problem. If you'll follow me into the parlor, we can begin right away. My wife Clara and Mrs. Middaugh, a member of my church, will serve as witnesses."

Angelina followed behind the minister, praying she looked like a woman about to marry the man she loved. Somehow she managed to plaster a weak smile on her face, certain her efforts did little to portray the desired image.

Reverend Morton spoke quietly with the other two ladies in the room, then turned to make the introductions. His wife, a plump woman whose graying hair was pulled up into a severe knot atop her head, and Mrs. Middaugh, slightly older and painfully thin, a pair of glasses perched on her long narrow nose, simpered under Kit's formal bow and soft greeting. When Angelina stepped forward, the expression on the women's faces changed. Instead of gushing friendliness, curt nods and tight-lipped glares met her murmured, "Pleased to meet you."

Taken aback at their hostility, Angelina wondered at the reason for their abrupt change. As she turned away, she heard Mrs. Middaugh speak to her companion. "Who does she think she is, Clara, working at one of *those* places and asking to be married by a man of God? Gracious me, I've never been . . ."

The woman's voice faded away, replaced by a loud buzzing in Angelina's head. Obviously Reverend Morton had wasted no time telling them he'd seen her at the Murray House during one of his monthly attempts to reform those he said made their living through sin and degradation. She always figured the reverend to be a fanatic about his calling, attacking anyone who didn't work in what he believed to be an acceptable profession, hoping to convert such sinners to his views. Apparently he wasn't the only one to judge others with such zeal.

She glanced over at Kit. There was nothing in his stoic expression to indicate he'd also overheard Mrs. Middaugh's comment. Feeling the cold stares of the two women boring into her back, Angelina moved woodenly to take her assigned place next to Kit and in front of Reverend Morton.

As the minister started the wedding ceremony, she barely heard his words, her thoughts dwelling on how she would be treated by others in town.

While working in El Paso, she had kept to the Murray House or the rooming house next-door. Her only venture outside of those two places was visiting her mother and sister every Sunday. She hadn't tried to avoid the people of town, there just hadn't been a reason for her to go anywhere. And since she couldn't afford to buy anything, there'd been no point in going shopping. Ruby had constantly warned all the Murray House girls about leaving the tenderloin. But at the time, Angelina thought the madame was only trying to make sure anyone under contract wasn't tempted to just walk away from her obligation. Now she knew Ruby hadn't been giving out false warnings.

Would everyone rebuff her like the two ladies now standing behind and to the right of Kit? She *had* worked in a brothel, she wouldn't deny that, but she shouldn't be condemned for trying to support her family. Realizing how self-righteous people could be, no one would care what had prompted her to take a job at the Murray House. She'd started out as a piano player and even after she'd asked to join the prostitutes, she had never truly become one. Although it didn't matter now.

She knew such a distinction would not be made by those who condemned her. The fact that she'd worked in a brothel, regardless of her position, would be the one and only detail the townsfolk would take to heart.

The knowledge that her employment at the Murray House would be more costly than she'd imagined was another staggering blow to her self-esteem. Though she'd known her reputation would suffer when she first agreed to Mr. Wentworth's suggestion, she'd never given much thought to how she would be received once she left James Murray's employ. Crossing that bridge had always loomed well in the future.

The price she would have to pay now painfully clear, she . . . Reverend Morton's booming voice jerked Angelina back to the present.

"I pray that God in all his divine wisdom," he nearly shouted, staring at her with those piercing black eyes, "will forgive you your past sins. Miss Coleman, you should get down on your knees and offer the Lord Jesus a prayer of thanks. You should be forever grateful to Mr. Dancer for his willingness to remove you from a house of sin. He has surely saved your soul from eternal damnation."

"Reverend," Kit said, when the man paused to draw a breath. "We're under a pretty tight schedule here. Could you cut the preaching and just get on with the wedding?"

Reverend Morton flashed Kit an annoyed glance, but gave him a curt nod.

Angelina breathed a sigh of relief, thankful Kit had halted the minister's sermonizing. She wanted nothing more than to have the ceremony end, then get out of town as quickly as possible.

In just a few minutes, her wish was fulfilled. She and Kit exchanged wedding vows, the Reverend Morton pronounced them man and wife, and they made their exit from the parsonage.

By the time she'd climbed up onto the wagon, a horrible pounding headache had started behind her eyes. Gripping the side of the seat with one hand, her back ramrod-stiff, she sat in silence as Kit checked to be sure his horse was tied securely to the rear of the wagon then climbed up beside her. When he directed the teams of horses down Utah Street her grip on the seat relaxed a fraction, some of the stiffness left her spine. At last she was going home.

Kit's voice jarred her from her musings. "Just what the hell was that all about back there?"

"What are you talking about?"

"You know damn well what I'm talking about, Angel. It was obvious you two knew each other, and I'm sure it wasn't because you attended Reverend Morton's church. Don't tell me he was one of your customers?"

Angelina gasped. Of all the things Kit could have said, accusing her of consorting with a minister had never crossed her mind. Though she seethed with anger inside, the pounding in her head forced her to speak in a low steady voice. "I'd never met Reverend Morton before tonight, but yes, I have seen him before. He made the rounds of all the places in town he claimed were spawning depravity, preaching about sin and damnation and that all heathens must change their ways. As to his being a customer of mine or any of the other girls at the Murray House, he never left the parlor. He'd storm in the front door, Bible raised in the air, shout his sermon, then leave."

"Why didn't you say something when I told you who was going to marry us?"

"I never knew his name. Everyone called him the zealot preacher. We just pretended to listen to his pious ranting when he showed up every month, then go about our business after he left. We never asked the man his name."

Kit grunted in reply, wondering if he'd ever forget where Angel had worked, or stop suspecting every man they met had been one of her customers. He didn't like himself much for what he'd said to her, but for some reason he had trouble controlling the spurt of jealousy when he thought about her past. He heaved a sigh. She was his wife now, and former prostitute or not, she didn't deserve such nasty insinuations.

"Listen, Angel, it's getting late. Maybe we should just stay in town tonight, then head for the ranch in the morning."

"No!" Angel snapped, making her head pound all the more. Lowering her voice, she added, "You told me we'd go to the ranch after the wedding. You can't change your mind now. I want to go home tonight."

"It'll be dark soon. Are you sure you want to make the trip tonight?"

"Yes, I'm sure. I don't care what time we get there, I just want to get out of this town. Now."

Hearing something in her voice, Kit said, "Okay, we'll do as we originally planned."

She sighed with relief, the ache in her head letting up. Barely noticing the buildings they passed, she kept her gaze locked on the mountains north of town, the mountains which formed the eastern border of her family's ranch. She had to concentrate on returning to the home she'd known for such a short time before moving into El Paso. She had to think about her mother and her sister, about how much work was yet to be done on the ranch, anything to keep herself from giving in to the threatening tears.

Knowing she could not allow herself to indulge in self-pity, she pulled herself together. By summoning the icy facade she'd used at the Murray House, she would never let her family know how much she— Kit's shifting on the seat snapped her back, reminding her there was another person in her future. For the next twelve months anyway.

Kit maintained the silence Angel seemed to prefer for a long time into their trip, wondering why she was so withdrawn. Was she still upset with him over his accusations about her and Reverend Morton? Or was she already regretting their marriage?

He transferred the reins to one hand, then reached over and squeezed her left hand, the wide gold wedding band he'd placed on her third finger cool against his palm.

"You okay, Angel?"

The soft tone and the concern she heard in his voice formed a lump in her throat. She swallowed, then turned to look at her husband. Her husband. The words sounded so strange. "Yes, I'm fine."

The flash of white teeth in his broad smile erased his earlier harsh words from her memory, scattering her thoughts like a handful of dirt tossed into the wind. A coil of heat careened through her body, a flush burned her cheeks, and her heart began a wild thumping against her ribs.

Seeing the darkening of her eyes, the heavy throbbing of the pulse at the base of her throat, Kit recognized her reaction for what it was. An answering flare of need sizzled through him, making him wish yet again he could take back the promise he'd made.

Trying to forget about the desire swirling around them like a thick billow of fog on a warm, rain-soaked morning, he forced himself to think of other things.

"How much farther?" he finally said, unwilling to tell her he knew exactly where they were going.

She glanced around, surprised to realize the sun had set while she'd been caught up in her thoughts. Peering into the rapidly falling darkness, she said, "We turn off another mile or so up ahead. There's a small trail to the east that leads right to the ranch."

He nodded, then shifted his gaze back to the road. Sensing Angel's eagerness to reach the ranch, he slapped the reins on the horses' backs. "Giddap, there, hosses."

Chapter Seven

James Murray jumped off the mule-drawn street car in front of the El Paso Bank. Though the front doors of the business were locked, he knew Elliot Wentworth always worked well past closing. Striding down the alley next to the bank, he headed for the building's side entrance. He stepped into the narrow hallway, then approached Wentworth's office. The door stood slightly ajar.

Hearing footsteps in the hall, Elliot Wentworth looked up from the papers on his desk. He was accustomed to having visitors show up at his office during the evening, and he was only mildly surprised to see who was standing in the doorway. Sitting back in his chair, he folded his hands across his belly.

"Well, well. Haven't seen you in a long spell, Murray. What brings you here tonight?"

James Murray moved across the thick Aubusson carpet, then sank into a chair across from the banker. Stroking one side of his moustache, he studied Elliot Wentworth. The man was somewhere in his early fifties, with thinning brown hair and heavy side whiskers. He could see the slight paunch beneath the man's smooth, well-manicured hands. A ruby ring winked in the lamplight from its place on the little finger of his right hand.

"I had a visitor today, Wentworth. A man asking questions about one of the women you sent to me."

One thin eyebrow raised. "And?"

"And, I don't like being asked questions I'm not prepared to deal with. You told me there would never be any problem with our arrangement." He dropped his hand from his moustache and pointed a finger at Wentworth. "You guaranteed no one would ever get wise to the plan you cooked up."

Wentworth jerked forward in his chair, his jowls bouncing with the movement. "Not *my* plan, Murray. It's yours, as well. You were involved just as much as I when we transformed my idea into a plan, and don't you forget it."

"Damnit, Elliot, no one has asked even one question about the employees I've gotten through you since we started working together. We have a good thing going here and I don't need someone interfering or causing—"

"Settle down, James. There's no need to get yourself all riled up. This is the first time anyone's asked about one of your employees or their contracts, so what are you so worried about?"

"The man who was doing the asking was a cold son-of-a-bitch, one who looked damned competent with the gun strapped to his hip."

"Who is he? Somebody with a beef against you?"

Murray shrugged. "Calls himself Kit Dancer, and as far as I can tell, paying off Angelina's contract has nothing to do with his looking to get back at me."

"Angelina? Is that the Coleman girl?"

"Yeah."

Elliot chuckled, leaning back in his chair and lacing his fingers back over his belly. "Well, I wouldn't waste my time worrying about Mr. Dancer, James. The Coleman place is a good ten miles from town and a damn poor excuse for a ranch. Besides, Angelina's mother is a lunger. Bed-ridden. So between making repairs and seeing that his mother-in-law is looked after, I'd venture to say Dancer won't have the time to poke around into our business dealings."

Murray stared at the banker for a long moment, then said, "You'd better be right, Elliot, 'cause I sure as hell don't want trouble."

"Look, if Dancer starts sticking his nose where it doesn't belong, I'll see to it the prying bastard is taken care of. Fair enough?"

Settling back in his chair, Murray twisted one side of his moustache. "Yeah, okay. Fair enough."

Kit pulled the horses to a stop in front of the Coleman ranch house, then turned to Angelina. Though night had settled in, a full moon cast enough light for him to make out her stiff posture and the way she clenched her hands in her lap.

"Are you all right?" he said.

She started, then turned her face toward him. Worry lines puckered her brow. "I'm fine. I was just thinking how . . ." She cleared her throat, unable to say what she'd really been thinking, that she'd been wondering how to tell her mother and sister about her sudden marriage.

"You were thinking how . . . what?" Kit prompted when she remained silent.

She shifted her gaze back to the front of the house. Finally, she said, "I was thinking how strange it feels knowing I won't have to go back to town and the Murray House anymore."

Kit's jaw tightened. "Will you miss working at the brothel?"

Swinging around to face him, her eyes wide, she said, "That's not what I meant. I'll miss some of the people, like Jenna and Lin-Shee. But I won't miss working there."

"What about the customers? You won't miss any of them?"

Giving him a questioning look, she shook her head. "No, of course not."

Allowing the muscles of his face to relax, Kit wrapped the reins around the brake handle, then jumped to the ground. Once again the promise he'd made to Angelina came to mind. Too bad he'd been foolish enough to be so gallant, otherwise he'd make damn sure she didn't miss any of the men she'd entertained at the Murray House. Just thinking of making her his wife in the physical sense caused his blood to warm.

Forcing his thoughts from the tantalizing picture his imagination had created, he removed their luggage from the back of the wagon. He set the bags on the front porch, then turned to help Angelina. As he wrapped his hands around her waist and lifted her down, it took all of his control not to pull her against his chest. Setting her on her feet, he gave in to temptation and pressed a brief kiss on her mouth.

Seeing the surprise in her eyes, he smiled. "Better get used to me kissing you every now and then," he said in a husky whisper. "We don't want your mother and sister to suspect the truth, that our marriage isn't a love match, now do we?"

Angelina fought the surge of desire singing in her veins. Though only a slight brushing of lips, Kit's kiss had shaken her badly. When she'd managed to regain her composure, she whispered, "No, I don't want them to—"

Angelina's words were cut off by the sound of the front door opening. A lamp in the room revealed the silhouette of someone standing in the doorway. "Who's out there?" the person shouted. "I have a gun, and I know how to use it."

"Oh for heaven's sake, Chloe. It's me. And you'd better put Papa's gun down before you hurt yourself."

"Angelina! What are you doing here?" Chloe replied, dropping the rifle from her shoulder. "I told Mama I heard something, but I never expected to find you out here. Leastways not on a weeknight." Two flashes of dark fur whisked around her skirt, ran across the porch, and disappeared into the night.

"Eros. Nyx!" Chloe called. "You two get back in the house." Shifting her gaze from the moonlit yard to her older sister, she said, "What are you doing here?"

Stepping away from Kit, Angelina turned toward the door. "I'm moving back to the ranch. How's Mama?"

"She's getting weaker, and she needs her medicine more often." Chloe eyed the man standing next to Angelina, her brow furrowed. "She'll be glad to know you're here to stay."

Following her sister's gaze, Angelina said, "Kit, I'd like you to meet my sister, Chloe. And, Chloe, this is Kit Dancer."

"Ma'am." Kit touched two fingers to his hat brim. The moonlight didn't reach under the porch roof, so he couldn't see Chloe's face. But the glow of the lamp behind her revealed a shape and height very similar to Angelina's petite willowy form.

"Mr. Dancer."

"No need to be formal. Call me Kit."

Her brow furrowing even more, she said, "All right, if you'll call me Chloe."

Angelina moved across the porch to stand in front of her sister. Seeing the confusion on Chloe's face, she whispered, "I'll explain everything later." Glancing over her shoulder, she raised her voice to say, "Kit, if you'll get our bags, I'll show you where to put them. Then I want to introduce you to Mama."

He nodded, then bent to grasp the handles of their luggage. When he straightened, Chloe had disappeared inside the house and Angelina waited for him in the doorway.

Stepping over the threshold, Kit blinked with surprise. The interior of the house bore no resemblance to the neglected exterior. The wooden floor had been waxed to a high sheen, the walls painted a soft cream color. On one side of the room, a large colorful rug lay beneath the overstuffed sofa and pair of chairs arranged around the fireplace. On the opposite end, a large archway revealed the kitchen with its large pedestal table and matching chairs sitting atop another brightly colored rug.

Kit followed Angelina across the parlor, through a second, smaller archway, then turned left down a hallway. At the end of the hall, Angelina stopped at a closed door.

"Just a minute and I'll light a lamp," she said, opening the door and stepping inside.

Kit heard the scratch of a match, then watched as the soft glow of lamplight illuminated the room. Cautiously, he moved forward.

The plank floor bore the same soft shine as the rest of the house. Pale blue curtains trimmed with lace hung at the single window. A four-poster bed covered with a patchwork quilt dominated the room. A chest of drawers and a large steamer trunk stood against one wall. A row of wooden pegs for clothes and a washstand took up another.

When Kit remained silent, Angelina said, "This is my . . . I mean, our room." In spite of her best efforts, she couldn't stop the blood from rushing to her face. "After we see Mama, I'll rearrange the drawers in the chest to make room for your things."

Kit gave her a nod, unable to take his gaze off the bed. This was something he hadn't considered. Sleeping in the same bed, only inches from his desirable wife, how was he going to keep his hands to himself? And what would he do about the nightmares?

He couldn't believe he hadn't considered this complication. But then, he'd lost the ability to think with his usual cool-headed logic ever since he'd first seen Angel. He squeezed his eyes closed, then drew a deep breath. Keeping his promise was becoming more and more difficult.

Angelina's voice pulled him from his troubled thoughts. Allowing his lids to drift upward, he turned to look at her. She was staring at him with those beautiful whiskey-colored eyes, her forehead crinkled with concern. He swallowed hard. "What?"

"I said, I'd like you to meet my mother now."

He nodded, then turned to follow her from the room, purposely keeping his gaze on the knot of hair at the back of her head, away from the enticing gentle sway of her hips.

Angelina opened her mother's bedroom door, then peeked inside. The lamp on the bedside table burned low. "Mama, are you awake?" she whispered.

Sarah Coleman stirred. "Angelina? Is that you?" Turning her head on the pillow, she smiled at the sight of her oldest daughter. "What are y'all doing here, darlin'? You were just here on Sunday. Is everything all right?"

Angelina approached the bed, chuckling softly. "Yes, Mama, everything is fine." She grasped her mother's thin hands with hers and squeezed. "I'm . . . I'm moving back to the ranch."

Sarah's mouth pulled into a frown. "What do you mean? What about your job, and the money we owe?"

"I'll explain all of that, but first I want you to meet someone." Turning toward the door, she motioned Kit to enter.

Pulling his hat from his head, Kit took a step into the room.

Angelina turned back to her mother, took a deep breath, then said, "Mama, I'd like to introduce Kittridge Dancer."

When Angelina moved away from the bed, Kit got his first glimpse of his mother-in-law. Sarah Coleman was a tiny woman, the large bed nearly swallowing her among the bedclothes. Propped up by a mound of pillows, her silver hair and pale, nearly translucent skin gave her an ethereal appearance.

Shifting her gaze from her daughter's face to where a man stood just inside the door, she offered him a smile. "Mistuh Dancer, I'm mighty pleased to meet a friend of Angelina's."

Kit saw Angelina's shoulders stiffen. Willing to let her explain their relationship, he said, "The pleasure is mine, Mrs. Coleman."

Two bright splashes of color appeared on her cheeks. In spite of her pallor, her eyes sparkled with life. "Thank you kindly, Mistuh Dancer. Will you be staying with us long?"

Before Kit could respond, Angelina said, "Mama, there's something I want to tell you."

Sarah shifted her gaze back to her daughter. "Yes, dear, what is it?"

Angelina cleared her throat. This was proving to be more difficult than she'd thought. Screwing up her courage, she blurted, "Kit is my husband."

"What?" Sarah's eyes went wide. "Did you say husband?"

"Yes, Mama. Kit and I were married in El Paso."

"Married in El Paso," Sarah repeated, stunned. "My goodness, dear, you sure know how to surprise a person. You never mentioned having a beau during your visits."

Her hands clenched in the fabric of her skirt, Angelina took a deep breath. She'd never lied to her mother, but she couldn't risk upsetting her with the truth. "I know, Mama. I . . . um . . . never said anything because I . . . uh . . . I wasn't sure how . . ." She flashed a desperate look at Kit.

He took another step into the room. "What your daughter is trying to say, ma'am, is that we haven't known each other for a very long time. And since she wasn't sure what my intentions were in such a new relationship, she thought it best not to mention me to her family. I hope you won't hold that against her."

Snapping out of her shock, Sarah said, "So where and when were you married?"

"The Reverend Morton married us in his parsonage at six o'clock . . . yesterday." She just couldn't bring herself to admit she and Kit had only been married a matter of hours, that there had been no wedding supper, no wedding night, as her mother undoubtedly assumed. Before Sarah could comment, Angelina said, "Sorry you couldn't be there, Mama. But we—"

Sarah smiled. "Don't be sorry, dear. I could never have made the trip. I'm just happy you finally stopped that foolishment about never marrying." Looking past her daughter at the man still standing just inside her room, she lifted one hand toward Kit. "Well, come closer, Mistuh Dancer and let me get a good look at you."

Kit exhaled slowly, then moved forward. When he stood next to the bed, he took the hand Sarah offered. Holding her fragile fingers gently in his, he bent and brushed his lips across her knuckles.

She blinked with surprise, then flashed him a bright smile. "Well, blast my old shoes, but it's been a month of Sundays since I met a true Southern gentleman."

The corners of his mouth twitching, Kit straightened, then dropped her hand. He waited silently while Sarah looked him over. Seeing the sudden knitting of her brows, his humor fled. He'd hoped the soft light in the room would prevent this. Trying to exude an air of indifference, he braced himself for the worst.

"My stars, Angelina," Sarah said, her face glowing with delight. "You've bagged yourself one fine-looking man."

"Mama! Shame on you. I can't believe you would say such things."

"Why ever not, dear? I was only speaking the truth. Didn't I always teach you and Chloe to tell the truth?" She turned to look up at her new son-in-law. "Surely there's nothing wrong in speaking the truth. Wouldn't you agree, Mistuh Dancer?"

Kit wondered if she had spoken the truth. Maybe she'd paid him a compliment because she was too kindhearted to tell him her true reaction to his looks. Staring into the depths of her snapping brown eyes, he tried to judge her sincerity. Her exaggerated wink gave him a start. Fighting down the urge to laugh, he finally said, "I'd like it if you'd call me Kit. And, yes, ma'am, I agree. There's nothing wrong in speaking the truth."

Glancing over at his wife, he wasn't so sure he should have agreed. If he told Angelina the truth about wanting to take back his promise, he could very well punch holes in Sarah's theory.

"I'd be honored to call you Kit," Sarah replied. "And I do hope y'all can come up with another form of address for me, anything but ma'am. I've no objection to your using my given name. Provided you feel comfortable with that, of course. Or maybe . . ." Realizing no one was listening, Sarah fell silent, content to look at her oldest daughter and her new son-in-law.

With her illness taking more and more of a toll, Sarah was delighted by the unexpected turn of events. She had worried so much about Angelina working in El Paso—though she'd tried not to let on—but now she would rest easier. Angelina had a man to take care of her, a man who—if she read the expression on his face correctly—deeply cared for his new bride. Sarah sighed, pleased one of her daughters had found a mate. Now if only Chloe would forget about her animals and do the same, she would die a happy woman.

As Kit continued to stare at Angelina, his eyes filled with blue fire, the heat of another flush crept up her face, a tingling rippled through her body. With every ounce of strength she could muster, she managed to wrest her gaze from his and turned to study her mother. *Chloe was right about Mama. She's definitely weaker.*

"Are you warm enough, Mama?" she said, straightening the bedclothes. "Do you need your pillows fluffed up?"

Sarah brushed her daughter's hands away. "Stop fussing over me. I'm perfectly—" A fit of coughing ended her declaration.

"Oh, Mama, I knew this was too much for you. We'll leave you now so you can get some sleep." Angelina started to turn away, but her mother's surprisingly strong grip on her arm stopped her.

"No, wait," Sarah managed to say between deep racking coughs.

After a few moments, the attack passed. Even paler than before, she laid back on the pillows, a linen handkerchief pressed to her lips. When she caught her breath enough to speak, her voice was slightly breathless, a mere whisper. "Please don't leave. I want to hear all about you and Kit. Wherever did you two meet?"

Angelina's gaze met Kit's for just a second, then skittered away. Before she could think of how to answer her mother's question, Kit spoke up.

"I met Angelina at her place of employment."

Angelina's eyes went wide. Would he forget the promise he'd made? "Yes, that's right," she said, before he could elaborate. "He called on me several times, then I accepted his invitation to take a walk with him."

"Down by the river," Kit added.

"Ah, the river," Sarah said with a smile. "Your father and I used to take strolls down by the river before we were married. The river is such a . . ." She yawned. ". . . a romantic setting for courting."

"Mama, it's late and you're exhausted. We'll leave now. Do you want your medicine?"

Sarah rolled her head from side to side on the pillow. "I don't believe I'll need it tonight, dear. All this excitement has left me plum wore out." She managed a weak wave toward the door. "Y'all run along. We'll talk more another time."

Angelina bent to place a kiss on her mother's forehead, then backed away from the bed. She tiptoed from the room, her husband moving silently behind her.

Back in what was formerly her bedroom, Angelina set to work. She unpacked her meager wardrobe, then emptied half the dresser drawers. When she was finished, she looked over at Kit's luggage: a pair of saddlebags and a small leather satchel.

A frown pulled at the corners of her mouth. Should she unpack her husband's bags, as well?

Kit watched her work from where he stood, one shoulder leaning against the doorjamb, thumbs hooked in his gunbelt. They hadn't exchanged a word since leaving her mother's room, but he rather enjoyed the silence while watching Angel.

Pushing away from the door, Kit said, "Don't worry about taking care of my things, Angel. I'll do that after I take care of the horses. They need to be unhitched and fed."

Angelina started, swinging a surprised gaze to meet his. "Fed? Heavens, I forgot all about eating. You must be starved. Can I fix you something to eat while you tend the horses?"

"You don't have to. I can rustle up something."

"Don't be silly," she said, moving past him to the door. "I brought a ham when I visited last Sunday, so there's bound to be some left over. I'll put on a pot of coffee and have everything ready by the time you get back."

He nodded, then followed her down the hall. "I'll bring in the supplies before I take the wagon down to the barn."

Angelina halted at the door to the kitchen. "Supplies? I didn't have time to buy anything before we left El Paso."

"I know. But I did. The back of the wagon is filled with boxes of food, sacks of grain, and other things I figured we could use."

"Oh." Angelina couldn't believe she hadn't noticed the supplies in the back of the wagon. She'd been so nervous about marrying Kit, then so upset with the way she'd been received in Reverend Morton's home, that she hadn't even thought about what had been beneath the tarp in the wagon bed. "That's very kind of you. Thank you," she said. "Do you need some help?"

"No, I can get them, and you don't have to thank me, Angel. Since I'll be living here, I intend to take care of you and your mother and sister. They're my family now, too."

Kit clenched his teeth, hoping he hadn't spoken rash words. He did intend to take care of his new family, the same way he'd intended to care for another family he'd been a part of. Unfortunately for his first wife and son, even the best of intentions hadn't meant squat in the end. *If only I'd taken his threat seriously. But this time, I swear I'll do a better job.*

Angelina saw the pain etched on Kit's face and wondered at the cause. "Are you okay?" she asked, reaching out to place a hand on his arm. His muscles flexed, the raw power of his strength evident beneath her fingers.

"Yeah," he replied. Seeing the concern on Angel's face, he pulled himself from his momentary lapse into the past, the ache in his heart easing. "By the way, who or what are Eros and Nyx?"

Stepping into the kitchen, Angelina chuckled. "Chloe's cats. My sister has always loved animals; she has a real gift when it comes to doctoring anything with fur or feathers. She's always taking in strays or injured critters, then setting the wild ones free when they're fit. Some of them end up being her pets, like Eros and Nyx."

Angelina turned pensive for a moment, thinking of Chloe's devotion to animals and wishing again her sister could have gone on with her schooling. Realizing Kit was waiting for her to continue, she said, "Anyway, another of Chloe's loves is mythology, so she names all her animals for Greek deities. Eros is always on the prowl for a willing lady cat so Chloe named him after the God of Love. And since Nyx's fur is as black as a chunk of coal, he was named for the Goddess of Night, though of course he doesn't know his namesake was female. If you see either of them when you go outside, try to shoo them to the house. Chloe doesn't like to let them run at night."

Kit smiled. "I doubt they'll listen to me. But if I see them, I'll try to shag them toward the house."

"Just tell them there's cream in their dish and they'll come running." Seeing the dubious look on Kit's face, she said, "I know, it sounds crazy. But I told you, Chloe really has a way with animals, and those two cats understand more than some people. I'll pour the cream, you just tell them it's here."

"Okay. Any idea where they might have gone?"

"Probably the barn. They're both good mousers, so my guess

is that's—Oh, that reminds me, when y'all go into the barn watch out for Hermes. Chloe's goat. Once he gets to know you, he'll be fine. Until then, watch yourself around him. He might try to butt you, or even take a chunk out of your hide if he thinks you have food you're not sharing. Chloe named him after the God of Thieves because he'll steal anything he can eat. Carrots. Apples. Boots. Gloves. You name it."

"You're pulling my leg, right?"

" 'Fraid not. Hermes will eat anything and everything, so hang onto your hat and don't turn your back on him."

Shaking his head, Kit left Angelina in the kitchen and went outside. After he unloaded the wagon, he led the team of horses across the yard and into the barn.

Keeping a careful eye on the long-haired goat on the other side of the barn, he unhitched the pair of Belgians, then turned them loose in the corral behind the barn. After untying Sid from the back of the wagon and putting the gelding in one of the empty stalls, he made sure all three horses had feed and water before heading back to the house. He washed up using the basin of water sitting on a bench beneath the overhang of the north side of the house, then entered the kitchen door and stepped inside.

Chapter Eight

Kit gave the kitchen a cursory glance, noting the food he'd brought had been unpacked and put away and a platter of thick slices of ham sat in the center of the table along with a crock of butter and a loaf of bread. The smell of fresh coffee filled the air.

Angelina looked up to see him standing just inside the door, then nodded toward the table. "Have a seat and help yourself. I'll get the coffee."

Kit dropped his hat on a hook by the door, then moved across the room and sat down. "I see Eros and Nyx came back." He nodded toward where the pair of cats sat crouched in front of a plate of cream, the tips of their tails flicking slowly as they lapped up their promised treat.

"Yes. They yowled at the back door not long after you went outside. I told you they'd come running at the mention of cream," she replied, taking a seat opposite him.

Shifting his gaze from the pair of cats to the food on the table, Kit picked up his fork and reached for the platter of ham.

Though Angelina hadn't felt hungry while she prepared the hurried meal, seeing how much Kit enjoyed the simple fare roused her appetite. The food was quickly eaten, and second cups of coffee poured.

"I've been thinking," Kit said after Angel set the coffeepot back on the stove and returned to her chair. Schooling his features to reveal none of his inner feelings, he kept his gaze on his cup when he continued. "It might be best if I slept in the barn."

Angelina's head snapped up. "No, you can't do that!" she said with more volume than she intended.

"Don't worry about Hermes," he replied. "I'll make sure he stays on his side of the barn."

Leaning across the table, she lowered her voice to a fierce whisper. "No, that's not what I meant. I wasn't talking about Chloe's goat. I meant, we have to look like we're married." In spite of her determination not to blush, she felt the heat creep up her neck onto her cheeks. "Married couples don't sleep like that: the wife in the house and the husband in the barn."

The corners of his mouth lifted in a crooked smile. "They might if they've had a spat."

"Stop teasing, Kit. I'm serious. We have to sleep in the same room and . . ." she swallowed, her cheeks burning even more, "in the same bed."

His smile faded. Wondering if his predicament could get any more complicated, he stared at her. Maybe he could change her mind. As quickly as the notion formed, he knew it was out of the question. The determination in her eyes and the stubborn tilt of her chin told him she wouldn't be swayed.

He ran a weary hand over his stubbled jaw. Somehow he had to dredge up the self-control to do as she wanted. Finally, he said, "All right, you've made your point."

Watching relief mix with the sadness in her eyes did strange things to his insides. Ignoring his reaction, he pushed his chair away from the table and stood. "Where's Chloe?"

"In her room. Once she knew her cats were safe, she said she was going to bed, though she's probably reading one of those old veterinary journals again."

"What about you? You've had a long day. Aren't you going to bed?"

"As soon as I clean up the kitchen and . . . um . . . make a trip to the backhouse," she replied, unable to meet his gaze.

"The back—? Oh, I take it that's what folks in Georgia call an outside privy?"

"Yes, though only homes far from town still have them."

Kit stared at her thoughtfully for a moment, then said, "You must've had a hard time adjusting to conditions here."

She shrugged. "Not really, though I do miss not having a room for bathing. Hauling a tub into the kitchen whenever I want to take a bath gets rather tiresome."

"Yeah, I imagine it would," he replied, filing the information away with what he already knew about the ranch's shortcomings. Moving across the room, he said, "I think I'll make that trip to the . . . uh . . . backhouse first, if that's okay."

At her nod, he opened the kitchen door and stepped into the darkness.

After he returned to the house, Angelina made her trip outside, returning a few minutes later and heading to the bedroom she would now share with Kit.

Her heart pounding a loud rhythm in her ears, she entered the room to find him staring out the window. Glad he had his back to the door, she took advantage of the moment and allowed her gaze to roam over the black shirt pulled taut by his wide shoulders and muscular back. Then dropping her gaze lower, she noted how his trousers hugged the contours of his thighs, hips, and derriere like a custom-fit glove.

She shivered, though not from a chill. The once unfamiliar but now increasingly less foreign spark of heat made another sizzling trip through her body. She had never felt anything so wonderful or so disturbing. What was it about him that—

"Did you bolt the doors?"

His voice brought her back to the present. "Yes," she replied in what she hoped sounded like a normal tone.

"Good," he said, loosening his gunbelt and slipping it from his hips. He refastened the buckle, then hung the leather belt on the wall peg nearest him. Glancing over his shoulder, he said, "Aren't you gonna get undressed? Or were you planning on sleeping in your clothes?"

"No, I was just . . ." She drew an unsteady breath. "Could

I . . . um . . . turn out the lamp before I change into my night-dress?"

Kit narrowed his gaze, his eyebrows pulled together in a scowl. He'd never known a soiled dove to be modest—usually they were eager to undress for a man, more than willing to flaunt their bodies in a shameless display. He shrugged. *Must be she's nervous because we're in her mother's house.* "Fine," he finally replied, moving to the side of the bed and sitting down. "Just let me get my boots off, then you can douse the lamp."

"Don't you need to unpack? I mean, don't you wear something to . . ."

Kit's hands stilled in the chore of tugging off his right boot. Damn! This was something else he hadn't considered. "Well, usually I prefer to sleep the way God made me." He heard her soft gasp.

For a reason he couldn't identify, her reaction to his frank words rubbed him the wrong way. His voice gruff, he said, "I never owned one of those ridiculous nightshirts, and I sure as hell don't aim to start wearing one now."

After a moment, his frustration eased. Turning to look at her, his voice was softer when he said, "Angel, listen, I . . ." Her wide-eyed gaze, the slight trembling of her mouth, halted what he'd been about to say. He sighed, then said, "All right. Out of consideration for you, I reckon I could sleep in my drawers."

Angelina relaxed her stiff posture. "Thank you," she murmured, dropping her gaze so he wouldn't see the tears of relief in her eyes.

After Kit removed both boots and tossed them aside, she reached for the lamp and turned down the wick. Only the silvery moonlight filtering through the window kept the room from total darkness.

As she removed her clothes, she could hear the rustle of Kit removing his on the opposite side of the bed. She pulled her nightdress over her head, buttoned the placket up to her chin, then threw back the quilt and eased under the top sheet.

In just a minute, Kit slipped into bed beside her. Clinging to her side of the bed, Angelina lay awake for a long time, thinking of the startling events of the last twenty-four hours. She no longer worked at the Murray House. Her debt had been paid. And most incredible, she was married to the man lying less than a foot away from her.

"Angel?"

She wished he wouldn't call her Angel, but the time didn't seem right to tell him. "What?"

"Did you really plan on never getting married?"

Rolling over onto her back, she stared up at the ceiling. As a young girl she had experienced the typical dreams of having a husband and children. But she'd given up such notions as Sarah Coleman's health continued to deteriorate. Instead of a family of her own, Angelina had dedicated her life to caring for her mother. After a moment, she said, "Yes. As soon as I finished my schooling, Mama started nagging me to look for a husband. I kept telling her I didn't want to marry, but she wouldn't listen."

"She didn't believe you?"

"No. I couldn't tell her the real reason—she would have gotten too upset—so I kept trying to convince her I just wasn't cut out for marriage. After we moved here and I started working in El Paso, she finally stopped talking about me finding a husband."

Kit mulled over Angel's words. Certain he knew the real reason for her not wanting to get married, he could understand not wanting to tell her mother about her lost innocence. Yet, given that situation, there was something else that went way beyond his understanding. Why would a non-virtuous woman want to postpone the consummation of her wedding vows?

" 'Night, Kit." Angelina said softly.

" 'Night," he muttered, flopping over onto his side. Thinking about Angel being so close, catching a whiff of her intoxicating scent, sent a rush of desire to his groin. He closed his eyes and clenched his teeth in frustration. *That damn promise I made is going to be the death of me.*

As sleep began tugging at Kit, he racked his brain for a way to rid himself of the constant hunger gnawing at his insides: the constant hunger to taste Angel's sweet mouth, to caress her sweet skin, to sink into her sweet body. He bit back a groan.

Staving off sleep for a few minutes more, he was determined to find an answer. He finally decided the only way to forget how much he wanted his wife was to immerse himself in work. Maybe if he worked himself to a frazzle and kept away from Angel, he would be too exhausted to want her.

Just before sleep succeeded in pulling him deeper into its folds, he frowned. *Yeah, right. I'd have a better chance of sprouting wings and flying.*

Angelina woke with a start. What was that sound? There it was again, sort of a half-sob, half-moan. As she shrugged off the last remnants of sleep, she turned her head on the pillow to look at Kit.

A shaft of silvery-white moonlight splashed across his side of the bed, revealing the rapid rise and fall of his chest, how his features were contorted in obvious pain.

Just as Angelina raised up onto one elbow, Kit groaned again, his hands curled into tight fists at his sides, his head thrashing from side to side. "Kit? Kit, wake up." When her words did not release him from the throes of his nightmare, she sat up. Scooting closer, she called to him again, then reached out and shook his arm.

Kit jerked in response to her touch, a shudder racking his entire body. "No, no," he murmured in a tortured voice. "I can't lose you, too."

"It's okay, Kit. It's okay. Wake up and look at me."

As her words penetrated the pain of losing his first wife and their son in the nightmare that had plagued him for five years, his panic began to ease. Taking a slow, deep breath, he opened his eyes to find Angel staring down at him, brow furrowed, her bottom lip caught between her teeth.

"Jesus," he moaned, rubbing a hand over his face. Every time he had the nightmare it was like reliving that awful moment all over again: the moment when his wife died in his arms, the lifeless body of their son clutched against her chest. The helplessness. The pain. The fury at the man who'd taken the lives of two innocent people. Realizing Angel was talking to him, he shoved the memories to the back of his mind. "What?"

"I asked if you're all right."

"Yeah."

"Do you want a glass of water, or something?"

He shook his head.

"Do you . . . do you want to talk about it?"

"No!" he said in a fierce whisper.

Even though she knew she risked riling his temper, she said, "Talking about it might help."

"Thanks for the advice, Angel, but I don't want to talk about it. Not now, not ever. Is that understood?"

"Yes. But if you ever change your mind, I'm—"

When he opened his mouth, she placed her fingers over his lips to halt his protest. "I know, you don't want to talk about it. But some day you might. And if you do, I just wanted you to know, I'm willing to listen."

Shifting her position, she stretched out next to him. "Would it help if I held your hand? Sometimes just knowing someone else is nearby keeps bad dreams away." When he didn't reply, she tucked her hand in his. For a moment his fingers remained stiff, unyielding. Then he relaxed, his grip tightening as he brought their intertwined hands up to rest on his chest.

"Better?" she whispered.

"Uh huh," he murmured in a sleepy voice, wiggling to a more comfortable position.

In just a few seconds Kit's breathing returned to the deep, even cadence of sleep. Angelina lay awake for a long time, wondering at the source of Kit's bad dreams. From the way he'd acted, this wasn't the first time he experienced the same nightmare. What had happened in his past to bring on such dreams, and why was he unwilling to talk about them?

The questions disturbed her more than she wanted to admit.

It was a very long time before sleep allowed her to escape from her troubling thoughts.

The next morning, Kit rose just as the blush of dawn sent a golden-pink cast across the purple sky. He dressed quickly, taking care not to wake Angel. He wasn't ready to face her yet, not after waking in the middle of the night from one of his nightmares to find her concerned face staring down at him.

He wished he could take her up on the offer to talk about the dream, but he couldn't. He couldn't admit his own stupidity had taken his family from him. No, that was a secret he'd take to his grave. He picked up his boots, then moved on stockinged feet across the wooden floor. Slipping from the room, he sat down in the kitchen to pull on his boots, then headed outside.

He drew in a deep breath of the sweet morning air. A warm westerly breeze stirred the bare branches of the cottonwood trees, hinting at the warmth of the day to come.

Walking toward the barn, he heard the clucking of what sounded like chickens. He glanced around the yard, finally spotting the source of the noise. A small wooden chicken coop surrounded by wire fencing stood beneath a stand of trees to the right of the barn. Sitting atop the coop's peaked roof, a fat rooster eyed his harem while the hens pecked at the ground.

At least the coop looked to be in good repair, Kit mused as he entered the barn.

After checking on the draft horses and his own mount, he spent the next hour walking the surrounding countryside, acquainting himself with the land where he would live for the next twelve months. Thinking of the ranch as only a temporary residence left a hollow feeling in his gut.

When he returned to the house, Angel and Chloe were chatting over a cup of coffee, their breakfast dishes pushed to the center of the table.

"Kit," Angelina said, her brow furrowed. "Where've you been? I was beginning to worry." She hoped her voice sounded like that of a concerned wife, rather than revealing what had prompted her question. Though his bags were still in their bedroom when she awoke and found him gone, she hadn't been able to squelch the fear that he'd changed his mind. Maybe after the nightmare, he'd decided he didn't want to stick around. Seeing him standing before her eased the fright clutching at her heart.

"I was just out walking," he replied, avoiding her gaze. "Looking around. Getting a feel for the ranch and trying to figure out what to do with the place."

"So, what do you think?" Chloe said before Angelina could respond.

Kit shifted his gaze to get his first good look at his sister-in-law, purposely delaying his answer until she'd gotten a chance to see his face in the full light of day. While she looked him over, he studied her. Though Chloe's hair was more blond than Angelina's, her eyes a much deeper brown, she bore a strong resemblance to her older sister. Each had the same delicate nose, high cheekbones, and slightly pointed chin.

When he realized Chloe had finished her visual examination and hadn't reacted as he expected, he cleared his throat then said, "I think the Diamond C would make one fine cattle ranch."

"Diamond C?" the sisters responded in unison.

"That's the name I've given the ranch." He turned toward Angel. "I never heard you call the ranch by name, so I figured your father hadn't gotten around to giving it one. What do you think about calling it the Diamond C?"

Angelina looked over at Chloe who smiled and nodded. "We should ask Mama," Angelina said, rising to fetch the plate she'd filled and left on the stove's warming shelf. "But we think the Diamond C sounds fine, except . . ."

"Except, what?" Kit prompted, accepting the plate and cup of coffee she handed him, then taking a seat at the table.

"Do you know anything about cattle or running a cattle ranch? We lived in a city before moving here and don't know the first thing about cows."

"Speak for yourself, Angelina," Chloe said. "I don't have any of George Dadd's books on cattle, but I've done a fair amount of reading about them. There are a number of articles in my copies of the *American Veterinary Journal*. Even though I've never treated cattle, I'm sure I could if the need arose."

Digging into his breakfast, Kit smiled. "I'm sure you could. And to answer your question, Angel. Yes, I know about cattle. I was raised on a cattle ranch. Though the terrain here is a little different than what I'm used to, there's still a good water supply and plenty of catclaw and mesquite to supplement the grass. Food and water, that's about all it takes to raise beef cattle."

"So, if we start raising cattle," Angelina responded, "what are we going to do with them?"

"I plan to check with the commander at Fort Bliss about getting a contract to supply his post with beef. If the army isn't interested, there are other markets. Selling the cattle won't be a problem. I figure the ranch can eventually support several thousand head, though we'll start out with two hundred. But first there are some things I want to do, like running some fence to keep the herd from wandering too far. If any cattle get into the *bosque* along the banks of the Rio Grande, we won't have a chance of finding them in that tangled mess of trees and shrubs. And then I want to add on to the barn so we can store feed in case there's a real hard winter or a severe drought next summer."

"Where are you going to buy the cattle?" Chloe asked.

"I'll be going into town in a day or two to see about some barbed wire. When I do, I'll send a telegram to a friend of mine. Between him and the ranchers he knows, I'm sure they'll be able to sell us enough head to start our herd. They can ship the cattle by rail which gives me enough time to get at least part of the fence strung before—"

The excited yelping of a dog halted Kit's words.

Chloe pushed away from the table and rose. "Uh oh. Sounds like Artemis has Nyx treed again. That blame cat doesn't know when he's well off, always teasing Artemis until she chases him across the yard and up the nearest tree. Guess I'd better get out there."

With a limping gait she hurried to the kitchen door and went outside. Kit stared after her, his brows pulled together. Turning back to Angel, he said, "Let me guess. Artemis is a dog?"

"Yes," she said with a laugh. "Artemis, named for the Goddess of the Hunt, showed up on our doorstep a few days after we moved here. She was in pretty bad shape; she'd been shot. Chloe removed the bullet and stitched her up, but the rest of us thought the poor thing wasn't going to pull through. Chloe was determined to do everything she could to save the hound. She even slept in the barn a couple of nights. In a few days, Artemis was strong enough to eat, and eventually she recovered completely."

Kit finished his breakfast in silence, then said, "Did Chloe get hurt?"

"Hurt? I don't know— Oh, you mean her limp." At his nod, she said, "She fell as a child and broke her right ankle. Unfortunately, the bones didn't set properly, leaving her with a permanent limp. It's been so long, I don't even think about Chloe limping anymore. That's just how she is."

"Isn't she self-conscious?"

Angelina tipped her head to one side, studying Kit's bland expression. "I don't recall that she was ever self-conscious. I remember she didn't even get upset when the doctor told her she'd always walk with a limp. And she's certainly never let that stop her from doing anything she's wanted to do, especially for her animals."

Kit sat back in his chair, drinking his coffee while contemplating Angel's words about his sister-in-law. Though the source of Chloe's injury wasn't visible to the eye, the resulting limp was just as obvious as his scar. So how could her family not think about it? Yet Angel claimed she didn't notice her sister's limp. And from what he'd seen, she didn't treat Chloe any differently. Was that why none of the Coleman women, first Angel then Sarah and Chloe, had shown any outward reaction to his scarred face?

"Kit?"

Angel's voice finally penetrated the depths of his thoughts. "What?"

"Are you all right?"

"Yeah, fine. What were we talking about?"

"Buying cattle. I'm not so sure about your plan, Kit. Mama, Chloe, and I might be able to pay for the fence. But there's no way we can buy even one cow, let alone two hundred."

"Don't worry. I'll take care of paying for the herd as well as the wire for the fence."

"But—"

He leaned across the table and placed a finger over her lips. "Now, don't say any more about it. I intend to take care of you and your family and I don't want to hear anything more about money. I can afford to buy everything we've talked about."

Seeing the pained look on her face, he relented to add, "If things cost more than I figure they will and I need you to pay for part of the supplies, I'll let you know. Okay?"

She nodded, unable to make her throat muscles work. The feel of his finger on her lips had stirred the cauldron of desire bubbling deep inside her body. The heat grew in intensity, sending rivulets of need outward, the heaviest concentration settling between her thighs. She pressed her knees together to stem the throbbing, though her efforts did little good.

Keeping her face averted, she heard him scrape back his chair, then the soft thud of his boots on the floor.

"I've got some work to do. I'll be making a list of what I'll need to get in town later on, so if there's anything you want me to add, let me know."

She nodded, unable to meet his gaze, unable to speak, her throat still clogged with emotions she didn't completely understand.

Once the door banged shut, she lifted her head. How could just his touch make her body react with such intensity? How long would it be before he kissed her again? The idea of tasting his mouth once more sent a shiver up her back.

Shaking off her wayward thoughts, she shoved her chair

away from the table and rose. *Angelina, for heaven's sake! You have plenty of other things you should be doing, not sitting here acting a like love-sick fool.* Her knees threatening to buckle, she dropped back onto the chair. Love! Was her reaction to Kit the beginnings of love? No, of course not. She barely knew the man, so she couldn't be falling in love. Besides, there was no future in loving a man who was a temporary fixture in her life. After twelve months he would pack up and leave the ranch, and her, for good.

Getting to her feet a second time, she forced herself not to dwell on the thought of Kit's eventual leaving—it was just too painful. Instead, she resolved herself to concentrating on the present, on displaying the picture of a loving wife to her mother and sister. How she could accomplish that and not allow herself to fall in love with Kit would be the hardest challenge she'd ever faced. But she would do it. She had survived working in the Murray House, so she would survive this latest obstacle.

Chapter Nine

"Kit, Mama'd like to see y'all when you're finished eating," Chloe said, entering the kitchen with her mother's supper tray.

Kit lifted his coffee cup, glancing over the rim at Angel. She stared back at him, panic evident in her eyes. After swallowing the last of his coffee, he set the cup down. "Thanks, Chloe, I'll go see her directly."

Pushing away from the table, he moved behind his wife. He bent to kiss her temple. "Don't worry, Angel, I'll remember my promise," he whispered, wondering why her back stiffened at his words.

Angelina exhaled slowly, then tilted her head back to look up at him. Why did he have to keep calling her Angel? She hated the name. Every time he used it she was reminded of her time at the Murray House, a time she was trying very hard to forget. But she'd never completely forget if Kit persisted in calling her—

"Are you all right?" His softly spoken words broke into her thoughts.

"Yes, I'm fine," she replied, dropping her gaze to the table. "You'd best get in to see Mama."

His brow furrowed, Kit straightened. He didn't have time to contemplate his wife's odd behavior. He'd been summoned to his mother-in-law's room—something he'd been expecting since his introduction to Sarah Coleman two days earlier—and he had to concentrate on the upcoming interview. Giving Angel's shoulder a gentle squeeze, he turned to leave.

Once he left the kitchen, Chloe said, "What's with you, Angelina? You've been acting mighty strange ever since y'all moved back here. Is there something wrong?"

Knowing she couldn't tell her sister the truth, Angelina shrugged. "Nothing's wrong. I'm . . . I'm just not used to having a husband around, I expect."

Her mother's supper tray still clutched in her hands, Chloe studied the face of her older sister for a long moment. Setting the tray on the table, she said, "I can't imagine having a man in my life day after day, demanding my attention and disrupting the time I spend tending my animals. So, I reckon being married must really take some adjusting to." When Angelina made no reply, she added, "You do care for Kit, don't you?"

Startled by Chloe's frank question, she rose from the table and started gathering up the dirty dishes. "Mama didn't eat much of her supper."

"No, her appetite hasn't been good for some time." When Angelina remained silent, Chloe said, "You didn't answer my question. Do you care for Kit?"

"Well of course I care. Do you think I would actually marry a man I didn't care for?"

Watching Angelina place a stack of dishes in the wash basin, Chloe replied, "No, I don't think that. But sometimes you act like y'all don't want him near you. That's not how married folks are supposed to behave."

Angelina closed her eyes, wishing her sister weren't so perceptive. "I can see why you'd think that," she replied, choosing her words carefully. "Kit and I didn't know each other very long before we got married, and even though we . . . um . . . care for each other, it's still going to take some time to get used to . . . everything." She could feel her sister's gaze boring into the back of her head, but she refused to say any more.

Chloe thought about Angelina's explanation for a minute, then turned to the stove. Lifting a kettle of hot water, she filled the basin. "Well, if y'all ever need to talk, I'm good at listening."

Grateful the subject was being dropped, Angelina managed a smile. "Thanks, Chloe. Here, I'll start the dishes, if you'll take the plate of scraps out to Artemis."

After Chloe went outside to feed her dog, Angelina added cold water to the basin then reached for the dish cloth. While she washed the supper dishes, her thoughts strayed from the disturbing conversation she'd just had with her sister to another conversation—the one taking place in the bedroom at the other end of the house.

Kit adjusted the chair next to Sarah Coleman's bed so that his left side would face her, then lowered himself onto the seat. Hands braced on his knees, he waited in silence.

Amused by his behavior, Sarah said, "Tell me something, Kit. Are you a vain man?"

Kit blinked with surprise. When Chloe announced he'd been summoned to this room, he figured Sarah wouldn't pull any punches. But this wasn't the direction he'd expected her questioning to take.

"I'm not sure I understand what you're asking," he finally replied.

"I'm asking if you're vain about your looks?"

Kit snorted. "No, ma'am. I'm—"

"Now what did I tell you about calling me ma'am?" she said before he could finish.

He cleared his throat, then said, "No, Sarah. I'm definitely not vain about my looks."

"Don't try to hornswoggle me, young man. If you're not vain, then why in the world do you always try to hide the right side of your face?"

Kit resisted the urge to squirm in his chair. "Believe me, vanity has nothing to do with it. I'm only trying to protect people with delicate sensibilities, like yourself."

"You're being ridiculous."

"I don't think so. No one wants to look at a face as disfigured as mine."

"That's tripe and you know it," Sarah snapped, setting off a coughing spell.

When she quieted, Kit said, "I have to disagree with you. I sure don't expect anyone, especially decent, well-bred ladies, to look at what I see in the mirror every day."

"Well, tarnation. If that isn't just like the foolish ravings of a stubborn man." She drew a labored breath. "Must I remind you, Kit Dancer, you married my daughter, a decent, well-bred lady?"

Kit's shoulders stiffened. "Yeah, I married Angel. But that's . . . different."

Seeing the hard set to his jaw, the way he tightened his hands into fists, Sarah pondered the complex man sitting beside her bed. At last, she said, "So, you met Angelina while she was working."

"That's right," Kit responded, not liking this new topic, the one he'd been expecting, any better than he liked the previous one. Knowing he had to pacify Sarah *and* keep his promise to Angel, he thought a moment before he continued. "I stopped by the . . . uh . . . place where she was working one evening."

Sarah sighed. "Don't try to spare me, Kit. I know where Angelina worked. Near broke my heart when she told me she was playing piano in a saloon theatre. I sure never meant for one of my girls to end up working in a place like that. If only . . . Well, none of that matters now. So, go on, Kit. Tell me about meeting Angelina."

"Like I said, I went there one evening, and that's when I saw this vision come down the stairs. As soon as I saw her, I knew I had to meet her."

"Must be you were real taken with my daughter."

Kit smiled. "Reckon I was."

"I can't tell you how much it pleases me that y'all took Angelina away from that place. I worried so much about her safety while she was in El Paso. She would never say much about what went on while she was working, but I've heard stories about the goings-on in those kinds of places." When Kit offered no additional information, she said, "Tell me, was my daughter in any danger?"

His gaze snapping to Sarah's face, he studied her pale features. Did she know more than she'd let on? Though he couldn't put his finger on the source of his suspicions, his gut instinct told him she did. Finally he said, "No, Sarah. She wasn't in danger."

The tightness around her mouth relaxed. "Oh, thank the stars. That certainly lightens the burden of guilt I've been carrying on my shoulders."

"Why would you be burdened with guilt?"

"If not for me being consumpted, I would have been the one taking responsibility for paying off my husband's debt. I would have been working in El Paso these past months, not lying here fretting about my daughter."

Kit reached over and patted one of Sarah's frail hands. "Now don't go blaming yourself. What's done is done. No need to get all worked up. Angel came to no harm, and now she's back to stay."

Sarah gave him a weak smile. "Yes, and we have you to thank for her return." After a moment, she said, "I don't know if Angelina told you, but she never socialized much. Always claimed she didn't hold with such foolishment. But I know she only said that so . . . well, never mind about that. I don't suppose you had the chance to do much courting, not with you up and getting married so sudden-like."

He shook his head. " 'Fraid not. I know our marriage must've come as quite a shock, especially since we hadn't known each other very long. But marrying Angel so soon was the only way I could end her employment. Does that make any sense?"

"Of course it does, Kit. I know exactly what you're trying to say. You couldn't stand the idea of the woman you fell in love with working in a saloon." She sighed. "How romantic!"

Somehow Kit managed to halt the scowl her words triggered. That wasn't what he'd meant, but if such nonsense pacified Sarah, he'd leave well enough alone.

A moment of silence passed, then Sarah spoke. "Promise me something, Kit. I know this probably sounds silly, I mean with you two already being married and all, but I'd like you to court Angelina, take her to social functions, show her the joys of living. After what she's been through, she deserves some happiness. I won't be around much longer and . . ."

When he opened his mouth to object, she shushed him by saying, "No, Kit, I won't sugarcoat the truth. Everyone's time comes eventually, and I know mine isn't far down the road. I'd like to pass on knowing Angelina got to experience some of the fun things in life. Will you do that for me, Kit? Will you make an old woman happy and promise to give my daughter part of what she's missed?"

Kit swallowed. He knew doing what Sarah asked of him would only make it harder to keep his hands off Angel, and harder to leave when his year as her husband ended. At last, he said, "With all the work that needs doing around here, there won't be a lot of time for courtin'."

"Oh balderdash. Surely you'll have some free time, an evening here or there, or a Sunday afternoon when you can take Angelina to a dance in town or on a picnic. Is that so much to ask?"

Kit drew a weary breath, then exhaled slowly. "Okay, Sarah. When I can, I'll do as you ask." Staring across the room, he murmured, "Maybe I can erase the sadness in her eyes."

Sarah gasped. "You noticed?" At his nod, she chuckled. "How silly of me. Of course you would. When you're in love, you notice things other folks don't see. Douglas and I were like that. He could always tell when I . . . . Well, that's not important now. We have to concentrate on finding a way to end Angelina's sadness."

"Could her father's death have anything to do with it?"

"I know she took Douglas's passing hard; we all did. But no, it wasn't until she started working in El Paso that I noticed a change. On her Sunday visits she looked so defeated, as if some terrible sadness had crushed her spirit. I can't remember the last time I heard her laugh. I tried to get her to talk to me, but she kept saying everything was fine. I don't know what made my daughter so sad, but I hope you'll be able to bring back the happy, carefree girl she used to be."

"Yeah, me, too."

After Kit pressed a good-night kiss on Sarah's cheek, he left her room, moved silently through the parlor to the front door, and slipped outside. As he stood with forearms draped over the corral fence, the evening breeze ruffling his hair, he went over his conversation with Sarah.

Though she hadn't admitted as much, he still had a feeling Sarah knew, or at least suspected, more about Angelina's employment in El Paso than she'd let on. He hoped she didn't know her daughter had worked as a prostitute. Thinking about the frail woman who was more concerned about her daughter's happiness than her own deteriorating health, Kit made himself another promise. As long as he was on the Diamond C, he would make damn sure she heard nothing about Angel's time in El Paso. If Sarah didn't already know the truth, he meant to keep it that way. Learning the whole story would serve no good purpose and only further weaken her already fragile constitution.

His thoughts shifted from keeping the truth from Sarah to what she had asked him to do. As much as the idea appealed to him, he knew courting Angel was a dual-edged sword. He longed to take her to a social gathering, hold her in his arms while he twirled her around the dance floor, see a bright smile light up her lovely face, hear sweet peals of laughter flow from her tempting mouth. Yet the notion of paying court to her also filled him with trepidation. The more time he spent alone with Angel, the harder it would be to honor another promise he'd made.

Pushing away from the fence, he lifted a hand to massage the back of his neck. *Damn. How did I get myself into such a sorry situation? And why the hell did I decide to stick around El Paso?*

Hearing the soft crunch of footsteps on the ground behind him, Kit turned around. Though he couldn't see her face in the fast falling darkness, he recognized her instantly. He also real-

ized he was looking at the answer to his questions. Angel.
Catching a whiff of her scent, he bit back a groan. The realization that he had a weakness for this woman didn't sit well
and made his voice gruff when he said, "What are you doing
out here?"

Startled by the tone of his voice, Angelina hesitated before
she said, "I just wanted some air. The house was stuffy."

Pushing aside his irritation, he managed to smile. "I'm disappointed, I thought maybe you had another reason for joining me."

"Well actually, I did. I wanted to ask how your talk went with
Mama."

"I didn't spill the beans, if that's what you're wondering," he
replied. "But that's not the reason I was thinking of. I thought
maybe you came out here to do some sparking with your husband."

Thankful the darkness hid her flushed face, Angelina found
the courage to retort, "I wanted no such thing. Washing dishes
made me warm, so I came outside to cool off. Then when I saw
you, I decided to ask about your talk with Mama."

"Too bad," he said, moving closer. "Sparking would be a lot
more fun." He ran the tip of one finger down her cheek.
"You're so soft, Angel."

She stiffened, pulling away from his hand.

"What is it?" he said, putting his knuckles under her chin and
forcing her to look at him. "How come you shrink from my
touch, Angel? You never used to."

"I . . . I just . . ." Taking a deep breath, she blurted, "I wish
you wouldn't use that name."

"Name? You don't like being called Angel?" His hand still
beneath her chin, he felt her shake her head. "Didn't anyone
ever shorten your name to Angel?"

"My papa, when I was little. But the last few months, being
called the Ice Angel . . ." She shuddered. ". . . changed how I
feel. I don't like the nickname anymore, and I'd like to be called
Angelina."

His mouth pulled into a frown, Kit dropped his hand. "Okay, if that's what you want." He heard her breath escape in a soft sigh. "If you've had enough air, would you let me escort you back to the house . . . Angelina?"

The emphasis he placed on her name eased the stiffness of her spine. "Thank you kindly. I'd like that."

Grasping her hand and looping it through his arm, he murmured, "My pleasure."

As they strolled across the yard, Kit said, "I'm heading for El Paso in the morning. Would you like to go with me?"

"Thanks, but I'll just stay here," she replied, the humiliation she'd felt in Reverend Morton's house returning in a rush.

"Are you sure?" he said, remembering his promise to Sarah. "We could have dinner at one of the restaurants in town, make a day of it?"

"No, I don't think so. I'd prefer to stay on the ranch."

Startled and surprisingly miffed by her rejection, Kit attempted to affect a light tone when he said, "Suit yourself. Maybe another time."

The disappointment Angelina heard in his voice made her glance up at the man beside her. Swallowing the reservations she had about ever wanting to go into town, she said, "Yes, maybe another time."

Kit pulled the team of Belgians to a halt in front of the Blinn Lumber Company on Overland Street, wrapped the reins around the brake handle, then jumped to the ground. After Angelina had turned down his invitation to accompany him, he'd considered riding Sid so he could make the trip to El Paso as quickly as possible. But since he needed the wagon to haul the barbed wire and tools he needed back to the ranch, he'd had no choice in the matter.

Unfortunately, the much slower draft horses gave him entirely too much time to think on the long ride to town. Time to think about the very desirable woman back at the ranch, time to fantasize about ending their platonic relationship. Drawing a deep breath to chase the erotic thoughts from his head, Kit headed toward the lumber company.

He paused just inside the double doors to let his eyes adjust to the dim interior, then moved farther into the store.

"Help you with somethin'?" the man behind the counter asked.

"Yeah," Kit replied. "I need some barbed wire."

"Sure thing. Anything else?"

"I need some staples, wire cutters, a couple spades and picks. Here . . ." He reached in his shirt pocket and withdrew a slip of paper. "I made a list."

The clerk studied the list, then said, "I've got everything except the wire. I've only got about half this much in stock, but I'm expecting a shipment later this week."

"I'll take what you've got. Can you have the lumber delivered with the rest of my wire?"

"Where to?"

"A ranch about ten miles north of town. Is that a problem?"

"Nope, I have a man who delivers for me up that way. But he may not be able to make it until sometime next week, or maybe the week after."

"No problem. I got plenty to do before I'll need the rest of the wire or the lumber."

"Fine. Let me write up your order, then I'll get directions to your ranch. Be right back."

Kit nodded, wandering around the store while he waited. He stopped to look at a handsaw, when a conversation in the next aisle caught his attention.

"Have you heard about Mavis Johnson?" a female voice said in a loud whisper.

"No, what about her?" a second woman replied.

"Well, it seems when her husband died he left her deep in debt. With no money to pay off what he owed the bank, Mavis had to take a job at . . . at one of those places."

"You're not suggesting Mavis is working at one of those awful houses over on Utah Street, are you?"

"That's exactly what I'm suggesting, because it's true. My

brother saw her there with his own eyes. She was waiting tables."

"Oh, good heavens, what a terrible thing to have happen."

"I know. But I guess she didn't have any choice."

"Even so, can you imagine working in a place where heaven only knows what goes on? Just the idea makes my skin crawl."

"Mine, too. Look, I have to go. My husband is waiting for me. I'll talk to you later."

After the two women left, Kit remained where he was, frozen in place by the conversation he'd just overheard. How many more women like Angelina and Mavis were working in the tenderloin because of a debt owed to a bank?

He clenched his teeth in silent fury. If only he could look into the dealings of James Murray and Elliot Wentworth. But with all the work ahead of him on the Diamond C, there was no way he could leave the ranch and start doing some checking.

After paying the clerk and giving directions to the ranch, Kit left the lumber company and headed for the telegraph office. Why had his life become so complicated? he wondered, and why couldn't things be like they were?

Remembering the woman who now bore his name, he didn't have to wonder any longer. Ever since he'd met Angelina, nothing had been the same. If not for that meeting, his life might not have taken such an unexpected turn. A turn, he was beginning to suspect, which would only lead to more pain. Yet in spite of knowing what lay ahead, he hadn't done anything to change the direction of his life.

Being completely honest with himself, Kit knew he didn't want to change his life's direction. Not for twelve months anyway.

Chapter Ten

Angelina leaned over the wash tub in the yard next to the house, scrubbing the week's laundry against the washboard. She rinsed each piece in a bucket of clean water, then piled the wrung-out clothes in a basket. Pausing in her chore, she glanced up at the sun. Only several hours had passed since Kit left to go into town, and though at least several more would have to pass before he returned, she found herself looking up at every little sound. She hadn't thought she would miss him so much.

The truth was, in spite of having known each other for such a brief time, she already cared for Kit. And even though they had married for reasons other than the usual ones, she knew he was a good man, a kind man—a man she suspected she'd already begun to love.

Pushing such thoughts aside, she wiped a hand across her brow, picked up the basket, then moved to the clothesline Kit had strung between two cottonwood trees. Shaking out her mother's things and hanging them on the line, Angelina drew a ragged breath. Though Sarah had tried to hide it, there were blood stains on her linen handkerchiefs, stains Angelina had finally managed to scrub clean. She bit her lip, determined not to let the sign her mother's disease had worsened bring on the threatening tears. She couldn't give in to a case of the doldrums, she had to be strong in order to hold her family together. Just like she'd held them together by working at the Murray House.

The Murray House. Would memories of her months there

ever fade? She pressed her lips together in annoyance. Not if people like the Reverend Morton's wife continued to treat her like vermin.

Hanging the last of the laundry on the line, she picked up the basket and headed back to the wash tub, her thoughts dwelling on the evening of her marriage. *Maybe Mrs. Morton and her friend were right. Maybe I am the lowliest of women.* After all, she had worked in a brothel. While it was true she hadn't crossed the line into prostitution, she had planned to, and would have if not for meeting Kit. Still, shouldn't there be a difference between a person's intentions and what they actually did?

Angelina squeezed her eyes closed for a moment. According to women like Mrs. Morton, the answer was cut-and-dried. No, there wasn't a bit of difference. How many others in El Paso would share the same opinion?

Angelina had never intended to tell anyone where she'd worked, clinging to the fragile hope that anyone she might come in contact with would never learn the truth. Such intentions were meaningless now. Someone had learned the truth, and she knew how fast word would get around. The gossipmongers in town would make gleefully short work of spreading the news of her fall from grace.

What about Kit, would he try to stop such talk? Or would he simply ignore it? The thought that his reaction might be the latter caused a wrenching pain in her chest. How could she expect her husband to defend her against accusations of having been a prostitute when that's exactly what he believed?

While she emptied the wash water, rinsed out the tub, then hung it on a nail under the eave of the house, Angelina tried to come up with a way to enlist her husband's support. Drying her hands on her apron, she stopped in mid-motion. There was *one* way to prove she hadn't been a prostitute. Just thinking about what she would have to do to supply that proof caused her breathing to become erratic and an intense heat to ignite low in her belly.

Her brow wrinkled in concentration, she turned to stare across the yard, barely noticing the way the late morning sun made the water in the creek sparkle like a thousand jewels.

Should she actually consider going through with what she was thinking? Moving toward the kitchen door, she gave a sharp nod of her head. Yes, the idea definitely bore some serious consideration.

Kit returned to the ranch just before sunset. After brushing what dust he could from his clothes, he entered the house through the front door. He stood in the middle of the empty parlor, uncertain where he would find his wife. Hearing the squawk of the cast-iron stove's oven door, he pulled his hat from his head and turned toward the kitchen.

"Hello," he called, stepping just inside the archway. Finding Angelina bent over in front of the stove, her shapely derriere pointed in his direction, he smiled. "Need some help?"

"Hello, yourself," she said, her voice muffled by the opened oven. As she shoved the covered pot back inside, then closed the oven door, she shook her head. "No, I got it." She rose and turned to face her husband. "Thanks anyway," she managed to say around the sudden lump in her throat. He looked so good standing on the other side of the room, idly slapping his hat against one thigh. So masculine, so powerful, so . . . She forced her mind away from the direction her thoughts had taken.

Moving around the table, she crossed the kitchen and stopped in front of him. She drew an unsteady breath, suddenly apprehensive about proceeding. But she knew if she decided to carry out the plan she'd begun formulating during his absence, she had to start laying the groundwork. Still, not knowing how he would respond to the *new* Angelina caused her an anxious moment.

Determined to continue, even with the risk of his adverse re-action, she took another step closer. Her gaze focused on the tuft of dark hair just above the top button of his shirt, she reached up to straighten his collar, then let her fingers brush his chest as she withdrew her hand. "Did you get everything you need?"

"Yeah . . . uh . . . I mean, no. I got most of the supplies, but the store didn't have enough barbed wire. The clerk said he'd have the rest delivered with the lumber for the barn in a week or so." He stared down at her through narrowed eyes. For some reason Angelina seemed different. There was still the sadness in her eyes, yet there was something more. He had the distinct impression she was flirting with him.

She nodded, a tiny smile playing about her lips. "Well, I'm glad you're back." She lifted her gaze to his face. "I missed you."

Kit's eyebrows rose sharply. "Did you? I didn't think—"

Angelina's mouth pressed to his halted what he'd been about to say. Before he had time to wrap his arms around her and deepen the kiss, she ended her surprise greeting and stepped back.

Realizing her actions had become even bolder than she had anticipated, she twisted her hands in the folds of her skirt. "I wasn't sure what time you'd be back, so I started supper late. I hope you don't mind, but it won't be ready for another hour."

Kit cleared his throat, trying to shake off his shock, then lifted his hat with a less-than-steady hand and settled it back on his head. "Fine. That'll give me time to unload the wagon and get cleaned up."

He started to leave, then stopped. He had to find out if his imagination had played a trick on him. Turning around, he took a step toward Angelina, then another. She didn't move away but stared up at him with those beautiful whiskey-colored eyes, sending his pulse into double-time.

When her gaze dropped to his mouth, he groaned and reached out to catch her around the waist. Pulling her into his arms, he lowered his head. He grazed her lips with his, then nibbled with gentle little bites before allowing his ministrations to develop into a full-blown kiss.

Forgetting her nervousness, Angelina rose on her toes and pressed closer, the tips of her breasts brushing against his chest. A low groan rumbled in her throat, answered by one from Kit. When he pulled her bottom lip into his mouth and gently suckled, heat like she had never experienced knifed through her. Knees weak, heart pounding against her ribs, she clung to him like her mother's clematis vine had clung to the trellis on the west side of their Savannah home.

"Angelina, where did you put—Oops." Chloe slid to a stop just inside the kitchen.

His sister-in-law's voice jerked Kit back to the realm of reality. Lifting his head, he stared down into the flushed face of his wife. His breathing ragged, he flashed her an apologetic smile. "Looks like we got caught."

Angelina swallowed hard. Unable to get a word past her tight throat, she nodded, then peeked around her husband. Her sister, a sheepish grin on her face, stood on the other side of the table.

"Sorry," Chloe said. "I didn't mean to interrupt."

"No problem, Chloe," Kit replied. "I was on my way out anyway." Lowering his head, he brushed a soft kiss on Angelina's mouth, then whispered, "Don't forget where we left off." After adjusting his hat, he turned and strode from the room.

Angelina stood stock-still, the delicious remnants of the kiss her sister had interrupted lingering throughout her body. She finally drew a deep breath and turned to meet Chloe's amused gaze.

"Well, well." Chloe grinned. "I guess y'all do care for him."

Out in the barn, Kit took care of the team of Belgians, then turned to the wagon. He removed some of the tools, but left the rest along with the barbed wire. He'd have to use the wagon to haul the wire up to the pasture where he planned to run fence, so there was no point in handling the heavy rolls more than once.

When he finished in the barn, he hesitated returning to the house. He had to regain control of his runaway libido before he could face Angelina again. Even though he'd given her the impression they would finish what they'd started, he'd done some thinking on that score while tending the horses and unloading the wagon.

The kiss she'd surprised him with, while thoroughly enjoyable, had seemed more like the work of someone who knew little about kissing—something a soiled dove would be well versed in, along with a whole passel of other ways to please a man. So, why did Angelina persist in playing the innocent? And what did she hope to gain by such behavior? That he still couldn't come up with an explanation for her conduct continued to rub him the wrong way.

And to confuse the situation even more, what would he do if she kept up the flirtation? Though he wanted her in the worst way, he wasn't sure her actions meant she was ready for their relationship to become intimate. So for the time being, he'd just have to bide his time, waiting until he figured out what she was up to.

Blowing out an exasperated breath, Kit stepped outside and closed the barn doors. Artemis lay sprawled in the dirt against the front wall of the barn.

Smiling when the dog thumped her tail in greeting, Kit hunkered down next to the hound. He scratched the dog's head while staring across the yard at the house. "Damn, helluva a note, Artemis," he grumbled. "When a man doesn't know what to make of his own wife."

The dog lifted her head, a pair of doleful brown eyes looking up at him. Kit chuckled. "Sure wish you could talk. You probably have all the answers in that canine brain of yours and could set me straight on a thing or two." Giving Artemis one last pat, he straightened. "Guess I'd best get washed up. Supper's bound to be ready by now."

Her ears perking up at the mention of food, Artemis jumped to her feet. She lifted her muzzle to the sky, let out one long ear-piercing bellow, then took off for the house.

Kit shook his head. "I swear that dog understands more than some people."

Rolling up his shirt sleeves, he started across the yard.

"All right, gals," Kit said the next morning. "First you mix a little water into the sand to make mud." He pointed to the pile of sand he'd dumped on the west side of the house. "But don't get it too wet. Then you add enough straw to hold the mixture together. Are you with me so far?"

"How do we mix everything together?" Chloe asked.

"I've seen Mexicans mix it with their feet."

"Their feet?" Angelina and Chloe cried in unison.

Kit smiled. "Yeah, they say they can tell when the mixture is just right by the feel." Seeing the looks of disbelief on the sisters' faces, he said, "Don't worry, I don't expect you to make adobe the Mexican way. You can use a spade."

Seeing their shoulders relax, he continued with his instructions. "Once you have the adobe in a workable consistency, fill each hole and crack in the house. Be sure to pack it in tight, then before the mud dries, smooth out the patches. Got that?"

Angelina looked over at her sister. When they'd offered to help Kit fix up the ranch, they hadn't expected him to tell them they could repair the crumbling adobe on the lower half of the house. But they'd agreed, though neither she nor Chloe had the slightest idea how to accomplish such a chore. Thankfully, Kit knew something about adobe. And after his explanation, the process didn't look all that complicated.

Seeing Chloe nod her agreement, Angelina turned back to her husband. "Yes, we got it. Y'all go ahead and start working on the fence. We'll do just fine."

Kit eyed the sisters for a minute, then nodded. "Okay. I'm heading for the north pasture, but I'll be back in a few hours to check on you."

After Kit left, Angelina drew in a deep breath, then moved closer to the pile of sand. "Well, I reckon we'd best get started."

"Reckon so," Chloe replied, reaching for the pail of water.

Wiping his face on his shirt sleeve, Kit looked over the work he'd accomplished in the north pasture. Though his back and shoulder muscles ached from swinging the pickaxe, he was pleased he'd managed to dig as many fence holes as he had in the rocky ground. At this rate, he could start stringing wire in a day or two. Glancing at the sky, he realized he'd been gone longer than he'd planned. He put the tools in the bed of the wagon, then climbed up on the seat and picked up the reins.

He stopped the horses in front of the barn, then jumped to the ground. Looking across the yard to the house, he saw no sign of Angelina or Chloe. Had they finished repairing the adobe already?

As he crossed the yard, he heard giggling coming from the back of the house. Stepping around the corner, he pulled up short.

Angelina and Chloe had taken the hems of their skirts, pulled them forward between their legs and tucked the fabric in their waistbands, forming makeshift trousers and exposing their bare legs from the knees down. If their bizarre attire wasn't enough of a surprise, the mud splattered all over their clothes and stuck in their hair definitely was.

Not wanting to make his presence known just yet, he took a step backward. Standing in the shadow of the house, one shoulder leaning against the wall, he watched the sisters mix up another batch of adobe.

After Chloe poured water onto the sand, Angelina stepped into the mud and began working the mixture with her feet.

Kit grinned. If he'd told them they had to use their feet, they would have pitched a fit.

Chloe threw a handful of straw into the mud, then jumped in next to her sister. The movement caught Angelina off guard and she slipped. She managed to catch her balance, then just as quickly lost it again.

"Chloe, watch out. I think I'm going to fall."

"Here, grab my hand."

Angelina tried to do as her sister asked, but just as she grasped Chloe's hand, both feet slid out from under her. Unable to stop her momentum, she sat down in the mud with a plop, pulling Chloe down beside her.

The sisters looked at each other with wide eyes and opened mouths, then suddenly burst into gales of laughter.

"Oh, my God, look at me," Angelina managed to say. "I'll never get this mud out of my clothes."

"You're right. I think our clothes are beyond cleaning. So, in that case . . ." Chloe reached into the mud, came up with a handful, and let it fly.

"Okay, you asked for it now," Angelina said, wiping the mud from the side of her face. Struggling to her knees, she threw herself at Chloe, sending them both sliding through the wet, sticky mess.

Biting his lip to keep from laughing, Kit left his hiding place and moved to where the sisters were rolling around on the ground.

Arms crossed over his chest, he looked down at them from beneath the brim of his hat. "If you *children* have had enough fun playing in the mud, don't you think you should finish patching the house?"

Angelina went still. Glancing up at her husband, she slowly opened her fingers and dropped the handful of mud she'd been about to smear in Chloe's hair. "We're not children."

"Oh really? You could have fooled me," Kit replied.

Sneaking a peek at Chloe, Angelina saw the laughter in her sister's eyes and burst into another fit of giggles. By the time Kit had managed to get them up onto their feet, her side ached from laughing so hard.

"You two better get cleaned up before that mud dries, otherwise you may lose a layer of hide when you have to scrape it off. Go on. I'll finish the house," he said, pointing them toward the creek.

"You want us to bathe in the creek?" Chloe said.

"You don't expect to go inside the house like that, do you?"

Chloe looked down at her mud-caked skirt and legs. "Reckon not. Come on Angelina, let's get this mess off us." She turned and hobbled toward the creek.

Before Angelina could follow, Kit grabbed her arm. "I'd offer to help you, but I have to use the adobe before it dries."

Her face flaming beneath the layer of mud, she replied, "I can manage just fine, thank you."

Watching her walk away, her gait awkward because of the mud weighing down her clothes, Kit chuckled. The real Angelina was beginning to emerge—the happy, carefree woman Sarah had mentioned—the woman he'd promised to try to bring back. More startling than the scene he'd just witnessed was the knowledge he found the new Angelina even more attractive than the one he'd met at the Murray House.

As he worked to finish patching the house, he tried to think of something besides the woman now bathing in the creek behind him. But no matter where he tried to fix his concentration, his mind kept circling back to her. How one slip of a woman—one who could fire his blood to such a fever pitch though he'd done no more than kiss her—could so completely take over his thoughts, was more evidence of how important she was becoming to him.

The laughing, playful minx he'd watched roll around in the mud with her sister was just the sort of woman he could share his life with, just the sort of woman he could love.

A sudden frown erased his previous merriment. *Watch it, Dancer, you're treadin' on thin ice with that kinda thinkin'.* Bending to scoop up another shovelful of adobe, he made a vow. Though he knew he'd already begun to care for Angelina, he vowed not to let his feelings get any deeper. Even when, or if, their relationship became intimate, he would force himself to feel nothing more than physical pleasure. Otherwise when his year as her husband ended, he'd never be able to leave. And he couldn't allow himself to do that to Angelina. He wouldn't keep her shackled to a disfigured man who wasn't capable of protecting his family. Even a former soiled dove deserved better than that.

Chapter Eleven

After her episode in the mud, Kit saw a distinct change in Angelina over the next ten days. She seemed to blossom before his eyes. She smiled more easily, even laughing on occasion— a sound he instinctively knew he'd never grow tired of hearing. And although the sadness in her eyes hadn't entirely disappeared, he knew it would, given more time.

Even the forward behavior she'd exhibited after his return from El Paso continued, much to his delight. She did nothing overt, just a subtle slipping of her arm around his waist, a light stroking of her fingers over his chest, or the initiation of a slow, thorough kiss. Yet each seemingly innocent action nearly drove him out of his mind with desire. If that was her intention, she was doing one hell of a good job.

Forcing thoughts of making love to his wife from his mind, he straightened from repairing a board on the corral fence. He hoped the rest of the barbed wire would be delivered soon so he could finish fencing in the pasture. He'd spent nearly every hour of daylight during the past week digging holes and setting fence posts. Now all that remained was stringing the wire.

Unwilling to just sit around and wait, he'd started on the corral fence. Pulling his hat from his head, he wiped a shirt sleeve across his forehead. Though it was only a little past noon, already his shirt was damp with sweat. The fall weather had been especially warm for mid-October, and looking at the cloudless, deep blue sky, he figured they were in for another scorcher. Of course, the day had started out plenty hot, right from the moment he'd opened his eyes.

He'd awakened at first light to find Angelina's head nestled on his chest, her left arm thrown across his hips. The silk of her hair tickling his neck and shoulder, the heat of her body burning him wherever they touched had nearly been his undoing. He gritted his teeth at the memory.

How he'd longed to toss her on her back and bury himself in her sweet body. Yet somehow, he'd managed to control his lust and move her away from him. He couldn't risk having her awaken and involuntarily brush her arm against his rock-hard arousal. If she'd touched him, even briefly through the fabric of his drawers, he knew he would have spilled himself right then. There was no way in hell he would chance embarrassing himself that way. Yet as he shifted her position—touching her soft curves and inhaling her womanly scent—he'd been only a hairsbreadth away from being sent over the edge.

Recalling the scene sent a surge of warmth through his blood and the return of the all-too-familiar dull ache in his groin. He inhaled a deep breath, then blew it out slowly. *Jesus. I can't take much more of this. I'm already damn near the end of my rope. If she doesn't tell me she's ready soon, I swear I can't be held responsible for my actions.*

Glancing across the yard, he could see the woman who continued to play havoc with his self-control. He smiled at the scene she presented. An old rag tied around her head, Angelina had dragged the parlor rug outside and finally succeeded in draping it over the clothesline. Picking up a rug beater, she took aim and gave the carpet a sound whack. A cloud of dust puffed into the air, followed by another after each wallop.

His smile broadened. She looked so domestic in her plain cotton dress and that ridiculous cloth covering her hair, not at all like the perfumed and painted woman he'd met at the Murray House. He scowled, his good humor replaced by a heavy dose of irritation.

Why couldn't he forget where he'd met Angelina, or that she'd worked as a prostitute? Turning away from the sight of his wife, a new thought occurred to him. Why did knowing what she'd previously done cause such a crushing pain in his chest?

Chloe had just removed the last of the burrs from Artemis's coat when the dog leaped to her feet, head cocked, ears lifted. Letting out an excited bellow, the hound crossed the yard to take up a sentry position at the head of the trail leading to the main road.

Following the dog at a slower pace, Chloe glanced down the trail. She didn't see anything yet, but Artemis's behavior told her someone or something was headed toward them. A minute later, she heard the rumbling sound of an approaching wagon.

As she watched from where she stood next to the barking dog, Chloe saw a freight wagon come into view, pulled by a team of bay Morgans. Her gaze moved over the four horses, their coats shining in the afternoon sun, barely noticing the man who handled the team with expert efficiency.

When the four-in-hand came to a halt in front of her, she studied the horse nearest her, brow furrowed in concentration. Taking a step closer, she crooned softly to the mare. The horse's ears flicked forward. "Easy, girl. I won't hurt you."

She crouched down to run a hand along the right fetlock, then straightened. Glancing over the backs of the horses, she turned her attention to the man sitting on the wagon seat. He sat still as a stone, face shadowed by the brim of his hat, feet widespread with boots braced on the wagon's footboard, thick forearms resting on heavily muscled thighs, large hands gently holding the reins between his knees.

The unexpected desire to feel those big hands touching her momentarily flustered Chloe. Shaking off the strange sensation, she lifted her chin to give him a pointed glare. "Mister, are y'all aware this mare has a windgall on her right front fetlock? She should be resting, not pulling a heavy freight wagon."

Jared McBride stared down at the young blonde, unable to believe his eyes. As incredible as it seemed, he felt as if he'd waited his entire life for this woman to appear—this petite blonde with huge dark brown eyes, eyes that looked ready to devour him, though out of desire or anger he couldn't be certain. He bit the inside of his mouth to keep from grinning. Who would have guessed he'd meet such a woman, not at a social function or at church as one would have expected, but on a ranch not five miles from his own place?

There was one fly in the ointment though, he acknowledged, evaporating his light mood. The woman of his dreams had the audacity to tell him how to take care of one of his horses. And that wouldn't do. No woman of his was gonna have a say in how he treated his animals. Realizing he was getting way ahead of himself, he tried to rein in his irritation. He wasn't entirely successful.

"And what would you know about windgalls, little lady?"

Chloe stiffened, her gaze narrowing at his condescending tone. "I know plenty. I've been tending animals as long as I can remember. And don't call me 'little lady.' "

Pushing his hat back with a thumb, Jared couldn't halt a chuckle. This little gal had grit; he'd give her that. He admired folks with grit, though in the past his admiration had always been directed toward men with that particular attribute. "I'd be pleased to call you by your name, ma'am, if I knew what it was."

"Chloe. Chloe Coleman." Something about his attitude made her add, "That's Miss Coleman to you."

"Pleased to meet you, Miss Coleman. I'm Jared McBride, and I take it this is the Coleman ranch, the Diamond C?"

"Yes. Have you got business here?" Rising on tip-toes, she peered over the side of the wagon. "Oh, y'all brought the rest of Kit's barbed wire!"

"Yes, and the lumber he ordered. Can you tell me where to unload it? I've got another delivery to make and I want to get there before dark."

"Didn't you hear what I said a moment ago? This mare should be rested, Mr. McBride. I wouldn't advise keeping her in harness any longer than necessary."

"You wouldn't, huh? Well, let me tell you something. I know Bess has a windgall, but I've been keeping a close eye on it. And since she's not favoring the leg, I plan to continue using her to help pull the wagon."

The stiffness in Chloe's shoulders relaxing, she studied his face for the first time. He had a squarish jaw with a slight cleft in the center of his chin, a thick dark moustache over a full mouth, and a slightly hawkish nose. His eyebrows were the same dark brown as his hair and slightly arched over the greenest eyes she'd ever seen. She had to swallow several times before she could get her voice to work. "Y'all're really watching the leg for signs of lameness?"

At his nod, she said, "Pull the wagon up to the barn, and I'll fetch Kit. While you're unloading, I'll take a closer look at the mare's leg."

"I appreciate the offer. But, there's no need for you to trouble yourself."

"It's no trouble, Mr. McBride."

"Like I said, I'm taking good care of Bess."

"I know, but it wouldn't hurt to have me—"

"Begging your pardon, Miss Coleman, but I don't need some woman looking after my horse. Everybody knows caring for animals is man's work."

"Do they really? Well, that's not the case on this ranch, Mr. McBride. Since that's how you feel—even though you're dead wrong—I won't touch your horse," she replied, turning and heading for the house. "Come on, Artemis, help me find Kit."

His lips drawn into a frown, Jared watched her stalk away, the tricolored hound bounding ahead of her. Starting at the blond hair woven into a loose chignon at the base of her slender neck, he gave her a final scrutiny. His gaze drifted lower, past the stiffness in her shoulders and back, her narrow waist and nicely rounded hips. Her slight limp made her bottom twitch from side to side in a real enticing swing.

As he directed his team of Morgans to the barn, he grinned. In spite of her prickly temper and fool notions about caring for animals, Miss Chloe Coleman was some kind of woman.

Kit came from the other side of the creek at Chloe's call, then headed for the barn to help unload the wagon.

"I appreciate your bringing my order all the way out here," Kit told Jared after introducing himself.

"No bother. I've made deliveries a lot farther from town than this. Besides, this place and my next stop are close to home."

"You live near here?"

"Yeah. I got a good-sized spread about five miles to the north. The Rocking M."

"That's a long way to go to work everyday."

"I only work as a teamster three days a week, less if there aren't many deliveries. The rest of the time I work on my ranch, raising quarter horses. Once I get the Rocking M on its feet, I can quit working for Mr. Blinn's lumber company."

After everything was unloaded, Jared accepted Kit's offer of a cool drink before continuing with his deliveries.

"If you don't mind my asking, Kit, what're you planning on fencing in with that wire?"

"Cattle. I ordered two hundred head a few weeks ago. I should be hearing any time on when to expect them. Listen, Jared, I've been thinkin'. Would you consider helping me string that wire? I'll match your wages as a teamster. I could probably manage myself, but it sure would go a lot faster if I had some help. Are you interested?"

"How much time are you talking about? I have a mare due to foal soon, and I don't want to be away when her time comes."

"The posts are already in, so I reckon it wouldn't take us more than three, maybe four days."

"Okay, you've got a deal." Looking over at where Chloe stood on the front porch of the house, Jared lowered his voice to add, "Do you let her treat your animals?"

Kit wiped a hand across the lower half of his face to hide his grin. He saw no reason to point out that most of the animals on the ranch belonged to his sister-in-law. "Yup, sure do. Chloe is mighty talented when it comes to caring for anything with four legs."

Jared shot a skeptical glance at him, then turned his gaze back to Chloe. "You don't say?" Though the idea of a woman treating animals still went against the grain of his beliefs, he tucked Kit's statement into the back of his mind.

"Chloe, are you going to help me move the parlor furniture back on top of the rug, or not?" Angelina said from the opened doorway.

"What? Oh, yes. I'll be there in a minute."

"What's so interesting, anyway?" Angelina stepped onto the porch and followed the line of her sister's gaze. "Who's that man talking to Kit?"

"Jared McBride. He's a teamster for one of the lumber companies in town."

"He brought the rest of the barbed wire?"

"Uh huh."

Angelina stared at her sister for a moment, then glanced over at the two men standing by the barn, then back at Chloe. A wide smile parting her lips, she said, "If I didn't know better, I'd say you were mooning over a man."

"Don't be silly. I have better things to do with my time," she replied, then added in a soft voice, "He is good looking, though." After a moment she said, "Do you think there's such a thing as love at first sight?"

Angelina blinked with surprise. "What?"

Chloe finally turned to look at her sister. "Never mind, it wasn't important," she said, moving past Angelina toward the door.

Confused by her sister's odd behavior, Angelina pulled her face into a frown. What was wrong with Chloe? Glancing at the two men standing in front of the barn, her frown deepened. Chloe interested in a man? No, it couldn't be. Her sister had never given a man a second glance, let alone shown even the slightest interest in one. Still . . .

Four days later, the barbed wire had all been strung, and the pasture was finally ready for its first herd of cattle. Still waiting to hear when to expect the two hundred head he'd arranged to buy, Kit spent another day finishing the repairs to the corral fence. Then first thing the following morning, he headed for the barn, planning to start the addition.

Stepping into the building's dim interior, Kit heard a soft voice coming from one of the stalls. He moved closer, finding Chloe examining one of the two quarter horses he'd purchased from Jared, a mare named Star.

"She's a beauty, isn't she," he said, draping his arms over the top of the stall door.

Chloe straightened and smiled at her brother-in-law. "Yes, her conformation is perfect. And she's a real lady. Aren't you, Star?" she crooned, running her hand down the horse's neck. Star nickered and bobbed her head.

"What about Belle? Have you had a look at her?"

Chloe glanced over at the next stall where the second mare stood quietly. "Belle's in great shape, too. You bought some fine horseflesh, Kit."

"I agree. But the credit should go to Jared. He's the one who bred and raised these two."

Seeing the way Chloe ducked her head at the mention of the man who'd spent nearly four days on their ranch, taking his meals at their table, Kit bit back a smile. "Unless I miss my guess, I'd say you're kinda sweet on him." When Chloe didn't respond, he said, "I think Jared might be sweet on you, as well."

Her head snapping up, she looked up at him with widened eyes. "Do you really think so?"

Kit chuckled. "Yes, I think so. You're all he talked about while we were stringing wire."

"Y'all aren't funning me, are you?"

"No, I'm serious."

"What about . . ." She swallowed, then said in a low voice, "What about my leg? Surely he mentioned my limp?"

"Nope, not a word."

Her eyes went even wider. "Truly?"

"Yes, truly. So, what about you? How do you feel about him?"

Chloe shrugged. "I like him well enough, I reckon. But he . . . he doesn't cotton to a woman doctoring animals, and you know how much taking care of critters means to me."

"Well, I wouldn't worry about that. If he really cares for you, what you are or what you've done won't make any difference."

"Thanks, Kit," she replied with a smile. "I appreciate your talking to me, and I'll remember what you said. If there's ever anything I can do for y'all, don't hesitate to ask."

Kit nodded, then removed his arms from the stall door and stepped back.

While he worked on adding a room for storing feed to the barn, he kept thinking about his conversation with Chloe. Though he believed the last statement he'd made, he wondered if the words would prove true in his own relationship. He did care for Angelina, a whole lot more than he should considering he wouldn't be a permanent fixture in her life, but could he ever completely forget about her past?

After waking up from another nightmare the night before and finding Angelina's arms around him, her soft voice whispering soothing words, he suspected he knew the answer. The nightmares used to plague him nearly every night, but since arriving at the ranch, he'd suffered only two of the torturous dreams—a reduction in frequency he was starting to believe directly attributable to the woman he'd married.

As she crossed the yard, Angelina watched Kit cut a board for the barn addition. He had stripped to the waist, his broad chest tanned from hours in the sun and slick with sweat, his muscles flexing with each movement of the saw.

Now that the moment was upon her, she wasn't sure she could get the words past the tightness of her throat. She'd spent a lot of time over the past few days thinking about the one way she could prove her innocence to Kit. In fact, she'd thought of little else. But now that she'd made her decision, she was at a loss on how to proceed.

The problem was, she hadn't made the decision just to prove

to Kit that she had never been a prostitute. The primary reason she wanted to change the nature of their relationship was the need burning inside her—the need to experience more than his kisses, the need to find relief from the constant ache to touch him and have him touch her, the need to become his wife in the true sense of the word.

So given all that, how did a woman go about telling a man she was ready and more than willing to make their relationship an intimate one?

When Kit straightened from his task, looked up to find her standing nearby, and flashed her a smile, she swallowed hard. Heart racing, she offered him a weak smile in return, then tried to speak. Her voice trapped somewhere inside her throat, no sound came out, making her already burning cheeks grow warmer.

"Did you want something?" he finally said.

"I . . . uh . . . I came to see if you wanted something cool to drink. I made lemonade."

"Sounds good." He laid the saw on a stack of lumber, ran an arm over his forehead, then accepted the glass she handed him.

Angelina couldn't pull her gaze away from his chest. Rivulets of sweat ran down his neck, over his collarbone, and disappeared in the dark hair covering the center of his chest. Her fingers twitched, longing to catch those beads of moisture, to run through the silky, dark whorls of hair, to—

"Are you all right? You're lookin' awfully flushed."

She lifted her gaze to meet his. "I'm fine."

"Angelina," Chloe shouted from the kitchen door. "Mama's asking for you."

"I'll be right there." The interruption reminded Angelina that she and Kit weren't alone on the ranch, causing second thoughts about what she'd intended to tell him. Having her mother and sister living under the same roof, their bedrooms just down the hall from hers, wasn't how she'd envisioned the first time she and Kit made love. Yet, what other choice did she have?

She glanced over at Kit who was finishing the last of his lemonade. Maybe he'd have an idea about—No! She couldn't ask him that. She'd just have to come up with something on her own.

"Thanks," Kit said, handing the glass back to Angelina, then reaching for the saw. "Oh, by the way. A messenger delivered a telegram awhile ago. The cattle I ordered will be arrivin' at the train station in the next day or so."

"You'll be going into El Paso to meet the train?" Her heart racing again, her palms grew damp.

"Yeah. I'll head into town in the morning. The cattle probably won't get there until the following day or even the day after that. But I'll have to arrange for a couple of men to help me get the herd moved from town to the ranch. So to make sure I have enough time, I want to be in town by noon tomorrow."

Gulping down her fear of rejection, she said, "Any chance you'd like some company?"

Kit's eyes widened for an instant, then narrowed under knitted brows. "You want to go with me?"

She nodded.

He stared at her for a very long time. "I just told you, I could be in town a couple of days waiting for the cattle. That means I'll be staying in a rooming house or a hotel, and I don't intend to rent more than one room."

"I don't want a separate room," she said in a low voice. "I want to stay with you, in one room, with . . . one bed."

His brow furrowed even more. "Are you saying you're ready for us to stop playing man and wife, and make it a real marriage?"

Though her face burned with another fierce blush, she held his gaze. "Yes, that's what I'm saying."

The furrows on his brow smoothing out, the corners of his mouth lifted in a smile. He took a step closer, then raised his hand and ran his fingers down the side of her face. "You won't be sorry, Angel . . . uh, Angelina. I'll make it good for you, the best you've ever had."

Though she should be angry at his reference to the other lovers he thought she'd had, she didn't let his comment rile her. She had other things on her mind. Giving in to temptation, she lifted one hand to his chest. The hair was soft to the touch, the muscle beneath warm and solid. His chest expanded with a sudden indrawn breath beneath her palm. She let her fingers drift downward, tracing the ridges of his ribs and skimming over his hard muscular stomach. She stopped her explorations just above the waistband of his trousers.

Kit exhaled his held breath in a long sigh. "Jesus, honey. I can't wait to get you alone in El Paso."

Jerking her hand away as if she'd been scalded, she forced herself to look into his face. The heat in his eyes ignited a flame deep in her belly. The fire spread lower, becoming a throbbing ache between her thighs. Slightly breathless, she whispered, "I can't either."

Chapter Twelve

"I have to go, Mama. Kit is waiting for me. Are you sure you don't mind if I'm gone a couple of days?"

"Of course, I don't mind, dear. Chloe and I will do just fine. Don't give us a second thought."

"But, I feel guilty leaving you two alone again."

"I don't want y'all feeling any guilt on my account." Sarah lifted one hand and gave a wave toward the door. "Go on, shoo. Both you and Kit have been working too hard around here. You're due for having some fun."

Hoping a blush wouldn't give away the *fun* she had in mind, Angelina bent to kiss her mother's cheek. "Promise me you'll do what Chloe tells you."

Sarah smiled up at her daughter. "Yes, I promise to mind your sister. Just enjoy yourself and try not to worry about us."

Angelina returned the smile. "Yes, ma'am, I'll try. We'll be back as soon as we can. I love you, Mama."

"I love you, too, child. Now git."

Angelina squeezed her mother's thin hand, gave her another kiss, then left her room and headed outside.

Kit sat on Sid's back, his wrists crossed over the saddle horn, the reins to Belle clasped in one hand. He straightened at Angelina's approach.

"Ready?" he said in a soft voice, sending a shiver of anticipation up her spine.

She nodded, then reached out to take the mare's reins from

him. By the time she moved to Belle's left side and stuck her foot in the stirrup, Kit had dismounted and was standing behind her. As he wrapped his large hands around her waist, another tingle shot through her, making her knees momentarily weak. Taking a deep breath, she forced herself to concentrate on getting on top of Belle's back. Grateful for Kit's assistance, she managed to put her weight on her left foot as she lifted herself and swung her right leg over the horse's back.

Only after she was settled in the saddle did she dare look at her husband. If she read the look in his eyes correctly, he'd been just as affected by helping her.

In spite of the heat in his gaze, his voice held a biting edge when he said, "I don't know why I let you talk me into leaving later." He scowled up at the sun. "By the time we get there, daylight will be about gone. Now we're going to have to run Sid and Belle most of the way. You'd better be up to a hard ride."

Wondering why he sounded so angry when he hadn't voiced a single objection to her request to delay their departure, she merely nodded.

Kit noted the flicker of pain in Angelina's eyes and wished he could call back his words. He hadn't meant to sound so gruff. But the frustration of not knowing whether she really wanted their marriage to become a real one, and the constant desire for her eating at his insides, made his temper flare at the slightest provocation.

He moved behind Belle and picked up Sid's reins. Forcing his muscles to relax, he swung up onto the gelding's back. He tugged at his hat, planting it more firmly on his head while searching for words to make up for his outburst. After a moment, he turned to look at her. She returned his gaze warily.

"Look, Angelina, I'm not angry with you. I'm just anxious to get the cattle on the ranch and get them settled, that's all. I didn't mean to take it out on you, okay?"

At her nod, he gave the brim of his hat another tug, then flashed a grin. "Come on, let's make tracks." He wheeled the piebald around, then jabbed his bootheels to the gelding's sides.

Angelina's spirits lifting, she smiled at his departing back. Jerking Belle's reins hard to the right, she urged the mare into a gallop.

Kit and Angelina arrived in El Paso at dusk and made their first order of business finding a place to stay. Kit suggested the Vendome Hotel on the corner of Utah and St. Louis Streets, and since Angelina had never stayed anywhere but the boardinghouse James Murray owned next to his bordello, she agreed.

Angelina waited with the horses while Kit went inside to register. He returned in just a few minutes to retrieve his saddlebags and her small satchel. Taking her arm, he escorted her into the hotel, past the lobby, then on to their room.

"This place isn't as fancy as some hotels in town," he said, opening the door and letting her pass in front of him. "But I thought it best to stay close to the train depot."

"Yes, that makes sense." Looking around the room, Angelina's gaze touched each piece of furniture, carefully skipping over the bed. She moved to the window and pushed the curtains apart. "The room is fine. And there's a nice view of the park across the street."

Kit joined her at the window, the warmth of his body settling over her like a fur-lined cape. "That's San Jacinto Plaza," he murmured near her ear.

He ran a finger across the nape of her neck, then up to trace the ear still warm from his breath. "I have to find a place to stable the horses. While I'm out, I'll start asking around about hiring a couple of men to help with the cattle. When I get back we'll find a place to have supper. Will you be all right while I'm gone?"

Thankful his plans kept her from having to come up with an excuse to go off by herself, she swallowed, then turned to look up at him with wide eyes. Her breathing slightly erratic from both his nearness and his touch, she said, "I'll be fine. How long do you think you'll be?"

"At least an hour, I expect. Maybe longer. Is that a problem?"

"No, I'll just . . . um . . . unpack my things and then maybe I'll . . . take a nap." Fearful the truth would be reflected in her eyes, she dropped her gaze.

He chuckled. "Too bad I have to go out. I'd sure enjoy staying here a whole lot more."

She peeked up at him from beneath her lashes, hoping she hadn't given him reason to change his mind about leaving. She had to talk to Jenna before her friend started working that evening.

Kit forced her chin up with his knuckles. "You're so beautiful." He bent to brush his lips across hers. "And you taste so sweet," he murmured before claiming her mouth for a long, mind-drugging kiss.

When he finally lifted his head, he took a deep breath, then exhaled slowly. "Jesus, you drive me wild." After giving in to temptation and sampling her mouth one last time, he whispered, "I'll be back as soon as I can."

Wanting to tell him to take his time, she bit back the words. "I'll be waiting," she finally said, praying it wasn't a lie.

Out of breath, Angelina arrived at the boardinghouse on Utah Street. She entered the house, pausing at the foot of the stairs until the stitch in her side eased. When she could breathe without pain, she ran up the staircase and turned toward Jenna's room.

Jenna adjusted the bodice of her peacock-blue dress, turning at the sound of the door opening. Her mouth dropped open, then immediately curved into a smile.

"Well, if you aren't a sight for sore eyes." When Angelina didn't return her greeting, Jenna's smile faded. "What are you doing in town? Is something wrong?"

"No, Jenna, nothing's wrong. Well, not exactly. Kit bought some cattle for the ranch and they're due any day by train. We're in town to wait for their arrival. But I do have to talk to you about something." She closed the door and moved to sit on the foot of the bed. Clasping her hands tightly in her lap, she said, "I need to know how to . . ."

Jenna took a seat opposite Angelina. "How to what?"

Angelina took a deep breath, then blurted, "How to keep myself from getting with child."

Jenna blinked. "What?"

"I know you said there are ways. During one of our conversations after I asked Mr. Murray if I could change jobs, you told me how you and other girls working in bawdy houses take precautions. But I guess I wasn't listening very well, because I don't remember much."

Jenna reached over and laid a hand on Angelina's knee. "Honey, you're a married lady now. Getting in a family way is the normal course of things. So why would you want to know about preventives?"

"Kit told me he doesn't want a family right away. And since I worked at the Murray House, he said I would know ways to keep from conceiving a child."

"You've been married for several weeks. Unless you've been using something to protect yourself, it may already be too late."

Angelina dropped her gaze to hide the blush she knew must be staining her cheeks. "No, I haven't used anything because there was no need. I mean, I didn't need to worry about the possibility of a child because we haven't . . . That is, we've never . . ." She gave up trying to get the words past the sudden tightness in her throat.

"Are you saying you and Kit haven't been intimate?"

Angelina nodded.

"I don't understand. He wanted you when he thought you were one of the Murray House lovelies. He even fought off the other men who showed interest in you so he could be the first to take you upstairs. Yet you're telling me, getting married changed that?"

"Not exactly. He . . . um . . . still wants me. But he hasn't done anything because he's keeping his word." She looked up to meet Jenna's confused gaze. "The day I agreed to marry Kit, he promised to give me time to get used to the idea, that he wouldn't make me his wife completely until I told him I was ready."

Jenna stared at her friend for a long moment. "So, I take it your being here means you're ready?"

"Yes," Angelina whispered, sure her face had turned as red as Jenna's painted lips.

"And that's why you want to know about preventives?"

She nodded.

Giving Angelina another long, thoughtful look, Jenna sighed. "Okay, but this will have to be quick. I've got to get to work in a few minutes. Now, listen carefully. There are several ways to prevent pregnancy, but a couple of them require the man's participation. He can wear a shield, or he can practice the age-old incomplete act of worship. As to the—"

"Wait," Angelina said before Jenna could go on. "What was that last one?"

"*Coitus interruptus.* Withdrawal. Now, do you know what I mean?"

Angelina bobbed her head once.

"Good, I was hopin' I wouldn't have to explain. Anyway, I don't imagine many men would want to sacrifice their pleasure by agreeing *not* to complete the act in the usual way. And even if they did agree beforehand, there's a good chance they'll conveniently forget at the critical moment, then claim they got carried away and couldn't stop. I wouldn't recommend that as a reliable way to prevent conception.

"Now, as to what you can do. You can get a syringe and one of the patent medicines available to use after . . . uh . . . intimacy. Or there are little sponges attached to a narrow ribbon available, or you could use what I prefer. A pisser made of—"

"A what?"

Jenna flashed a smile. "No, I guess you wouldn't know what that is. That's what I call a female preventive made of India rubber. Their real name is pessary, though I've also heard some of the gals call them Dutch Caps. Anyway, both the sponge and the cap have to be used before you have relations. Then of course, if you're unsuccessful in prevention, you can always buy an abortifacient."

Angelina gulped. "You mean, cause a miscarriage?"

Jenna nodded. "I've known girls who used them and got the results they wanted. Just don't ever resort to other methods of trying to unfix a pregnancy. I heard about a woman who used a knitting needle on herself. She messed up her insides something awful and suffered a terrible death."

Shuddering at the thought, Angelina said, "Where do I get one of the other things you mentioned?"

"You can find most of them at one of the druggists in town, but they're all closed by this hour. I'm guessing you're in need of something tonight. Am I right?"

Angelina's face burned in another blush. "Yes."

"Well, you're in luck. A girl in my line of work can't be too careful, so I always keep extra piss—I mean, pessaries on hand." Jenna rose and moved to her dresser. "I'll explain how to use it, then I have to skedaddle."

Angelina spent as much time as she dared in the hotel's bathroom, then gathering up her things, she opened the door to the hallway. After dining at Beach's Restaurant across from the Grand Central Hotel, she and Kit had taken a stroll through San Jacinto Plaza before returning to their own hotel.

Needing some time alone, Angelina had announced her plans to take a bath and excused herself. Now scrubbed clean, her hair loose and still damp, she made her way to the room where Kit awaited her return. Every nerve ending was abuzz with the thought of what the rest of the evening had to offer, and there was also a knot of apprehension in her stomach. What if she couldn't go through with it? Or what if she hadn't followed Jenna's instructions correctly?

Opening the door and finding Kit lounging on the bed, her misgivings vanished. She was already this man's wife on paper. Now she wanted to become his wife physically.

"There wasn't anyone waiting when I came out of the bathroom, if you'd like to use it."

Kit swung his feet off the bed and stood up. Pulling a clean set of clothes from his saddlebags, he rubbed a hand across his bristled jaw. "Yeah, I would like to soak awhile, then scrape off this stubble. I won't be long."

He moved across the room, opened the door, and stepped into the hall.

Once the door closed, Angelina sprang into action. She put away her dirty clothes, pulled back the bedspread, then dug through her satchel until she found the things she wanted. After setting the small jar and her hairbrush on the bedside table, she reached for the buttons of her shirtwaist. She undressed quickly, then slipped into bed. The sheets felt wonderfully cool against her heated, bare skin.

She smiled. No wonder Kit liked to sleep naked. She sat up long enough to give her hair a few more strokes of her brush, then pulled the sheet up to her chin and lay back to await her husband.

Time seemed to stand still as she strained to hear the bathroom door open then the clomp of his boots in the hall. Her heart feeling like it was about to take flight from her chest, she glanced at the bedside table to make sure the jar was within easy reach. On impulse, she rose up on one elbow and lowered the wick on the lamp. Settling back on the bed, she tried to remember what Jenna had told her during their talks before what was to have been her premiere appearance in the ranks of prostitution. Jenna had explained about what men expected, what they liked, how to please them.

She wiggled to get more comfortable, wondering if she should have worn a nightdress. Maybe Kit would think her too bold. Maybe he would think—

The door swinging inward ended her worrying about what he would think. She would soon find out.

His eyebrows lifting slightly at finding the room nearly dark and Angelina in bed, Kit resisted the urge to comment on her eagerness. Instead he said, "Is the bed comfortable?"

"Yes, it's fine."

The husky timbre of her voice sent a very erotic message to the lower half of his anatomy. Turning the lock on the door, he moved into the room and dropped his bundle of clothes beside his saddlebags. He sat on the edge of the bed and pulled off his boots, then rose to shrug out of his shirt.

When his hands went to the buttons of his trousers, Angelina silently berated herself for turning down the lamp. Now that she was finally getting the chance to see all of her husband, she wished her first view could have been in much brighter light.

She watched him push his trousers down over his hips, then held her breath as his drawers followed. Tossing his clothes aside, he turned toward her.

Her gaze moved from his face, drifting downward and stopping at the puckered patch of skin just beneath his left shoulder. In response to her furrowed brow, he said, "Knife wound. A souvenir from my last job as a bounty hunter."

"Does it pain you?"

"No, it's completely healed."

"Good," she murmured, then moved her gaze to the center of his chest with its thatch of dark hair.

Kit allowed Angelina to look her fill with amused indulgence. But after a full minute of letting her ogle him, he was ready to end the game. Grabbing the top sheet, he flipped it to the foot of the bed.

Startled by his actions, Angelina started to cover herself with her hands, then stopped when she heard him inhale sharply. The heat in his eyes sent an equally hot stab of need racing through her body.

Thinking she was even more beautiful than he'd imagined, Kit placed a knee on the mattress, then eased down next to her. Bracing himself on one forearm, he reached out to touch her face. As he trailed his fingers over her cheek, down her neck, then lower, he watched her expression. When his hand settled over one breast, her eyes widened slightly, her lips opening.

He leaned closer. "Are you sure this is what you want?"

"Yes," she replied in a breathless whisper. "I'm sure." As he lowered his head, she wrapped her arms around his neck. Lifting herself off the mattress, she rubbed her breasts against his chest, moving her mouth back and forth almost frantically under his.

When she tried to press closer, he jerked her arms from around his neck and pulled his mouth free of hers. "What the hell are you doing?"

She blinked up at him, unsure why he sounded angry. "But, that's what Jen—I mean, isn't that how you want me to act? Didn't you like what I was doing?"

"You said the key word. Act. That's exactly what you were doing. Your other customers may have appreciated your acting abilities, but I don't. I want everything that happens in this bed to be a natural reaction to what we do to each other." He lowered one hand to cup the creamy mound of one breast. "No acting. No pretending. Do you understand what I'm saying?"

Unable to find her voice, only able to feel the gentle kneading of his fingers on her left breast, she nodded.

"Good," he murmured, before closing the distance between them and covering her mouth with his once more.

This time she did none of the things Jenna had told her would ignite the desire of the bordello customers. This time she just let herself feel. When Kit coaxed her lips apart and slipped his tongue into her mouth, she gasped at the incredible bolt of heat spreading to every part of her body, then intensifying to a tingling throb between her thighs.

She gripped his upper arm with one hand, her fingers biting into his flesh. Her hips came off the bed of their own volition, bringing a groan from deep within Kit's chest.

He shifted his hand lower, feeling the ridge of each rib, then the concave silk of her belly. When his fingertips touched the downy nest at the base of her stomach, he groaned again, his hips rocking forward to press his swollen sex against her thigh.

Lifting his mouth, he drew a deep shuddering breath. "I've never wanted a woman as much as I want you," he murmured, bending his head for another kiss. Before he could anticipate

her actions, she pulled away and dropped her hand from his
arm.

"What is it?"

She squirmed beneath the weight of his upper body, one
hand reaching for the bedside table. As her fingers wrapped
around a small glass jar with a black and gold label, his brows
pulled together. "What are you doing?" he demanded in a soft
whisper.

"I was just getting the La Clyde's. It'll . . . um . . . make it
better for you. It's a lub—"

"I know what the hell it is. But I won't be needing any artificial help." Seeing the apprehension in her eyes, he nodded toward the jar of white petrolatum. "Why do you think we need
that stuff?"

Dropping her gaze, she said, "I just thought you'd be in a
hurry to—Anyway, I figured it wouldn't hurt so much if I used
the La—"

"Hurt so much? Jesus, what do you think I am? I would never
take a woman who wasn't ready for me." He drew a deep
breath, trying to curb his irritation. "I swear we won't need a
lubricant from a jar. I'll make sure your body prepares itself for
me."

Feeling her body respond to his words, she knew he'd spoken the truth. She dropped the jar on the table, then moved
her arm back to his shoulder and pulled him closer.

Kit didn't need more of an invitation, but immediately set
out to make his words reality. He kissed her, tenderly at first,
then with increased pressure. This time she eagerly opened
her lips for him, accepting his tongue and reciprocating with
hers, seeking out the warmth of his mouth.

He continued to caress her breasts with his hands, rubbing
the tips until her nipples stood up in tight little peaks. Then he
shifted positions, replacing his fingers with his mouth. When his
lips closed over one nipple and suckled gently, she gasped, her
hips jerking in reaction.

Lowering one hand, he pushed his fingers through the silky
hair at the apex of her thighs, then cupped her with his palm.

With one finger, he traced the curve of her most private place, bringing another gasp from her lips. He pushed lower and gently massaged the tender pebble of flesh until it hardened. As he slipped one finger into her body, a groan vibrated in his chest.

She was unbelievably hot and moist, and most definitely ready. Knowing he couldn't wait any longer, he shifted his position and rose over her.

For a moment he just stared at the sensual picture she made, lying in an enticing sprawl, eyes heavy with desire, lips swollen from his kisses. But as he pushed her legs apart and settled on his knees between her spread thighs, the picture changed. Squeezing her eyes shut, she held her bottom lip between her teeth and clenched her hands into fists.

"Look at me, Angelina," he ordered in a soft voice.

Slowly her eyelids lifted, uncertainty swimming in their golden-brown depths.

"I swore I'd make sure you're ready for me, and believe me you are. You have nothing to fear. I won't hurt you. Did someone use you badly? Is that why you're so tense?" All the while he talked to her, he eased his hips forward. When his arousal touched between her thighs, she flinched.

"Don't stiffen up on me, honey. Just relax. Let your muscles relax." As the stiffness left her legs, he whispered, "That's it. Relax and just feel." He pushed forward a little more, the tip of his manhood entering her. The silken heat of her pulled at him, drawing him deeper. He bit back a groan.

Unable to wait any longer, he pulled her legs up around his waist, then drove into her with one steady stroke.

Angelina cried out as he broke through the barrier he had never thought to encounter, then turned into a wildcat. Twisting beneath him, she lifted her hands and pushed at his shoulders. His snarl to be still ended her struggles.

Shocked to his toes by what had just happened, the part of his brain still capable of logical thought told him he should stop. But the rest of his brain was quick to overrule the order. He'd been wanting this woman for far too long and been without any woman a lot longer, so there was no way he could stop what he'd started.

Clutching the pillow on either side of her head, he began moving with slow, gentle thrusts, hoping to spare her more pain. His good intentions soon were forgotten. The only thing he could think about was finding completion.

After only a few more quick hard strokes, he groaned, then let his climax overtake him. His mouth pressed to her neck, he pushed his hips against her one last time, then went still.

Several minutes passed before his senses returned enough to remember the staggering discovery he'd just made. Not saying a word, he rolled to his side. He remained silent until Angelina stirred next to him.

Turning his head on the pillow, he said, "Would you mind telling me why you never mentioned I was marrying a goddamn virgin?"

Chapter Thirteen

Angelina turned toward Kit and met his glare with an icy one of her own. "Would you have believed me, if I had?"

The muscles in his jaw worked. "Who in their right mind would even suspect a woman working in a whorehouse was a virgin?"

Sitting up, she reached for the sheet at the foot of the bed and pulled it around her. "My point exactly."

Staring at her through narrowed eyes, he wondered how he'd managed to shackle himself to the exact kind of woman he'd tried so hard to avoid, the kind of woman he had no business having for a wife. The Lord works in mysterious ways, was one of his mother's favorite sayings and certainly fit the turn his life had taken.

"Okay," he said at last. "You've made your point. Did Murray force you to become one of his whores?"

"No. It was my choice."

"Your choice!" His voice rose to a roar. "What do you mean it was your choice?"

"I told Mr. Murray I no longer wanted to play piano in the parlor, that I wanted to work with Jenna and the other girls. He granted my request and told Ruby to see about some dresses for my new position."

"Did it never occur to you that you weren't playing dress-up in those low-cut gowns? That in your new *position*, you'd have to allow some rutting male to take you upstairs where he'd take something more precious—your virtue?"

She shot him a peeved look. "Of course, I knew that. Besides, you were the rutting male who just couldn't wait to take me upstairs and have your way with me. You've got a lot of nerve, acting like I'm the one at fault when your behavior was no better."

"Damnit, I didn't know you still had your maidenhead," he snapped. "Most whores of my acquaintance are not virgins for Christ's sake."

Unable to believe the conversation he was having with his wife, Kit pinched the bridge of his nose. When he dropped his hand, he spoke in a much calmer voice. "Why would you choose to do such a thing?"

Ignoring his question, she shifted, wincing at the stickiness between her thighs. "I'd like to . . . uh . . . get cleaned up, if you don't mind."

"Fine," he replied, scooting up so he could lean against the headboard.

She rose to her feet, the sheet still wrapped around her, and marched across the room to the washstand. After moving the folding screen to block Kit's view, she poured water from the pitcher into the bowl, then allowed the sheet to drop away.

While giving herself a quick sponge bath, Angelina wondered how she could have fallen in love with such an obstinate, infuriating—

Love? She gripped the front of the washstand to keep from falling. Could it be true? Had she fallen in love with Kit? The answer was both immediate and adamant. Yes, she loved him, for all the good it would do. He was only in her life temporarily—he'd made that abundantly clear—so how could she have allowed herself to fall in love with him?

The how didn't matter now. What did matter was making sure he didn't leave before his year was up. Would this latest turn of events change his mind? A man should show some gratitude at finding out he'd married a woman who'd never known a man. Yet, Kit had sounded anything but grateful. In fact he'd sounded down right furious. Was it because she hadn't told him the truth, or was there another—The voice of the man filling her thoughts interrupted her line of thinking.

"What are you doing back there? We're not through talking about this. And don't use all the water. After I wash up, we're going to continue our conversation."

Angelina was struck with the sudden urge to stomp over to the bed and dump the basin of water over his head. If only she weren't standing without a stitch on, she might have given in to temptation. "Just hold your horses. I'm nearly finished." After pulling on the nightdress she'd shunned earlier, she poured the used water into the chamber pot, then refilled the basin.

Stepping from behind the screen, she kept her gaze carefully averted from her husband. "I poured water for you," she said in a cool voice. She dropped the sheet on the foot of the bed, then moved to her side and took a seat on the edge of the mattress.

"Thanks," he grumbled, getting to his feet and stalking across the room.

He washed himself then rinsed the cloth in the basin, the reddish tint of the water—proof he'd taken Angelina's maidenhead—filling him with a satisfying sense of pride. He shoved such feelings aside. He couldn't allow himself to feel anything for Angelina—other than lust, of course, though perhaps now even that would wane. Yet just thinking about her silken warmth, her eager mouth, he knew his desire hadn't diminished in the least. In fact, even with her lack of experience, he'd never known such incredible satisfaction. Too bad he'd left her unfulfilled.

Next time he would stroke her and kiss her until she was out of her mind with need, then he'd make sure she scaled the lofty peak of release. Next time . . . He frowned. *Don't even think about a next time, Dancer. You're gettin' way ahead of yourself.* She'd been a virgin for Christ's sake, not the experienced woman of the world he'd expected, and therefore probably knew nothing about preventing pregnancy.

He emptied the basin, then pulled on a clean pair of drawers. After he folded the screen and moved it out of the way, he tried to avoid looking at Angelina. But against his will his gaze immediately sought the woman who was becoming much too important to him.

She was still sitting on the edge of the bed, her back stiff as a board, pulling a brush through her hair in slow, deliberate strokes.

Taking a deep breath, Kit moved around the bed and took a seat next to her. When she didn't react to his presence, he grabbed the hand holding her brush. "Here, let me," he whispered.

Angelina looked up, her eyes wide with surprise. After a moment, she shrugged and relinquished the brush. Her posture rigid, she turned her back to him and balled her hands into fists in her lap.

Using gentle pressure, Kit ran the brush through her hair, the silky strands swaying with each stroke, the golden highlights glimmering in the soft lamplight. After a few minutes of his silent ministrations, the stiffness left her back. A tiny sigh escaped her lips.

"Now," he said in a soft voice. "I want to hear why you asked to become one of the Murray House whores."

Angelina drew in a deep breath, then exhaled slowly. "I already told you how I ended up working for Mr. Murray, and you know about the contract I signed."

"I read it, remember? That's why we're married."

"Yes, well, when I started working at the Murray House I was given my choice of jobs. Since I couldn't imagine allowing even one man I didn't know to touch me or . . ." She cleared her throat. "So anyway, because I've always been musically inclined, I chose to be the piano player in the main parlor. I didn't mind the work overly much, except for when some of the customers tried to convince me to give up the piano for more interesting sport. When they wouldn't take no for an answer, I kind of withdrew, hiding behind a wall I built in my mind. That's when they gave me that awful nickname."

"The Ice Angel," Kit said.

"Yes. How I hated the name. But at least when I was the Ice Angel the customers stopped badgering me and I could finally play the piano in relative peace."

"If you enjoyed playing the piano, why did you quit?"

"Money. The wages I made didn't go very far. After paying for my room and board and buying food for my mother and sister, there wasn't much left to pay Mr. Murray. It would have taken me years to pay off what I owed."

She paused for a moment, drawing another deep breath. "Every time I went home Mama was weaker, and I was so afraid something would happen to her before I could pay off my contract and move back to the ranch. When I found out the girls working as who—I mean, as Murray House lovelies made a lot more than me, even after paying the ten dollar monthly fee to the city, I decided to change jobs."

"Just like that, you decided money was more important than your virtue?"

"No, it wasn't 'just like that.' I spent a lot of time thinking about my decision, and I talked at length with Jenna. She didn't want me to go through with it, but my mother and sister are the only family I have, and they were relying on me. I was willing to do whatever was necessary to take care of them."

Kit mulled over her words for a minute, his hands still working the snarls from her hair. Finally he said, "So, the night we met was to have been your first time?"

"Yes."

His hands abruptly stilled. "Jesus, Angel, how the hell could you do it? How could you have been willing to sacrifice your virginity that way? In a whorehouse, to a man you didn't know, to a man who paid for your time."

She turned around to face him, lips pressed into a fierce line, dark eyes blazing.

"Don't you lecture me, Kittridge Dancer. You don't know what it was like, constantly worrying about my mother and sister, not knowing when or even if I'd ever get to live with them again. I'd have been willing to do anything, do you hear me, anything to speed up paying off my contract." Her bosom heaving beneath her cotton nightdress, she lifted her chin and pinned him with a fierce glare. "And another thing. I asked you not to call me Angel."

Kit blinked down at her flushed face, a myriad of emotions roiling inside him. Surprise at her outburst. Empathy for the predicament she'd been in. And the strongest emotion: white-hot desire. Seeing the fire in her eyes and hearing it in her voice caused his physical hunger for her to soar to an all-time high.

The first time he'd gazed into her eyes, he knew there was a woman of fire hidden beneath the sadness. He'd tasted a bit of her fiery nature in her kisses, suspected it throbbed just beneath the surface of her body. And now he knew he'd been right. It was all he could do not to smile.

"Sorry," he said at last. "The name just slipped out."

She stared up at him, brow knitted, lips pulled into a frown. Finally her features relaxed and she offered him a small smile. "I'm sorry, too. I didn't mean to sound so cross."

"No need to apologize," he said, reaching around her to lay the hairbrush on the bedside table. "It's been quite an evening for both of us. Why don't we try to get some sleep?"

She nodded, not at all sure she'd be able to sleep. Getting to her feet, she helped Kit smooth out the wadded-up top sheet then tuck the ends under the mattress.

She watched him slip into bed, then adjust his pillow. Once he was settled, the sheet pulled up to his waist, she crawled in beside him.

After a few moments of silence, he said, "I hope I . . . uh . . . didn't hurt you. If I'd known, I might have been able to spare you some pain."

"No," she replied. "You didn't hurt me. There was some . . . discomfort, but it passed quickly."

He turned to look at her. She lay on her back, staring at the ceiling. "I'm sorry you didn't enjoy it more, Angelina. I would have taken more time if I'd known."

"Will you stop saying that. You didn't know, so let's just drop it, okay?"

"Okay, we'll drop it. But, I want you to know I didn't mean to sound so harsh earlier."

"You were just saying what you feel. Besides, you had every right to say what you did."

"What do you mean?"

"As you just reminded me, by deciding to become a whore I allowed myself to sink to the lowest of depths, so I deserve whatever I get."

Kit jerked upright in bed. "What the hell are you talking about? You made the decision to turn to prostitution, but you never had to go through with it. I married you and took you away from that place."

"Yes, and now I'm your whore," she whispered. "All bought and paid for."

"Is that what you believe? That I paid off your contract and married you just to make you my personal whore?"

Not giving her a chance to answer, he grasped her chin between his thumb and forefinger and forced her to look at him. "Have you forgotten the promise I made not to make us truly man and wife until you were ready? Would a man who did what you've accused me of doing make such a promise?"

She stared up at him, an enormous lump wedged in her throat. Forcing herself to swallow, she finally said, "I . . . I guess not."

Slowly, he relaxed his grip on her chin, then moved his fingers to caress one downy cheek. "Good, now go to sleep." He pressed a quick kiss on her lips, reached over to turn out the lamp, then lay down and pulled her into his arms.

With Angelina's head resting on his chest, her warm body tucked against his, Kit closed his eyes. Though he was tired, his body relaxed, his mind remained wide awake, going over the events of the evening.

Reality had been nothing like what he'd envisioned for the first time he made love to Angelina. Of all the things he'd imagined, her being a virgin had never even entered his mind. The last thing he wanted in a wife was purity. Hell, he hadn't even wanted a wife, hadn't even considered remarrying, until he saw

Angelina at the Murray House and learned how she came to be working there.

He drew a deep breath and exhaled slowly. How could he have allowed his life to become so damn complicated? He still couldn't believe he'd had the misfortune to be attracted to the one woman in the bordello who turned out to be a virgin. God, what a mess his life had become.

Feeling the woman in his arms relax, her breathing slow, Kit recalled her words about asking to become one of the Murray House whores. As incredible as her story sounded, he couldn't fault her motives. He knew all too well the importance of safeguarding the well-being of a person's family. Still, knowing she'd made the decision to give herself to any man who paid the price twisted his insides into a knot. Recalling her words about how he'd acted no better than the other rutting males vying for her time, and remembering how he'd shoved aside all competition so he could be the first to partake of her charms, the knot in his gut pulled tighter. *Shit, I was no better than the rest of the horny bastards, sniffing at her skirts like a stallion on the scent of a mare in season.*

But what if he hadn't returned to El Paso, or gone to the Murray House on the night of her debut as one of the lovelies? What if he hadn't paid off her contract and married her?

The idea of another man being the first to taste her passion hit him like a physical blow, making his chest ache, his lungs struggle to fill with air. Though his faith had been all but lost after the deaths of his first wife and son, he felt the sudden need to offer a prayer. He closed his eyes and whispered his thanks for protecting the woman sleeping in his arms until he'd entered Angelina's life and taken her away from the fate awaiting her.

He kissed the top of her head, still finding it hard to believe his usually accurate evaluation of people had failed with Angelina. Right from the start, he'd had her pegged all wrong. She wasn't an experienced prostitute, nor had she lost her innocence to a hot-blooded suitor. Of course, in fairness, even if his instincts had told him she wasn't what she portrayed herself to be, he wouldn't have listened. After all, finding a virgin working in a bawdy house was a definite exception to the rule.

Though he'd been surprised by Angelina saying she was ready to make their relationship a physical one, her words didn't begin to compare to his surprise when he took her innocence. Did she have an ulterior motive for offering herself? Did she think once he'd breached her maidenhead he would feel obliged to stay even after a year? Though he didn't think Angelina's mind worked that way, he couldn't be sure.

As he drifted to sleep, that last question continued to nag at him, spawning another disturbing thought. Now that he'd experienced the welcoming heat of her body, he wasn't sure he could just walk away from her when the time came.

Angelina came out of the depths of sleep with a start. Lying perfectly still, she waited for her fuzzy senses to clear. She was curled on her side, and Kit lay spoon-fashion behind her, one arm draped over her waist. He groaned, the muscles in his legs and arm jerking in spasms. Realizing she'd been awakened by another of his nightmares, she rolled onto her back.

"Kit? Wake up, Kit." Rising up onto one elbow, she gave his shoulder a shake. "Come on, Kit. Wake up." He groaned again, then gave a low keening cry. The eerie sound made the hair on her nape stand on end.

Wondering what could have happened to cause him such heartrending nightmares, she shook him again. "Kit, please wake up." Finally his groans stopped and his eyes flickered open.

"Kit, are you all right?"

He blinked several times, then looked up at her shadowed face. Drawing a deep cleansing breath, he rubbed a hand over his face. "Yeah," he finally said. "I'm fine."

"Have you always suffered from nightmares?" she asked, smoothing a lock of hair off his forehead.

"No."

"Then what happened to make you suffer from them now?"

"Drop it, Angelina."

"But, I just want to help you, Kit. I'm not trying to pry. If you'll talk about—"

"The nightmares are about my first wife and our son, okay? Now go back to sleep." He rolled onto his side, facing away from her.

"Your wife? But Reverend Morton married us, or . . . or isn't our marriage legal?"

"It's legal. Bethany and Thad are dead."

Angelina's mouth dropped open. She knew Kit had to have a past, but he'd never volunteered anything and she hadn't tried to pry. Yet learning of his first marriage and the son born to that union shocked her to the core. Snapping her mouth closed, she started at his back, a hundred questions tumbling over one another in her head.

"What happened to—"

He rolled back to face her, his movement so swift the rest of her question stuck in her throat.

"I said, go back to sleep, Angelina."

Unable to see his face in the darkened room, she heard the hard edge to his voice that told her his features were set in that stony expression she was getting to know so well. The expression that said the subject was closed.

With a sigh, she sank back onto the bed. Reaching across the distance separating them, she searched for and found his hand. Her fingers entwined with his, she closed her eyes.

Too keyed up to sleep after Kit's recent disclosure, she managed to lie still so she wouldn't disturb him. In a few minutes, he relaxed next to her, his breathing slowing. She sighed. *At least one of us is able to get back to sleep.*

Her thoughts drifted back to the day they'd walked down to the river in El Paso. Remembering his answer to her question about wearing black, Angelina realized she now knew why he'd called the color appropriate. Her heart cramped with the pain he must have felt. She knew how much it hurt when she lost her father. But she couldn't imagine losing a spouse and child.

Then a more painful thought struck. What chance did she have of winning the heart of a man who continued to mourn his first wife? Biting her lip to hold in a sob, she finally slipped into a fitful sleep.

Chapter Fourteen

Kit pulled Angelina closer. Her soft bottom pressed against his insistent arousal, causing a moan to rumble deep in his chest. The sun had been up for several hours, but he didn't want to stir from the bed. He wanted to hold his wife a little longer.

He shifted his hips, increasing the pressure of his throbbing flesh against her body. Another moan escaped his lips before he could stop it.

"Kit? Are you awake?"

He swallowed. "Uh huh."

She turned in his arms. "When I heard you moan I thought you might be having another night—" His fingers on her lips halted her words.

"That was a moan of pleasure," he whispered, mischief dancing in his pale blue eyes, the morning sun gleaming on his dark hair. "Remind me to show you the difference sometime."

She pulled her brows together. He certainly wasn't acting like the angry, interrogating man he'd been the night before. Just as she started to ask about the change, he covered her mouth with his.

Kit had meant to give her only a brief peck, a quick good-morning kiss, but his body had other ideas. Hiking up her nightdress, he lowered one hand to her thighs. Her skin was as soft and smooth as the finest silk, and touching her sent his desire into another realm.

He pushed her legs apart, his fingers seeking the heat he knew lay nestled between. Touching the downy patch of hair brought him back to reality with a jerk. What was he doing? As he strove for control, he removed his hand from her leg and ended the kiss. "I'd better stop," he said in a gruff whisper. "While I still can."

"Why do you have to stop?" she said, her mouth wet from his kiss.

He bit back another groan. "Because I don't want to get you with child. Last night was risk enough, and I won't increase the odds with more carelessness."

"But, you don't have to worry about getting me with child."

"What are you saying?"

"Before we were married, when I said you didn't need to worry about leaving even if there was a child, you told me I should know ways to prevent—"

"I know what I told you. But you're a virgin, or rather you were until last night, and most virgins don't know the first thing about preventing pregnancy."

"I didn't know anything about it, not for sure. But I went to see Jenna last night while you took care of the horses. She told me about the different kinds of preventives men and women can use. Since you said it was my responsibility, I figured you weren't planning on wearing what she called a shield, or willing to practice the incomplete act of worship. So I decided to use Jenna's recommendation: a pessary. Maybe you've heard them called Dutch Caps or the name Jenna used—a pisser."

Kit nearly choked. Hearing her say such words so matter-of-factly caused his face to grow uncomfortably warm.

When he didn't comment, she continued. "Jenna keeps extras, so she gave me one and explained how it has to be inserted before we—"

"That's enough," he said, frowning down at her. "I don't want to hear any more." Though he'd been the one to bring up preventing conception in the first place, he'd never discussed the subject with a woman in such detail. And while he found her unexpected candor refreshing, he was also inexplicably embarrassed by her frank words.

Surprised to see a dull splash of color spread across his cheeks, she said, "Okay. But I was just trying to tell you I followed Jenna's instructions last night. There won't be a child; I was protected."

"That was last night," he replied, her declaration easing his concern that he might have impregnated her. "But this is morning."

It was Angelina's turn to feel the hot sting of a blush. "Jenna said it wasn't necessary to remove the protection right after we . . . um . . . well, afterward, so I didn't."

The tightness of Kit's muscles relaxing, he smiled. "Good," he murmured, his manhood seconding his response with a throbbing jerk.

Pulling her flush against him, he ran one hand up her back, his fingers tunneling through the heavy mass of her hair. "I want to make it good for you," he said, his tongue tracing the outline of her lips. "I want you to tell me what pleases you." He pulled her bottom lip into his mouth, nibbling and suckling until she squirmed against him.

Lifting his head, he stared down into her flushed face. "Did you like that?"

Dazed, she managed a small nod.

"Then you must tell me when I do other things you like," he said, lowering his head to her throat. He kissed his way over the soft skin, up to her ear, then across her cheek. "God, you smell so good." His breath was hot on her face, his heart pounding hard against her breasts.

"Kiss me," she whispered in a raspy voice. "I like it when you kiss me."

He chuckled. "Good girl. Now you're getting the hang of it." He shifted one arm to grasp her left hand and pull it lower. "And, I want you to touch me."

Her fingers brushed the hard, pulsing length of his manhood, bringing a groan from deep in his chest. When he closed her hand around him, his back arched, his hips bucked forward. "Squeeze, honey. Like this." He tightened his fingers over hers. "Ah, that's it. Now, move your hand on me. Up, then down."

Her compliance made him groan again. "You're a fast learner," he whispered, removing his hand and settling his mouth over hers in a fierce kiss.

Angelina was fascinated with the feel of him. She wondered how such hardness could be so incredibly soft to the touch, like the finest of satins. As her hand moved in the rhythmic motion he'd shown her, she could feel him swell and harden even more within the circle of her fingers. Her body answered his need with a throbbing, moist heat between her thighs, a fervent hunger like none she'd ever known.

As if Kit sensed her need, he ended the kiss, then pulled her nightdress up around her waist. Placing his hand on her stomach, he began massaging her belly in slow, circular motions. He moved lower, inch by frustrating inch, until she was ready to scream.

Her hips lifted off the bed, her breathing harsh. "Please, Kit."

"Please, what?" he murmured near her ear. "Tell me what you want."

"I want . . . I want you to touch me," she finally managed to say.

His hand moved lower, cupping the mound covered with silky hair. "Do you want me to touch you here?"

She squirmed, trying to ease the ache, but unsure how to find relief. "Yes, but . . ."

"But, you want me to touch you more intimately. Like you're touching me?"

"Yes," she said, her voice rising to a near scream.

He smiled. "That's easily remedied." His fingers pushed lower, separating the petals of her feminine center. Her thighs fell open in blatant invitation. As he slipped one finger inside her, she cried out. He stopped immediately. "Did I hurt you?"

"No," she murmured, her eyes dilated with the fire of desire. "It didn't hurt. Please don't stop." She gripped him harder, moving her hand in a faster rhythm.

He grasped her wrist to halt her movements. "That's enough."

"Did I do something wrong?"

"No," he replied with a smile. "You did everything too damn good. Much more and I would have . . . well, never mind. I want to concentrate on pleasuring you, and I can't think straight with your hot little hand wrapped around me like that."

Releasing her wrist, he brought his hand back to her parted thighs. He ran a fingertip back and forth over the sensitive nubbin of flesh in soft gentle strokes until it hardened from his ministrations. Moving to insert a finger into her tight passage, he continued to flick at the hard kernel of flesh with his thumb.

Angelina sucked in a surprised breath, the blood pounding in her temples, the pressure building deep inside her belly. She felt as if she were floating, as if she were no longer connected to her body. Her hips started moving, lifting then lowering, matching the strokes of Kit's finger and thumb. Heat, intense and all-consuming, swept over her. The pressure continued to build, spreading outward in ever widening circles until she thought she'd surely die if she didn't find relief from such exquisite torture.

Kit's voice penetrated the fog of her need. "You're almost there, honey. I can feel your muscles tightening. Just relax and let it come."

The words had barely left his mouth when she exploded. Hands clenched in the sheet, hips bucking in a frenzied rhythm, her head thrashed on the pillow as wave after wave of incredible sensation washed over her. Heels digging into the mattress, she pushed against his hand one last time, then dropped back on the bed. She drew in a shaky breath, then exhaled on a long sigh.

"Jesus, Angelina, you're amazing," he whispered, rolling over and settling on his knees between her thighs. He eased himself inside her, then pushed forward until his entire length was buried in her honied depths. The last of the tremors from her climax caressed him, milking his manhood and snapping his control.

Bracing himself on his forearms, he began moving in deliberately slow strokes. But the memory of her powerful release and the hot, slick tightness surrounding him soon drove him into a much faster rhythm.

"Wrap your legs around me," he managed to say through clenched teeth.

She immediately did as he asked, driving him deeper. He paused for a moment, hoping to regain his control. But as soon as he started moving again, there was nothing he could do to stop the onrush of his own release. Throwing back his head, he pushed into her as far as he could, then spilled himself in one throbbing spurt after another.

For a few moments the only sound in the room was the harsh rasp of his breathing. When his strength returned, he relieved Angelina of his weight and rolled onto his back.

"I'm sure glad I got you out of the Murray House," he said when his breathing slowed. "Otherwise, you would've been on your back more than all the other gals put together."

Angelina's breath caught in her throat. His bringing up the Murray House hurt more than she wanted to admit. He now knew she hadn't worked as a prostitute, so why did he continue to make references to a time in her life she was trying very hard to forget?

When the answer came, it hit her like a physical blow. She clamped her lips together to hold in the sob threatening to erupt from deep in her chest. The motivation for his comment had to be her wanton behavior of a few moments ago. She could think of no other reason to account for his painful remark.

Was she not supposed to find making love a pleasant and fulfilling experience? Perhaps soiled doves were allowed to feel pleasure, but not wives. Her mother had explained the rudiments of what went on between a man and a woman, but the discussion had not included whether or not she should derive pleasure from the act.

Maybe Kit made the statement as a warning. But, if that were true, why did he insist she tell him what pleased her? Unless he still considered her a former prostitute, not in the physical sense but guilty by association. This marriage business was becoming much more difficult than she'd anticipated, made all

the more complicated by the love filling her heart for the man
lying beside her.

"Aren't you getting up, lazy-bones?"

Kit's question made her turn her head on the pillow, surprised to see him standing on the opposite side of the bed, fully
dressed. She'd been so caught up in her thoughts she hadn't felt
him leave the bed nor heard him pull on his clothes.

Swallowing hard, she forced a smile to her lips. "Who are
you calling lazy-bones? You've only been up a few minutes
yourself and it must be nearly nine."

"Quarter till," he responded with a grin. "Come on, time's
a wasting."

Angelina sat up, then swung her legs over the side of the bed.
"What's the big hurry?"

"I want to be at the train station when the nine-forty-five ar-
rives, which doesn't leave us much time to grab some breakfast."

"Do you think your cattle will be on the train?"

"That's *our* cattle, and yeah, I think there's a real good possibility they'll be arriving this morning. Now, get a move on.
I'm so hungry my belly thinks my throat's been slit."

In spite of her somber mood moments before, Angelina
chuckled. "All right, all right. I'll hurry." She grabbed her
clothes, then turned to look up at him. "Would it be all right if
I went down the hall? There's something I have to . . . um . . .
take care of."

"You don't have time to take a bath. We have—" Remembering the discussion they'd had before their second taste of
marital relations, he realized a bath wasn't the reason she
wanted the privacy of the hotel bathroom. He cleared his
throat, then said, "Okay, go ahead, but make it quick."

While they ate a hurried breakfast, Angelina remained quiet,
uncertainty over her earlier quandary still plaguing her.

"Is something wrong?" Kit asked. "You're awfully quiet."

"No, nothing's wrong. I was just . . . thinking."

"No harm in that, I reckon. Anything I can help you with?"

She shook her head, reaching for her coffee cup and lifting

it to her mouth. Realizing she couldn't reveal the reason for her silence, she took a sip of coffee, then said, "I forgot to ask. Were you able to hire some men to get the cattle back to the ranch?"

"Yeah. The man at the livery gave me a couple names. He claimed both men had worked cattle before and would probably help me out."

"Did you talk to them?"

He nodded. "They'll be ready to move the herd as soon as I let them know when we'll be heading for the Diamond C."

"That's good."

Kit pulled his brows together, the corners of his mouth turned down. "Are you sure you're okay?"

Her gaze snapped up to meet his. "Yes, I'm fine. Shall we go?"

Checking his pocket watch, he nodded. "The train will likely be late, but just in case it's not, we'd better get over there." He rose, then helped Angelina from her chair.

After paying their bill, he looped her arm through his, then directed them toward the Southern Pacific train depot.

As Angelina walked beside Kit, two ladies made their way down the platform steps and headed toward them. Angelina felt the muscles of his arm tense beneath her hand. She cast a brief glance up at him and realized the reason for his reaction. He'd neglected to pull the brim of his hat down enough to shadow his face as was his normal practice.

The ladies passed them, offering smiles of greeting. Angelina smiled in reply and heard Kit's murmured, "Morning, ladies."

Once the women were out of earshot, she pulled him to a halt. Staring up at him, she said, "Now, was that so bad?"

He turned to look down at her, the corners of his mouth pulled down. "What?"

"Letting strangers see your face."

He exhaled heavily. "I guess not."

"What made you change your mind about letting people see your face?"

"I'm not sure I've changed my mind, not completely at this

point. But something your mother said got me to thinking she might be right."

"Mama? Well, she is a mighty smart woman."

"Yeah, she is. She made me realize my scar isn't as hideous—"

"Hideous?" she replied in a fierce whisper. "Kit, you have a scar, a thin red line of slightly puckered skin. A slight imperfection. Nothing more."

"A few weeks ago, I would have argued with you. But, as I started to say, your mother made me realize my scar isn't as hideous as I once thought. In fact, it's nothing compared to what a lot of folks have to live with. I keep thinking about that poor bastard at the Murray House, the one who had the kerosene lamp explode practically in his face. If he survived, can you imagine the scars he'll be left with?"

"Yes, they must be terrible." She squeezed his arm. "I'm just glad you're no longer so sensitive about your looks."

"I wouldn't go so far as to say that." He started toward the platform steps, pulling her along with him. "I'm still not comfortable with the idea of people looking at me, but I reckon with time it'll get easier."

Angelina remained outside the depot while Kit went in to inquire about the arrival of the westbound train. Thinking about how he had begun to overcome his self-consciousness about his scar took her mind off her own problems for a few minutes. But now that she was alone again, her troubled thoughts flooded back.

She took a seat on a bench, watching a dust devil swirl up the dirt street and wondering what lay ahead in her marriage to Kit. Should she continue to enjoy his touch, in spite of what he would think of her? Or should she try to temper her response to what he expected from a wife?

When he returned a few minutes later, he flashed her a smile, then said, "The train's only fifteen minutes late, and the clerk says he received a wire early this morning to make sure there was someone here to help move a couple hundred head of cattle into the stock pens on the other side of the tracks. We can head for home as soon as the cattle are unloaded."

In spite of the gloom still hanging over her, Angelina couldn't help smiling at Kit's excitement. "That's wonderful. Should I go back to the hotel and pack our things?"

"It'll be at least a couple of hours before we can start moving the herd. So if you'd rather wait in our room until then that's fine."

Rising from a bench in front of the depot, Angelina said, "Yes, I believe I would. I'll pack our things, then wait for you to fetch me."

"Come on, I'll walk you back to the hotel."

"That's not necessary."

"It may not be necessary, but I want to. Understood?"

She nodded, then started back down St. Louis Street.

At the door to their room, Kit pulled her into his arms. "I'd like nothing more than another night with you in that bed, but I'm anxious to get the herd settled in their new home on the Diamond C. You understand that, don't you?" At her nod, he lowered his voice to add, "I can't leave until I've had another taste of your sweet mouth." He lowered his face, capturing her lips with his.

As he deepened the kiss, Angelina felt the familiar throbbing start between her thighs, the tips of her breasts tighten. All he had to do was touch her and she was afire with longing. Now that she'd tasted the end result of her need, the incredible explosion awaiting her as her desire peaked, her body's reaction to his touch was even stronger.

Her back stiffened. It was much too early to allow herself to be pulled into the web of physical pleasure. She hadn't made a decision about what she was going to do, and his kiss only confused the issue. Using every bit of her willpower, she tried to ignore the desire racing through her veins. She made no effort to fight him, but neither did she do anything to encourage his attention.

Releasing her, he held her at arm's length. He studied her face, but saw nothing in her expression to reveal why she'd abruptly withheld herself from participating in the kiss. With their cattle arriving soon, he didn't have time to ponder her behavior. "I'll let our hired hands know we'll be moving out later this morning, then settle up with the livery owner and take our horses over to the stock pens at the train station. I'll be back as soon as I can."

Nodding, she stepped into the room and closed the door behind her.

She packed what few personal items they'd brought with them, then stood looking out the window at the sun-splashed street.

With nothing to fill her time, thoughts of Kit likening her to a prostitute returned once again. So what was she going to do? She could forget about what he thought of her and allow herself to enjoy the pleasure he wrought from her so easily. What did it matter how passionately she responded when he would be gone from her life in less than twelve months anyway. Still, she couldn't bear knowing such behavior placed her on a par with soiled doves in his eyes.

She wondered if her punishment for working in a bawdy house had finally been doled out.

From the time she'd first started her employment at the Murray House, she feared God would eventually punish her for working in such a place, regardless of the circumstances that put her there. When she volunteered to become a prostitute, the possibility of divine wrath changed to virtual certainty. But then after Kit entered her life and offered to marry her, she experienced a ray of hope that she might be forgiven. After all, agreeing to marry a man she didn't know and, at the time, didn't love in order to save her family could certainly be viewed as a very noble gesture—perhaps reason enough for acquittal.

She should have known better. The truth hit her so hard she nearly crumpled to the floor. Grasping the window frame to steady her quivering knees, she swallowed the sudden lump in her throat. Her true penance had finally been revealed.

In order to prevent the man she loved from thinking of her as a harlot, she must not allow herself to experience the pleasure she knew awaited her in his arms. It seemed so unfair, to just recently learn of the incredible enjoyment she could derive from Kit making love to her, only to have it snatched away just as quickly. Fair or not, that was the unsavory dish served up to her.

Chapter Fifteen

Kit shifted his gaze from the cattle plodding their way toward the Diamond C to Angelina's position on the opposite side of the herd. She hadn't said more than two words since they left El Paso several hours earlier, but rode in silence, staring straight ahead and barely acknowledging his presence. Something obviously weighed heavily on her mind, probably the same thing filling his thoughts.

Giving his head a little shake to clear the puzzle of his wife's change in behavior, he turned his attention back to the herd of longhorn cattle. He glanced at the men he'd hired, one rode ahead of him, the second was riding drag.

Relieved the two were experienced hands, Kit figured if they kept their current pace, they would arrive at the Diamond C in an hour or so and have the cattle settled in the north pasture an hour past that.

Satisfied the men had everything under control, his thoughts again drifted to Angelina. While he was glad the cattle had finally arrived, he wasn't so sure about returning to the ranch house and, more specifically, sharing a bed with Angelina. Her sudden coolness had thrown him completely off kilter.

She'd made it plain she wanted more than kisses and caresses from him. Yet now that the deed was done, she had withdrawn into a shell of cool indifference, the incredible sadness back in the depths of her eyes. Such a change left him with only one

conclusion to draw: She regretted offering her maidenhead
and hadn't found a way to tell him.

He gave a snort of disgust. Wasn't that just like a fickle
woman! Pulling his hat lower, he kicked Sid into a trot. Maybe
if he moved closer to the front of the herd, where he couldn't
see Angelina, he could keep his mind on other things.

But it didn't matter where he rode, she was never far from
his thoughts, the memory of her trembling with her first climax
vivid in his mind's eye.

By the time the last longhorn had entered the fenced pasture
and Kit had closed and latched the gate, he'd made a decision.
Figuring Angelina's sudden coolness was for the best, he vowed
to control his own desire and not touch her. Since he'd be leaving eventually, maintaining a platonic relationship would be the
wisest choice. But would he be able to keep his vow? If she continued the cold shoulder, he probably could. But if she reverted
to the Angelina who touched and kissed at the slightest provocation, he was in big trouble. He already desired her more
than he should and it wouldn't take much to push his already
inflamed libido into action.

Watching the cattle saunter across the pasture, he blew out
an exasperated breath. The next eleven months were going to
be the longest he'd ever known.

Angelina knew Kit wondered why she'd withdrawn from
him. She could see the confusion and questions in his eyes, but
she was too embarrassed to explain.

After saying hello to Chloe and spending a few minutes with
her mother, Angelina unpacked her bag, changed clothes, then
headed for the kitchen. While measuring flour into a large mixing bowl, she couldn't shake thoughts of her husband or the
events of the past day and a half. In the span of less than forty-
eight hours she'd lost her virginity, discovered she'd fallen in

love with Kit, and had her behavior while in the throes of passion likened to that of a harlot.

It was the last that continued to plague her. Why should she care that Kit thought her actions whorish? What difference would it make if she experienced the same incredible pleasure again? He didn't return her love, so why— Her hands stilled in their task.

Ah, there was the rub. The love she'd so recently acknowledged growing in her heart for Kit wasn't returned. As she reached for a cake of yeast, Angelina realized her newfound love made her see things differently. No longer did she think of her marriage as short-lived, or of Kit as her temporary husband. In order to make her fanciful imaginings reality, she would have to figure out a way to keep Kit from leaving after their agreed year of marriage. The key to that end, she decided, was getting him to return her love.

How to accomplish such a task could be a problem, since she knew little about the male of the species. But she did know one thing that should prove useful. Kit desired her physically. So if she was ever going to get him to fall in love with her, she would have to make a concerted effort to be the kind of wife he wanted—which meant withholding her response whenever they made love. A difficult assignment, but she prayed it was not impossible. Sacrificing the pleasure she'd experienced in the arms of the man she loved didn't seem too high a cost. Not if behaving in a manner befitting a wife atoned for her shameful behavior *and* earned his love.

In spite of her decision and her determination to carry out her plans, she was struck with a sudden fear. Perhaps devising such a strategy would be for naught. Perhaps Kit had been so put off by her wanton display he no longer wanted to make love to her. Shoving that painful thought aside, she added part of the yeast cake to warm water then poured the mixture into the bowl of flour. Though she tried to concentrate on making bread, her mind insisted on dwelling on the night ahead.

What would happen when she and Kit retired? Would he

reach for her, or simply turn his back? She drew in a deep shaky breath, wishing she knew the answers.

Unfortunately, she was forced to wait to get the answers she sought. At the supper table Kit announced his intention to spread a bedroll by the north pasture, spouting some nonsense about making sure the cattle didn't spook during their first night in a strange place.

Her suggestion of letting one of other men take his place was met with a surprised glance, then a terse reply. "They were hired to help drive the cattle to the ranch, nothing more. As soon as I paid 'em they headed back to town."

Fearful his decision had as much to do with wanting to stay away from her as needing to play nursemaid to a herd of long-horns, Angelina didn't press him for more of an explanation.

Kit returned to the ranch house a little after noon the following day, his back aching from sleeping on the ground. He'd spent many a night stretched out on his bedroll on land just as unforgiving as the rocky north pasture, but he'd never suffered any physical consequence. *Guess I must be gettin' soft.*

He stopped Sid in front of the barn then dismounted, the motion causing another twinge in the small of his back. Idly rubbing the tight muscles, he frowned. Was softness the result of being married to Angelina and sleeping in a comfortable bed every night? His frown deepened. He sure as hell didn't want to start spending his nights on his bedroll, but that would solve the problem of being too close to temptation. If he didn't sleep next to his wife maybe—

"How did the cattle do last night?"

Angelina's voice jerked Kit from his thoughts. She must have seen him ride in and immediately headed for the barn. Realizing he must've been so firmly caught in the snare of his thoughts that he hadn't heard her approach, he called himself every kind of fool. *Good way to get yourself killed.* Or someone you care for, his guilt-ridden inner voice goaded, sending a prickle of fear up his spine.

Schooling his features not to reveal the emotions churning inside him, he swung around to face her. "They did fine. Settled down nice as you please."

"Good. I was . . . worried about you." Lifting one hand to brush a strand of hair off her face, she shifted her gaze to the corral where the two mares stood dozing.

"No need. Both the cattle and I did just fine."

"I'm glad," she whispered, casting a quick glance in his direction, then looking back at the horses in the corral.

Kit studied her in silence for a moment. She didn't seem quite so cool today, or was that just his fanciful imagination?

"Things okay here?"

She nodded. "Everything's fine." She took a deep breath, her breasts straining against the fabric of her dress and enticing his gaze to their lush fullness. "Will you have to spend the night in the pasture again tonight?"

He swallowed. Though he knew he should give her an affirmative answer, he found he couldn't form the words. Instead he said, "No. The cattle should be fine."

Turning back to Sid, he lifted the left stirrup and hooked it on the saddle horn. When he bent down to loosen the cinch, he sucked in a sharp breath. "Jesus," he murmured, grabbing his back.

"Kit, what is it? Are you hurt?"

"Just a little crick from sleeping on the ground," he managed to say. "It'll be fine once I work the tightness out of my muscles."

"Chloe keeps a bottle of liniment at the house. She uses it on her animals, but she says it works just as well on human aches and pains. Should I get it for you?"

"No, that's not necessary." He finished loosening the cinch and straightened. Liniment. Now there was something that might work—not on his back, since he was sure exercise would ease the tightness, but on his randiness for Angelina.

Pulling the saddle from Sid's back, he said, "Maybe I'll use it later. Before I go to bed." Most liniment he'd ever used stunk to high heaven, which was the reason he usually shunned such concoctions. But maybe using the vile stuff was warranted this time. Filling the bedroom with the medicinal odor of liniment was sure to kill the notion of undertaking any conjugal activity.

"Did you and Angelina enjoy y'all's time in El Paso?" Sarah asked, watching Kit sit down in the chair by her bed and stretch his legs out in front of him.

"We weren't there very long," he began carefully, "but in spite of the cattle arriving the day after we did and our having to start back right away, we enjoyed the trip. I had hoped . . . Well, never mind that."

She offered him a weak smile, then said, "Tell me about El Paso. I didn't get to see much when we arrived, what with going directly from the train to the wagon Douglas hired for the ride here. I used to ask Angelina to tell me about the town, but she would never say very much."

It was on the tip of Kit's tongue to say Angelina hadn't said much because during her six months in El Paso she'd been restricted to the tenderloin—not an area of town a daughter would normally discuss with her mother—but he swallowed the words. Crossing one ankle over the other, he started talking about El Paso. He tried to concentrate on what might be of interest to Sarah, but found his knowledge of the town's social amenities sorely lacking.

Before meeting Angelina he'd only been to El Paso a couple of times, both during his tenure as a bounty hunter. And since his prey usually holed up in the seedy section of town, he spent the majority of his time there as well. Unfortunately his intimate acquaintance with the goings-on of the tenderloin left him little to tell Sarah that wouldn't scorch her ears.

Finally when Kit could think of nothing more to say, he glanced at his mother-in-law and found her eyes closed. He waited a few minutes before rising from his chair. When he was certain she was asleep, he got to his feet, turned down the lamp on the bedside table, then moved silently toward the door.

Entering the bedroom at the opposite end of the hall, he found his wife brushing her hair in front of the dresser mirror. His fingers twitched at his sides, remembering the feel of the thick strands, itching to run through their silky texture again. Ignoring the urge, he moved to his side of the bed and sat down.

"Mama's asleep?"

"Yeah. I think my talking put her to sleep."

She turned from the mirror. "What were you talking about?"

"She wanted to hear about El Paso. I told her what I could but . . ." He shrugged. "I guess I was kinda boring. Next thing I knew she's sound asleep."

Angelina chuckled, then quickly sobered. "I doubt that. She's been awfully tired lately."

"I know. Should I send word for her doctor to come by?"

"No. He's supposed to be here later this week. So unless her condition worsens, there's no need to send for him early."

After a few moments of silence while he pulled off his boots then shrugged out of his shirt, she said, "How's your back?" Her gaze skimmed across his shoulders, then down his spine and across the smooth expanse of muscle. "I could . . ." She cleared her throat. "I could rub some of Chloe's liniment on your back, if you'd like."

As much as the idea of Angelina running her hands over his back appealed to him, he shook his head and said, "Thanks, but the soreness is gone." He refused to consider why he hadn't lied or used the liniment for a purpose other than a sore back. "All I need is a good night's sleep."

To prove his point, he rose, shucked his trousers and drawers, then settled between the sheets with a huge yawn.

"Well, good night then," she murmured. Turning back to the mirror, she gave her hair several more strokes, then placed the brush on the dresser.

She moved to her side of the bed where she stood staring down at her husband. His eyes were closed, thick dark lashes brushing his cheeks, tousled black hair a stark contrast to the whiteness of the pillow slip.

Drinking in his relaxed features, strikingly handsome regardless of the scar he found so offensive, she closed her eyes for a moment in an effort to calm her racing heart. When her gaze returned to his face, she blinked in surprise. The pale blue eyes she found so incredibly beautiful were focused on her in an unwavering stare.

"Aren't you coming to bed?" he said in a soft whisper.

Unable to speak, she managed a nod, then reached to turn out the lamp. She waited for her eyes to become accustomed to the darkness before lifting the top sheet and sliding in next to him.

Feeling the heat of her body so close, inhaling her sweet scent, Kit rolled onto his left side, his right hand moving slowly to settle on her arm. He would probably live to regret his actions, but now that he'd experienced her passion, knew the pleasure awaiting him when he slipped into her warmth, his determination to stay on his side of the bed went out the window.

Instead of listening to his mind's warnings to honor his decision to abstain, he let his hunger for the woman lying beside him override reason.

Running his fingers up the sleeve of her nightdress, he scooted closer. For a moment he tried to haul in on the desire surging through his veins with little success. *This is insanity. She's not a virgin, and we're married. So what's the harm?* Using such logic and the rationalization that since they would be together for another eleven months before going their separate ways, there was no reason to deny himself her sweet body.

He dipped his head to within inches of hers. "Are you safe?" he whispered.

As the meaning of his question dawned, a flush heated her face. "Yes," she answered in a breathless voice, thankful she'd taken a chance and used her protection.

Exhaling the breath he'd been holding, Kit lowered his mouth to hers. The kiss was gentle at first, then progressively more demanding. When he parted her lips with his tongue and slipped into her mouth, she moaned and grasped his shoulders to pull him closer.

While he continued to kiss her, he lifted her nightdress until it was bunched around her waist. His fingers trailed across the heated skin of her belly, inching lower to the treasure awaiting him between her thighs. He eased a finger through the downy hair and touched the pouty pearl of flesh nestled there. She gasped, her thighs falling open at his intimate intrusion.

He worked the pad of his finger back and forth over the nubbin, feeling it swell with each movement. Another moan rumbled in her throat, her hands tightening around his neck, her hips lifting off the mattress.

"Slow down, honey. No need to get so riled. Just lay back and try to relax," he murmured, placing kisses along her jaw and down her neck.

Angelina stiffened, his words hitting her like a bucket of water. How could she? She'd promised herself she wouldn't act like a harlot, yet she was doing exactly that. And worse, he'd been forced to remind her he didn't want such behavior.

Closing her eyes, she dropped her arms to the mattress, forcing herself to lay quietly while he shifted and rose above her. As he lifted her hips off the bed and joined his flesh with hers, it took every bit of self-control she could summon to remain still. When he started moving in slow easy strokes, she bit her lip, hoping the pain would block out all other sensation.

Kit paused, his eyebrows pulled together in confusion. "Is something wrong?" he said between deep breaths.

She swallowed, then whispered, "No."

"Am I hurting you?"

Shifting slightly beneath him, again she whispered no.

"Then, why . . ." Her movement tightening her intimate hold on him, the rest of his words ended in a sharply drawn breath. In spite of his determination to wait until Angelina finished with him, he knew he wasn't going to make it. His hips bucking against hers in an increasingly faster rhythm, he gave in and let his climax overtake him. With a half sob, half groan, he pressed his face into her pillow, his release pulsing again and again within her silken depths. Somehow he managed to keep himself braced above her, his elbows and knees bearing his weight. After a minute, he roused from his orgasm-induced lethargy and rolled to his side.

When his breathing slowed to normal, he said, "Are you sure you're all right?"

"I'm fine, just tired," she replied, stifling a yawn. Hoping to end the conversation, she rearranged her nightdress, pulled the sheet up to her chin, then rolled onto her side.

Staring at her back, Kit scowled. Damn, would he ever understand women? How she could change from hot and eager to cold and detached in the blink of an eye went completely beyond his knowledge of the fairer sex.

Stretching out on his back, he closed his eyes. He knew he should have kept his hands—and other parts—to himself. But fool that he was, he had to go and let lust overrule common sense.

The truth was, he knew if he had it to do over again, he would do exactly the same thing. In fact, being totally honest with himself, he knew as long as they were together he would continue to give in to his desire to possess Angelina.

So what would he do if she persisted in acting the accommodating but unresponsive wife? He was willing to accept her story of being tired once. But if she continued with such nonsense, she'd tell him the truth or there would be hell to pay.

Chapter Sixteen

Late the following morning, Angelina and Chloe had just finished changing their mother's bed when the excited barking of Artemis drifted into the room from the front of the house.

Chloe gathered up the pile of bed linens which would have to be boiled to prevent the spread of her mother's disease. "I'll go see—"

The sound of a fast approaching horse followed by a male voice shouting, "Hello, the house," halted her words.

"That sounds like Jared," Angelina said, making one final adjustment to her mother's bedding, then straightening to meet her sister's surprised gaze. "Were you expecting him to call?"

Her brow knitted, Chloe shook her head. "I'd best go see what he wants." Dropping the bed linens, she hurried from the room.

Chloe returned a few minutes later. "Angelina would you mind saddling Star while I gather up my supplies? I'll be leaving with Jared as soon as I can get ready."

"What's happened and where are you going?" Angelina said, following Chloe down the hall.

"One of Jared's mares is having a hard time. He said she should have foaled hours ago, but something's wrong. I'll be at his place as long as I'm needed."

Angelina nodded, then headed for the door.

In a matter of minutes, Chloe had packed her veterinary supplies in one bag, stuffed a change of clothes in another, and stepped through the front door onto the porch.

Leaning against a post, Jared stood motionless, staring across the yard. Hearing her approach, he snapped to attention.

"Ready?"

She looked up at him. Deep lines of fatigue bracketed his mouth and creased his forehead. "Yes, as soon as Angelina saddles Star we can leave."

"She's already saddled," Angelina called from a few feet away. Leading the mare to a spot next to Jared's lathered roan, she handed the reins to Chloe. "Good luck."

"Thanks," she replied, hooking her bags over the saddle horn, then sticking her left foot into the stirrup and mounting.

Angelina turned to Jared. "I hope you'll take good care of my sister."

"No need to ask," he said, then added for her ears alone, "She means too much to me."

Angelina waited on the porch until her sister and Jared disappeared down the trail, a thick cloud of dust kicked up by their horses' hooves swirling in their wake.

Rolling up the sleeves of her shirtwaist, Chloe moved as quietly as possible through the barn and into the stall Jared indicated. She set her bag down on the straw-covered floor, then knelt beside the mare Jared called Abby, a liver chestnut with black points.

"Easy girl. I won't hurt you," she crooned, running a hand down the well-shaped head and over the silky black mane. "I'm here to help you deliver your foal."

After finishing her examination, Chloe turned to look up at Jared. "How long has she been in labor?"

He ran a hand through his hair, shifting his gaze to the mare. "Since early last night."

"Early last—Have y'all taken leave of your senses?" she said in a fierce whisper. "Why didn't you come for me sooner? Was all that talk about it being a man's job to take care of the animals just that?"

"No, it wasn't just talk," he replied just as fiercely. "I take damn good care of my animals. But this isn't Abby's first foal, so I figured she'd get along fine if I gave her a little more time. But then a little more time became a little more and I just kept thinking . . ." He pushed his fingers through his hair again. "Hell, I don't know what I was thinking."

"That's for sure," Chloe responded, reaching for her bag. "The foal's in the wrong position. I'm going to try to move it." After pouring disinfectant over her hands and arms, Chloe began the painstaking process of repositioning the foal while keeping up a litany of soft crooning to reassure Abby.

When she was satisfied she had realigned the foal's forelegs into the proper position, she sat back on her heels and waited. It soon became apparent Abby was too weak to successfully deliver without further assistance.

"Jared, pour that disinfectant over your hands and arms. Quick. We've got to pull the foal."

"Have you ever done this before?" he said, kneeling on the straw beside her.

"No, have you?"

At his negative reply, Chloe said, "Well, unless you've got another idea, this will be the first time for both of us."

When Jared shook his head a second time, she pointed to the bottle of disinfectant. "Now hurry. Abby is near worn out. If we don't deliver this foal right away, you could lose both of them."

After following her instructions, he moved into position. Using the mare's contractions to ease the process, they worked in tandem to carefully and purposely pull Abby's foal into the world.

"A filly," Jared said. "And the spitting image of her dam."

Watching Abby to make sure she had suffered no ill effects from the difficult birth, Chloe smiled at the excitement in his voice.

"What about Abby?" he said, turning to look at his mare. "Is she going to be okay?"

"She's tired. But I think after a few hours of rest, she should be able to get up and tend her baby."

Jared nodded. Exhaling a sigh of relief, he shifted his attention back to the foal.

"Oh God, something's wrong. Chloe, the filly isn't breathing right."

"Here let me see," she ordered in a firm voice, moving in front of Jared. "Did she reject the milt?"

"Yes," he replied, pointing to what looked like an oval-shaped piece of liver lying in the straw. "I checked her mouth right away, then I saw the milt, so that's not the problem."

Chloe began massaging the filly with brisk movements, but there was no response. Holding one of the foal's nostrils closed she blew gently into the other.

"What are you doing?" Jared said.

"Forcing air into her lungs," she replied between breaths.

Sitting back on his heels, Jared watched in stunned silence as Chloe continued her ministrations. In just a few seconds the foal began breathing on her own.

When she was satisfied the danger had passed, Chloe carefully moved the filly closer to her dam's head. "Okay, Abby, she's all yours now."

Giving a soft whinny, Abby lifted her head and ran her tongue over her foal in a loving caress. Once she'd licked the filly dry, Abby lay back on the straw to rest. The foal slept close by.

"What are you going to name her?" Chloe said, repacking her bag then rising to stand next to Jared.

"I haven't thought about it. You're the one who saved her, so you should be the one to name her."

Chloe stared at the foal for a moment. "Tyche."

"What?"

She turned to look up into his face. "I'd call her Tyche."

He scowled down at her. "What the hell does that mean?"

"Tyche was the Greek Goddess of Fortune. I think it's a perfect name, don't you?"

"I'm not so sure," he replied, moving his gaze from Chloe to the sleeping filly. "But I like the idea of picking a name having something to do with her good fortune in making it into the world." He suddenly brightened. "Hey, how about calling her Fortune?"

Realizing not everyone was as taken with Greek mythology as she, Chloe smiled. "Yes, Fortune would be just fine."

"Great," he said, returning her smile. "Come on, I'll show you where you can get cleaned up. Then I'm going to have me a drink."

"It's a mite early for liquor, don't you think?"

"I'd agree with that if I hadn't been up all night with Abby. Would you care to join me? I've got some mighty fine brandy."

"I've never had brandy. But my nerves are still pretty shaky after the close call with Abby and Fortune." She took a deep breath. "Yes, I believe I will join you."

Sitting at the table in Jared's kitchen, Chloe took a sip of the brandy he poured for her, the warmth of the liquor seeping through her body. "Um, this is wonderful. Just what I needed."

What she needed, Jared thought, was to have her lips, still wet from the brandy, thoroughly kissed. Instead of voicing such thoughts, he said, "You're very good with animals."

Dark eyes snapping, the corners of her mouth turned down. "As I recall, I told you I was. But y'all wouldn't believe me."

"Yeah, well, now I do," he grumbled, then louder said, "Where did you learn about caring for animals like that?"

"Self-taught, mostly. Though I've done a great deal of reading. *American Veterinary Journals* and any books I can get my hands on. Someday I hope to go to school to learn more."

"School? You can't be serious?"

Her chin came up. "I most certainly am. Texas Agricultural and Mechanical College offers a course in veterinary science, and it's my dream to enroll there someday."

"Damnit, Chloe. A woman's got no business taking a course in how to care for animals. She should be looking after her husband and children."

"And just what would have happened to your mare and her foal if this woman hadn't been there to help?" Not waiting for him to respond, she shook a finger at him. "And don't give me another of your lectures about a woman's proper place, do you hear me, Jared McBride? I refuse to sit here and listen to more of that consarned drivel."

Setting her glass on the table with a thump, she rose. "I'm going to check on Abby and Fortune."

Jared jumped to his feet. "Wait! I didn't mean to upset you. It's just that you're behaving in ways I'm not used to. I was taught women take care of the house and men take care of everything else. That's how it was with my parents and their parents before them." He stepped in front of her. "Don't be angry with me, Chloe. Please."

She looked up to meet his gaze, her dark brown eyes still blazing with the last remnants of her pique. Taking a deep breath, she exhaled slowly. "All right. I'm not angry. Now if you'll excuse me. I want to make sure Fortune is able to nurse."

She tried to step around him, but his hand on her arm stopped her. "Wait, I'll go with you."

"Shouldn't you get some rest?"

"No." His voice dropped to a husky whisper. "I'd rather be with you." The look he gave her ignited something hot and delicious deep in her belly, a sensation she'd been experiencing more and more when in Jared's company.

Her face heating with a mixture of a blush of pleasure and a flush of embarrassment, she didn't know what to say. When discussing animals or defending her choice of vocations, she never had trouble finding something to say. But as soon as the conversation turned to anything of an intimate nature, her self-assurance fled, leaving her tongue-tied and decidedly uncomfortable.

Sensing Chloe's uneasiness, Jared said no more, though there was plenty he wanted to say. Like how beautiful she was, how much he enjoyed being near her, hearing her laugh, seeing her smile. He wanted to reach out and touch her but forced his arms to remain at his sides. Soon, he promised himself. Soon.

Kit returned from checking on the cattle just before dark. He unsaddled Sid, then gave the gelding a rubdown before turning him loose in the corral. After washing up, he entered the kitchen and dropped his hat on its usual peg.

Noting only two places set at the table, he said, "Chloe hasn't returned yet?"

"No," Angelina replied. "Jared sent one of his men over a few hours ago to tell us Chloe would be home first thing in the morning."

"Everything okay with his mare?"

"Yes, she had a filly. But I guess the mare was pretty tuckered out, so Chloe thought she should stick close by tonight."

Kit nodded, pulling out a chair and taking a seat. "How's Sarah?"

"About the same. If we have a nice warm day soon, would you carry her outside? I'll make a pallet for her on the porch."

"Do you think it's wise this time of year?"

"As long as the sun's shining, the porch will protect her from the wind. Spending time in the open air was one of the things we were told would help her consumption." She finished putting the food on the table and took her seat.

"Mama used to enjoy sitting on the porch for an hour or so each day. Then, when she got too weak to make it out there by herself, Chloe and I helped her. But now she's even weaker and . . ."

"I'd be happy to carry her to the porch," he said, reaching across the table to squeeze her hand.

She managed a smile. "Thanks. She really likes you, you know."

"I like her, too," he replied, returning her smile, then withdrawing his hand and reaching for the bowl of potatoes.

"She thinks you're a real gentleman. Polite and very charming."

Kit shrugged, setting down the bowl of potatoes and picking up the meat platter. "She doesn't know I worked as a bounty hunter. If she did, she'd change her tune about me."

"No she wouldn't." Seeing his dubious look, she added, "She already knows." His eyebrows shot up. "When she asked me what line of work you were in, I had to tell her something. And since the only work I knew you'd done was bounty hunting, I told . . . Anyway, she found nothing wrong with it. I'm sorry if I spoke out of turn."

"No harm done, I reckon," he said, spooning gravy over his potatoes. After a few minutes of silence, he cleared his throat, then said, "I was a sheriff before I took up hunting criminals for their bounty."

"A sheriff? Where?"

"Taylor County."

"How come y'all quit being a lawman?"

"I had my reasons." Seeing she was about to ask another question, he added, "Personal reasons."

She stared at him for a long moment, then said, "Was it because of what happened to your wife and son?"

He slammed his hand down on the table with such force the dishes rattled. "Look, Angel, I don't want to talk about it. Now either pick another subject, or keep quiet."

Unruffled by his sudden display of temper and his gruff tone, Angelina realized she had the answer to her question. Then she realized something else: Kit's calling her Angel no longer felt like a raw sore being prodded with a sharp stick.

Filling her plate, she contemplated the latter. Being called Angel still stirred up memories she would prefer not recalling. Yet, what had softened her reaction? Why did the nickname no longer spawn a heart-wrenching pain in her chest? She could think of only one answer to those questions. Love. Falling in love with Kit was having an unexpected impact on every aspect of her life.

Kit stayed up later than usual that night, sitting at the table, a stack of paper and a pencil in front of him. When he left the ranch, he wanted to be sure Angelina and Chloe had instructions on how to care for the Diamond C's herd of cattle. Though the time for his departure was still many months away, he figured he'd best start now, since there was a lot they would need to know.

Besides, the task kept his mind off his sleeping wife and what he'd be doing if he were in the bed next to her.

Trying to read what he'd just written about caring for orphaned calves, he found the words all blurred together. He rubbed his eyes, then tried again. It was no use, he was just too exhausted to continue.

With a weary sigh, he pushed away from the table, picked up the sheaf of papers, and turned toward the parlor.

Angelina fought sleep as long as she could, hoping Kit would come to bed before she lost the battle. Just when she thought she would have to give in to the insistent pull of slumber, she heard his footsteps in the hall.

Keeping her eyes closed, she listened to the click of the door closing, the soft thump of his boots hitting the floor one at a time, the rustle of fabric as he removed his clothes. Just thinking of his naked body sliding into the bed sent her heart into a wild rhythm.

She waited until he'd settled next to her, then carefully let out the breath she'd been holding. "Did you finish what you were doing?"

Kit started at hearing her voice. "I thought you were asleep."

"Not yet," she replied, rolling to face him. "I guess I must be getting used to sharing my bed, because I couldn't fall asleep without you next to me."

He made a sound, much like a moan, from deep in his throat. "You shouldn't be getting used to having me here. It will only make it tougher on you when I leave."

"I know," she whispered, a slight catch in her voice. "But I can't help it." She longed to reach out and touch him, to feel the hard muscles of his arms, to run her fingers through the silky hair covering the center of his chest. Uncertain if such actions fell into the same category as her behavior in El Paso, she didn't move.

Kit drew a deep breath, willing his body to stop reacting to Angelina's nearness. He wasn't successful. Cursing his inability to keep a clear head when she was near, he reached over and pulled her into his arms. "Leaving is gonna be hell on me, too," he murmured before capturing her lips with his.

The thought of having to leave the woman lying so temptingly against him lent an urgency to his need to lose himself in her welcoming heat. His kisses and caresses bordered on the frantic before he pushed her to a sitting position then pulled her nightdress over her head.

Tossing the cotton gown across the room, he stared at her, wishing it wasn't the middle of the night. He wanted to see her naked body in the brightness of full daylight, not cast in shadows by the meager moonlight filtering through the curtains at the window.

He cupped one breast with his hand, his thumb gently rubbing the already peaked tip. Her nipple tightened even more from his touch. He inhaled sharply, his breath hissing through his clenched teeth. Jesus, he'd never wanted anyone, not even Bethany whom he'd desired from the time he was eighteen, the way he wanted Angelina.

"Lay back, honey, and let me love you," he whispered, gently pushing at Angelina's shoulders. She did as he asked, opening her thighs when he nudged them apart with his knee.

He kissed her long and hard, his fingers stroking her breasts, then her belly, then between her thighs. Somehow Angelina managed to keep her response to his kisses and touch in check, though it was a difficult battle. Then he slipped one finger inside her. As a white-hot streak of desire sizzled through her body, her hips jerked upward, a gasp escaped her lips. Much to her horror, she felt a gush of wetness between her thighs. She squeezed her eyes closed. *I mustn't feel anything. Please, don't let me feel anything.* Gritting her teeth, she steeled herself, hoping it would be over soon.

Kit pulled Angelina's legs up around his hips, then leaned forward to join them as one. He had guided only the tip of his manhood into her damp flesh when her inner muscles abruptly tightened, preventing him from an easy entry.

"Are you okay?" he whispered, his blood pounding so loud in his ears he barely heard his own words.

"I'm fine," she replied.

He waited for a moment, expecting her to relax. But her muscles remained unyielding. Refusing to cause her pain by using force to gain entry, he withdrew. When his blood cooled enough to allow rational thought, he said, "Are you gonna tell me what's bothering you?"

"I . . . I don't know what you mean."

"The hell you don't. Last night and again just now you suddenly act like you don't want me to touch you. Now talk."

She cleared her throat. "I don't know why you're so angry. I was just trying to be the kind of wife you want."

"The kind of—You think I want a wife who doesn't feel anything, who doesn't respond, who just lays under me like a cold fish?"

Swallowing hard, she whispered, "Yes."

"Where the hell did you get a harebrained idea like that?"

"From you."

"Me?" His voice rose to a near roar.

"Shh. You'll wake Mama."

"Don't move," he said, the mattress dipping as he shifted his weight.

She heard the scratch of a match, caught a whiff of the acrid smell of sulphur, then blinked as the bright glow of lamplight filled the room.

Climbing back into bed, he turned his confused gaze on her.

"Now, tell me exactly how I gave you the idea I wanted a frigid wife."

Resisting the urge to cover her nakedness, she pushed herself up to sit against the headboard. She ran her tongue over her dry lips and tried to forget her lack of clothes. "It was while we were in El Paso," she said, her voice no more than a whisper.

"Which time? When I first met you, or last time, when we went to get the cattle?"

"The last time."

Kit searched his memory of the hours they'd spent in El Paso but found nothing to explain Angelina's ridiculous notion. "Go on."

"In the morning, after we . . . um . . . were intimate, you said you were glad you got me out of the Murray House." Hoping he'd remember the rest of what he'd said so she wouldn't have to continue, she glanced up at him. When he stared at her from beneath knitted brows, then nodded for her to continue, her hopes were dashed. She took a deep breath, then before she lost her nerve, said in a rush, "Then you said I acted like a whore. If how I behaved made you think of me that way, I decided that wasn't how you wanted a wife to—"

"Whoa. Wait a minute," he said. "Back up a bit. I never said you acted like a whore."

"Yes you did. You said, I—" He pressed a finger against her lips.

"I know what I said. I think my exact comment was, you would've been on your back more than all the other gals put together. Believe me, I was *not* calling you a whore."

Seeing she didn't look convinced, he scooted closer. Lifting a lock of her hair off her shoulder, he rubbed it back and forth between his thumb and forefinger. "What I meant was, if you'd stayed at the Murray House and word of your incredible passion got out, you would have been the most popular gal in the place. I wasn't saying your passionate response made you a whore. Honey, the truth is, most whores don't really respond at all. They take men to their bed because that's what they get

paid to do. They might act like they're enjoying it, like the way
Jenna told you to act, but usually their customers are in too
much of a hurry to worry about what they're feeling. And if they
don't receive any pleasure— Well, they probably figure it's just
part of the job."

He continued rubbing her hair between his fingers for a few
moments, then said, "I'm sure you won't believe this. But what
I said was meant as a compliment. A backhanded one, I admit.
But that's truly how I meant it. After tasting your passion, I
couldn't believe how lucky I was to have found such an incredibly responsive woman."

When she didn't respond, he placed his knuckles under her
chin and forced her to meet his gaze. She stared up at him, her
mouth trembling.

"Do you believe me?"

"Yes, but . . ." She took a deep breath. "Does that mean you
want a wife who enjoys your kisses, and your touch and . . .
everything?"

He chuckled. "Absolutely. I still haven't quite grasped how
you jumped to the conclusion that I wanted a wife who is no
more than a body beneath me, but let me put that notion to
rest once and for all. I want a wife who not only enjoys my kisses
and my touch . . . and everything, but who isn't afraid to show
her reaction or be willing to try something new."

Angelina's eyes widened. "New! You mean there's more?"

Chapter Seventeen

"Yes, my innocent wife," Kit replied with a chuckle. "There's a lot more. Let me turn out the lamp, and I'll show you."

"No," she said, grabbing his wrist to halt his movement. Her face burning, she whispered, "I want to see you."

Like a bellows transforming smoldering coals into red-hot flames, her softly spoken words rekindled his desire with lightning speed. "Good idea," he murmured in a husky voice. He pushed away from the headboard then scooted down to stretch out on his left side. Looking up at her, he patted the mattress next to him.

Accepting the invitation, she shifted positions until she lay on her right side facing him.

"You want to try something new *and* you want to see me while we make love. You are becoming a very demanding wife," he said in a whisper, bending his head to nuzzle her neck.

The gentle nibbles of his lips and the throbbing of his arousal against her belly told her his words were not a complaint.

"Are you up to satisfying my demands?" she said.

"What do you think?" he replied, pushing his hips toward hers and pressing his hardened length more firmly against her.

Lowering her hand between their bodies, she wrapped her fingers around him. When he moaned at her touch, she smiled. "Yes, I definitely think you'll meet the challenge without a problem." She tightened her fingers, then slowly moved her hand up and down on his sleek length.

"The only problem will be my finishing in your hand if you don't stop what you're doing."

"Are you sure?" Applying a little more pressure, she increased the rhythm of her movements.

"Yeah," he said through clenched teeth, his breathing becoming more labored. "Jesus, I can't take much more."

Leaning back to see his face, she noted the tightness of his features. She gave him one last squeeze, then reluctantly released her grip.

He waited for his breathing to slow, then lifted her left leg and draped it over his right hip. Carefully opening the petals of her damp flesh, he guided himself into her slick heat. The feel of her surrounding him, tugging him deeper, was incredible.

His eyes clenched shut, he fought for control. It required all his concentration, but he finally managed to check his raging desire and keep it at a manageable level. Only then did he allow his eyelids to drift upward.

Angelina lay staring up at him, eyes dilated, cheeks flushed.

Rocking his hips forward, then retreating, he whispered, "How does this feel?"

"It's . . . um . . . different."

"If I'm not in the best position to take you to completion, just tell me how to make it better." He bent to press a brief kiss to her lips. "Bringing you to climax gives me a great deal of pleasure, so I want you to be honest with me."

"Maybe if we . . ." She wiggled her hips, changing the angle of his penetration and increasing the friction on her sensitive flesh. She sucked in a surprised breath. The shifting of their positions, though only a small adjustment, sent an instantaneous stab of need surging through her body. The intense throbbing of her pulse settled between her thighs.

He started moving his hips, rocking forward and burying himself as deeply as possible, then pulling back to nearly withdraw. Moving his mouth near her ear, he murmured, "Do you want me to touch you?"

When her dazed senses grasped the meaning of his words,

she couldn't stop a blush from rushing to her already heated cheeks. Wondering if she would ever get over being embarrassed when he said such intimate things, she nodded.

While capturing her lips in a long, deep kiss, Kit shifted slightly so he could get one hand between their bodies. His fingers moved through the soft nest of feminine curls and found the hardened pebble of flesh. She gasped into his mouth.

Moving his fingers in a slow, intoxicating rhythm, his hips following the same cadence, he directed her to the pinnacle of pleasure. Her stomach muscles tightened, as well as the ones surrounding him deep inside. She pulled away from his mouth, her breathing ragged.

"Kit, I . . ."

"Yes, honey. I know. I know," he crooned, bending to take the rosy tip of one breast into his mouth. The nipple, already a tight bud, hardened even more as her orgasm began.

Her entire body went taut as a bowstring, then a deep shudder rippled over her. With a soft keening cry, spasm after spasm racked her body. Head thrown back, fingers digging into his arm, her hips continued to meet his thrusts in near frantic movements. After pushing against him one final time, she gave another cry, then went limp.

Her inner muscles still quivering from her intense release, Kit carefully removed his hand, knowing she would be extremely sensitive. Staring down at Angelina, he shook his head in disbelief.

What he'd told her a few minutes ago hadn't been the truth, not entirely. He knew bringing her to climax gave him pleasure. But he never realized the full extent of his pleasure until that moment. Feeling each of her deep shuddering spasms and knowing he was the one to direct her to such a mind-shattering release was very nearly as satisfying as reaching his own completion.

The shocking discovery made him frown. What the hell was wrong with him? Nothing had ever taken the edge off his own need, not even with Bethany—the only woman he'd ever loved. So what had caused the difference? The answer hit him instantly: Angelina. Realizing everything was different, more intense with her, his frown deepened. The idea that he hadn't heeded his own advice about keeping his emotions out of his relationship with the woman lying beside him didn't sit well. In fact—

Angelina stirred, pulling him from his painful musings. He looked down at her, watching as she opened her eyes and smiled up at him. Her dazzling, thoroughly satisfied smile scattered his thoughts in a thousand directions.

"Are you all right?" she whispered.

He swallowed. Unable to force words through his tight throat, he managed a nod.

She studied him in silence for a moment, then lifted a hand and ran her fingers through the hair on his chest. Rubbing a fingertip back and forth over his left nipple, she said, "Aren't you going to . . . um . . . finish." She shifted her hips closer to him, the movement contracting her inner muscles and massaging his partially aroused manhood still encased in her tight passage.

He groaned, surprised by how quickly the fires of his desire sparked back to life. "Oh, God," he said in a hoarse voice. "You feel so good."

"What do you want me to do?" she murmured. "Tell me how to give you pleasure."

"Jesus," he rasped, just having her ask how to please him affected his senses like an aphrodisiac. "Just kiss me," he managed to say, the blood pounding so loud in his ears he could barely hear his own words.

Angelina lifted herself up to press her breasts against his chest, her face close to his. She teased his lips with her tongue, then plunged deep inside his mouth, wringing the rumble of another groan from his chest. He could have sworn the sound came all the way from his toes.

Desperate to get closer, to sink even farther inside her, he grasped her shoulders, then in one motion pushed her onto her back and settled between her thighs. As soon as they were in the new position, Angelina wrapped her legs around his waist.

"Yes, Angel, yes, that's right," he murmured, pushing even deeper and stretching her tight sheath with his pulsing hardness.

She moved with him, lifting her hips to meet each thrust, grinding her pelvis against his at the culmination of each stroke, whispering words of encouragement in his ear.

Somewhere in his barely functioning brain, Kit knew he'd never experienced anything even close to the desire roaring through his veins. As he'd discovered just minutes earlier, he also knew Angelina was responsible. Refusing to dwell on what his discoveries signified, he closed his mind to everything except the velvet heat of the woman beneath him.

Pumping his hips faster and faster, the heat continued to build until without warning he exploded. He clamped his lips shut to hold in the shout clamoring to escape his throat. After several more quick thrusts, he pushed forward one last time then froze. Holding himself perfectly still above her, he spilled his seed in one powerful throbbing eruption, followed by another, then another.

After what seemed like an eternity, his heart ceased pounding against his eardrums, his breathing slowed to normal. His legs and arms quivering with a weakness brought on by his formidable climax, he managed to roll off Angelina and flop onto his back. Though physically drained and sexually sated, mentally he was far from relaxed. The intensity of what he'd just experienced, coupled with his thoughts just prior, swamped his mind, leaving him strangely edgy.

Long after Angelina slipped into a deep slumber, Kit lay awake, trying to figure out exactly what he felt for his sleeping wife. Not liking the direction his thoughts had taken, he rolled onto his side and willed himself to fall asleep. Much later, he finally drifted into a light doze, only to have his dreams filled with the whiskey-colored eyes and honey-tasting lips of a temptress he could no longer resist. A temptress he feared was creeping into his heart in spite of his best efforts to lock her out.

By noon of the next day, Kit had managed to push the thoughts plaguing him about his feelings for Angelina to the back of his mind. Figuring if he didn't allow himself to think about it, he wouldn't have to deal with the repercussions, he finished his usual morning chores then headed to the house for dinner.

Chloe had returned an hour earlier and was helping her sister set the table when he entered the kitchen.

Angelina gave him a timid smile, her cheeks flushing with color. He wanted to return her smile, but turned away instead, making a big production out of removing his hat and hanging it on one of the pegs by the door.

"What are your plans for the day?" Angelina asked Chloe, after all three of them had taken their seats at the table.

"I'm going to take a long nap," she replied, stifling a yawn. "I was up off and on most of the night, checking on Jared's mare and new foal."

"What about Jared?" Angelina said. "Why didn't he spell you part of the time?"

Chloe smiled. "Oh, he wanted to, all right. But since he was up the entire night before, I shooed him off to bed. He finally agreed when I told him I planned to stay in the barn so I'd be close to Abby and Fortune."

"We should start raising horses," Angelina mused aloud. Turning to Kit, she said, "How about breeding Sid to Star or Belle? Wouldn't they have fine looking foals?"

He laid his fork down on his plate and reached for his cup. "That might prove a bit tricky."

"Miracle's more like it," Chloe added with a grin.

Seeing the confusion on his wife's face, Kit took a sip of coffee, then said, "Sid's been gelded."

"Oh, I forgot." Ignoring the flush she knew stained her face, she turned to her sister. "Jared has stallions. Maybe we can pay him to—"

"I'm way ahead of you," Kit said, cutting her off. "I've already discussed stud fees with Jared. He thinks Star will come into season first, but probably not before spring. When she does, he'll bring his best stallion to the Diamond C for a week."

"A week? Doesn't the stallion need to . . . um . . . well, make love to Star just once?"

Somehow Kit managed to swallow the threatening laughter. "Horses don't make love, Angelina. The stallion covers the mare. And as for the week, according to Jared, it's important to let the stud cover the mare at least a couple of times while she's in season to insure she conceives."

Meeting Angelina's wide-eyed stare, his breath caught in his throat. Based on the look on her face, their talk of horses mating had brought other thoughts to her mind, thoughts he was beginning to read with ease.

He shifted in his chair, hoping to ease the sudden tightness beneath the fly of his trousers. Casting a quick glance at Chloe, he saw her mouth twitch and the amusement dancing in her eyes before he looked away.

Sensing the highly charged air between her sister and her brother-in-law, Chloe said, "Well, if y'all will excuse me. I'll check on Mama, then I'm heading to my room for that nap."

Once Chloe had left the kitchen, Angelina took a deep breath and exhaled slowly. "So, what about you, Kit? What are your plans for the afternoon?"

"I thought I'd finish the addition on the barn. All that's left is the roof, then slapping on a coat of paint."

Rising, she started stacking the dishes. "I'll help you if you want. I'm pretty good with a paintbrush."

Kit pushed his chair back from the table, then rose. "Don't you have work to do in here?"

"No, I did all the chores that needed doing this morning."

"What about Sarah? Didn't you want me to carry her outside? Surely you'll want to stay with her."

"The sun's not warm enough today. Besides, after I gave her a sponge bath this morning and changed her gown, she was exhausted. Maybe tomorrow." She turned from setting the dishes in the sink. "So, do you want my help, or not?"

Seeing there was no way he could refuse without sounding rude, he said, "Change into some old clothes, then come down to the barn." Snatching his hat off the wall peg with more force than necessary, he crammed it on his head then stomped out the door.

Kit was on the roof of the barn addition by the time Angelina left the house a few minutes later. She paused halfway across the yard, content to just look at her husband. Bareheaded, shirt sleeves rolled up to his elbows, muscles straining, and jet-black hair ruffling in the breeze, he took her breath away. She wondered how she could survive never being able to look at him again.

Praying she never had to find out, she started toward the barn. She stopped by the ladder and called up to him, "Where's the paint?"

"Inside. To the right of the door." He glanced down at his wife and bit back a smile. She'd followed his instructions and changed into a dress long past its prime, one she'd obviously outgrown some years ago. But in spite of the garment being worn thin in places, too short, and much too tight across the bodice, Kit thought Angelina couldn't look more appealing if she were clothed in a dress made of the finest silk. Forcing such thoughts aside, he turned his attention back to the roof.

Finding the pail of paint and brush right where Kit said they'd be, Angelina carried them back outside. After tying an old rag around her hair, she opened the pail and dipped the brush into the paint.

By the time Kit announced he'd finished the roof, she had painted the front of the addition and started working on the side. She glanced up as he came down the ladder, then returned to her painting.

Dropping a hammer and a bag of nails, he reached for the rag tucked in one of his trouser pockets. As he wiped his face and neck on the piece of toweling, he took a couple of steps back. Looking up to admire the finished barn addition, he braced his hands on his hips, the strip of white cloth flapping in the breeze against one thigh.

"Looks good, don't you think?"

Angelina looked up at the addition, then over to her husband. She opened her mouth to reply, but a loud bleat halted her words. "Oh, no!" Looking around the barnyard, she finally spotted Hermes. "Kit! Put it away. Hurry, Kit, put the rag away."

His brow furrowed, he shifted his gaze from the barn to her. "What are you—" The sound of running hooves and a shrill bleat brought his head around with a snap. Head lowered, Hermes was bearing down on him at full speed. Hoping to ward off the charging goat, Kit wadded the piece of cloth into a ball and threw it as far as he could, but Hermes never broke stride. Realizing the only way to avoid getting butted was to run like hell, Kit turned toward the corral fence.

Angelina dropped the brush and rushed toward Kit and Chloe's irate pet. Forgetting about the pail of paint, she caught her shoe in the wire bail and went down hard on her knees. The pail swayed back and forth before finally tipping over, spattering over a sprawled Angelina, and sending a rivulet of paint across the hard-packed ground.

Slipping and sliding, she struggled to her feet, looking up just in time to see Hermes cut to his right and block Kit's dash to the fence. With a loud snort, the goat lunged, catching Kit squarely on his right thigh.

Gritting his teeth against the pain throbbing in his leg, Kit hoped to avoid another blow of Hermes's horns and again headed for the fence. He managed one step before his right knee buckled. Unable to maintain his balance, he lost his footing. He went down onto his knees with a grunt, then pitched forward into the dirt. A little cloud of dust puffed up around him, then drifted across the barnyard.

Angelina stood staring at her unmoving, prone husband and the goat standing nearby. No longer interested now that his prey lay flat on the ground, Hermes gave one last snort then moved off to find other entertainment.

Finding her voice, she said, "Kit? Kit, are you all right?" She moved closer, dropping onto her knees beside him.

He drew in a deep breath, coughed to clear the dust from his throat, then said, "Yeah, I guess." He rolled over onto his back and slowly straightened his legs. He grimaced. "Other than my thigh feeling like it's on fire and swallowing half the dirt in the barnyard, I'm just dandy." He carefully rose up onto his elbows, keeping his gaze glued to the twitching tail of the departing goat. "What the hell got into him?"

"It was the piece of toweling. Hermes saw it flapping against your leg and it set him off. I told you to watch out for him."

"You told me he eats anything and not to turn my back on him. You never said he'd knock me on my butt just 'cause I've got a piece of cloth in my hand."

"Guess I forgot to mention he doesn't like anything waving or fluttering. Chloe figures he must see it as some kind of threat."

He blew out an exasperated breath. "Damn obstinate goat," he grumbled, shifting his gaze to his wife. Seeing the splotches on her face and the laughter shining in her eyes, he scowled. "What the hell's all over you, and what's so all-fired funny?"

"Paint." She swiped at her face with the sleeve of her dress. "I tripped over the paint pail when I . . ." A giggle slipped out. ". . . when I tried to . . ." She giggled again. ". . . when I tried to head off Hermes." Her giggle turned into a full-fledged laugh. "I'm sorry. But if you . . . if you could have seen how you—" Clapping one hand over her mouth and grabbing her stomach with the other, she collapsed on the ground.

Watching his wife roll around in the dirt, her shoulders shaking with laughter, his scowl deepened. In spite of not finding the incident the least bit amusing, his lips suddenly twitched. He must have looked like a damn idiot, trying to outrun a goat. No wonder Angelina was laughing so hard. The corners of his mouth lifted in a smile. God, what a wonderful sound.

Then a startling thought hit him; he'd never heard Angelina

laugh. Though he'd probably have one hell of a bruise and be sore as the devil for the next few days, he no longer cared. A little pain was well worth the price to hear the infectious peals of his wife's laughter.

The last of his irritation slipping away, he caught the light-hearted mood. Dropping back on the ground, his howl of laughter joined hers.

Chapter Eighteen

"Lord have mercy, what happened?" Chloe said, stepping aside as Angelina helped Kit hobble into the kitchen.

"Hermes took exception to the rag Kit was holding. Before I could stop that blasted goat of yours, he put his head down and charged. He caught Kit square on the thigh."

"Oh, Kit, I'm sorry. I'd break him of that horrible habit if I knew how. Did he hurt you bad?"

"I don't think so," Kit replied, sinking onto the chair Angelina pulled out for him. "The skin's not broken, but the muscle is bruised pretty good. Nothing real serious."

Turning to her sister, Chloe said, "What about you? How in the world did y'all get yourself covered with paint?"

"Just my own clumsiness. Will you help me tote the bathtub in here? Kit and I both need a bath."

"Sure. Y'all won't believe this, but a few minutes ago, I could have sworn I heard laughter coming from the barn. With the sorry state you two are in, I reckon I must've been mistaken."

Angelina turned to meet Kit's gaze. Her sides still aching from her earlier bout of hysterics, she was certain she'd gotten the laughter out of her system. But she was wrong. The smile teasing his mouth and his outrageous wink set her off again, which in turn triggered his booming laugh.

Chloe looked at first one, then the other, thinking they must have lost their minds. Realizing her sister had never been as happy as she'd been since bringing Kit home as her husband,

Chloe said, "So my hearing hasn't gone bad. Well, I can't say as I see the humor in being covered with paint or being butted by a goat, but whatever makes you happy is fine by me."

After soaking in a hot bath, Kit insisted he could work and spent the afternoon cleaning up the spilled paint in the barnyard, then brushing what was left in the pail on the barn addition. By nightfall he regretted not taking Chloe's advice to stay off his feet. His thigh vehemently protested his decision by tightening into a painful charley horse. He headed back to the house, cursing the long-haired goat responsible for his limp.

Unable to find a comfortable position, he found sitting at the supper table pure misery. Grateful when the meal ended and he could excuse himself, he pushed away from the table and shuffled into the parlor. With a weary sigh, he collapsed on one end of the sofa, stretching his injured leg out in front of him.

Resting his head on the back of the sofa, he closed his eyes. He could hear the rattle of dishes, the murmurs of Angelina and Chloe as they cleaned up the kitchen.

He must have dozed off, because he was jarred awake by Angelina's voice. Opening his eyes, he looked up to find her standing in front of the sofa. "Hmmm? Did you say something?"

"I asked if I can get you anything," she replied.

"Yeah, a glass of whiskey."

"I think there's a bottle of the bourbon Papa liked around here somewhere. I'll see if I can find it, then I'm going to rub some of Chloe's liniment on your leg."

The smooth whiskey affected him in more ways than he'd figured. The throbbing in his leg eased in direct proportion to the warming of his blood. Whether the latter stemmed from the liquor or the idea of his wife's hands on his leg, he couldn't be sure.

Half an hour later, Angelina helped him into the bedroom and stripped him down to his drawers.

"You just get comfortable while I go fetch the liniment."

When she returned to their room, he lay sprawled on the bed, naked. Her pulse quickening at the sight, she reminded herself he was in no condition to do more than sleep.

Sitting next to him on the edge of the mattress, she opened the bottle and poured some of the contents into her hand.

"This isn't necessary," he said, watching her put the cap back on the bottle and set it on the floor. "You don't need to stink up the room with some putrid home remedy. I'll be fine without it."

"This doesn't smell bad, and maybe you would be fine without Chloe's liniment, but I'm not taking any chances. She said using her special formula will take the soreness away a lot quicker. So hold still while I rub it in."

He sniffed the air tentatively, relaxing when he realized she was right. The odor wasn't half-bad.

"What's in that stuff?"

"Chloe combines spirits of turpentine, oil of origanum, and black oil with a little gum camphor, aqua ammonia, and some other things I can't remember. Then she mixes all those ingredients in a quart of alcohol."

"Alcohol? Maybe I should just take a swig of her *special* concoction."

"Oh, no, you don't. This isn't for your insides. Now stop making excuses and let me do this."

A smile tugged at his mouth. "You'll be gentle with me, won't you, ma'am?" he said in a soft drawl.

His teasing tone sent a shiver up her spine. "You have my word, Mistuh Dancer. I'll be as gentle as a lover's caress."

Her response had an immediate effect. Not on the leg she massaged with firm strokes, but on another part of his anatomy, a part just inches from her hands. He should have covered himself, he realized too late. But getting out of his clothes and into a prone position on the bed had required more effort than he'd anticipated, leaving him too weak to even reach for the top sheet. His bone-deep fatigue had pushed aside the lecherous notions filling his head, convincing him the only thing he wanted was a good night's sleep.

He'd been dead wrong.

In spite of his exhaustion and his determination to ignore her erotic touch, his body had other ideas. Closing his eyes, he could only lay there, his erection jerking and swelling more and more as she rubbed the liniment into his thigh.

Though Angelina tried to keep her eyes focused on her hands, tried to concentrate on working the knot out of his black-and-blue thigh, her gaze as well as her thoughts persisted in straying. Fascinated with how his arousal grew larger and larger until it throbbed against his belly, she drew a deep shaky breath, then reluctantly withdrew her hands.

"Does your leg feel any better?" she said in a strangely raspy voice.

He didn't respond right away. Eyes still closed, he finally said, "Some."

"Chloe said there should be improvement by morning." She rose, then moved across the room to pour water into the bowl on the washstand. After washing and drying her hands, she went around to her side of the bed and sat down.

"Kit?"

"Yeah?"

"Is there something I can do?"

"No, you've done all you can. All my leg needs now is time."

"I wasn't talking about your leg. I meant, is there something I can do to . . . that is, is there some way we can take care of your other . . . well, need?"

His eyes snapping open, he turned to look at her. "My what?"

Staring down at her lap, she twisted her fingers in the skirt of her dress. "I couldn't help seeing how you . . . um . . . how you changed when I massaged your leg. Doesn't that mean you're in need?" She lifted her head and met his gaze. "Do you ache to make love the way I do?"

"God, yes," he said with a groan. "I ache something fierce."

"Then, isn't there a way we can take away our aches without hurting your leg?"

Kit's rampant arousal jerked again. Swallowing hard, he said, "Yeah, I imagine there is. Get undressed, then we'll figure out a way."

Her eyes flared hot and potent, sending another stab of desire to his groin. Clenching his teeth, he prayed he could stop the unraveling of his control before it was too late.

"I didn't use my protection because I wasn't sure you'd . . . I just need a minute or two." Leaping off the bed, she opened a dresser drawer and quickly found what she wanted. "If you'll close your eyes, I won't have to leave the room."

He wanted to point out she needn't be embarrassed, after all, they were married and weren't strangers to each other's bodies, but he kept such thoughts to himself. Instead, he agreed and obediently closed his eyes.

A few minutes later the mattress dipped as she climbed into bed beside him. "Okay," she said. "What do I do?"

He allowed his eyelids to lift. She was on her knees next to him, naked, eyes wide, hair splaying in glorious disarray over her shoulders and down her back. He bit the inside of his cheek to keep from grinning at the eager expression on her face.

"First, come down here and kiss me."

Scooting closer, she leaned over and pressed her mouth to his. When her hardened nipple brushed his chest, a low groan rumbled in this throat. He reached up to cup one breast, rubbing his thumb back and forth over the tip until it tightened even more. After giving equal attention to her other breast, he moved his hand lower.

She moaned, craving his intimate touch, then shifting to give him better access. He obliged her, his fingers gently caressing, softly prodding until she trembled with need.

Pulling his mouth from hers, he whispered, "Straddle my hips."

She lifted her head and stared down at him. "Are you sure I won't hurt you?" she replied in a breathless voice.

"Not if you don't put all your weight on my thigh. Now, come on, straddle me."

Careful not to touch his thigh, she did as he asked. One knee on either side of his hips, she held herself above him, keeping her balance by bracing her hands on his chest.

"Like this?" She looked down at him expectantly, unsure what to do next.

He smiled up at her, lifting one hand to push a strand of hair behind her ear. "Perfect. Now lower yourself and take me inside."

Reaching between them, she circled his pulsing erection with her fingers. He felt like hot velvet, all smooth on the outside, yet throbbing with raw power from within. She lowered her hips. He groaned when the tip of him brushed her inner thigh, his hips bucking up in reaction.

"Did I hurt you?"

"No. God, no," he replied. "Hurry, just hurry."

Loving the power in his raspy command, Angelina rubbed him against the damp flesh between her thighs. A sharp spear of desire ripped through her. Her blood pounded heavily against her eardrums.

Caught in a trap of her own devising, she abandoned the delaying tactics of her teasing game. She inhaled a deep breath, then dropped her hips in one sudden motion, driving him into her welcoming heat. Continuing to push down, she took him deeper and deeper, until her pelvis was pressed firmly against his. She paused, savoring the delights of this new position and the delicious feel of him filling her. Her shoulders quivered with a shudder of pleasure.

"So, what do you think?" he said, his voice unsteady. "Did we find a way to ease your ache?" He reached up to cover her breasts with his hand, gently squeezing the soft mounds.

"Yes," she replied, arching her back to push her breasts more fully against his palms. "This is . . . wonderful." She exhaled on a long sigh.

He chuckled. "Yeah, it sure is."

When he said no more and made no offer to move, she wiggled her hips in frustration. "Come on, Kit. Are y'all going to do something, or not?"

"I can't move my leg much, so you're gonna have to do the work tonight. You don't mind, do you?" He gave her nipples a playful pinch, smiling at the flare of desire in her eyes.

"No, I don't mind, but I don't know what . . ."

"Just do whatever feels good to you, honey."

"But what if it doesn't feel good to you?"

His smile broadened. "Believe me, if it feels good to you, I'll like it just as much. Hell, I'll love it." He moved his hands down to her waist. "Here, I'll help you get started, then you can take over whenever you want."

He lifted her, then lowered her, simulating his strokes when their positions were reversed. She gasped at the incredible heat gripping her belly. After repeating the pattern several more times, he dropped his hands to the bed. Angelina soon found the rhythm on her own, then added a small rotation of her hips on the downward stroke.

"Jesus," he hissed, finding his self-control again on the verge of total mutiny. He grasped the sheet in his fists, his hips coming off the bed to meet each of her descending motions, to bury himself deeper in her slick tightness. No longer did he worry about his bruised thigh. In fact, as he dug his heels into the mattress for better leverage, the slight discomfort in his leg barely registered in his feverish brain. He knew only the overwhelming need to find his release.

Somehow he cleared the fuzziness from his mind enough to determine if Angelina was close to joining him in the throes of orgasmic bliss. Refusing to scale the peak alone, he forced his senses to right themselves, willed his blood to cool.

When the fire raging through him had been sufficiently dampened to allow him to think rationally, he opened one fist to release the sheet clenched in his grip. Moving his hand to the apex of her thighs, he found the swollen bud. She gasped at his first touch. He moved his fingertips over the distended flesh, working it between his thumb and forefinger. Her erratic breathing and the tightening of her muscles told him she was very close to her climax.

She whimpered, eyes closed, head thrown back. A shiver racked her body. She momentarily froze, then began bucking her hips faster and faster, rubbing against his fingers in a near frenzy. With a low moan erupting from her throat, the spasms began.

Her release rekindling his banked need, Kit lifted his hips to push into her pulsing center once, then twice. By the third stroke, the flames of desire were a full-fledged inferno. Holding her firmly around the waist, he continued thrusting into her, his breathing harsh.

The last of the tremors rippling through her body sent him plunging over the edge. Needing to hold her close, he pulled her down on top of him. Her face pressed to his neck, her breasts flattened against his heaving chest, he said, "Oh God, honey. I'm going to—" He gave a strangled cry, the incredible strength of his climax momentarily robbing him of the power of speech.

At the zenith of his release, he arched up to push into her one last time, every muscle tense with anticipation. "I love you, Angel," he groaned, his manhood emptying his seed with a series of powerful throbs. "I love you."

Long seconds passed before the tenseness seeped from his body, before the harsh pants of his breathing began to ease.

Still caught up in the euphoric afterglow of her own release, Angelina wasn't sure she'd heard Kit correctly. And a few moments later, after he'd caught his breath and rolled her onto her back, she was certain she had imagined the words. Sneaking a peek at him from beneath her lashes, she swallowed the sudden lump in her throat. His features—furrowed brow, clenched jaw, mouth turned down in a frown—were not what she'd expect on a man who'd just declared his love. She forced her painful discovery aside, her gaze moving down his body to the bruise on his thigh. The discoloration looked darker.

Watching him idly rub his thigh, she said, "I'm sorry I hurt your leg. We shouldn't have given in to our lust."

Her comment momentarily chased Kit's gloomy thoughts. He stopped the movements of his hand and turned his head on the pillow. "You didn't hurt my leg, and I'm glad we gave in to our lust, as you put it. For a few minutes there, our lustful goings-on took my mind off my thigh." Seeing she didn't look convinced, he added, "You have my word, Angelina. My leg's no worse than it was, so stop fretting."

"Don't tell me to stop fretting, Kittridge Dancer. I can fret about you all I want," she responded in a moment of pique. Realizing how she must have sounded, she managed a smile before saying, "I didn't mean to snap at you. It's just that . . ."

"It's just what?"

She shrugged. "Nothing. I'm just tired." She rolled onto her side, facing away from him. " 'Night."

He scowled at her back. *What's the matter with her?* He shifted his gaze to stare at the ceiling. *Or with me? We're both acting like we got into the loco weed. Especially me. What the hell was I thinkin', saying words I don't mean?* He squirmed to get more comfortable, grimacing when the movement stretched the muscle of his thigh.

By the time he finally drifted off to sleep, he'd convinced himself he'd spoken in the heat of the moment. Nothing more. He didn't—he couldn't—love Angelina. He couldn't betray Bethany that way. Besides, Angelina was too good for him, and she sure as hell deserved more than he could give her.

The following morning, Kit awoke to find the bed beside him empty. Scowling at having slept later than he normally did, he rose and reached for his clothes. He dressed as quickly as he could, then headed for the kitchen.

Though his leg was still a little stiff, he noticed a marked improvement over the night before. Damn good thing, because there was no way he could spend the day in the house. He needed some time to think, and he couldn't keep a clear head with the object of his thoughts in such proximity.

He ate a hurried breakfast, grateful Chloe was at the table, her presence a deterrent to any conversation of a personal nature. Draining his coffee cup, he pushed away from the table. "I'm riding up to the pasture to check on the herd. See you two later."

"Are you sure you should be riding?" Angelina said.

He met her gaze long enough to see the concern in her eyes, then turned away. "I'm fine. My leg's a lot better."

Angelina turned to her sister. "Chloe, aren't you going to say something?"

"Kit's the best judge of how he feels. If he says he can ride, I say let him." She rose from her chair. "I'll go see if Mama wants anything to eat."

Pressing her lips into a thin line, Angelina shifted her gaze from her departing sister's back to her husband. "When will you be back?"

"I don't know," he replied, heading for the door. "I'm gonna ride the fence line and make sure the wire is still strung tight. So it'll be sometime late this afternoon or early evening before I make it back."

"Did you forget Reverend Gray is coming today? He visits Mama on the first Saturday of every month and always stays for supper."

He pulled up short. "Damn, I did forget," he grumbled under his breath. In no mood to meet the minister who preached the word of God to the shut-ins around the El Paso area, he racked his brain for an acceptable way to get out of meeting the man who'd been such a comfort to Sarah. Coming up empty-handed, he exhaled a sigh of resignation, then said, "You and Chloe can keep the reverend entertained this afternoon. I'll be back in time for supper."

Before she could reply, he grabbed his hat, crammed it on his head, then jerked open the door. Stepping outside, his irritation made him pull the door shut behind him with more force than necessary.

The resounding bang made Angelina flinch. She stared at the door for a long moment, wondering if she'd ever understand her husband's moods. Shaking her head, she turned to clear the breakfast table.

Kit struggled with his emotions the better part of that day as well as a good share of the next several days, searching for an acceptable excuse for his shocking declaration of love. Caught up in the heat of the moment was the most plausible explanation, but he was experienced enough to know that hadn't been the case. While sex with Angelina was undeniably the most satisfying he'd ever known, that fact alone didn't justify his suddenly spouting words of love.

The only conclusion making any sense was one he refused to accept. He'd already been over that ground; he couldn't actually love Angelina. He just couldn't! Discounting the notion that he might be wrong, he continued to search for an answer.

By the time Kit returned to the ranch late one afternoon a week later, he'd made a decision. He had to distance himself from Angelina. He had to get away from the ranch for a while so he could put everything in perspective. Once he did that, once he'd resolved the conflicting emotions eating at him, he would be back in control.

Since the cattle were now content in their new home, his presence was no longer a necessity on the ranch. And since he'd been planning on checking into the business dealings of Elliot Wentworth and James Murray, the timing was perfect for him to go into El Paso for a few days. There was only one detail of his plan yet to be resolved, a matter he hoped to settle over supper by talking to Jared.

As he gave his horse a rubdown then forked some hay into the stall's hayrack, Kit was struck with a heavy dose of the lonesome blues. He snorted with disgust. He hadn't even left and he was already missing his wife.

His lips set in a grim line, he pounded his fists against the top of the stall. Sid's head came up with a start. Sidling out of his master's way, the gelding eyed him curiously.

"Sorry, boy. Don't mind me, I'm just . . . Hell, I don't know what I am anymore."

After making sure the horse had fresh water, Kit left the barn, his thoughts again in turmoil. *Damnit, this has got to stop!* Trudging across the yard, he almost wished he'd never returned to El Paso. Almost, if not for a whiskey-eyed, honey-lipped woman whose phenomenal passion, he feared, had branded his very soul.

Chapter Nineteen

Supper with Jared as their guest that evening was jovial and filled with laughter, their neighbor's presence relieving the tension between Angelina and her frustrating husband. Seeing Kit sitting across the table from her, smiling and relaxed, made her heart swell with love even more. If only he could be this way all the time, she mused, rather than withdrawn or preoccupied like he'd been since he'd spoken words of love over a week ago.

Trying not to let her somber thoughts dampen the light mood, she said, "Could I offer you gentlemen something stronger?" Rising from her chair, she moved around the table to stand next to Kit's chair. Unable to resist, she laid a hand on his shoulder, hoping he wouldn't object. To her surprise, he covered her hand with his and gave her fingers a squeeze.

Since the night he'd broached the subject of love, he'd avoided physical contact with her, keeping his distance whenever they were in the same room. Only at night, after she'd doused the lamp on the bedside table, did he offer to touch her.

In the darkness of their room, as if the blackness hid his identity, he became a tender yet demanding lover, taking her to heights of passion she had never imagined possible. He rarely spoke during those nightly ventures into the world of indescribable pleasures of the flesh, and then only to issue terse whispers of instruction.

Angelina longed to be the one to break the silence on their feelings. She wanted to tell him of her love, but she remained silent. Until he came to grips with whatever demons he was fighting, she refused to expose her heart and risk having it trampled. Though he'd not spoken of loving her, to Angelina his kisses, his caresses, his body claiming hers each night spoke louder than words ever could. Still, she refused to admit her love for fear she had misread his actions.

Now that he had openly touched her in the presence of others, she felt her first surge of hope. Perhaps he was winning his inner battle and would soon overcome whatever plagued him.

Taking advantage of having Angelina out of his field of vision, Kit tightened his grip on her hand to keep her from moving. He wasn't used to taking the coward's way out, but he just couldn't bring himself to make his announcement when he could see the reaction on her lovely face. "By the way, Jared. I have a favor to ask."

"Sure thing, Kit. Name it."

"I have some business to take care of in El Paso which will likely keep me away for a few days. And I was hoping you could look in on the women while I'm gone." Angelina's hand stiffened beneath his, but he kept his gaze focused on Jared.

"When are you figuring on leaving?" he replied.

"First thing tomorrow. Is that a problem?" Though Kit had made the decision to go into town for a few days, he still struggled with the guilt of leaving the women alone and unprotected.

The situation reminded him of another time when he'd left his family alone. If only he hadn't left that day. If only he'd taught Bethany how to use a gun, maybe things would have turned out differently.

At least he hadn't allowed that oversight again. During the past few days, he'd taken first Angelina, then Chloe up into the mountains and taught each of them how to fire a rifle. He'd been relentless in his instruction, insisting they practice until

their arms ached from holding the rifle. Only when their aim
became deadly accurate did he experience an easing of his apprehension about leaving them alone. Jared's granting his request would alleviate his anxiety a little more.

"Not in the least," Jared said. "I'd be more than happy to
oblige. That'll give me an excuse to come by every day." He
glanced over at Chloe.

"As if you need an excuse, Jared McBride," she replied with
a smile, her cheeks rosy with a blush.

"Good, I'm glad that's settled." Kit released Angelina's hand.
"Now, how about that drink?"

"Don't mind if I do," Jared said, his gaze still on the younger
Coleman sister.

Angelina withdrew her hand from Kit's shoulder and moved
woodenly across the kitchen. If only Kit would look at her the
way Jared looked at Chloe. *Stop feeling sorry for yourself. You know
full well he may never return your love, so don't go hanging your heart on
something that might never be.* Though she knew she should take her
own advice, doing so was not easily accomplished. She wanted
Kit to love her so much it was nearly impossible to accept the
fact that no matter how much she believed he already cared
for her, no matter how much she hoped and prayed, there was
still no guarantee her wishes would come true.

Sighing, she pulled the bottle of bourbon from the cupboard
and picked up two glasses. Somehow she managed to force her
lips into a smile before turning to face the man who had captured her heart. The man who could just as easily cause her im-
measurable heartbreak.

The rest of the evening passed without Kit's impending
absence coming up again. Though Angelina wanted to ask Kit
exactly what business he had in El Paso and why it would take
him away from the ranch for a few days, she didn't broach the
subject. She didn't want to start what could end up being a
heated discussion in front of Jared and Chloe. Her questions
would have to wait until later.

When Jared announced it was time for him to leave, Kit offered to walk out with him. Leaving Jared at the front door, Kit said, "I'll get your horse while you say good night to Chloe."

Smiling his thanks, Jared turned to look down into the face of the woman who filled his thoughts more and more often. "I enjoyed supper," he said in a soft voice. "The chicken was mighty tasty."

"I'll tell Angelina you said so," she replied. Swallowing her apprehension, she added, "To be perfectly honest, Angelina fixed the entire meal. I'm not very good in the kitchen." If their relationship was going to progress any further, he had to know the truth.

"Is that so?" he replied, amused by her pained look. "Well, to be perfectly honest in return, I'm not interested in you because of your abilities in the kitchen, or because you clean a house better than anyone else, or for any other domestic skill you happen to possess."

She looked up at him with wide eyes. "Y'all aren't funning me, are you?"

Chuckling, he pulled her into his arms. "No, darlin' girl, I'm not funning you. I'm most definitely serious." He lowered his head and pressed his mouth to hers in a gentle kiss.

She swayed closer, her lips soft and pliant beneath his. Wrapping his arms around her, he deepened the kiss, moving his mouth back and forth on hers with increasing pressure. The approach of Kit leading his horse forced Jared to pull away much sooner than he wanted to. His mouth just inches from hers, he whispered, "I'll see you soon, darlin'." He released her and took a step back. "Sweet dreams."

Chloe stared up at him, her eyes still wide, her mouth wet from his kiss. " 'Night," she murmured, her voice quivering with her first taste of passion.

A pang of longing swept over Kit, the scene between Chloe and Jared a poignant reminder of what he could never have. Shoving aside the pain such thoughts spawned, he handed the reins to Jared.

"Take care of the women while I'm gone," Kit said in a soft voice.

Sensing something in Kit's tone, Jared said, "You have my word."

As Angelina got ready for bed, she went over various ways to ask Kit about his plans. She didn't want to stir his anger and have him withdraw behind another wall of silence. Yet she wasn't sure she knew how to open the discussion in a way to prevent such an occurrence. Sighing, she undressed, pulled a nightdress over her head, then picked up her hairbrush.

She had just finished brushing her hair and climbed into bed when Kit entered their bedroom.

He moved across the room, the limp from his confrontation with Hermes completely gone. "I forgot to ask what the doctor said when he came to see your mother this afternoon," he said, sitting down on his side of the bed and turning to face her.

"Dr. Irvin agrees Mama's a lot weaker. But he says we're doing all we can for her."

"What about her coughing up blood?"

"He said that's a normal progression of the disease. He told us not to let her catch a chill now that the weather has turned cool, and to get her to take as much nourishment as we can. Unless we send for him sooner, he promised to come back in a couple of weeks."

Kit nodded, wishing there was some way he could comfort her. Turning away, he pulled off his boots then got to his feet. "Angelina, I need to ask you some questions," he said, working the buttons free on his shirt.

She stared at him for a long moment, wondering what he would look like in a color other than his standard black. Maybe she'd make a shirt for him while he was gone. The trunk in her mother's room contained several lengths of fabric. Something in blue would be a nice complement to his eyes. Bringing her thoughts back to the present, she lifted her gaze to meet his. "What questions?"

Tossing his shirt aside, his hands dropped to the fly of his trousers. He thought better of taking off all his clothes, so he loosened the first button, then sat down on the bed again.

"I'm going into El Paso to do some investigating into James Murray's business relationship with Elliot Wentworth."

Her eyes widened. "Why would you want to do that? You got me out of my contract, so what more is there to gain?"

"What about the other women with contracts like yours? Shouldn't someone do something to help them?"

"Other women? Who are you talking about?"

"You lived with the girls at the Murray House for six months. Didn't the subject of contracts ever come up?"

"Mr. Murray told me I wasn't supposed to discuss my terms of employment with anyone else."

"Come on, Angelina, I know you must've talked to Jenna. She was your closest friend there, wasn't she?"

"She's still my friend, and yes, I did talk to her about my contract. I told her as little as I could, but she guessed some of what I didn't tell her."

"Do you think she had to sign a contract like yours?"

Angelina shook her head. "No, she worked at the Murray House by choice. That's all she's ever known. Her mother was a prostitute in Dodge City, and Jenna grew up in one house of ill-fame after another. She planned to leave all of that behind as soon as she turned sixteen. She dreamed of moving to California, finding work in a respectable business, and eventually marrying and raising a family. But on her fifteenth birthday, her mother sold Jenna to a customer who liked young virgins."

"Jesus," Kit muttered under his breath.

"Jenna lost more than her innocence that night—she also lost all hope of her dreams coming true. A few months later, the man who'd bought her dumped her at a brothel in Fort Worth. Seeing no other choice, she moved to El Paso and started working as a prostitute."

After a long pause, Kit said, "What about the other girls?"

Caught up in memories of the pain she saw in Jenna's eyes while her friend related her story, Angelina started at his voice. She cleared her throat, then said, "The only other employee I knew very well was Lin-Shee, and she worked in the Murray

House kitchen. The other girls kept pretty much to themselves, but I don't think any of them had contracts like mine. I'm sure Jenna would have mentioned it if they had."

"Did Jenna or the others ever talk about Murray's other businesses?"

"We all knew the Murray House wasn't the only business he owned. The White Horse Saloon and another bawdy house called The Shamrock are the two we heard about most. I never met anyone who worked in either of those places, but I can't speak for the other girls."

Another few minutes passed in silence, then Angelina said, "I still don't understand why you want to do this. Do you suspect Mr. Wentworth and James Murray of doing something wrong?"

"Too many things about how those two conduct business sound just a little too suspicious for me, especially the dealings of Wentworth. Like how he showed up right after your father's funeral claiming there was a loan due his bank. How he conveniently knew of a way for you to keep the ranch when you couldn't come up with the money on your own."

"You don't think Papa took out a loan at Mr. Wentworth's bank?"

"No, I think Wentworth just told you that to get what he wanted."

"But he showed us the loan papers with Papa's signature."

"You told me it looked like your father's signature, but you couldn't be sure he actually signed the note."

"That's true. So if it wasn't Papa who signed those papers, who did?"

"That's one of the things I aim to find out."

Angelina mulled over his words for a moment, then said, "Do you have any idea where to start?"

"When I went into town to order the barbed wire, I overheard two women talking about a Mavis Johnson. Do you know her?"

Angelina shook her head.

"Well, anyway, one of the women said Mavis had to go to work in one of the town's bawdy houses because she couldn't pay off her recently buried husband's bank loan. I plan to find this Mavis Johnson and talk to her. How much do you wanna bet Elliot Wentworth is behind her change in circumstance?"

"Kit, you can't do this." She sat up and reached over to grab his arm. "Please, don't go. If those two are behind such underhanded dealings, there's no telling what else they're capable of doing."

"I'm going," he replied in a soft but firm voice. "Someone has to stop those two before more innocent women fall prey to their slick scheme."

Seeing the hard set of his jaw, the determination in his pale blue eyes, she swallowed the knot of fear in her throat. Though he hadn't completely eliminated her concerns about the possible dangers facing him, she dropped her protests. Realizing he needed the time away to resolve whatever was troubling him, she said, "Promise me you'll be careful."

"I can take care of myself, so don't—" The glare she gave him and the tightening of her fingers on his arm made him add, "Okay, I promise I'll be careful."

Relaxing her grip, she removed her hand and dropped back onto the bed. "I'll still worry about you," she whispered.

"I told you, I'll be fine. Besides, I'll only be gone a few days. I don't like the idea of leaving the three of you alone here, so with or without the answers to my questions about Wentworth, I'll be back before you have a chance to miss me."

"I'll miss you as soon as you ride away from the ranch."

Kit nearly said he would miss her as well, but he held the words back. With no chance of their marriage becoming permanent, there was no point in giving her false hope.

"It's late," he finally said, getting to his feet. "And I want to get an early start."

He shed his trousers, then eased under the top sheet beside Angelina. "I'll let you decide whether to tell your mother and sister the reason I'm going into town."

"I'll tell Chloe, but I don't want to upset Mama with talk that

Mr. Wentworth might have pulled the wool over our eyes. She's been through enough."

"You all have," he replied.

Angelina balled one hand into a fist and pounded it on the mattress between them. "I should have done more checking. I should have talked to more people. I should have found a way to prove Papa never took out that loan."

"Don't go blaming yourself."

"Why shouldn't I? After Papa died, I became the head of my family. I was supposed to be taking care of my mother and sister, and what happened? I let some sneaky banker convince me we'd lose the ranch if I didn't come up with the money."

"That's enough."

"Then, to make matters worse, I end up working in a bawdy house. That's no way for the head of a family to—"

"Angelina, I said, that's enough," he snapped, rising onto one elbow.

She blinked at his sharp tone, looking up at him with anguish-filled eyes. He reached over and ran the backs of his knuckles across one cheek. "Listen to me. I want you to stop torturing yourself. You did what you thought had to be done, what you thought was right. No one can find fault with that. Do you understand what I'm saying?"

Biting her lower lip, she nodded.

"Good. Now come here and let me hold you." He shifted positions, slipping one arm under her and pulling her close. Her head laying on his shoulder, a hand curled in a fist over his heart, she trembled against him.

He slowly stroked her hair, murmuring soothing words near her ear until her trembling stopped, her fingers relaxing on his chest.

For a moment he thought she'd fallen asleep, then she stirred, lifting her head off his shoulder. She kissed his chin.

"Thank you," she whispered.

"You're welcome," he replied, fighting the temptation of the proximity of her mouth. Though he had no intention of making love to her that night, determined to leave in the morning without another memory of her passion fresh in his mind, he couldn't resist sampling the sweetness of her lips.

The kiss he meant to be only a gentle peck soon took another route, turning into a scorching excursion down a path of fiery, uninhibited desire. Head reeling, heart pounding in his ears, he finally pulled away. The rasping pants of his breathing mingled with hers in the room's quiet.

When his control returned, he reached over to turn out the lamp. " 'Night, Angel."

She pressed a kiss on his chest, then sighed, her breath warm across his skin. " 'Night."

Kit closed his eyes, torn between hoping for sleep to come quickly and wanting to stay awake so he could remember every minute he held her in his arms. A long time later, sleep finally won the battle.

Chapter Twenty

Kit arrived in El Paso just before noon the next day and made his first order of business finding a place to stay. After taking a room at the boardinghouse he used before and arranging for Sid's care at a nearby stable, he stopped at the post office to see if there was any mail for the Diamond C.

The clerk handed him a veterinary journal for Chloe and several letters addressed to him. Recognizing his brother-in-law's bold scrawl on each of the envelopes, he realized he had never written or wired Blaine to let him know the cattle had arrived safely.

At a restaurant on Overland Street he ordered a steak, then read Blaine's letters while he waited for his meal to arrive. The first letter was cordial—the only comment of a personal nature, his lamenting the loss of another housekeeper—though there was no mistaking the underlying irritation at not having heard from Kit. But the second letter was true Blaine. Never one to mince words, he got straight to the point.

Damnit, Kit. What the hell's going on out there? I don't hear from you in nearly four years, then all of a sudden you send a wire saying you want to buy two hundred head of cattle. I did as you asked and had the cattle loaded on a train, but I have yet to hear one blasted word from you. I certainly hope the reason for your silence isn't that fool notion you're in some way responsible for the deaths of Bethany and Thad. No one in our family blames you. Isn't it about time you

*let go of your guilt and got on with your life? I had hoped your re-
quest to buy cattle was an indication you were finally settling down,
but now I don't know what to think. I want some answers, Kit. If
I don't get some sort of message by the end of next week, I'll get on
a train for El Paso and find out for myself. Blaine.*

In spite of being reminded of the guilt he'd carried around
for five years, Kit managed a smile. The man who'd been a
close friend since childhood, then later his brother-in-law, always did have a short fuse. He was the exact opposite of his sister Bethany, who had the sweetest, most gentle disposition of
anyone Kit had ever met. Checking the date of Blaine's letter,
he cursed under his breath. Kit knew the man didn't make idle
threats. If Blaine Delaney said he'd get on a train, Kit knew he'd
damn well do exactly that. Even running a large cattle ranch
and caring for two young daughters wouldn't prevent Blaine
from making the trip if he deemed it necessary. And since a
week would be up in two days, Kit had to get a wire sent as soon
as he finished eating.

Though he would have preferred taking the time to savor his
meal, he ate his steak as quickly as he could, paid his bill, then
headed for the telegraph office.

He wrote out his message, then reread his words.

*Blaine Delaney. Double Star Ranch, San Angelo. Sorry for the delay
in writing. Cattle arrived safe. Money wired to your bank. Appreciate your help. Will explain everything in a letter to follow. Give
my love to the girls. Kit.*

He handed the paper to the telegraph operator, hoping his
message would satisfy Blaine enough to make him stay in San
Angelo.

Leaving the telegraph office a few minutes later, Kit's
thoughts remained on his friend and brother-in-law. Blaine
was right. It *had* been almost four years since they'd seen each
other. Bethany and Thad had been dead less than a year when

Kit learned Blaine's wife died giving birth to their second daughter.

Though he didn't want to go to San Angelo, fearing the memories would tear him apart, he knew he had to make the trip. He had to be there for the man he loved like a brother. Kit arrived too late to attend the funeral, which was just as well since he wasn't sure he could have faced Blaine's parents, who were also his in-laws. After offering what comfort he could to his grief-stricken friend, he stayed long enough to visit the graves of his wife and son, then rode out of town. He hadn't been back.

Heading for the city marshal's office, Kit decided he would make San Angelo his first stop when he left El Paso. Blaine would break out a bottle of his favorite Irish whiskey while they caught up on the past four years. Of course Kit had no intention of admitting his liberal drinking of whiskey wouldn't be in celebration of his arrival at Blaine's ranch, but an attempt to drown memories of the woman he'd left in El Paso.

The pain he'd suffer when he left Angelina brought a new thought to mind. If he could successfully prove Elliot Wentworth was involved in an illegal scheme to embezzle money from local citizens, the contract Angelina signed would be worthless. Which meant they no longer had to remain married for a year; which in turn, meant he could leave town much earlier than he'd originally planned.

The possibility should have chased away the despondency hanging over him of late, should have buoyed his flagging spirits, yet it did neither. Instead, he experienced a combination of near-panic and a profound sense of loss at the prospect of leaving Angelina much sooner than he'd anticipated.

Forcing his thoughts back to the reason he was in town, he took a deep breath and exhaled slowly. He had to keep focused on Wentworth's dealings as an unscrupulous banker, resolutely ignoring how his investigation would impact his future.

He spent a few minutes talking to the city marshal, asking about the local banks and whether there had been any complaints lodged regarding their business practices. He kept his questions relatively general and mentioned no bank or employee by name. Conspiracy and graft involving the local law was a possibility Kit had already considered, so he used the pretext of looking for a reputable bank to finance a land purchase as the reason for his questions.

The marshal claimed to have taken no formal complaints against the El Paso Bank, only the inquiry by Angelina and one by another woman, Carol Ann Wagoner, four months after Angelina's.

"What can you tell me about this Miss Wagoner?" Kit said.

"That's Mrs., or rather, Widow Wagoner now. Her husband died suddenly a few weeks before she came to my office. She was kind of a pretty little thing. Didn't look to be more than twenty-one or -two. Bright green eyes and copper-colored hair."

"So what did you tell her?"

"Just like I told Miss Coleman, I suggested Mrs. Wagoner see a lawyer. Since I can't do anything unless a crime's been committed, there was nothing else I could do to help either one of them women."

Kit thanked the marshal for his time, then headed for Utah Street. Since it was only mid-afternoon, he hoped to catch Jenna at the boardinghouse.

He passed the Murray House, still not open for business but repairs underway, then headed for the rear of the house next-door. His knock was answered by a small Chinese woman.

"You must be Lin-Shee," he said. "May I come in?"

Lin-Shee eyed him for a long moment, then bowed her head and stepped back to allow him to enter the kitchen.

"You man who marry Missy An-ge-rina?" she finally said, her penetrating stare never leaving his face.

"Yes, I married Angelina."

"What you do here? Something happen to her?"

"No, Angelina's fine. She's at the ranch. I came here to ask some questions about how women like Angelina end up working for James Murray."

After a moment, she said, "I have work to do. But . . ." She took another step back and waved for him to come farther into the room. "Come, sit. I work. You ask questions."

Moving across the kitchen, he took a seat at the large table in the middle of the room. "Jenna wouldn't happen to be here, would she?"

"She upstairs. You rather ask her questions?"

"Actually, I'd like to ask both of you some questions."

"You rike some rem-on-ade?"

Kit bit the inside of his cheek to halt a smile. "Yes, I'd like some lemonade."

Lin-Shee poured a glass and plunked it down in front of him. "I go get Jenna now."

A few minutes later, she returned with a slightly disheveled Jenna. Nodding when Lin-Shee asked if she wanted coffee, Jenna took a seat opposite him.

She ran a hand through the tangle of her toffee-colored hair, then gave Kit a weak smile. "I must look a fright, but when Lin-Shee told me you were here, I wanted to get down here as quick as I could."

Kit returned her smile, thinking she looked a lot younger without the makeup and trappings of the Murray House lovelies. "You look just fine. I don't want to take a lot of your time, but I was hoping I could ask you some questions." He sat back in his chair, pushing his hat off his forehead with one thumb. Allowing people to see the right side of his face was getting easier; nonetheless, he found himself holding his breath while waiting for Jenna's reaction.

He watched her gaze shift to his scar, but other than the slight widening of her eyes, she didn't react at all.

"Sure thing," Jenna replied, feeling just a little bit jealous of her friend for bagging such a good-looking man. Even the scar didn't detract from his looks. "I don't have any plans until evening, so ask all the questions you want."

Releasing his breath, he said, "For starters, do either of you know if any of the other girls have contracts like Angelina's?"

"Not for certain." She accepted the cup of coffee Lin-Shee

handed her, then reached for the sugar bowl. "What about you Lin-Shee?"

When the Chinese woman shook her head, Jenna said, "Angelina told me she wasn't supposed to discuss her contract, so I reckon Mr. Murray said the same thing to anybody else with that kind of arrangement. But I did hear one of the new gals mention a contract one day. I think it slipped out, 'cause she changed the subject and never mentioned it again."

"What's her name?"

"Stella Roberts. Or is it Robertson? Yeah, I think it is. Anyway, she started as a waiter girl at the Shamrock about three weeks ago."

"Any idea where she came from before she started working for James Murray?"

"She never said anything to me." Jenna dumped a spoonful of sugar into her cup. "But I overheard her telling the bartender she came here two years ago from east Texas."

"Do you think she'd talk to me?"

"Don't rightly know. She keeps pretty much to herself, so no one really knows her very well."

"What about you, Lin-Shee? Do you know anyone else who signed a contract to work for James Murray?"

"One woman who work in kitchen of Shamrock. She ask about extra work she can do. Say she need money to pay off contract."

"How long has she worked for Murray?"

"I say, maybe two month."

"Do you know her name?"

"I not remember name. I see her just one time. When I go to Shamrock to help when their cook take sick."

"What else can you tell me about her? Her age, what she looks like?"

"She young. I guess maybe twenty year. Eyes same as grass, hair bright as new penny."

"Carol Ann Wagoner," Kit said with a smile.

"That her name?"

"From your description, I'd say that's her." He took a long

swallow of lemonade, then said, "Do either of you know a Mavis Johnson?"

"I don't think so," Jenna replied, looking over at Lin-Shee.

"I not know name, either."

"Well, it was a long shot. I'd appreciate your asking around, though. Maybe someone else you work with knows her."

"Sure." Jenna stared into her cup, absently stirring her coffee. "Kit, can I ask you a question?"

"Go ahead."

"Why are you asking us about who has contracts and such?" She lowered her voice to a whisper. "Is Mr. Murray in trouble?"

"No one's in trouble. Not yet, anyway. I've just started looking into how he gets some of his employees. Angelina said I could trust you two, so I want you both to promise not to discuss this with anyone else."

"We promise, don't we?" Jenna replied, turning to Lin-Shee who bobbed her head in agreement.

"Good. Now I need you to tell me where I can find both Stella and Carol Ann. I want to pay each of them a visit."

The following morning, Kit made plans to visit the El Paso Bank and have a chat with Elliot Wentworth. He couldn't tip his hand, so he'd come up with a reason to meet with the banker that shouldn't arouse any suspicion.

As he walked through town on his way to the bank, Kit thought about his conversations with the two women Jenna and Lin-Shee had told him about.

Stella Robertson had refused to talk, telling him in no uncertain terms to get out and to leave her alone. He didn't doubt her rude dismissal had been triggered by her fear of having Murray find out she'd been talking to someone. Maybe after she had some time to think about it, she would come around.

At least Carol Ann Wagoner had been more amiable. After getting over her initial apprehension, she accepted his offer to help her and answered his questions. Remembering what she'd told him, he clenched his jaw in fury. As she recited how she ended up working for James Murray, he felt as though he'd gone back in time, as if he were listening to Angelina recite the tale. Other than Carol Ann being the wife of the deceased, the women's stories were identical.

Approaching the door of the El Paso Bank, Kit mentally rehearsed his plan one more time, then entered the building. His request to one of the clerks, a smallish man with thinning red hair and wire-rimmed glasses, brought an immediate response.

"Our manager, Mr. Wentworth, is the man you need to see. If you'll wait here, I'll see if he's free. Who should I say wants to see him?"

"Kit Dancer. Of the Diamond C Ranch."

The man's brow furrowed. "Diamond C? I don't believe I know that ranch."

"It's the name I recently gave the Coleman place."

"Coleman?" The man's voice rose to a squeak. Shoving his glasses back onto the bridge of his nose with a forefinger, he cleared his throat. "I'll . . . I'll be right back."

Kit nodded, then turned to gaze out the front window. Looking at the reflection in the glass, he could see the man hurry across the lobby to a closed door, knock, then enter the room.

In just a few minutes, the man returned. "Mr. Wentworth will see you now."

Turning, Kit said, "Thank you, Mr. . . . ." He looked down at the nameplate on the man's desk. "Richfield."

The man bobbed his head, pushed his glasses back in place again, then took a seat.

Striding into Wentworth's office, Kit shut the door behind him, then turned to face the man sitting behind his massive desk. "I appreciate your seeing me without an appointment, Mr. Wentworth. I'm sure you're a very busy man."

"I can always find time for a potential customer. I believe Mr. Richfield mentioned you're interested in securing a loan, Mr. Dancer, is it?"

"Right."

"Well, have a seat and tell me what you have in mind."

Sitting in one of the leather chairs in front of the man's desk, Kit crossed an ankle over the opposite knee. "I came into some property recently, and I'm looking to increase the size of my spread."

"This property you're referring to is the Coleman place?"

"Yeah, now called the Diamond C."

"Last I knew, the ranch was in a pretty shocking state of disrepair. So, I'm not so sure I could loan you money if you're planning on putting the place up as collateral."

"Oh, right, since you loaned money to old man Coleman to fix up the ranch, you would've looked the place over. Too bad about Coleman dying and not telling his family about the loan." Kit waved his hand in a dismissive gesture. "Well, that's in the past now. Listen, don't go worrying about collateral. I've done so much work on the ranch you wouldn't recognize the place."

Wentworth's eyebrows lifted. "Is that so?" He leaned back in his chair, his fingers intertwined over the paunch of his stomach. "Tell me, how much money do you want to borrow?"

"Actually, I don't know yet."

"Then why are we going through this exercise?" Wentworth replied, tapping his thumbs together.

Silently amused by Wentworth's obvious irritation, Kit kept his expression bland. Dropping his foot to the floor, he braced his elbows on his knees and leaned forward. "I don't know how much I want to borrow because I haven't found the property I want to buy. And I came here today because I figured you'd be the man who would know when some prime property is about to go on the market."

"And why would I know that?"

"With your business connections, the large number of people who deal with the bank, you'd know which landowners are in financial trouble and which ones are facing foreclosure. Just the kind of information an ambitious ranch owner like me is looking for."

Wentworth stared at him for several long minutes, the only sound in the room the soft ticking of a pendulum wall clock. Finally the tapping of his thumbs stopped. He unlaced his fin-

gers and straightened in his chair. "Okay, Mr. Dancer. I'll keep
my ears open for a piece of property which may interest you.
Should I send a message to the Diamond C if something becomes available?"

Kit smiled. "Certainly." Getting to this feet, he offered his
hand. "I hope to hear from you soon, Mr. Wentworth."

After their handshake, Kit started to leave, then said, "Oh,
by the way. I need to open an account."

Smiling for the first time—that oily smile Angelina mentioned—Elliot Wentworth rose and came around his desk.
"Mr. Richfield can take care of that for you." He crossed the
room and opened the door. "I just remembered I have an appointment, so I'll escort you to his desk on my way out."

A few minutes later, Kit finished signing the forms the bank
clerk shoved in front of him and left the El Paso Bank. On the
way back to his boardinghouse, he kept thinking about Richfield's nervous behavior after Wentworth's departure.

While opening an account, Kit had casually asked the bank
clerk some carefully selected questions. Morris Richfield was
originally from Boston, had worked in a bank for fourteen
years—ten back East and the remaining years in El Paso as a
clerk for Elliot Wentworth. The man was married and had six
children, the youngest chronically ill.

A man with that much experience wouldn't get all flustered
when he opened an account for a customer, something he
would have done countless times. In fact, now that Kit thought
about it, Richfield's nervousness had started not long after his
arrival at the bank—in fact, right after the name Coleman
came up in their conversation.

Strolling up San Antonio Street, Kit decided it wouldn't
hurt to give Morris Richfield some additional scrutiny. The
man just might know something that could help him prove
Wentworth a first-class shyster.

Chapter Twenty-One

Elliot Wentworth entered the storeroom at the rear of the White Horse Saloon, out of breath, his forehead dotted with sweat. James Murray looked up from the pad of paper where he was recording his liquor inventory and frowned.

"For Christ's sake, Elliot, what's gotten you so rattled? You look like you ran over here."

Wentworth pulled a linen handkerchief from his jacket pocket, mopped the cloth across his face, then said, "I did run, damnit. And the reason I did is to tell you I was just paid a visit by Mr. Dancer."

"Dancer? Kit Dancer?"

"Do you know anyone else with that name?" Wentworth snapped, lowering his weight onto an overturned wooden crate.

"What did he want?"

"He says he wants a loan to buy more property, and he thinks I have an inside track to properties coming onto the market."

Murray finished counting the cases of bourbon stacked against one wall of the storeroom, noted the count on the pad of paper, then turned to face his visitor. "Did he say anything about Douglas Coleman's loan?"

"He mentioned it."

"And?"

"He didn't seem concerned. In fact, he acted like that kind of thing happens every day."

"So you don't think he suspects anything?"

"That's the hell of it. Everything he said made sense. So if he suspects something, he did a damn good job of hiding it."

Murray laid down his pad of paper and pencil. "Tell me exactly what he said."

After Wentworth recited his conversation with Dancer, Murray twisted one end of his moustache while contemplating what he'd just heard. Dropping his hand to his side, he said, "Perhaps he does want to buy more property. He's right about you being the logical person to contact, since as he pointed out, you are in a position to know when a landowner is in trouble, or when a foreclosure is about to take place."

"Are you saying we shouldn't worry?"

"Not entirely. Until we know for sure exactly what Mr. Dancer is up to, we'll just take care not to do anything to arouse his suspicion. No new unpaid loans sprung on unsuspecting next of kin. No new contracts to get those folks out from under their debt and into my employ. Got that, Elliot?"

"Yeah, James, I got it. Now, I'm sure you want to get back to your work, so I'll be leaving." Getting to his feet, he tucked his handkerchief back into his pocket, then straightened his tie.

"Be sure to let me know if Dancer pays you another visit," Murray said. He started to turn away, then swung back to face Wentworth. "Oh, and don't forget what you said after I told you he paid off Angelina Coleman's contract." When Elliot didn't reply, Murray added, "You told me if Dancer started sticking his nose where it don't belong, you'd see to it the prying bastard was taken care of, remember?"

"Yeah, I remember." Brushing at the sleeves of his jacket, Wentworth muttered, "Damn filthy storeroom." He tugged his vest back into place, then headed for the door.

"Next time you need to talk to me, Elliot, send a message. Under the circumstances, I don't want you coming here."

"Go to hell," Wentworth replied under his breath.

Sitting in a rocker in her mother's bedroom, Angelina applied tiny, even stitches to the pieces of blue wool. In the two days since Kit left for El Paso, she'd found time to make a paper pattern from one of his shirts, pin the pattern to a length of fine-woven wool, then carefully cut each piece of fabric.

Since her mother now slept through the better part of her afternoon visits, Angelina began the painstaking process of sewing the shirt while rocking in what had been Sarah's favorite chair.

"You're making a shirt for Kit?" Sarah said, breaking the silence that had settled between them.

Glancing over at her mother's flushed face, Angelina hid her worry over Sarah's deteriorating health and managed a smile. "Yes. I think he'll look good in blue, don't you?"

Sarah nodded, then said, "I never wanted to pry, but his wearing only black did strike me as strange."

Angelina debated whether she should say anything, then after a moment took a deep breath and said, "Kit was married before and had a son. I don't know what happened to them, except they died five years ago. It must have been terrible though, because Kit still has nightmares about their deaths."

"Is that why he wears black?"

"I think so. He told me once the color was appropriate. I wasn't sure what he meant until I found out about his first wife's death."

Noticing a tightening around her daughter's mouth and the furrowing of her brow, Sarah said, "Is there something wrong, dear?"

Laying her sewing aside, Angelina dropped her head against the back of the rocker. "Mama, Kit and I didn't get married because we fell madly in love. He married me to get me out of my contract with Mr. Murray."

Sarah's eyes widened. "Well, if that don't take the rag off the bush," she whispered. A few minutes passed while she digested her daughter's startling admission. "Well, y'all may not have loved him when you two said your vows, but you love him now, don't you?"

Eyes closed, Angelina drew in a deep breath, then exhaled on a sigh. "Yes."

"So why are you looking so gloomy-faced?"

Opening her eyes, she met her mother's gaze. "I love Kit, Mama, but I'm not sure how he feels about me."

"What do you mean, you're not sure? Hasn't he told you he loves you?"

"Well, yes, but . . ." The heat of a blush creeping up her neck, she dropped her gaze to the rag rug beside the bed.

"Well, child, if he's said the words, I don't under . . . Oh, now I see. Did Kit happen to say he loved you in a moment of passion?"

Certain her face was as red as the currant jelly she used to make in Georgia, Angelina nodded.

"Darlin', y'all needn't be embarrassed. You've been a grown woman for quite a spell now. So it's high time you experienced the passion between man and a woman. When I got too sick to share your father's bed, I felt so guilty about denying him the passion we'd always enjoyed." She paused to catch her breath. After a moment, she said, "Tell me something, Angelina, is it good between you two? I mean intimately?"

Swallowing hard, she again met her mother's gaze. "Yes, but I want more than passion with Kit, Mama. I want him to love me."

"Well, from what I've seen of your husband, I'd say he already does. But he's probably still mourning his first wife. As soon as he realizes he has to let go of the past and live for the present, he'll come to see what's in his heart."

Picking up her sewing, Angelina sighed. "I hope you're right, Mama."

During the two days since his visit to Elliot Wentworth's office, Kit spent his time looking for other women who'd lost a loved one and subsequently ended up working in one of the businesses in the tenderloin. By the time he'd finished checking as many of the places as he could, no new names had been added to his list. Either that list was already complete, or others were unwilling to talk.

He also tried to find out more information about the clerk at the El Paso Bank. Morris Richfield was indeed married with six children. And just as the man had told him, the youngest child was ill most of the time and required frequent doctor visits. The family lived in an adobe house at the edge of town—a small structure which didn't look large enough to hold such a large family.

Kit could find no evidence that Richfield had ever been in any trouble with the law since his arrival in El Paso, and from all outward appearances the man was honest, hard-working, and devoted to his wife and children. Still, there had to be some reason for the unaccountable nervousness the man exhibited during Kit's visit to the bank.

Perhaps he should send a wire to Boston. Maybe someone at the bank where Morris Richfield had worked before moving his family west could supply some helpful information.

After sending a telegram to the manager of the Bank of Massachusetts in Boston, Kit walked around town. Since he couldn't proceed with his investigation until he received a reply to his inquiry, which could be days, he knew he probably should head back to the ranch.

Though he'd tried to keep thoughts of Angelina from interfering with his work, they were never far away. He missed her more than he'd imagined possible. While the days passed quickly, the nights went on forever. He wasn't sleeping well, though not because he was plagued by nightmares. No, his sleeplessness was caused by the woman waiting at the Diamond C and the truth he'd been forced to face the night before.

After supper, he returned to his room and sat down to write the letter he promised Blaine Delaney. While detailing the events of the past weeks, he made a very disturbing discovery.

Though he'd tried not to besmirch his love for Bethany, had fought to keep his heart true to her memory, he could no longer deny his feelings for Angelina.

He loved her.

Overwhelmed by the mixture of pain and joy such a realization gave him, he'd been unable to finish the letter to Blaine. Instead, he'd lain awake for hours, contemplating what he was going to do about his traitorous heart.

Now, in the full light of day, he made one decision. Whether he and Angelina had their originally agreed upon twelve months, or only until he could find the evidence necessary to get Elliot Wentworth arrested and convicted, he would still do as he'd planned and leave when the time came.

Even if he did love her, there was no way she deserved to have him for a husband one day longer than necessary. A man with his contemptible history had no business staying married to such a fine woman. He would rectify the situation as soon as possible.

Wanting to pay another visit to Jenna and Lin-Shee before leaving town, he decided heading back to the ranch could wait until first thing the next morning. Since it was only a little past noon, he'd have to wait to talk to the Murray House employees until at least mid-afternoon. With a few hours to kill, he headed for the stable where he'd boarded Sid. He'd take the piebald out for some exercise, find a place to eat dinner, then head over to Utah Street.

Kit found Lin-Shee in her usual place in the rooming house kitchen. "Afternoon, Lin-Shee, can I come in?" he said when she opened the door.

She nodded, then said, "You want me fetch Jenna?"

Removing his hat and stepping into the kitchen, he said, "Yeah, if it's not too much trouble."

"No trouble. I be right back." After she went into the hall and called up the stairs for Jenna, Lin-Shee returned to her work.

Jenna came into the room a few minutes later wearing a dressing gown of lavender silk, her hair piled atop her head. "Have you made any progress in your investigation?" she asked, sliding into a chair at the table.

"Not much. How about you two? Have either of you found out if there's a Mavis Johnson working in one of Murray's businesses?"

"I not find her," Lin-Shee replied.

"Neither have I," Jenna said. "But she could be going by a different name. A lot of us have names we use while we're working, so maybe she's using hers all the time."

"I reckon that's possible." Kit scowled, idly slapping his hat against one thigh. "I may never find her if that's the case."

"No need to look so down in the mouth. If she's in town, we'll find this Mavis woman."

Kit exhaled heavily. "I hope you're right, Jenna. So far I don't have any proof of wrongdoing, only suspicions. Even without talking to Mavis Johnson, Angelina and Carol Ann Wagoner may have given me enough to take to the marshal. But on the other hand . . ."

"On the other hand you have five fingers," Jenna replied with a smile.

"What? No, I meant—" Hearing Lin-Shee's giggle, Kit's scowl lifted, slowly changing to a smile. He stared at Jenna for a long moment. Finally he said, "Have you ever considered leaving the Murray House?"

Jenna's toffee-colored eyebrows shot up. "Me? Leave here?"

"Yeah. Have you ever thought about getting into a different line of work?"

"All the time, but I don't know anything else," she replied in a low voice. "Besides, who would hire me?" She absently traced the wood grain of the tabletop with her fingers.

"Can you cook and keep house?"

"She cook good," Lin-Shee replied before Jenna could answer. "Make pie sometime. Everyone say best they ate."

"Oh, Lin-Shee, stop bragging on me." She gave Kit a shy

smile. "I do like to cook, but I don't get the chance very often. And I reckon I can keep house as well as most folks."

"What about children? Do you like children?"

Jenna's smile widened. "Sure. I love children even though I haven't been around 'em much, not with growing up in a string of bawdy houses. I'd even like to have my own someday. Though that's probably just foolish talk." Her smile fading, she shifted her gaze back to the table.

"If you had the chance to leave here and start over somewhere, would you take it?"

She lifted her head, brows drawn together over narrowed eyes. "What are you talking about?"

"I was just curious. Would you be willing to start over?"

"That depends on where I'd be headed and what I'd have to do when I got there. But, yes, I would sure consider a chance to leave this life."

Kit tucked Jenna's answer into the back of his mind, then lifted his hat and settled it on his head. "Well, I'd best get going. I'm heading back to the ranch in the morning. If either of you learn anything you think I should know, just leave word at Blinn's Lumber Company. My neighbor, Jared McBride, works there a few days a week, and he can deliver any messages to me."

"We'll be sure to let you know if we find Mavis Johnson, or hear anything else that might help you." Jenna rose from the chair, tightening the belt of her dressing gown. "Tell Angelina Lin-Shee and I said hello."

"And say to Missy An-ge-rina, we think about her mama."

"I'll do that." He moved to the door. "Unless I hear from you sooner, I'll be back in town in a week or so." Pulling the brim of his hat lower, he nodded, then left the rooming house.

Angelina was washing the parlor window when she saw Kit ride into the yard. Just the sight of him kicked her heart into a faster cadence. She longed to run outside and throw herself into his arms, but thought better of the idea. Until she could gauge his mood, she would display none of the love filling her heart.

Kit unsaddled Sid and turned the gelding loose in the corral, then picked up his saddlebags and left the barn. Now that he'd acknowledged his love for Angelina, he was torn between wanting to run to the house and walking across the yard as slowly as possible. He settled for a pace somewhere in between.

He entered the house through the side door, relieved to find no one in the kitchen. Removing his hat and hanging it on its usual peg, he turned toward the parlor, then pulled up short. Angelina stood in the archway, hands tucked in the pockets of her apron.

Clearing his throat, he finally managed a mumbled hello. When she didn't offer to step out of his way, he said, "Is there a problem?"

"No. I just wondered how things went in El Paso."

"I talked to Jenna and Lin-Shee. By the way, they said to tell you hello and that they're thinking about Sarah. I also went to see the marshal and he told me about another woman who talked to him about the El Paso Bank's practices after her husband died. When I had a talk with Mrs. Wagoner, who's now working for James Murray, the story she told me is almost an exact copy of what happened to your family."

"Mr. Wentworth claimed her husband had taken out a loan at his bank?"

"Yeah. And when she said she couldn't repay the money, he came up with the idea of her going to work for Murray. I wonder how many other women the sorry son-of-a-bitch has pulled that trick on? I longed to ask him when I went to his office, but I kept quiet."

"You went to see Elliot Wentworth?" Her eyes went wide and the color drained from her face.

"Sure did. It's like they say, if you want the truth, get it straight from the horse's mouth—though in Wentworth's case, the mouth isn't the part of a horse I would liken him to. Anyway, I decided I'd go see him under the pretense of wanting to borrow money to buy more land, a reasonable request to make of a banker. And I figured my visiting his office would throw him off the scent. If he thought I had any suspicions about his business practices, he wouldn't expect me to approach him personally."

"How did he react when you told him your name? What did he say?" She took a step closer. "Do you think he believed you?"

The floral scent of the soap she favored drifted up to his nose, causing his pulse to quicken, his blood to warm. Forcing himself not to move, he swallowed, then said, "There's no doubt he was surprised. But I think I convinced him I wanted to buy more land with a loan from his bank. As to whether he really believed me . . ." He shrugged. "Well if he didn't, he's damn good at putting on a convincing front."

"Yes, he's very good," she murmured. "So what happens now?"

"I'm doing some checking on one of Wentworth's employees and Jenna and Lin-Shee are helping me try to find Mavis Johnson. For now, there's not much I can do except wait."

Nodding, Angelina moved past her husband. "Are you hungry?"

Kit wanted to haul her into his arms and whisper, "Yes, for you." But somehow he managed to keep the words locked inside. Realizing she was waiting for an answer, he said, "No, I had a late breakfast. I'm gonna put my things away, then ride up to check on the cattle."

After he stashed his saddlebags in their bedroom, he returned to the kitchen. He stepped around Angelina, careful not to touch her, and grabbed his hat from the peg. "Did Jared come by while I was gone?"

"Yes, he rode over every morning and sometimes in the evening, too." Thinking about her sister and Jared and the love blooming between them, Angelina's mouth curved into a wide smile.

"Is something funny?"

The smile vanished. "No, I was just thinking about how it must feel to have someone. . . . Never mind, it doesn't matter." Snapping out of her momentary lapse, she said, "I have to finish the parlor window. Will you be home in time for supper?"

"Yeah."

When he didn't offer to kiss her, Angelina swallowed her disappointment and headed back into the parlor. She had hoped his sudden reticence toward her before he'd gone into town would disappear by the time he returned. Realizing she had wasted her time hoping, she attacked the rest of her household chores with a vigor spawned by frustration.

There had to be a way to get Kit to love her. There just had to be.

Chapter Twenty-Two

Over the next five days Angelina's frustration with her husband continued to grow. He insisted on maintaining his distance, careful not to touch her whenever they ended up close to each other and allowing their lips to meet in only the briefest of kisses. He now permitted the latter because she'd swallowed her pride and practically pinned him to the wall with a good-bye kiss several mornings after his return. She wouldn't have taken such a drastic step if he hadn't persisted in leaving the house or falling asleep without so much as a peck on the cheek.

Something had happened during his trip to town, something that made him act as if their previous intimacy had never existed. But he'd offered no explanation for the change. Thrown off kilter by his behavior, Angelina had yet to give him the shirt she'd sewn during his absence for fear of a less-than-charitable reaction.

Watching him ride away from the ranch, she decided it was time to gulp down another dose of pride. Whatever demons Kit was fighting, she was determined to slay each one. Whatever the reason for his putting up the wall between them, she was determined to knock down the barricade. If she didn't, the survival of her love and their future together would be in serious jeopardy. She straightened her shoulders, ready to take the first step in the arduous assignment she'd given herself.

She packed a basket of food, carefully wrapped the shirt she'd made for Kit in brown paper, then went looking for her sister. She found Chloe in the barn, sitting on the straw-covered floor and holding a bedraggled light-colored cat.

"Don't tell me, another stray?" Angelina said.

Chloe looked up from the cat curled in her lap. "Yes, isn't she a beauty? I've named her Selene."

"Beauty? Looks like she hasn't had a decent meal in days."

"Maybe she is a little on the thin side. But I'll have her fat and sleek in no time."

"I'm sure you will." Angelina smiled, then said, "So which god is Selene?"

"The goddess of the moon." Chloe stroked the cat's head. "Doesn't the silvery-white of her hair remind you of the moon?"

"I guess," Angelina replied. "I have a favor to ask. Will you stay in the house with Mama until I get back?"

Chloe smiled as Selene's blue eyes closed to mere slits, a loud purr rumbling in the feline chest. "Where are y'all going?"

Shifting her gaze to the rear of the barn, Angelina stared out the window toward the foothills. In a low voice, she said, "If the mountain won't come to Muhammad . . ."

"What are you talking about?"

"Nothing." She walked over to Belle's stall. "I'm taking a basket of food up to Kit in the pasture. I . . . I don't know when I'll be back." She slipped a bridle on the mare, then reached for the saddle blanket.

Chloe flashed her sister a smile. "Ah, a picnic. How romantic."

"I hope so," Angelina mumbled under her breath, lifting the saddle onto Belle's back then tightening the girth.

"Don't worry, Angelina," Chloe replied, picking up Selene then getting to her feet. "I'll stay with Mama, so take as much time as y'all want."

"Thanks. I just have to change into my riding skirt, then I'll be ready to leave." She led Belle out of the stall and toward the barn door.

"I'll go back to the house with you. I want to introduce Selene to Eros and Nyx, then get her something to eat."

A few minutes later, Angelina had kissed her mother good-bye, tucked the present for Kit in one of the saddlebags, tied a blanket and the basket of food behind the saddle, and swung onto Belle's back. Waving at Chloe, she turned the mare toward the foothills, then urged her into a trot.

Kit thought he heard the approach of a horse, but discounted the sound as his imagination. There was nothing but a couple hundred head of cattle, Sid, and him on that part of the Diamond C. Then another metallic ring of a shod hoof on rock convinced him he wasn't imagining things. His privacy was about to be invaded.

Rising from where he'd been sitting in front of a thicket of catclaw, he adjusted his hat brim to shade his eyes from the sun's glare and watched a horse approach.

"Damnit," he groaned. Not only were his thoughts filled with Angelina, but now he would have to suffer through having her nearby, inhaling her intoxicating scent, fighting his desire until he could get her to leave.

Angelina pulled Belle to a halt a few feet from where Kit stood with legs spread, arms crossed over his chest. She swallowed the sudden spurt of apprehension his forbidding stance caused and dismounted.

"What the hell are you doing up here?"

Though she longed to box his ears, she managed a bright smile. "Since it's such a nice day, I thought we could have a picnic."

"A picnic?" A muscle ticked in his cheek. *Great! Just what I need, a goddamn picnic with the woman I can't afford to have around. All it'll take is one slip of my control and I'll be all over her like stink on a fresh pile of horse manure.* Uncrossing his arms, he rubbed a hand over his face, then blew out a resigned breath. He'd just have to make sure his control didn't slip.

"Where do you want the blanket?" he said, moving to Belle and untying the rolled blanket from behind the cantle with jerky motions.

Angelina looked around, finally selecting a relatively flat

patch of ground with no cactus and only a few rocks. Kicking the stones out of the way, she turned to help Kit. The blanket still clutched in his hands, he stood several yards away, staring at the western sky.

"What is it?" she said, following his gaze to the fast-moving dark clouds. A gust of wind swirled up the foothills, rattling the bare branches of the mesquite trees dotting the hillside.

"Looks like we're in for a storm. And a real rip-roarer from the way those thunderheads are moving." Throwing the blanket over his shoulder, he turned to Angelina. "There's a cave farther up the arroyo. We should be able to make it there before the storm breaks. Get back on Belle, then follow me."

He strode over to where he'd tied Sid to the catclaw, jerked the reins free, then swung into the saddle. Making sure Angelina was behind him, he directed the gelding deeper into the foothills.

The wind picked up even more, sending clouds of dust and dried leaves swirling over the rocky ground. Lightning streaked the sky and thunder rumbled in the distance by the time Kit stopped at the mouth of a cave cut into the rock.

He dismounted and turned to watch Angelina swing from her saddle. "The cave is big enough for both of us and the horses. I'll go first. You follow with Belle."

At her nod, he led them to one side of the wide though fairly shallow cave where they left the horses. He had just spread the blanket for Angelina on the opposite side of the cave when the first wave of rain cut loose.

While she removed the food from the basket and arranged it on the blanket, he moved to the mouth of the cave. His mouth drawn into a frown, he leaned against the stone wall, thumbs hooked in his gun belt.

Angelina glanced over at where her husband stood watching the downpour in brooding silence. "Everything's ready, Kit."

He didn't move for a moment, then she saw his shoulders lift then lower as if he had to steel himself to turn and face her. Forcing herself not to give in to self-pity, she managed to keep her voice light. "I brought cold chicken, cheese, deviled eggs, a jar of lemonade, and apple fritters."

"Great," he said, moving to the blanket and lowering himself onto the opposite side.

Angelina filled two plates, then opened the glass jar and poured lemonade into a pair of tin cups. Handing a plate and cup to Kit, she tried to calm her racing heart. She had no trouble deciphering his stiff posture, forbidding demeanor, and curt tone. She knew he'd rather be anywhere but in that cave with only her for company, but she was determined not to let his lack of interest derail her plans.

When Kit reached for the piece of chicken on his plate, she stared at the chicken leg on hers. There was no way she could choke down the meat; her already nervous stomach would never tolerate it. Finally she picked up a piece of cheese.

Kit managed to finish the chicken, then pushed his plate aside. There was no point in pretending he was hungry for food when Angelina sat just a few feet away. And seeing how she took tiny nibbles of cheese while the rest of her plate went untouched, he knew she had no appetite either. Coming to the cave wasn't a good idea. He should have insisted they head back to the ranch house, even though they could never have made it before the storm hit. Still, getting soaked to the skin would have been preferable to the tension in the cave.

He tried to keep his gaze focused outside the entrance to the cave, yet he was acutely aware of every move his wife made. Out of the corner of his eye, he saw her lift the cup of lemonade to her mouth, the soft skin of her throat work with her swallow, the way she dabbed her lips with a linen napkin.

"Are you finished?"

Her question jerked him from his musings. "Yeah. Sorry, guess I wasn't very hungry." He shifted positions, sitting with his back against the wall of the cave, his legs stretched out in front of him.

"Neither was I," she replied, cleaning off the plates and placing everything back inside the basket. When she turned from her task, she found him staring at her, the blue of his eyes darkened by the unmistakable heat of desire.

Her heart going into a wild rhythm, she scooted closer to the center of the blanket. Making a show of tucking the fabric of her skirt around her legs, she hoped to slow the heavy pounding of her pulse. She kept her gaze lowered, silently willing him to make the first move. *Come on, Kit, touch me. Just touch me so I'll know you still want me.*

When a few minutes passed and Kit made no offer to follow her unspoken pleading, Angelina knew she had to be the one to make the first move. Another few minutes passed while she summoned the courage to force his hand. She would get him to give in to the desire burning in his gaze, or make him tell her why he no longer wanted an intimate relationship. Though the former was infinitely preferable to the latter, one way or the other she intended to know the truth.

She drew a slow, steadying breath, then pulled her skirt out from under her legs and rose to her knees.

Hearing the rustling of fabric, Kit turned toward Angelina. His eyes widened at the look on her face—a look he had no trouble interpreting. Though he knew he should move, he found his muscles frozen in place.

"Angelina, I don't think this is a good idea. It's cold and damp in here, and there's only the one blanket. You wouldn't be very—"

"Shh. I don't want to hear your excuses," she whispered, moving closer until her mouth was just inches from his. "Tell me you don't want me and I'll stop."

"Not want you? Hell, I could never not want you, honey. But I still don't think we—"

This time her kiss halted his words. Though his breathing quickened at the first brush of her lips, he staunchly kept his hands at his sides.

She leaned closer. The tip of one breast grazed his chest. Even with the fabric separating their bodies, Kit felt the hardness of her tightened nipple. He drew in a deep breath and

caught the musky scent of her desire. She was ready for him.
With that one tantalizing thought his control shattered.

Groaning, he brought his hands up and grasped her waist.
In one easy motion, he lifted her off the blanket and settled her
on his lap. He moved one hand to hold her face, while he deepened their kiss. His lips explored hers, gently at first, then more
insistently until she opened her mouth. He plunged his tongue
inside, testing and teasing until she wiggled restlessly in his
arms.

Wrenching her mouth from his, she whispered, "Can we lie
down now?" Her voice was breathless, her cheeks rosy with her
desire.

Kit tried to hide his amusement, but couldn't stop a chuckle
from escaping. "You wouldn't be a tad anxious, would you?"

"Yes," she replied, reaching for the front of his shirt. "It's
been so long." Though her fingers trembled, she managed to
free all the buttons. Pushing the fabric aside, she ran her hands
over his bare chest. "I love touching you," she murmured, a
deep sigh accompanying her words.

"Jesus." No longer amused, but burning with the need to take
what she blatantly offered, he said, "Am I to assume you've
thought of *everything* regarding this picnic?"

She looked up at him, her eyebrows pulled together. "I don't
know—" Her confused expression suddenly cleared. "Oh, that!
You needn't worry. I'm safe."

Exhaling the breath he'd been holding until he knew if Angelina had remembered to use her protection, Kit slid her off
his lap onto the blanket. "Let me help you undress."

In a few minutes, Kit had her out of her clothes and managed to take off his own. Seeing the gooseflesh on her naked
body, he stretched out on his side next to her. "I shouldn't have
stripped you down to the skin. You'll catch a chill."

"No, I won't. You'll keep me warm," she said, wrapping one
arm behind his neck and pulling him down so his body nearly
covered hers.

After a long, thorough kiss, she whispered, "See. It's warmer
in here already."

He smiled against her lips. "Actually, it's getting downright hot in here."

"Umm," she replied, lowering her head and running her tongue across his collarbone. "One part of you is definitely hot." She lifted her hips off the blanket to press her belly more fully against his arousal.

Grasping a handful of her hair, he held her head still as he captured her mouth in another blazing kiss. Demanding and unrelenting, his lips plundered hers. With his free hand, he ran his fingers down her neck and over the crest of one breast, pausing to give the distended nipple a gentle squeeze.

She moaned, squirming impatiently beside him, one hand flexing in the hair on his chest. "Easy, honey. Don't you want to make this last?"

"No," she snapped, though the heat in her voice had nothing to do with anger.

Kit chuckled, bending to take the tip of one breast into his mouth. She inhaled sharply, arching her back to allow him better access. He suckled her for a moment before releasing the hardened nipple. Rising up onto one forearm, he smiled down at her. "Okay, you win. I'll see you find relief quickly, my impatient wife. But then I'm going to slow the pace. Before you reach your peak a second time, we'll take it nice and easy. Deal?"

Angelina looked up at him with wide eyes. Not only was he planning on making love to her, but unless her mind had been clouded by the desire pounding in her veins, he said she would experience her release more than once. Just the thought sent a shiver of excitement across her skin.

"Do we have a deal?" he whispered.

"Yes," she managed to say, then dug her nails into his arm. "Just hurry. Please."

Shaking his head, he smiled. "That bad, huh?" Not waiting for a response, he lowered his head for another kiss while moving his hand over her sleek belly to rest his palm on the mound of soft curls. He could feel the pounding of her pulse beneath his hand, the heat of her on his fingers. She lifted her hips in silent entreaty, making a sound of frustration in her throat when he didn't touch her.

He waited until he ended the kiss before inching his hand lower. Parting her damp folds, he kept his gaze riveted on her face, watching her features glow with ecstasy as his fingers found and rubbed the swollen nubbin of flesh.

Angelina could have sworn she was on fire. Kit's touch had ignited a firestorm in her body, the hottest flame raging out of control between her thighs. She lifted her hips in rhythm to the stroking of his fingers, her breathing changed to harsh pants, and the throbbing tension continued to build.

As the pressure reached the summit, her breath caught in her throat. She went utterly still for a heartbeat. Then sobbing Kit's name, she pushed against his hand harder and faster. As wave after wave of incredible spasms washed over her, the tenseness seeped from her body, until she collapsed in replete exhaustion.

From his first intimate touch, Kit never took his gaze from her face. He'd watched in fascination as he guided her to her peak. And just as he'd told her before, knowing he'd given her pleasure was as satisfying as if he'd experienced his own release. Though he still found the change in his attitude astonishing, he also accepted the transformation as absolute truth.

"Was that quick enough?" he murmured, bending to press a kiss to her mouth.

"Perfect," she replied, offering him a dazzling smile.

"I'm flattered." He returned her smile. "Ready to try it my way?"

"Yes, only I'm not sure I'll be able to . . . um . . . reach such perfection again."

"I think you can." Seeing the doubt on her face, he said, "Shall I prove it to you?"

At her nod, he shifted to kneel between her thighs. He pushed her legs farther apart, then traced the exposed petals of flesh with his fingertips.

She flinched at the contact, not from pain but the unbelievable jolt of desire his touch caused. He flashed her a smile, triumph shining in his eyes.

He stroked her one more time, his fingers coming away damp with her essence. "I want to taste you," he said in a harsh whisper, staring at the place his fingers had caressed.

When the meaning of his words sank in, she stiffened. "No," she said, rising onto her elbows and trying to scoot away.

"Yes," he replied, grabbing her legs to keep her from moving. "If you don't like it, I'll stop. Okay?"

After a moment, she gave him a nod and tried to relax her body. Dropping back onto the blanket, she watched in fascination as his dark head lowered to between her spread thighs. When he kissed her most intimate spot, she inhaled sharply. But the incredible sensation of his kiss was nothing compared to the laving of his tongue over her sensitive flesh. As the heat of a few minutes before returned, hotter and more intense, she cried out. The sound punctured the quiet of the cave, bouncing off the rock walls and momentarily blocking out the splatter of the rain.

He continued licking and nibbling, each touch of his tongue and lips sending her higher and higher on her journey to completion. The throbbing between her thighs intensified, the pressure building until she thought she could stand no more. When he suckled the hard kernel of flesh, she gave another cry. Her feet flat on the blanket, she lifted her hips, grinding her pelvis against him.

Kit grasped her bottom to keep her pressed to his mouth. Alternating the flicking of his tongue with the tugging of his lips on her swollen bud, he heard her gasp, then felt the first of her contractions.

Angelina bucked against him in frantic thrusts, the spasms going on and on, each more intense than the last. Finally with a sob, she pushed one last time, then went limp.

He eased her hips back to the blanket, then settled between her spread thighs. With a single smooth thrust, he entered her still-pulsing body. He gritted his teeth. Taking it nice and easy as he'd told Angelina he would could easily prove to be an impossible task. Encased in her hot center, controlling the urge to find instantaneous relief was in all probability beyond his ability. Still, he was determined to try.

Keeping himself braced above her on his forearms, he began moving in slow strokes. He rocked forward, then pulled back to nearly withdraw. Each thrust took him closer to the brink. And then before he could stop it, he was there, sailing over the edge with a strangled cry. His hips continued pumping until the throbbing of his release slowed, then stopped.

Weak with exhaustion, he pressed a kiss to her ear then collapsed atop her.

Angelina ran her hands up and down his back, savoring the warmth and weight of his body. Turning her head, she caught his earlobe between her teeth. She bit him gently, then soothed the soft skin with her tongue.

He chuckled. "I hope that's not your way of saying you want me again, because I don't think I have the strength."

"No, I was just trying to make sure I had your attention."

He kissed her neck. "Believe me, honey," he murmured, his voice lazy and relaxed, "you definitely have my attention."

"Good." She swallowed, then before she lost her nerve she said, "I love you, Kit."

Chapter Twenty-Three

The silence in the cave was deafening to Angelina. Though she hadn't been certain what Kit's reaction would be to her declaration of love, she hadn't expected him to get up and pull on his clothes without so much as a word.

She sat up, pushing a strand of hair away from her face. He stood just a few feet away from her, yet the distance might as well have been miles. As she reached for her drawers and camisole, his voice startled her.

"The rain's stopped. We can head back as soon as you get dressed."

His casual tone was just too much. "We're not going anywhere until we talk."

He swung around to face her, his expression shuttered. "There's nothing to talk about."

"Yes, there is. I just told you I love you and you're acting like I never opened my mouth."

"Look, Angelina, I don't want to get into this with you. So just put—"

"We *are* going to get into this, damnit," she said, her cheeks burning with a flare of temper. "I love you, Kit Dancer. Nothing you can say will change that. And what's more, I think you love me, too."

When he remained silent, she said, "You love me, don't you?"

"All right," he replied, his voice rising to a near-shout. "I love you, but that doesn't change anything."

"What do you mean it doesn't change anything?"

"You know as well as I do that our marriage was never meant to be permanent. We got married to get you out of your contract. We agreed to stay married for the required time. That's it. Period."

"No, that's not it. When we got married, we didn't love each other."

"That doesn't matter. Our marriage is still temporary. As soon as I find enough evidence to have Wentworth arrested or twelve months pass, I'll be leaving."

"But—"

"There's nothing more to discuss. Now get dressed."

Angelina stared up at him, shocked and hurt by what he'd just told her. He loved her, but that didn't change anything. He still planned to leave.

Swallowing the threatening tears, she reached for the rest of her clothes then got to her feet and finished dressing. As she carried the basket over to Belle, she remembered the shirt she'd labored over. She secured the basket to the saddle, then flipped open the saddlebag and withdrew the package.

She gazed at the brown paper for a long moment, then turned on her heel and headed back to where Kit was folding the blanket.

"Here," she said, shoving the package against his chest. "I made this for you while you were in El Paso. I had hoped to give it to you during a happier moment, but . . ." She drew a shuddering breath. "But, apparently there won't be one."

Before he could respond, she said, "If you don't want it, burn it or throw it away. I don't care what you do." With that, she turned and stalked away.

The blanket dangling from one hand, the package Angelina had thrust at him clutched in the other, he stared at his wife's stiff back. He closed his eyes. *Christ! Will life ever get any easier?*

Opening his eyes, he draped the blanket over one shoulder and unfolded the brown paper. He stared at the blue wool for a long moment, then tentatively touched the soft fabric with the tip of one finger. His heart heavy, he swallowed hard. He already considered himself a first-class louse for the way he'd talked to Angelina, and now her thoughtfulness made his dwindling self-respect sink even lower.

Glancing over at Angelina, Kit wished he could find the words to explain, but he was so mixed up inside. Nothing was like it used to be, when he had no trouble knowing exactly what he felt, exactly what to say and do. He drew a deep breath, then slowly exhaled. Rewrapping the shirt and moving across the cave to his horse, he knew he had to try to find the words.

"Angelina, I'd like to explain."

She turned a cool glare in his direction. "Unless you're going to tell me you want to stay married, then I don't want to hear it."

"I can't tell you that, but I still—"

"I said," her voice rose sharply, "I don't want to hear it." Grabbing Belle's reins, she moved to the mouth of the cave, the mare following behind her.

Kit stared after her, a terrible pain wrenching his insides. He'd done the unforgivable. He allowed himself to fall in love with Angelina when his heart already belonged to another. He had never meant to hurt Angelina, yet through his reckless words and actions he'd done exactly that.

The ride home was accomplished in silence, for which Angelina was grateful. If Kit had insisted on saying whatever he'd tried to say in the cave, she would surely have lost what remained of her control. And she had no intention of crying in front of him. Since he thought so little of their love, she refused to let him see how much she'd been hurt by his words. Sitting rigidly atop Belle and staring straight ahead, she held her pain inside, her brain too numb to think about her future. When the ache subsided she'd decide what she should do, but not when the wound was still fresh.

The following afternoon, Kit headed over to Jared's ranch. He wasn't sure if choosing the Rocking M as his destination was a wise decision, nor what he would say when he got there. But with Blaine nearly four hundred miles away, Kit's need for male companionship had led him to another man he now counted as a friend.

Jared came out of the large horse barn at Kit's approach. He watched his neighbor dismount then loop his gelding's reins over the top rail of the corral fence.

"Didn't expect to see you on such a blustery day," Jared called from the barn door. "With the temperature taking a nose dive after the storm that blew through yesterday, I figured most folks would stick close to home."

Kit pulled the collar of his jacket tighter around his neck, thinking the temperature inside the Diamond C ranch house wasn't much different than outside. Saying Angelina had been cool toward him since their exchange at the cave was like saying the size of Texas was fair to middling.

Turning toward Jared, he managed a smile. "Guess I'm not like most folks. I was just checking on the cattle and decided to ride over."

Jared nodded, seeing the tightness in Kit's expression but making no comment. "Well, come on up to the house. A swallow or two of whiskey should go a long way in warming up your blood."

Once Kit sat down in Jared's parlor and took several healthy gulps of whiskey, the tension of the past twenty-four hours began seeping from his body. Dropping his head against the back of the chair, he stretched his legs out in front of him. "How're Abby and her filly?"

"Doing just fine. Fortune's gonna be as fine a horse as her

mama, thanks to your sister-in-law. I would've lost both Abby and Fortune if it hadn't been for Chloe."

Kit nodded, then after a long pause he said, "Jared, I have another favor to ask. I'll be leaving soon and I'd like you to promise you'll take care of Sarah, Angelina, and Chloe."

"How long you figure to be gone this time?"

"I'll be leaving permanently."

"Permanently? I don't understand. You and Angelina are married."

"Yeah, we're married. For now." After another long pause, he said, "You ever been in love, Jared?"

Jared chuckled. "Yup. In fact, I'm pretty smitten right now."

Kit smiled. "Figured as much." He took another swallow of whiskey, then stared into the amber liquid in his glass.

"What about you? You ever been struck with Cupid's arrow?"

"Yeah."

"You don't sound very happy about it."

Kit lifted his gaze to the man sitting in a chair opposite him. "That's 'cause I should never have allowed myself to fall in love with Angelina."

"I don't follow you. What's so bad about loving Angelina?"

"I was married before, to a woman I'd known since we were practically kids. When she and our son were killed five years ago, I swore no one would ever take her place."

"And now you're feeling guilty because you fell in love with Angelina?"

"I should feel guilty. Don't you see, by loving Angelina I'm betraying Bethany and the love we shared."

"I think you're wrong, Kit. You're not betraying your first wife."

"You don't know anything about it," Kit said with more heat than he intended. "Unless you've lost the woman you loved and the child you helped create, you don't have one damn idea what it's like."

"No, I haven't lost a wife and child. But I know there are different kinds of love. There's the love we have for those we've lost—the kind that's soft and gentle, you know, like a cherished memory. And then there's the love we have for the living—a more powerful, wild, feverish kind of love. Do you follow what I'm saying?"

"I'm not sure," Kit replied.

"Let me ask you something. You say you love both Angelina and Bethany, your first wife?"

Kit nodded.

"And, you'll never stop loving Bethany, right?"

Kit nodded a second time.

"Then I don't see the problem. Loving Angelina hasn't changed how you feel about your first wife. I'm sure Bethany would want you to get on with your life. Finding someone else to love doesn't mean you're supposed to forget the past, and it sure doesn't mean you're betraying her."

Kit lifted his glass and swallowed the contents in one fiery gulp. He mulled over Jared's words for a few minutes, then said, "You remind me a lot of a friend of mine, Bethany's brother. If he were here, he'd probably tell me pretty much the same thing."

Kit straightened in his chair, then got to his feet. "Thanks for the whiskey and the talk."

Jared rose, too. "Any time, Kit."

"Listen, I'd like your promise to look after the women. It could be a few weeks or a few months, but whenever I leave, I'll feel better knowing you're looking out for them."

"You still figuring on leaving?"

"Yeah. Even if what you said is true, Angelina deserves— that doesn't matter now. Anyway, I'm still planning on moving on. I'd appreciate your not mentioning our conversation to Chloe or Angelina."

"All right, if you think that's best."

"Yeah, I do."

"Then, you have my word," Jared replied, offering his hand.

After shaking hands, Kit said, "Well, I'd best get back to the Diamond C."

"Give Angelina and Sarah my best, and tell Chloe I'll be over to see her on my way home from town tomorrow evening."

"I'll do that." Handing Jared his glass, he headed for the front door where he picked up his hat and jacket.

Settling the hat on his head, Kit turned back. "You planning on asking Chloe to marry you?"

"I was gonna ask her on Christmas Eve. But seeing how that's a whole month away, I don't know if I can wait that long to find out what her answer will be."

Kit smiled, shrugging into his jacket. "I wouldn't worry about Chloe saying yes. Your time would be better spent making sure the barn is in tip-top shape. You know how finicky she is about where her animals are kept."

Still stunned by Kit's announcement, Jared managed a chuckle. "You're right about that. Guess I'd best do a bang-up job of mucking out the horse stalls before I ask for her hand."

"Good idea," Kit replied, then opened the door and left the house.

While Kit gave Sid a rubdown after the ride home from Jared's place, he heard the barn door open.

"Kit, are you in here?"

His pulse speeded up at Angelina's voice. "In Sid's stall," he replied.

He heard her approach the stall at the back of the barn, but didn't turn from his work. He kept moving the curry comb in steady strokes across the gelding's black and white hide, though his mind was focused on the woman now standing less than six feet away.

"Kit, I'd like to talk to you for a minute."

Her soft voice sent a ripple of pleasure up his spine. Clearing his throat, he said, "Fine."

"I . . . um . . . I'd like for us to call a truce."

"A truce?"

"Yes. Just because we don't agree about . . . well . . . certain things, that doesn't mean we can't get past what happened yesterday. I think it would be best for everyone if we made an effort to get along."

Kit's hand stilled on Sid's withers. He looked over his shoulder at his wife. She looked pale, the dark smudges beneath her eyes a stark contrast to the rest of her face. Even her hand looked unusually pale against the dark green of her woolen shawl. "Really?" He tilted his head to one side, lifting his eyebrows. "And who is everyone, Angelina?"

"I don't want to upset Mama. Our being at each other's throats is sure to distress her, and I don't want to take any chances with her fragile health." She pulled her shawl more tightly around her shoulders. "I'd like us to go back to pretending we like being married."

Kit wanted to say there was no need to pretend, but he held the words inside. Instead, he drew a deep breath, then blew it out slowly. "Okay, for Sarah's sake, I reckon I can go along with what you're asking."

She gave him a genuine smile, the first one since their ill-fated picnic the day before. "Thank you," she murmured, before turning to walk away.

"Wait," he said, "I'll go with you. Just let me give Sid some feed."

Walking back to the house a few minutes later, Kit's arm draped over her shoulder, Angelina let herself pretend they weren't acting. For just a moment, she allowed herself to imagine what it would be like to have Kit beside her for the rest of her life. Then with a sigh, she pushed the dream back into its hiding place deep inside her heart.

Two days later just as the weak winter sun was beginning to slip from the sky, Jared arrived at the ranch. Jumping down off his wagon, he hurried over to the porch and knocked on the door.

Hoping Chloe would be the one to answer his knock, he was disappointed when he saw Angelina behind the opened door.

Jared pulled his hat from his head. "Evening, Angelina. I need to speak with Kit."

Stepping away from the door, she said, "Come on in. Kit's getting cleaned up for supper. Would you like to join us?"

"No, I don't want to impose again. You feed me enough as it is."

"Don't be silly," she replied taking his sheepskin-lined jacket. "You're always welcome here. And besides, I made one of your favorites. Beef stew and biscuits."

Jared smiled. "I'm mighty tempted, but I really can't stay more than a few minutes." He lowered his voice to add, "Any chance you can teach your sister to cook as well as you?"

Angelina chuckled. "I've been trying, Jared, but being a good cook just doesn't interest her. I'm afraid I can't promise you won't get a bellyache or two from her cooking after you two get married."

"Did Kit tell you I plan to ask her to marry me?" he said in a hushed voice.

"No, I just took it for granted. Since you two spend so much time together, I figured getting married would be the next step. Listen, I won't say anything to Chloe."

"Thanks, and don't fret none about her cooking. I'm willing to take my chances."

"It's a good thing, because I'm about ready to give up on teaching her. I'll fetch Kit."

Jared moved across the room to warm himself in front of the fire while Angelina went into the kitchen.

"Kit, Jared stopped by to see you. He's waiting in the parlor."

Seeing the expectant look on Chloe's face, Angelina added, "I already asked him to stay for supper, but he said he couldn't."

Kit laid the towel next to the sink, then moved toward the parlor. "I'll be back in a minute. Go ahead and start eating without me."

He returned to the kitchen a few minutes later. "Chloe, Jared would like to say hello before he leaves."

After his sister-in-law hurried from the room, Kit took his seat at the table. As Angelina ladled stew onto his plate, he said, "Jared brought a message from Jenna."

Angelina's gaze snapped to his face. "What did she say?"

"She found Mavis Johnson. The woman took sick about a month after she started working for Murray, and she just recovered enough to go back to her job this week."

Passing the plate of biscuits, Angelina said, "What are you going to do?"

Kit took two biscuits then reached for the crock of butter. "I'll go into town to talk to her."

"Will you have to stay very long?"

"No, probably not. Until I hear something from the bank back East, I—Would you like to go with me?" When she didn't respond right away, he added, "We can make the trip in one day." He didn't want to give her the wrong impression about his invitation. Since agreeing to call a truce, they'd slipped back into their former relationship with one exception. They hadn't resumed their previous intimacy.

"Are you sure you wouldn't mind if I went along?"

"Of course not. I'd be happy to have the company."

"Well, I really should get Mama another bottle of her medicine. We could use flour and coffee, and the chicken feed is getting low. But that would mean taking the wagon."

"If we leave at first light, we can still be back before dark."

Angelina broke open a biscuit and spread butter on each half. Finally, she said, "Okay, I'll go."

After supper that evening, Kit went in to see Sarah. He hadn't broken his promise to Angelina not to talk to her mother about his checking into Elliot Wentworth's business practices, but he really needed to see if she recalled anything that might prove useful to his investigation. When he mentioned his intentions to Angelina, she was still against his broaching the subject with her mother. But when he agreed to end the conversation at the first sign of Sarah's getting upset, Angelina gave in.

"Evening, Sarah," he said, pulling a chair close to her bed and sitting down.

She looked over at him, her pale lips curving into a smile. "You've changed, Kit."

"How's that?"

"You don't hide the right side of your face anymore. Did you get over that nonsense about your scar?"

He chuckled. "Not entirely, but I'm gettin' better at it, thanks to you and your daughters. You all made me see I was wrong to think no one should have to look at my face."

"Oh, I wouldn't say that. I reckon there are lots of women who'd *like* to look at your face. Not because of your scar, mind you, but because you're a right handsome man."

Kit shifted in his chair, the heat of a rare blush creeping up his neck. Clearing his throat, he said, "Thanks, but I didn't come in here to talk about my looks. I wanted to ask you about the loan Elliot Wentworth said your husband took out at his bank."

"Douglas never took out that loan, I don't care what that jackleg Wentworth says, but there was no way we could prove it."

"How do you know your husband didn't get a loan?"

"Douglas and I were as close as two people could be. He never withheld anything from me, nor I him. There's no way he would have borrowed money and not told me."

"So how do you suppose Wentworth got your husband's signature on the loan papers?"

"Someone else signed his name. It looked like his signature, but I'll go to my grave knowing it wasn't him who signed those papers."

"Then how do you account for Wentworth's claim?"

"The man's lying through his teeth. I think he forged Douglas's signature."

"Or had someone else forge it," Kit said in a low voice.

"That's possible, I reckon. So, tell me, why are you asking me all these questions?"

"Because I've found out about some other women who've been coerced into signing contracts with James Murray to pay off money borrowed from Wentworth's bank—loans none of them knew about until their husbands passed away. And if I can find enough evidence, I intend to see the man arrested for embezzlement."

"Why that lickspittle!" she said, a blush adding a splash of deep rose to her cheeks. "If I could get out of this bed, I'd—" A cough cut off her angry words.

"Haul in your horns, Sarah," Kit said with a smile when her fit of coughing passed. "I'll take care of Wentworth, but I need you to tell me everything you can remember from the time you first arrived in El Paso."

Seeing her struggle to catch her breath, he reached over and placed one hand over hers. "Take your time, Sarah. There's no rush."

Chapter Twenty-Four

Late the next morning, Kit pulled the team of Belgians to a halt in front of the building housing W.A. Irvin & Company on South El Paso Street. Securing the reins around the wagon's brake handle, he turned to Angelina.

"Irvin? Isn't that the name of the doctor who visits your mother?"

"Yes, Dr. Irvin and his brother own the business, and he helps out in the shop when he isn't seeing patients."

Kit nodded, then said, "Are you sure you don't mind if I go see Mrs. Johnson while you're buyin' supplies?"

"Of course not. It'll save time if we go our separate ways to do our errands. When I finish here, I'll go to the grocer a couple of doors down, then come back to the wagon and wait for you."

"I know you usually trade at Mr. Cooper's store over on St. Louis Street. So, if you'd rather do your business with him, we can head over there when I get back."

"Don't be silly. I don't need much, so I'm sure Stuart and McNair will have everything. You go on and talk to Mavis Johnson, I'll be fine."

"I need to check the telegraph office to see if any wires have come in for me. I'll go there first, then head over to Utah Street."

He jumped to the ground, circled around the team of horses,

then helped Angelina from the wagon. Touching her, even in such a non-intimate fashion, made his fingers itch to run through her hair, to caress the silken warmth of her naked body.

"I might be gone more than an hour," he said, his thoughts turning his voice husky. "Are you sure you'll be warm enough."

"The sun's warm today. And besides, I have my shawl in case it turns cool. I'll be fine."

He dropped his hands from her waist, forcing his mind back to the reason for the trip into town. Giving her a smile, he gave in to temptation and brushed his knuckles across her right cheek. "Be back soon."

Angelina nodded, a lump in her throat. If only Kit would open his eyes and view their marriage with less pessimism. Then perhaps he would see they were meant to be together, their love nothing to dismiss. She watched him walk down El Paso Street, the sun glinting off his black silk shirt. Though she knew he'd kept the shirt she'd made for him, he still hadn't worn it, or even taken it out of the dresser drawer as far as she knew. Grateful he hadn't taken her heated words to heart and burned or thrown out the garment, she still feared the time and effort she put into making the shirt might have been wasted.

When he disappeared from sight, she sighed then turned toward the door of the druggist.

In response to Kit's inquiry, an old man mopping the floor of the Shamrock's parlor told him Mavis Johnson was washing glasses in the small kitchen at the rear of the building. Walking through the brothel, Kit noted the place was less gaudy than the Murray House, apparently catering to a less affluent clientele. The place smelled of cigar smoke and cheap whiskey.

He opened the kitchen door and stepped over the threshold.

"I'm washing as fast as I can," the room's lone occupant replied. The woman stood with her back to the door, her arms immersed in a tub of soapy water.

"I'm sure you are, Mrs. Johnson. But I'm not here to check on your work."

Mavis Johnson swiveled around, wash water dripping from her hands and soaking the apron wrapped around her narrow waist. She was petite, probably in her early twenties, with dark brown hair and pale gray eyes. "Who are you, and how do you know my name?"

"I'm Kit Dancer, Mrs. Johnson and I know your name because I did some checking. I came here to ask you a few questions."

"What kind of questions?" The woman pinned him with her narrowed gaze.

"Questions about the El Paso Bank, the manager, Elliot Wentworth, and a loan the bank made to your husband."

Her mouth pulled into a frown. "And what possible reason could you have for wanting to ask questions like that?"

Kit moved closer and lowered his voice. "It's my belief Mr. Wentworth is embezzling money by falsifying loan documents. Your husband did do his banking with the El Paso Bank, didn't he?"

"Yes. He opened an account not long after we moved to El Paso last year." Her gray eyes widened. "You're not saying that man Wentworth had my husband killed, are you?"

"No, I'm not accusing Wentworth of murder. At least, I don't think he'd go that far. My theory is he waits for the untimely passing of one of his customers, then presents the widow with loan papers containing a forged signature of the departed and claims the death of her husband makes the balance due in full. When he receives payment, either by the widow managing to come up with money on her own, or like you, by getting Murray to pay off the bogus loan in exchange for your name on a contract, the money goes directly into Wentworth's pocket."

A dark blush sprang to her cheeks. "Why that low down, good for nothing horse's patoot. If I could get my hands—" Drawing a deep breath, she said, "I knew he was lying when he said my husband had borrowed money from his bank, but I had no way to prove it."

"Tell me about your husband."

"Charles worked as a tailor and hoped to open his own shop someday. But he never planned to take out a loan; he didn't believe in going into debt. Each week he set aside a little of his salary. But we'd only been married a short time and our savings were no way near enough to pay what Mr. Wentworth said I owed after Charles died."

"Did your husband tell Wentworth about his plans to open a tailor shop?"

"I don't know. It's possible, I suppose. Mr. Wentworth found out somehow though, 'cause he told me Charles said he wanted the loan to buy a building for his own business."

"The man is clever, I'll give him that," Kit replied. "He manages to find out just the right information to make the loan sound plausible."

"Yes, and his showing up the day after the funeral, with the appropriate words of sympathy and that pained look on his face when he handed over the loan papers, made his claim that much more believable."

"I'm sure the timing of his arrival is planned in advance. Taking advantage of the family's grief to hit them with a debt while they aren't thinking clearly has to be part of his scheme. A scheme he has successfully pulled a number of times."

"You mean I'm not the only one he's done this to?"

"No, ma'am. My wife was also coerced into signing a contract with James Murray to pay off a loan to Wentworth's bank. And I know of several other women with similar stories."

Mavis's mouth fell open, the color on her cheeks deepening. "Well doesn't that just frost your ballocks."

Kit nearly choked. "Yes, ma'am, it does," he managed to say before allowing a bark of laughter to escape. When he regained his composure, he said, "Can you tell me who signed as witness on the loan document Wentworth showed you?"

"I believe his name was Richmond, or Richland. No wait, it was Richfield. Morris Richfield."

Kit's jaw tightened. Richfield again. He was the witness on both the Coleman and Wagoner loans, as well. The man was looking more and more like a conspirator of Wentworth's, though whether the relationship was entered into willingly or by coercion remained unknown.

"Mrs. Johnson, I hate to interrupt your work, but I'd really like you to tell me the whole story of your dealings with Elliot Wentworth."

"Call me Mavis. And don't worry about interrupting my work. Time will go faster if we talk while I finish these glasses."

Angelina wished Dr. Irvin a good day, then tucked the package containing her mother's medicine into her purse and turned to leave. Back on El Paso Street, she turned north and walked the short distance down the boardwalk to the storefront bearing the sign Stuart and McNair.

Opening the door, she stepped inside, the mixed scents of spices and freshly ground coffee assailing her nose. Smiling at the wonderful combination of smells, she carefully closed the door behind her. Since she'd never shopped at any grocer other than Cooper, Gamble & Company, she spent some time walking up and down the aisles.

After acquainting herself with the store's merchandise, she made her selections and took them to the counter.

She paid for her purchases, smiled her thanks at the clerk, then picked up her package. Pivoting to leave, she took one step then smacked squarely into someone's chest. She tottered backward and might have fallen if not for a pair of male hands grabbing her upper arms.

When she'd regained her balance, she said, "Forgive my clumsiness. I wasn't watching where I was going." She lifted her gaze from the package still clutched in her arms and met a pair of narrowed gray-green eyes. Instantly recognizing the man, she swallowed hard, praying he wouldn't remember her.

The first words out of his mouth crushed her hopes. "Say, ain't you that Angel woman?" His eyes narrowed even more, then widened. "Yup, you're her all right. Don't you know you're not allowed in this part of town, dovey."

Clearing her throat, Angelina said, "You must have me confused with someone else. Now if you'll excuse me." She tried to step around him, but he refused to release her.

"No, I ain't confused. I remember you from the Murray House. You was the pi-anny player before you started working as one of them . . . what did they call their soiled doves? Oh, yeah, lovelies. But it don't matter what they call you over on Utah Street, a whore's still a whore in my book. And on the off chance you ain't heard, there's a city ordinance against whores leaving the tenderloin."

Lowering her voice, Angelina hoped to get rid of him by saying, "Okay, you're right, I used to work at the Murray House. But I don't anymore. I left there a few months ago."

"Don't matter none. Once the taint of a whorehouse gets on your skin, you cain't never wash it off. I'd head back to Utah Street if I was you, dovey, then stay there."

The heat of a flush burning her face, she said, "I can't go anywhere if you don't take your hands off me."

The man tipped his head back and laughed. She was certain her face must have turned scarlet, and tears of humiliation clogged her throat and stung the backs of her eyes. When the man fell silent, she whispered, "Please, just let me leave."

With another laugh, the man dropped his hands, then gave her bottom a swat as she scurried by him. Mortified by his behavior and the sound of his laughter ringing in her ears, she rushed outside, not caring that she closed the door behind her with a resounding bang.

Keeping her head lowered, Angelina hurried down the street. When she arrived at the wagon, she climbed up onto the seat and sat down with a sigh. She should have known better than to come into town. Just because her last visit hadn't resulted in someone recognizing her, she'd begun to think it wouldn't happen. What a fool she'd been to believe the townsfolk would overlook her previous employment.

Her hands curled into fists on her lap, she kept her gaze on the team of draft horses and wished Kit would hurry.

Kit left Mavis Johnson with a promise to keep her informed of his progress finding evidence against Wentworth and started back to where he'd left the wagon and Angelina.

He was extremely pleased with his visit to the Shamrock and his conversation with Mavis Johnson. Too bad his earlier stop at the telegraph office hadn't been as helpful. After learning there had been no reply to his telegram to the bank in Boston, he sent two more: a second wire to the bank and the other to the Boston police.

In spite of his disappointment at not receiving an answer from Richfield's former employer, Kit was satisfied he was making headway in his investigation. If he had more time, he'd pay the bank clerk another visit. But going to the bank during the day, when Wentworth would likely be present, would be a waste of time, and besides, he'd promised Angelina they would get back to the ranch by dark.

As he approached the wagon, he saw Angelina on the seat and quickened his steps. When he noticed her slumped posture, the smile beginning to form on his lips faded.

He hurried the final few yards and approached her side of the wagon. "Angelina?"

He called to her a second time before she moved. When she shifted her gaze from the horses to him, his breath caught in his throat. Her face was very pale, that familiar sadness back in her eyes.

"What is it? Did something happen?"

She ran her tongue over her lips, then said, "Can we leave now?"

"But it's only a little past noon. I was planning on taking you to the Link Restaurant for dinner before we started back. Are you sure you don't want to change your mind?"

"No, I just want to go home."

"Okay, but what about the chicken feed? Should I stop on the way out of town?"

She weighed his words for a moment, then gave him a nod and scooted over to make room for him on the wagon seat.

Climbing up next to her, Kit unwrapped the reins from the brake handle then guided the team down the street. His gut in a knot over what could have happened, he didn't mention it until after he bought a sack of chicken feed and started the trip to the ranch.

A few miles outside of town, he glanced at Angelina and said, "You gonna tell me what happened back there?"

Squaring her shoulders, she shook her head.

"Honey, if you don't tell me what happened, I can't help you."

A few more minutes passed in silence, then she drew a deep shuddering breath. "I was just leaving the grocer. I didn't know there was anyone behind me, and when I turned to leave I ran into another customer, a man. He grabbed my arms to keep me from falling, and then I apologized for my clumsiness. That's when I recognized him."

"From the Murray House?"

"Yes, he was a regular there."

"And, I take it he recognized you, as well."

"He used to hang around the piano, making lewd remarks along with some of his drunk cronies. When I saw him today, I foolishly thought he might not remember me. You know, with me not wearing face paint and him being sober—but he knew who I was."

"So what happened after he recognized you?"

"Nothing happened, exactly. He just said some things and I tried to explain . . . and then . . . then he let go of me and I left the grocer and went back to the wagon."

"What *things* did he say?"

"He . . . um . . . said I was in the wrong part of town. I tried to deny it at first, hoping he'd think he made a mistake, but he didn't fall for it. Then when I told him I no longer worked at the Murray House, he said it doesn't matter, that—" A sob escaped before she could stop it. "That I already had the taint of a whorehouse and I . . ." her voice dropped to a whisper. ". . . can never wash it off."

"Oh, Jesus." Kit pulled back on the reins and directed the team of Belgians onto the side of the road. When the wagon came to a stop, he dropped the reins and reached for Angelina.

Wrapping his arms her, he held her tight. "Don't take what he said seriously."

"But it's true," she replied, her words muffled by his chest and the tears clogging her throat. "I'd forgotten how cruel people can be. Like how Reverend Morton's wife acted like I was a piece of trash. I don't know how I could've been so stupid to think my past would never come up." She drew a shuddering breath. "I'll never be able to go into town again."

"That's not true."

"Yes, it is. If I go to town, there's always the chance I'll run into someone else who recognizes me, or someone who's heard about me."

He rubbed one hand over her back, trying to soothe her suffering. "People move away, others forget. With time, no one will remember, and those that do won't care about your past."

Pushing out of his arms, she looked up into his face. "Yes, they will. I worked in a whorehouse, Kit, that makes me a whore."

"You weren't a whore."

"You thought I was."

"Yes, I admit, when we first met, I thought you were. But I later learned appearances can be deceiving."

"Don't you understand? *I* asked Mr. Murray to let me become one of the lovelies; he didn't approach me about changing jobs. And if things had worked out differently, I would have gone through with it." She dropped her gaze.

"You didn't, though."

"But I fully intended to, so what's the difference? No one in town cares that I didn't take even one man into my bed while I worked at the Murray House. They already see me as a who—"

"Listen to me, Angelina," he said, grasping her arms and giving her a gentle shake. "You went to work in a brothel out of loyalty to your family. While that isn't how most soiled doves end up in that profession, your decision doesn't taint you in any way. And it sure as hell doesn't mean you deserve the harsh treatment that sorry bastard gave you in the grocery today."

When she started to object, he placed a finger on her lips. "Shh. Let me finish. I know you were prepared to sacrifice your body to provide for your mother and sister, but that doesn't make you a bad person, either. Being willing to lose your innocence in a brothel takes a lot more courage than what most folks would do for their families. That includes men as well as women. But we both know you didn't make that sacrifice. And even if you had, your heart and soul would still be pure, and I . . ." he lowered his head and brushed a kiss across her lips. "I would still have fallen in love with you."

Angelina squeezed her eyes closed for a second, sending a tear trickling down each cheek. "Oh, Kit," she said in a quivering voice. "Do you really mean that?"

"Of course I do. Now come here and let me hold you for a few minutes. When you're feeling better, we'll head for the ranch."

Her heart close to bursting with love, Angelina snuggled against the hard muscles of her husband's chest. She sighed, wishing they could stay like that forever.

The growling of Kit's stomach pulled her from the moment of contentment. "I'm sorry I ruined your plans for dinner."

"Don't be," he replied, his chin resting atop her head. "Actually, I don't mind not eating in a restaurant since you're a better cook than any in town. But I suggested we go to the Link for dinner because I wanted you to enjoy a meal you didn't fix."

Straightening, she smiled up at him. "You really are a kind man."

"Me, an ex-bounty hunter?" he said in mock outrage. "Kindness is not a trait that bodes well for anyone chasing after someone with a price on their head."

"That may be," she replied with a trace of a smile. "But

you're definitely kind." Lifting her hands to his face, she held him still while she proceeded to plant a very thorough kiss on his mouth.

When she pulled away a few seconds later, her breathing was as ragged as his, her heart beating in a rhythm to match the wild cadence of his pulse.

Though he longed to find a place to make love to her, Kit managed to curb his desire enough to say, "Shall we go home now?"

She nodded. Home. It was the first time she could remember him calling the ranch home. Once he got the business of Wentworth's illegal dealings over with, would Kit still think of the Diamond C as home, or would he simply forget the place existed and move on as he claimed he would?

Fearing the answer, Angelina refused to let her hopes get too high. If the love she and Kit felt for each other was strong enough to survive, then it would, and her fears would prove groundless. And if their love wasn't strong enough, well, she'd just have to deal with the aftermath when the time came.

Chapter Twenty-Five

The next several days passed in a blur for Angelina. Her
mother's worsening health and Chloe's near giddiness after accepting Jared's marriage proposal kept her from dwelling on
the memory of her recent visit to El Paso. And Kit's attentive-
ness had been equally helpful along those lines. He helped her
with the household chores whenever he could spare the time
from his own work, held her close every night until she fell
asleep in his arms, and not once had he mentioned her experience in town.

Early one afternoon, Angelina entered the kitchen to find
Chloe pouring over a catalogue of dress patterns. "Find something you like?" she said, looking over her sister's shoulder.

"Yes, but I'm not a very good seamstress, so . . ."

"I can help you make your wedding dress."

"Thanks," Chloe said, looking up at her with a wan smile.
"But I'm not sure we'll be able to get married on Christmas Eve
like we planned."

"What do you mean?"

Chloe lowered her voice to a whisper. "Christmas is only a
month away, and you know what the doctor said. When consumption is this far advanced, hemorrhage or exhaustion can
take patients at any time. Mama is failing so fast I'm afraid she
won't last until Christmas."

Angelina squeezed Chloe's shoulder, wishing she could offer
some comforting words about their mother's condition. Finally

she said, "I think we should make you a dress, and if . . . if something happens to Mama, you'll still be able to wear it."

"But what about a period of mourning? I wouldn't be able to marry Jared for a year, and he may not be willing to wait that long."

"Mama would have a fit if you waited a full year after her passing. You know she doesn't hold with that tradition. And besides, I wouldn't worry about Jared. He loves you, so he'd wait as long as necessary. Now come on, show me the pattern you like." Pulling out a chair, she sat down next to her sister.

Kit sat on a stool in a corner of the barn mending a bridle, the fading light from the shortened days necessitating the use of a lantern. Nearly a week had passed since the day he and Angelina had gone into town, and though he'd considered going back to El Paso and talking to Morris Richfield, he hadn't. He tried to convince himself he stayed at the ranch because of Sarah's health, but the truth was, digging up enough evidence to have Wentworth arrested would force Kit to make a final decision about his future—a decision he dreaded making.

The excited bark of Artemis pulled him from his musings. Moving to the barn door, he watched Jared pull his team of horses to a halt in front of the house. By the time Kit put the bridle away, doused the lantern, and stepped through the barn door, Jared had left the house and was halfway across the yard.

"Everything okay, Jared? From the way your horses are lathered, you must have run them all the way from town."

"Actually, I did, but don't tell Chloe. She'd have a conniption." He reached into his jacket pocket and withdrew several envelopes. "I brought these to you. The telegraph operator seemed to think you'd be real anxious to get them. He hightailed it over to the lumber company as soon as they came in this afternoon, hoping to catch me before I left town."

Kit took the envelopes from Jared. "Thanks. I appreciate your bringing them by."

"No problem. When you asked me to check the telegraph office whenever I was in town, I figured you must be waiting for something real important."

"Yeah," Kit replied, turning the envelopes over in his hands. "Yeah, these could be very important."

"Well, I think I'll go back to the house and talk to Chloe. I only had a chance to tell her hello when she came to the door since I wanted to find you right away."

"Thanks again, Jared. I owe you one."

"No need. That's what neighbors are for." He grinned. "And besides, we'll be brothers-in-law soon."

"Right," Kit said, able to summon only a feeble smile.

Jared saw the distracted look on Kit's face and wondered if he was still thinking of leaving. Resisting the urge to ask, he said a hurried good-bye, then headed to the house.

Kit stared after his neighbor for a few seconds, then looked down at the envelopes in his hands. He turned and went back into the barn, took the lantern down from its peg, and relit the wick. Taking a deep breath, he opened the envelopes and withdrew the telegrams. Noting the sender of each, he selected the one from the manager of the Bank of Massachusetts in Boston and held it closer to the lantern.

Sorry for the delay in replying, out of town on business. Morris Richfield worked here for just under ten years, first as a clerk then as my personal assistant. He left the bank's employ in '81 after a discrepancy in a customer's account was discovered. We could not prove he was involved, but since he was responsible for the account in question, we thought it best to terminate his employment.

The second telegram was from the chief of the Boston police.

In response to your inquiry about a Morris Richfield, he was the center of an investigation several years ago regarding the possible forgery of bank drafts on an account at the Bank of Massachusetts. The charges were dropped before the case went before a judge. To

*my knowledge, that one incident was Richfield's only brush with
the law. As I recall, he left town after the case against him was dismissed to take a job in your city working for his brother-in-law. Sorry
but I can't remember the man's name.*

Kit stared at the second telegram, his mouth slowly curving
into a satisfied grin. "No problem, Chief, I already know his
name," he murmured. Tucking the telegrams into his shirt
pocket, he doused the lantern a second time, then headed for
the house.

Finding Angelina in the parlor mending a tear in one of his
shirts, he took a seat in the chair opposite her. "Where are Jared
and Chloe?"

"They went to check on Mama."

He nodded, then said, "I have some business to take care of
in town, so I'll be heading there in a few minutes."

She looked up from her sewing, her brow wrinkled with concern. "Is it about the telegrams Jared brought you?"

"Yeah, there's someone I have to talk to."

"How long will you be gone?"

"I'm hopin' I'll be back by this time tomorrow. Would you
like to go with me?"

She shook her head, her gaze fastened on the shirt in her
hands.

"You can't stay away from town for the rest of your life."

"I know." She sighed, her fingers stilling in their task. "I've
been thinking about what you told me on the ride home from
town last week, and I realized you're right. I know I have to
face the townsfolk who condemned me, show them I'm not the
immoral person they think I am, give them the opportunity to
see I should be forgiven for what I did. But it's . . ." She lifted
her head and met his gaze. "It's just too soon."

The pain in her eyes hit him like a fist in the gut. Kneeling
in front of her chair, he grasped her hands with his. "I understand, honey. When the time is right, you'll go into El Paso with
your head held high and show those sanctimonious bastards
Angelina Dancer is one of the finest women in these parts."

Her lips curved into a wide smile. "With such enthusiastic words of encouragement, how can I fail?"

The brightness of her smile set his heart to pounding hard against his ribs, warming his blood with lightning speed. Leaning closer, his voice dropped to a husky whisper. "There's no way a special woman like you could fail, Angel . . . I mean—"

She pulled one hand free of his grasp and pressed her fingers to his lips. "No, that's okay. You can call me Angel."

Removing her hand from his mouth, he pressed a light kiss on her fingertips. "I thought you didn't like the name because it reminded you of when you were at the Murray House."

"I didn't like it when we first moved to the ranch. But now I don't mind." Seeing one of his eyebrows arch in question, she added, "You just told me I can't stay away from town forever, that I can't run from what I did, and I agree with you. I know I have to not only face my past but also forgive myself. And I also have to deal with how the folks in town will undoubtedly treat me until they can forgive or at least forget what I did. But I know I can do it because I've already come to terms with part of my past, the part where I was the Ice Angel. So if you want to call me Angel, I have no objections."

"Are you sure? I don't want to bring back bad memories."

"You won't. The name conjures up only one memory now. A very special memory of the night I met the man I love."

A lump filling Kit's throat and tears stinging the backs of his eyes, he was shocked by the force of the emotion her words evoked. He swallowed hard, then said, "I . . . uh . . . guess I'd better get a bag packed."

"Can I help?"

"No. No, that's okay. I can do it. I'll be back in a minute."

Before Kit rode away from the Diamond C, he pulled Angelina into his arms for a very long, very deep kiss. He didn't know why he allowed himself to participate in such torturous behavior. He just knew he couldn't leave without tasting the sweetness of her mouth, without feeling her soft curves pulled snug against him.

When he finally released her, he needed all his willpower not to open his mouth and say, "I love you, Angel." But the look on her face as she gazed up at him told him she'd heard the words anyway.

Kit arrived in El Paso just past eight that evening. He rented a room at the Vendome Hotel, then swung back onto Sid's back and went looking for Morris Richfield.

When his wife said he wasn't home, Kit feared she wouldn't volunteer his whereabouts, if in fact she knew them. To his surprise, Mrs. Richfield said her husband was attending a meeting at the Masonic Lodge on the corner of San Antonio and Utah Streets.

Since the lodge was only two blocks from his hotel, Kit stabled Sid then walked the rest of the way on foot. Unwilling to interrupt the Masons' meeting, he waited outside the single-story adobe building.

When the men filed out several hours later, Kit stood in the shadows, never taking his gaze from the door. At last Morris Richfield appeared in the doorway, deep in conversation with another man. The two shook hands, then parted company.

Moving quietly, Kit approached the bank clerk. "Hold on there, Richfield."

The man jumped, then swung around to face Kit, one hand clutched to his chest. "Great heavenly days, you nearly scared me to an early grave. Who are you, and what do you want?"

"The name's Dancer. You should recognize the name, since you opened an account for me a few weeks back."

"Yes, yes, I remember." He jabbed at the nose piece of his glasses. "Why are you looking for me at this time of night, Mr. Dancer?"

"I need to talk to you, in private. Got any suggestions on where we might have that conversation?"

"What . . . what do you want to talk about?"

"Something real important, Morris. Now what about a place for us to have our discussion?"

"We could go to my house. My wife and kids will be in bed by now."

Kit thought about his suggestion for a moment, then said, "Yeah, okay. Lead the way."

Once he'd taken a seat in the small parlor of the Richfield house, Kit refused the man's offer of a drink, then said, "I'd leave the whiskey alone, Richfield. You're gonna need a clear head for that conversation I mentioned earlier."

Ignoring the advice, he downed a double shot, refilled his glass, then turned to face the man dressed in black. "All right, Dancer, what's on your mind?"

"I want to talk to you about Elliot Wentworth's business practices, in particular the loans he extends to his customers."

Running a finger around the inside of his collar, Richfield sank into a chair opposite Kit and said, "I'm only a clerk. I have nothing to do with Mr. Wentworth's decisions on making loans."

"I don't doubt that, Morris." Kit paused for a moment, letting his companion's nervousness build. "You know what I find real strange? I find it strange that so many of the El Paso Bank's customers end up dying a few months after Elliot Wentworth gives them a loan. Don't you find that strange, Morris?"

"There's no way a banker can know which of his customers will die before they pay back a loan. So I . . . I don't know why you're telling me all of this."

"Oh, I think you do, Morris. You might be interested in knowing I've talked to all the recently widowed women in town whose husbands, according to Elliot Wentworth, owed the bank money. And you know what, Morris? Not one of those women believes her husband had taken out a loan without her knowing anything about it. I find that mighty peculiar."

Richfield made a whimpering sound, but otherwise remained silent.

"I also find a couple other things peculiar. Like how you signed as the witness on every one of those loans, and how the customer's signatures looked so much like the genuine article. That last one got me to thinking about who at the bank had access to a customer's records. Do you see where I'm heading with this yet, Morris?"

"I wasn't the only one to have access to the bank customers' records."

"No, but you're the only one who lost a previous job over the suspected forging of a bank draft."

Richfield sucked in a sharp breath, his complexion turning a pasty white.

"How did you find out about that?" he whispered.

"I sent a telegram to the Bank of Massachusetts. The manager was more than happy to supply information about the termination of your employment."

"But I didn't do anything wrong. The man who claimed I took money out of his account was a valued customer of the bank, and I always handled his transactions personally. He came in on a regular basis to withdraw money, but he was getting on in years and sometimes he'd forget to sign the bank draft. When I noticed his oversight, I signed his name the way I'd watched him do a hundred times."

"So, you never took any money from the man's account?"

"No. I swear I didn't. When the bank manager told me I'd been accused of forging the man's name to take money from his account, I couldn't believe it. I tried to explain, but no one would listen."

"I understand the charges were dropped."

Richfield took another swallow of whiskey, then said, "Yes. The man's family realized his declining health could be the reason he made the claims about me, so they decided to drop the charges."

"But you lost your job anyway?"

Richfield nodded. "The bank's board of directors decided I couldn't be trusted and thought it best to let me go even though I hadn't been found guilty of anything."

Kit studied the man's face, now flushed from the liquor. "Is that when you came to El Paso?"

"I couldn't stay in Boston. Word would have gotten out sooner or later about the . . . er . . . problem at my previous job, so none of the other banks in town would have hired me. I don't know what we would have done if I hadn't been offered a job at the El Paso Bank."

"The offer would have come from your brother-in-law, Elliot Wentworth, right?"

Richfield's head snapped up from his contemplation of his whiskey glass. "If Elliot hadn't given me a second chance, my wife and I and our four children would have been thrown out on the street. I could have ended up begging to support my family."

"And what did Wentworth want in exchange for offering you a job?"

"Nothing. He said he was moving here to be the manager of a new bank and wanted to know if I'd like to work for him. He even allowed me to sign a note for enough to buy this house once we arrived in town."

"What happened to make you agree to forge customers' signatures on loan papers for Wentworth?"

Richfield tugged at his shirt collar again. "You have to understand. Things haven't been easy for me since I moved my family to Texas. I now have six children and the youngest is sickly most of the time. Elliot was kind enough to extend the terms on my note, and he even gave me more money to help with the doctor's bills. We couldn't have gotten by without his help."

"I do understand, Morris. You had a rough couple of years. But something happened to convince you to do what Wentworth wanted. Didn't it?"

Richfield lifted his glass, his hand visibly shaking. He downed the last of the whiskey, then blew out his breath in a low sigh. "I'm tired of carrying this inside, so I'll tell you. You're right, something did happen. About a year ago, Elliot told me the bank's owners were pressing him to collect on my note or they would insist he start foreclosure proceedings. I was in a panic until he said he'd come up with a way to help me pay off what I owed."

"I can guess what he wanted you to do, but what did he promise you in return?"

"He said he would use a portion of the money he collected on each fake loan as payment against my note. I knew I'd never be able to pay what I owed on my salary, but I was still reluctant to get involved in something illegal."

"What did he threaten you with if you didn't go along with his scheme?"

"If I didn't forge the loan papers, he planned to ruin me. He said he would take my wife and children into his home and send me packing. I love my wife and children and I couldn't risk having them taken from me."

"And Wentworth knew you couldn't go to the law without implicating yourself," Kit mused aloud.

"Yes. Elliot knew how scared I was over the mess in Boston, so I'm sure my squealing on him was never a consideration."

"Will you go to the marshal and tell him what you just told me?"

"No, and if you tell him anything, I'll deny it."

"You can't go on living a lie, Richfield. Does your wife know what you're doing? Does she know you're running the risk of being arrested and sent to prison?"

The man pushed at his glasses again. "How could I tell her? The man who got me into this is Molly's brother. I wouldn't do anything that might change how she feels about me."

"You couldn't do that, Morris," a soft female voice replied from a shadowed doorway.

Richfield blanched, his knuckles turning white where they gripped his empty glass. "Oh my God, Molly! How long have you been standing there?"

Kit watched as a slightly plump woman, her dark brown hair braided into a single thick plait, moved across the room and took a seat next to her husband.

"I heard most of the conversation between you and Mr. . . . ?"

"Dancer, ma'am."

"Are you with the police?" She clutched her dressing gown closed over her full bosom with one hand.

"No, I'm not the law, but I do have an interest in this. My wife's family was one of Wentworth's victims."

"Oh, dear Lord," Molly murmured. "Morris, you have to help. What Elliot's been doing must stop."

Richfield turned to look at his wife. "Molly, if I tell the marshal what I know, Elliot will be arrested. It could be a long time before you see him again."

"I don't care. I can't stand to think of what he's done, not only to you but to all the other folks he's cheated. I'm ashamed he's my brother."

Richfield fell silent for a moment, then said, "But Molly, lass, if I tell the authorities about Elliot, I'll also have to tell them what I did."

"Surely they'll understand you were forced into helping Elliot." She turned to Kit. "If my husband goes to the marshal and tells everything he knows, can you promise us he won't be arrested?"

"Like I said, I'm not the law around here, so I don't have the authority to promise anything. But if Morris agrees to testify against Wentworth, I would think his cooperation might convince the marshal not to arrest him as an accomplice. You have my word I'll do everything I can to make sure he stays out of jail."

Richfield slumped against the back of the sofa. After a moment, he straightened and said, "I'll testify. Let's go see the marshal right now. I want to get this over with as soon as possible."

"But, it's late, Morris," Molly said. "Are you sure you wouldn't rather wait until morning?"

"No," he replied, getting to his feet. "I want to get this over with. I want to talk to the marshal now, provided Mr. Dancer will go with me."

Rising from the chair, Kit settled his hat on his head. "We may have to shag the marshal out of his bed, but I'm willing to do that."

Richfield planted a firm kiss on his wife's mouth and gave her a fierce hug, then followed Kit from the house.

Chapter Twenty-Six

On the way to find the marshal, Kit asked Richfield if he knew anything about Wentworth's dealings with James Murray.

"Nothing specific," Morris replied. "I'd say they've known each other for close to three years. Elliot likes to play poker, and he spends a lot of time in Murray's gambling hall. But I don't know about any other dealings between them."

"Besides making payments on your note, do you have any idea what Wentworth did with the money from the loans he had you forge?"

Richfield shook his head. "The only thing I can say is Elliot has highfalutin tastes. Everything has to be the best or the most expensive, or he isn't interested. He and my Molly are as different as day and night when it comes to spending money. Molly can stretch a dollar farther than—" He cleared his throat, then said, "Sorry, I got off the track there for a minute. As I was saying, other than Elliot liking high-priced fripperies and his penchant for gambling, I wouldn't hazard a guess on what he does with the money, that is if there is any left to spend."

"Well, his days of living high on the hog are about to come to an end," Kit replied.

"Won't break my heart," Richfield mumbled, pushing his glasses back into place. "He never let Molly forget how she married beneath her."

* * *

Kit slept in late the next morning, having arrived at his hotel room after the visit he and Morris Richfield made to the marshal's office only an hour before daybreak.

He rolled over in bed, wishing Angelina lay curled up next to him, wishing he could reach out and touch her. He pushed those thoughts aside. Soon enough he would have to deal with his wife and his future, but not just yet.

Sitting up and throwing his legs over the side of the bed, he ran a hand over his jaw. A bath and a shave were the first order of the day, then a late breakfast, and another visit to the city marshal. He wanted to be sure Elliot Wentworth was behind bars before he headed back to the Diamond C.

After leaving the marshal's office several hours later, Kit decided to make one more stop before going to the stable where he'd boarded Sid.

Arriving at the clapboard house on Utah Street, he entered the front door and found the interior abuzz with female chatter. When Jenna spotted him from where she stood with the other Murray House employees at the opposite end of the hall, she moved away from the others and approached him.

"What's going on?" he said, nodding to the group of women.

"We just heard Mr. Murray was taken to the city marshal's office early this morning for questioning."

"That right?"

Jenna saw the twinkle in his eyes and gave his arm a playful punch. "Yeah, that's right, and you know all about it, don't you?"

"Well, I wouldn't say I know everything, but I have a pretty fair idea about what's going on."

"So, tell me," she said in a hushed voice. "Did that banker get taken to the marshal's office, too?"

"Yes. Elliot Wentworth was arrested late last night on charges of embezzling money from at least a half-dozen bank customers."

"Is the marshal going to arrest Mr. Murray?"

"There's a real good possibility."

"So where does that leave all of us?" Jenna waved toward the other girls still talking at the other end of the hall.

"I don't know. The only thing I can say for sure is, if any of you signed contracts with Murray to satisfy a faked debt with the El Paso Bank, those contracts will be declared null and void."

"Have you told those other women, Mavis Johnson and Carol Ann Wagoner, about this?"

"No, the marshal was gonna take care of telling them since he had to get their statements. He also planned to tell Stella Robertson about Wentworth's arrest. Maybe that'll get her to open up."

"It sure enough ought to," Jenna replied, then added, "I bet Angelina will be thrilled when she finds out what you did."

Kit shrugged. "Reckon you're right. So what will you do if Murray gets thrown in jail and his businesses close for good?"

"I've got some money saved, so I'll probably stick around town for a while to see what happens. I haven't thought beyond that yet."

"Listen, Jenna, before I go there's something I'd like to say. If you ever decide you want to try something different, you know, to change your life like we talked about before, I hope you'll get word to me. I have a friend in San Angelo who could give you a new start."

Jenna smiled up at him. "I appreciate that, Kit, and I'll keep the offer in mind. You take care of Angelina, hear, and give her my best."

"I'll do that. Good luck, Jenna."

"Same to you. Bye, Kit."

As he started the ride back to the ranch, Kit thought about his offer to Jenna. He hoped she would decide to get out of her line of work. She was so full of life, and she had a wonderful sense of humor—just what the often staid Blaine needed. And his friend was perfect for Jenna as well, generous and equitable. Kit suddenly scowled. When the hell had he become a match-maker?

Kicking Sid into a lope, he pushed his opinion about Jenna and Blaine from his mind, only to find thoughts of Angelina taking their place. Though still loath to do so, he knew the time had come to think about his wife and make plans for his future.

In so many ways, he felt like he'd known Angelina and her family for far longer than just two months. And in just as many ways, he wished he could get to know her even better—a lifetime wouldn't be long enough. He had the Coleman women as well as Jared to thank for making him see he'd been overly sensitive about his looks. He no longer thought of his scar as hideous, unfit for a feminine gaze. While he was still slightly uncomfortable having his face scrutinized by strangers, he no longer went out of his way to avoid such an occurrence.

Regardless of his changed opinion about his scar, he still wasn't the kind of husband Angelina deserved. She deserved a better man than he—a man who could protect his family, not let them be slaughtered by a madman.

In spite of loving Angelina, Kit knew he had only one choice. In a few days, after he was certain the charges against Wentworth would stick, he'd pack his few belongings, swing into his saddle, and head out. Though he knew it was the right decision, having made it didn't improve his spirits. In fact, the hollow feeling in the pit of his stomach and the wrenching ache in his heart worsened his mood.

When Kit arrived at the Diamond C there was a buggy in front of the ranch house. Recognizing the rig and dun mare as that of Reverend Gray, Kit didn't bother taking Sid to the barn. He had barely pulled the gelding to a halt beside the dun when he jumped to the ground and flipped the reins over the porch railing.

His heart pounding with dread, he crossed the porch in two strides, opened the front door, and stepped inside. Spotting his wife sitting in the parlor, her head resting against the back of the sofa and her eyes closed, he started toward her.

"Angelina?"

Angelina's eyes popped open. "Kit! I didn't hear you come in."

"I know. What's going on. Why is Reverend Gray here? It's not Saturday."

"Mama had a real bad spell after you left yesterday, and she asked to see him. I rode over to Jared's to see if he could locate the reverend."

Kit cursed under his breath. More proof he wasn't worthy of the lovely woman sitting before him. History was repeating itself. He hadn't been home when she needed him, just like—

Her voice jarred him back to the present.

"The reverend's been sitting with Mama for about an hour."

"How's Sarah doing?"

"She seems a little better today. At least I think the danger has passed this time."

"Where's Chloe?"

"Lying down. We were both up with Mama all night, so I sent her to bed as soon as Reverend Gray arrived."

"That's where you should be," Kit said, taking a seat next to her on the sofa.

"I'll rest later."

"I don't want you taking sick. You'd be no help to your mother if you're confined to your own bed." He reached over and pulled her into his arms. Using slow easy movements, he rubbed her back and shoulders, gently working the tightness from her muscles.

"Umm, that feels wonderful," she murmured against his chest.

He kissed the top of her head. "Just relax, Angel." He continued massaging her back until she sighed and the stiffness left her body. Holding her close, he loosened the knot of hair at her nape and ran his fingers through the strands of golden-brown silk. She snuggled closer, bringing a smile to his lips.

After just a few minutes, she went limp against him, her breathing slowed to the even pattern of sleep. When Reverend Gray entered the room a short time later, Kit shifted so he could ease Angelina into a prone position on the sofa. Once he was certain he hadn't awakened her, he rose to speak with the minister.

"How is she?" Kit said in a low voice.

"She's asleep." Reverend Gray, a man in his early twenties with wavy light brown hair and a close-cropped beard, tucked his Bible into his coat pocket. "Sarah has been such a strong woman, never complaining for a minute about how she's suffered for so many years. But I think she's ready to let God take her into his care. All she talked about was seeing Douglas and telling him how both their daughters had found such fine men."

Kit swallowed the lump in his throat. "Thank you for coming and sitting with Sarah. You're a big comfort to her."

"That's why I chose working for the Lord, to comfort His flock along with preaching His word."

"Can I get you a cup of coffee, Reverend?" Kit said, then, remembering the man wasn't a teetotaler, he added, "Or maybe something stronger?"

"Yes, I believe I would like some coffee." When Kit started to turn away, the reverend said, "On second thought, you might add just a splash of bourbon."

Sitting at the table, the two men sipped their whiskey-laced coffee in silence for a few moments, then Reverend Gray said, "Even though I believe we leave this life for a better world, I sometimes have a hard time dealing with the mortality of those I serve."

"Yeah, especially a fine woman like Sarah."

"That she is. The finest. And she's lucky to have two daughters so devoted to her care. Folks don't come much better than the three Coleman women."

"I agree." The lump was back in Kit's throat.

"She's so relieved both Angelina and Chloe will have someone to take care of them. I don't know how many times, both today and during my last visit, she told me how much she approves of having you as a son-in-law."

Kit swallowed with some difficulty. If Sarah knew the truth about him, she'd snatch her approval away with record speed.

"And of course, she approves of Jared just as much."

"Who approves of Jared?" Angelina said, passing through the archway into the kitchen.

"Your mother," Reverend Gray replied, pushing away from the table and getting to his feet. "Thanks for the coffee, Kit. I think I'll go back and sit with Sarah for a little while."

After the man left the room, Kit turned to his wife. "You shouldn't be up; you only slept a few minutes."

Angelina managed a smile. "I'm fine. Truly." Seeing the skepticism on his face, she said, "I mean it, I'm fine. So you can stop your worrying."

Kit didn't respond. He couldn't very well tell her he'd worry about her, regardless of the miles separating them, until he drew his final breath. Because if he did, he'd be forced to reveal his reason for making such a statement. And he couldn't tell her of his plans—not yet.

Angelina poured herself a cup of coffee and took a seat at the table. "I was so glad to see you when you got back that I forgot to ask what happened in town?"

"Morris Richfield was the one doing the actual forging of customers' names, but at Elliot Wentworth's behest. Wentworth threatened to take Richfield's family away from him if he didn't follow orders."

"No wonder the poor man went through with it."

"He didn't want to at first, but when the only alternative was financial ruin and the possibility of never seeing his wife and children again, he felt he didn't have a choice."

"How did Mr. Murray get involved?"

"It seems Wentworth enjoyed poker, and unfortunately for his wallet, he enjoyed the game a little too much. He'd run up some sizeable debts at Murray's gambling hall, and when Murray went to him to collect, they worked out a deal. Part of the money Wentworth collected from unsuspecting widows went to pay off the money he owed Murray. Or, as happened in most of the cases, when the widow had no way of paying him, he'd get her to sign a contract with Murray, who in turn reduced Wentworth's debt by a prearranged percentage."

"What a devious mind Elliot Wentworth has, figuring out a way to pay off his debts using someone else's money. What about Mr. Murray? Will he be arrested for his part in this?"

"That depends. If he knew Wentworth was having bank loans forged—which I suspect he did—then he's sure to be arrested as an accomplice. But if he can convince the authorities he knew nothing about the banker's illegal dealings, claiming he was only an unknowing participant, then I reckon he might not face prosecution. That'll be up to the judge."

"So what will happen to the clerk? He was an accomplice, too."

"Yes, but he was coerced into participating in the scheme, and I doubt Murray was. Because Morris agreed to testify against Wentworth, the marshal is going to talk to the judge about waving the forgery charges he faces. I don't think there will be a problem."

"I hope not," Angelina replied. "It sounds like he was just a pawn in Wentworth's plan. What's that rat going to get out of this?"

"Prison time, and he'll probably be ordered to make restitution."

"Serves him right."

"Yeah," Kit said. "It sure does."

The next several days were filled with constant worry over Sarah's worsening condition. She would seem to rally for a few hours, even an entire day. But the improvement was always short-lived. Her breathing became more and more labored, her appetite completely fled, and getting her to swallow even the smallest amount of water happened less frequently.

Kit insisted on taking his turn sitting beside her bed to give Chloe and Angelina some relief. And just like the sisters, he would spend his time in Sarah's room reading aloud, talking to her though she was rarely strong enough to respond, or simply holding her hand.

Watching his mother-in-law lose her battle was hard enough, but seeing what it did to Chloe and Angelina nearly tore him apart. Neither of the young women ate more than several bites of food, and the blue smudges beneath their eyes attested to their lack of sleep.

On the evening of the fourth day since Kit's return from town, he watched Chloe replace Angelina at Sarah's bedside from the bedroom doorway, his brow furrowed with concern for his wife.

He stepped back to allow Angelina to pass in front of him, then followed her down the hall.

"Come on," he said, cupping her elbow with one hand. "You need to get some sleep."

Too weary to argue, she nodded and managed to drag one foot after the other to their bedroom.

Kit helped her out of her clothes, then slipped a nightdress over her head. He lifted the covers and nodded for her to get into bed.

"Aren't you going to lie down with me?" Seeing him hesitate, Angelina said, "Please, Kit. I'd like you to hold me."

He nodded, then moved to his side of the bed, where he removed everything but his drawers, then slipped in beside her. Slipping his left arm under her shoulders, he pulled her close.

"Better?" he whispered, pressing a gentle kiss to her temple.

She nodded against his chest. After a few minutes, she said, "I don't know how much longer she can linger like this."

"I know. Try not to think about it right now. You're exhausted and you've got to get some rest."

"Kit, I . . ." she drew a shuddering breath. "I don't know what I would have done without you these . . ." her voice broke, ". . . these past few days."

"Shh, honey. Don't. Just close your eyes and try to sleep."

Squeezing his eyes closed against the pain ripping through him, he pressed another kiss to her temple, then started rubbing her back with one palm. He moved his hand up, then down her spine, gently kneading her tight muscles with his fingers. A quiver racked her body as she drew another ragged breath, then slowly relaxed before slipping into a deep slumber.

Kit soon followed her into the land of dreamless sleep, her head still on his chest, his arm still wrapped around her waist.

Certain he'd only been asleep for a few minutes, he was jolted awake. Opening his eyes a crack, he glanced toward the window and blinked with surprise. He'd slept longer than he thought; the first blush of dawn was just tinting the sky. Before he could figure out what had disturbed his sleep, Angelina bolted upright.

"What is it?" he said.

"Chloe. I heard Chloe calling me," she replied, scooting over to light the lamp on the bedside table, then swinging her feet to the floor.

She had just slipped into her dressing gown when the door opened.

"Angelina . . ." Chloe called again, her voice thick with tears. "Mama's gone."

"Oh, Chloe, you should have called me sooner."

"There wasn't time. She was breathing real easy one minute, then . . ." she paused to draw a deep breath. "Then the next minute she slipped away from us."

Tears running down her face, Angelina held her arms out to her sister and closed the distance between them. With a sniffle and a hiccup, Chloe stepped into her sister's embrace.

For a moment Kit sat motionless in bed, completely unnerved by the combined sobs and tears of the two women. Then, rising and pulling on his clothes, he crossed the room and wrapped an arm around each of them. "I'm so sorry," he murmured, holding them against his chest in a fierce hug. "I'm so sorry."

When the women quieted, Kit eased his hold, but didn't release them completely. Keeping a hand on each sister's shoulder, he said, "I should go tell Jared, and I'll need to notify Reverend Gray. Will you two be okay if I leave you alone for a little while?"

Both women sniffed loudly, then each nodded.

"Maybe one of Jared's men can fetch the reverend," Chloe said. "That way you can come back with him."

"I'll ask him. But if there's no one he can send, I'll have to go. Understood?"

"Yes, just be careful," Angelina replied, lifting her gaze to meet his. She was very pale, her cheeks tear-stained and her eyes filled with pain.

Pressing his lips to her forehead, he whispered, "I'll be back as soon as I can."

Chapter Twenty-Seven

Kit returned to the ranch less than an hour later, thankful he'd been spared a trip into town. One of Jared's hired hands had been dispatched to find Reverend Gray and arrange for an undertaker to have a coffin delivered, allowing Kit to ride with Jared back to the Diamond C.

After putting their horses in the barn, Kit started across the yard, Jared falling into step beside him.

"The next few days are gonna be real rough on those two gals," Jared said. "It's a damn shame, losing both their father and their mama just a few months apart."

"Yeah, I know," Kit replied, his voice a raspy whisper.

"They're gonna need us more than ever now," Jared added.

Kit nodded, closing his eyes against the raw pain cramping his insides. Yes, Angelina was going to need him, and what did he plan to do? Walk out of her life as soon as possible after her mother had been laid to rest. Sighing, he opened his eyes. But what other choice did he have? Staying any longer than he deemed absolutely necessary would only make it harder on Angelina when he finally did leave.

Realizing Jared was speaking to him, he glanced over at the other man. "Sorry, I . . . uh . . . I guess I was caught up in my own thoughts there for a minute."

"No problem. I was wondering if there's anyone else we should have notified about Sarah's passing."

"She didn't know anyone in town besides Dr. Irvin and Rev-

erend Gray. I told your man to stop by and tell the women Angelina used to work with, so I reckon we've taken care of everyone."

Jared nodded, then made the rest of the walk to the house
in silence.

Reverend Gray stood at the head of the freshly dug grave,
his Bible clasped in his hands. "Thank you for joining us here
today. We have gathered to pay tribute to Sarah Coleman. She
was a very . . ." His voice quavered. "She was a very special
lady, and one we shall all miss greatly." Pausing to regain his
composure, he looked around the grave site at the handful of
mourners attending the service.

He lifted his face to feel the warmth of the afternoon sun, to
look at the deep, clear blue winter sky. This was just the kind
of day Sarah would have enjoyed. How she loved to sit outside
on a warm, sunny afternoon. Calling on his theology school
training, he set aside his own pain at Sarah's passing and continued in a stronger voice. "Though our hearts are heavy at the
loss of a mother and a dear friend, rejoice in the knowledge that
Sarah's pain and suffering have ended, that her passing has
taken her to a pain-free world. For the Lord has taken her into
his care and given her eternal life."

Angelina listened to the reverend eulogize her mother with
dry eyes; after a day and a half of weeping, she had no more
tears to shed. She stood beside Kit, one hand tucked securely
in his. To her left were Chloe and Jared, also holding hands.
On the opposite side of the grave stood Dr. Irvin and his wife,
the two men who worked for Jared, and Jenna.

Dear Jenna. Angelina couldn't believe her friend had made
the trip from town to attend the service for her mother, even
renting a buggy for the long ride. But Angelina was so glad
Jenna had decided to come. Since there'd only been time for
them to exchange a quick hello before the service, Angelina
hoped they'd have a chance to talk later.

Kit's shifting next to her pulled her back to the present. She turned to look up at him. His eyes were bloodshot. Deep lines bracketed his mouth. Since her mother's passing early the morning before, he hadn't left her side for more than a few minutes at a time. As she moved her gaze over his face, her heart nearly burst with love. She knew he grieved for her mother, she could see it in the depths of his eyes. Yet, she saw something else as well, something that had nothing to do with losing his mother-in-law. He still planned on leaving.

Some of the tears she'd shed in the previous twenty-four hours had been for the loss of the man she loved. When he finally told her his plans, which she knew would be soon, she would try to convince him to stay. But there was a very real possibility he wouldn't listen, that her declaration of love would do nothing to change his decision. She inhaled a shuddering breath, praying she had the strength to survive without him.

Reverend Gray ended the service by reading the Twenty-third Psalm. After everyone echoed his Amen, the minister lifted his head and nodded toward Angelina and Chloe.

Angelina pulled her hand free of Kit's and stooped to pick up a handful of soil. She straightened, then tossed the dirt into the yawning hole of the opened grave. The rattle of gravel on the wooden coffin made her flinch, the sound overly loud in the quiet setting beneath a large cottonwood tree. The small knoll not far from the stream behind the ranch house was the place Sarah had selected as her husband's final resting place. And now she was being committed to the same ground.

Angelina's voice was a mere whisper when she said, "Goodbye, Mama. We love you."

She returned to Kit's side, leaning against his solid strength as he put an arm around her shoulders and pulled her close. She looked over at Chloe, giving her a watery smile of encouragement.

Repeating the actions of her sister, Chloe bent to scoop up a handful of earth, then took a step forward to toss the dirt into the grave. Her shoulders rippling with a shudder, she managed to swallow the lump lodged in her throat. "Tell Papa we miss

him, Mama. Just like . . ." she swallowed again. "Just like we
miss you." With a sob, she turned and stumbled into Jared's
arms.

The sorrow enveloping the Diamond C eased over the next
few days, allowing for the daily routine of the ranch to slowly
return to normal. Kit watched Angelina and Chloe lose their
haunted expressions with a silent sigh of relief. They were
bouncing back much faster than he'd anticipated, even smiling and laughing over treasured memories of their parents. If
Angelina continued showing signs of improvement, he would
tell her his plans in a day or two.

Five days after the funeral, Angelina excused herself from the
dinner table, then rose and walked toward the kitchen door.

"Where are y'all going?" Chloe said, watching her sister take
her shawl from a peg.

"For a walk."

"I'll go with you," Kit said, shoving his chair away from the
table. He turned to Jared who had been almost a permanent
fixture around the ranch recently. "Would you mind helping
Chloe clear the table?"

"Sure thing. Then I should be heading home."

"I think I'll ride with you," Chloe said. "It's been a while
since I saw Fortune. Y'all don't mind, do you, Angelina?"

"Of course not. Go on and have a good time."

"Come on, Jared. Let's hurry and take care of these dishes,
so we can get going."

Jared chuckled. "Yes, darlin'. Then how 'bout we race to the
Rocking M?"

"Race?" Chloe's eyes sparkled. "You're on."

Kit helped Angelina with her shawl, then grabbed his jacket
and hat. Stepping outside and closing the door behind them,
he said, "Where do you want to walk?"

"I want to go to Mama's grave. I have some flowers—more
like weeds, actually—that I want to lay on her grave."

He took one of her hands in his, then said, "Okay, let's go."

When they reached the grave site, Angelina carefully laid the bouquet on the mound of dirt covering her mother's grave. Taking a step back, she frowned. "I wish I had some real flowers, instead of these pitiful weeds. Mama loved the flowers we grew in Savannah. We had a beautiful garden, and she used to spend hours every summer sitting among our flower beds." Angelina looked across the foothills. "I hate to disappoint her, but even in the spring there aren't many flowers around here."

Kit pulled her into his arms. "Stop it."

"Stop what."

"Stop torturing yourself by worrying about the flowers you can pick for Sarah's grave. She wouldn't care if you brought flowers or weeds, as long as you're the one who brought them."

"I suppose," she murmured, pressing the side of her face to his chest.

"You and Chloe did a fine job caring for Sarah. No one could have done better than the two of you. Don't ever forget that. I know you'll miss your mother and it'll take a long time for the pain of her passing to fade, but at least you won't have to live with the guilt of knowing you didn't take good care of her."

Angelina lifted her head and leaned back within the circle of his arms to look up into his face.

"Why would you say that?"

"What?"

"That at least Chloe and I won't have to live with the guilt. We know we did our best for Mama, so there's no reason for us to feel guilty."

When he didn't respond, she said, "That little speech wasn't about Chloe and me, was it? You were talking about yourself."

Kit drew a long slow breath. While he didn't relish what would unfold in the coming minutes, he knew the time had come to tell her the whole story. At last he said, "Come on, let's walk for a while."

He led her from her parents' graves and headed down toward the stream. They followed the meandering streambed deeper into the foothills for a short distance, stopping beneath a stand of cottonwood trees. In the summer the spot would be shaded by a thick canopy of leaves, but in early December the bare branches allowed the winter sun to warm the boulders scattered among the trees.

Kit directed Angelina to sit on one of the boulders, then sat down beside her. He stared up the arroyo for a few minutes, watching the shadows cast by the bare cottonwoods dance and sway over the rocky ground.

Angelina reached over and placed a hand on his arm. "Kit, you're planning on leaving, aren't you?"

He turned to look at her, his brows pulled together and lips pressed together in a firm line. Now that the moment was upon him, he couldn't make himself say the words. He started to shake his head, but the tightening of her fingers on his arm stopped him.

"Don't deny it, Kit. I know something's been bothering you. I saw it in your face days ago."

When he didn't respond, she said, "Are you going to tell me why?"

"Yes, you deserve to know that much." He shifted his gaze back to the rocky terrain, then began speaking in a low voice. "I grew up on a cattle ranch along the Concho River. Bethany's family moved to San Angelo when I was sixteen. She was two years younger, and I think I fell in love with her the first time I saw her. I proposed two years later, and as soon as she turned eighteen we were married."

Angelina fought to control the incredible pain his words inflicted, determined not to do or say anything that would halt his discourse. She clenched her hands in her lap and tried to concentrate on what he was saying.

"I wanted to try something besides cattle ranching so I decided to become a lawman. My first job was working for the city marshal in Fort Worth. Thad was born shortly after we moved there. Bethany wasn't very happy with city living, but I convinced her to stick it out for a while longer so I could get enough experience to look for something else. After we'd been there a couple years, I started sending telegrams to some of the smaller towns around the state, asking to be considered for any future openings. In the summer of '79, I received a wire that I'd been elected Sheriff of Taylor County."

"I don't know much about Texas. Where's Taylor County?"

"You came through it on your trip from Georgia. Do you remember passing through Abilene?"

At her nod, he said, "Abilene was founded after the railroad selected the route for their tracks. Now it's the biggest town in the county, but while I was sheriff, Buffalo Gap was the largest as well as the county seat. Bethany, Thad, and I had a small place not far from Buffalo Gap, and we both thought it was a good place to raise a family. Thad turned four that next spring, and Bethany worried about never being able to have more children. She was afraid I would be disappointed in her. I told her it didn't matter if our family never got any bigger, but she wouldn't believe me. When she became pregnant the next year, she was ecstatic. I'd never seen her so happy. Then my stupidity took Thad and Bethany and . . . and the unborn child she wanted so much."

He fell silent, the muscles in his jaw working as he stared straight ahead.

"Tell me what happened, Kit." Though Angelina didn't want to hear any more about the first woman Kit had loved and still mourned, she knew his inner wounds would never heal unless he talked about what had caused them.

"One of the saloon owners was having trouble with a customer who got drunk and turned nasty. I threw the man out on the street and told him to find a bed somewhere or else he could sleep it off in jail. He staggered away, so I figured he took my advice and by morning would be heading out of town. The next evening he went back to the same saloon. When the bartender refused to serve him, the man pulled a knife and threatened to use it if the bartender didn't hand over a bottle of whiskey. I arrived before anyone got hurt and hauled him outside. I told him I didn't know what was eating at him nor did I care, but the folks in Buffalo Gap didn't take kindly to strangers making trouble. I went with him to retrieve his horse, then escorted him to the edge of town, where I made it clear I never wanted to see his face in Buffalo Gap or Taylor County again.

"He took exception to my throwing him out of town and reached for his knife. When I drew my gun and leveled the barrel at him, he thought twice and moved his hand away from the knife handle. He finally rode away, but not before he cursed me up one side and down the other. I'll never forget his final words. He looked me square in the eye and said, 'You better stick close to that wife and kid you're so fond of, 'cause they ain't long for this world.' "

"Oh, dear God," Angelina whispered. "He didn't . . ."

"Yeah, he did. I figured he was just taking out his anger by saying something he knew would rile me, so I didn't put much stock in his threats. I should have arrested him when I had the chance. But I was so sure he'd leave the county, I didn't even tell Bethany. If I had, at least she would have kept a gun close by. Maybe then she would've had a chance against that son-of-a-bitch."

The hard edge to his voice sent shivers up Angelina's spine. "What happened?" she said, preparing herself for the worst.

He took a deep breath as if steeling himself for what came next. "Just to be safe, I stuck around home for a week, but when there was no sign anyone was watching my moves, I figured he was long gone. Since I'd been neglecting my job, I left the following day to ride up to Phantom Hill in the next county to take care of some business. Whenever I traveled that far from home, I always stayed the night and returned in the morning.

"But something bothered me all afternoon, something I couldn't put my finger on. I only knew I had to get back to Bethany and Thad. As soon as I completed my business, I started home. It was past midnight when I arrived at the house. The parlor looked like it had been turned upside down and shaken. The other rooms hadn't been disturbed, but Bethany and Thad were gone and the back door was wide open.

"I lit a lantern and tried to pick up a trail. An hour later I found them. Bethany was . . ." He paused to draw another deep breath.

"Kit, you don't have to go on."

"Yes, I do. I . . . I've never told anyone the entire story. Bethany was lying against a tree, Thad clutched in her arms. He was dead. His throat had been slit. Bethany had been cut several times, but not so severely to cause a quick death. Clinging to life, she had prayed I would find them before it was too late. The loss of blood was making her delirious and she talked in disjointed ramblings. But I managed to piece together what happened.

"Apparently the bastard had been watching the house ever since I ran him out of town. On the day I left for Phantom Hill, he must have followed me awhile to make sure I wouldn't be returning right away. When he went back to our house in the afternoon, Bethany said he told her he knew I was miles away by then and couldn't save my family. She fought him as long as she could, but he only laughed at her efforts to stop him. When he got tired of the game, he hauled her and Thad out the back door and away from the house.

"She . . ." He squeezed his eyes closed against the painful memories swamping him. After a minute, he swallowed then resumed his recitation. "She told me after he took his knife to Thad the bastard turned on her. She finally realized the only way she could survive was to pretend to be dead. When the man left, she waited as long as she dared, then crawled over to Thad's body. He was already gone, yet she continued to hold him, even when . . . even when she lost the baby."

Angelina's stomach lurched. Swallowing hard, she swayed and nearly fainted. Placing her hands on the boulder at her sides, she gripped the stone as hard as she could.

"As Bethany died in my arms, she apologized to me for losing both our children." His voice rose sharply. "God, I couldn't believe she would actually blame herself. I was the one at fault. I was the one who killed my children and my wife, as surely as if I'd used the knife on them myself."

"Kit, no! That's not true."

"Yes, it is true." He turned to look at her, the hard look in his eyes boring into her. "Didn't you hear what I said? I didn't take his threats seriously enough. I didn't stay around to protect my family. I went off and left them alone while a deranged killer watched my every move. I'm the one who has to live with the guilt of knowing I was responsible for their deaths."

"But—"

"Let me finish." When she nodded, he said, "I took Bethany and Thad back to San Angelo for burial, then I went after him. I tracked him for a month before I caught up with the sorry bastard. When he saw me, his face twisted in a sinister grin as he reached for his knife. I was ready to fight; I'd thought of little else for weeks. He outweighed me and was deadly with that knife, but he made a mistake and I ended up with the weapon. He tried to get away, but I was quicker. I pinned him to the ground, then killed him with his own knife."

"Is that when you got the scar?"

"Yeah. He managed to cut me before I got the knife away from him and plunged it into his heart. I was a sheriff, sworn to uphold the law, yet I took a life like it meant nothing."

"But he pulled his knife on you. You were only defending yourself."

"But, I should have taken him in. Once I disarmed him, the fight should have ended right then."

"You don't know that. He might not have given up, but continued to fight. He could have ended up killing you. Don't second guess your actions, Kit."

"I'm not. What's done is done. I only told you everything so you'd know why I have to leave. You deserve a better husband than me—one who can protect his family. Don't you understand, Angelina? I'm not worthy of you or your love."

Chapter Twenty-Eight

Angelina sat in stunned silence, digging her fingernails into the boulder. She knew the deaths of Kit's first wife and son had been a devastating blow, yet she hadn't been prepared for the reality of the situation. She finally understood the source of the pain she'd seen on his face and heard in his voice so many times. No wonder he suffered nightmares.

Forcing her hands to relax, she turned to look at him. "Kit you're not to blame for what happened to your family."

He shifted his gaze in her direction, his eyes a cold, chilling blue. "The hell I'm not." His voice was as icy as his glare.

"Listen to me. You couldn't have known that man would do what he threatened. People make threats all the time, but they never actually carry them out." When he started to open his mouth, she held up one hand. "I'm not through. Okay, so you misjudged the man. You made a mistake, a very costly one. But you can't hold yourself accountable for something you had no control over, and you can't live the rest of your life filled with guilt. It's destroying you, can't you see that?"

When he didn't respond, but continued to stare at her, she said, "Don't you remember what you told me on our way home from town a few weeks ago?"

His eyebrows pulling together in a frown, he said, "I remember what I told you, but that doesn't have anything to do with me."

"But it does. What you told me also applies to you. You have

to come to terms with your past. You said I had to forgive myself then move forward with my life. Now it's your turn to do
the same. Once you've forgiven yourself, then you'll be able to
set your pain aside and remember your first wife and son with
only love, not the guilt-ridden love that's eating away at your
insides."

He shook his head. "You make it sound so easy, but it doesn't
work that way."

"I know it won't be easy. But, I'd help you, Kit. I'd be there
every step of the way to get you through this . . . that is, if you
wanted me to."

He gave her a wistful smile. "I know you would, Angel.
You'll make some lucky man a wonderful wife."

"I want to be *your* wife, no one else's."

"Even after what I just told you?"

"Of course I do. I love you, Kit. You're the man I want to
spend the rest of my life with. But if you truly don't feel the same
way, then I . . . I guess there's nothing I can say to keep you
here."

"Angelina, I do love you, I want you to know that. Some of
what you said makes sense, and I promise to think about it. But
I can't do that here. I have to get away from the ranch, so I can
clear my head and decide what to do with my life. As soon as
we go back to the house, I'll pack my things."

She nodded, the enormous lump clogging her throat preventing her from speaking. Sliding off the boulder, she got to
her feet and pulled her shawl more tightly around her shoulders. She felt a sudden chill that had nothing to do with the air's
temperature.

Less than an hour later, Angelina stood on the porch watching Kit lead Sid from the barn. In spite of her best efforts, she
couldn't blink back her tears. Brushing the moisture from her
cheeks, she gave him a tremulous smile.

"If I don't return by the end of the week, I won't be back."

"Okay." She glanced around the yard. "If you don't come
back, I'll probably go back to Georgia. I'm only telling you that
in case you ever need to get in touch with me."

"But what about Chloe? She and Jared are still planning on getting married and living on his ranch. Would you really move that far away from your only family?"

"There's no way I could run this ranch by myself, and besides . . ." she pressed a fist to her mouth to stop the trembling of her lips. "Staying here would be too painful."

"Angel, I'm so sorry. I wish . . . well, it doesn't matter what I wish anymore. I'd better go."

She stepped closer, rose on her toes, and brushed a brief kiss across his mouth. "I've laid my ghosts to rest. Now you need to do the same. Take care of yourself, Kit."

Before the tightness in his chest eased enough for him to speak, she whirled around and nearly ran back into the house. He stared at the closed door for a moment, then exhaled a weary breath. Moving to Sid's side, he stuck his foot in the stirrup, swung into the saddle, and never looking back, kicked the gelding into a trot down the trail to the main road.

When Chloe returned to the ranch several hours later, she found Angelina curled up in one of the parlor chairs, her eyes puffy and red.

"What is it, Angelina? I thought y'all got over crying for Mama."

"I did. My tears aren't for her."

"Well, are y'all going to tell me why you're crying?"

"Kit left a couple hours ago."

"Left? Where did he go?"

"I don't know, but I don't think he'll be back."

Chloe dropped onto the sofa facing her sister. "You don't think he'll be back, like in *never?*"

Angelina nodded.

"I think y'all had better start from the beginning and tell me what this is about."

"Yes, you're right." Angelina paused to gather her thoughts, then she said, "When I went to El Paso to work for Mr. Murray, I wasn't a piano player in a saloon theatre. I worked in the Murray House which is one of the many bordellos in town."

"A bordello?" Chloe's eyes went wide. "You weren't one of the women who . . . you know?"

"Not at first." Ignoring her sister's gasp, she said, "I played the piano in the main parlor for a few months, but I wasn't paying off the contract I signed fast enough on piano player wages, so I asked if I could become one of the lovelies—that's the name given to the Murray House prostitutes."

"Oh, Angelina, how could you do such a thing?"

"Chloe, I was worried sick about you and Mama out here all by yourselves and Mama's health getting worse all the time. I didn't see any other choice. Anyway, on the night I was to make my debut, I met Kit."

"Don't tell me, he thought you were a—"

"Yes, that's exactly what he thought. Now stop interrupting so I can finish telling you my story before I start crying again."

Over the next few minutes, Angelina recited the events of the past two months, then concluded by saying, "So now you know everything, including why Kit decided he had to leave."

"But if he loves you, surely he'll come back."

"I wish I could believe that. But he's burdened by so much guilt, and he's convinced he isn't worthy of me." She managed a weak smile. "And to think a few weeks ago, I thought I wasn't worthy of him because I worked in a bordello and planned to become a prostitute. What a tangled mess my life has become. The only thing I can hope for is that Kit's love for me will be strong enough to survive everything pressing down on him."

Kit stopped in El Paso long enough to buy a few supplies. Wanting no distractions, he left town in search of a place to camp. The Huego Mountains, twenty-five miles to the east, had a good water supply so he headed in their direction. He arrived at his destination well past dark, and made camp near one of the water-filled natural rock tanks.

After starting a fire and eating a quickly prepared meal, he stretched out on his bedroll. Now that he'd found the solitude he'd been craving, he realized he no longer enjoyed having only his horse for company. The ground was harder than he remembered; the silence grated on his nerves. When falling asleep proved impossible, he finally gave up and sat by his campfire staring across the desert toward the Franklin Mountains—toward Angelina.

His heart cramped with love just thinking her name. Pinching the bridge of his nose, he knew he would love her for the rest of his days. But what of his love for Bethany? Turning his search for answers inward, he carefully analyzed his feelings.

He still loved Bethany—he always would—but without his being aware of it, that love had changed into a sweeter, gentler love, not the wild, vibrant love he felt for Angelina. A small part of his heart would always belong to his first wife, but she was gone and there was nothing he could do to bring her back. He had to turn his attention to the living, to the love occupying the rest of his heart: his love for his present wife.

He shook his head with disbelief. Jared had been right. During the past few weeks, Kit had been mentally hitting himself over the head for thinking he was betraying Bethany by loving Angelina. Now he knew that wasn't the case at all.

Having resolved one issue, his thoughts turned to earlier in the day and his soul-baring conversation with Angelina. Had he been wrong to wear his guilt like a shroud for the past five years? He spent a long time thinking about what he'd told Angelina after their last trip into town and how she tried to apply some of what he'd said to his situation. Was forgiving himself the key to finding inner peace?

He pondered that question and many others throughout the night. By the time the sun rose above the eastern horizon signaling the beginning of a new day, Kit was prepared to embark on a new beginning of his own.

Though he'd recently wished for things to be as they once were, he now welcomed the changes in his life. For the first time in many weeks, he no longer felt mixed up inside, no longer felt confused by his conflicting emotions. His thoughts clearer than they'd been in years, he was prepared to put the past to rest and get on with his life. Reaching that conclusion was like having an enormous weight lifted off his shoulders.

Absolutely sure of what he wanted, he moved to where he'd dropped his saddlebags the night before. He opened one flap and carefully removed the package wrapped in brown paper.

Angelina sat at the table watching dust motes float through the shaft of late afternoon sunlight pouring in the kitchen window. Kit had only been gone a day, but it felt like a year. If he didn't return she had no idea how she could pick up the pieces of her broken heart and get on with her life. But she meant what she'd told him—if he chose to make the separation permanent, she would leave the Diamond C. Though she was not at all enthusiastic about returning to Savannah, at least she knew people there—people who didn't know about her sojourn in a bawdy house. That was one plus.

She heaved a weary sigh, thinking she should get up and do something to take her mind off her future. Deciding to make an apple pie, she rose from the table and gathered the ingredients she'd need.

Once the crust was made, she began mixing the dried apples and spices for the filling when she suddenly straightened. Artemis's excited barks drifted in from the yard. Wiping her hands on a towel, she went into the parlor and peeked through the lace curtains at the window.

She saw the cloud of dust first, then heard the staccato beating of hooves. When the horse came into view, a black and white piebald, her breath caught in her throat. As she squinted to make out the rider, her brow wrinkled in concentration. She was certain the horse was Sid, but the man on the gelding's back wasn't wearing black.

"His shirt is blue," she murmured. "Oh, my God. It's blue! Chloe. Chloe! Kit's back!"

Not bothering with a shawl, she jerked open the front door. Lifting her skirts, she crossed the porch and broke into a run.

She was halfway across the yard when Kit pulled Sid to a skidding stop a few feet away.

He leaped from the saddle and closed the distance between them. Wrapping his arms around her waist, he lifted her off her feet and held her firmly against his chest. Her name on his lips, he lowered his head to seek the sweetness of her mouth. After thoroughly kissing her and being thoroughly kissed in return, he eased his hold and set her back on her feet.

She looked up at him, her face flushed. Her voice sounded breathless when she said, "I was so afraid you wouldn't come back."

"I know. I'm sorry I frightened you, but I needed time to put everything in perspective, to untangle my twisted thoughts. You were right, Angelina. I have to put my guilt over my part in the deaths of Bethany and Thad to rest. And to do that I have to forgive myself."

"Have you?"

"Not completely. But I know I can, if you're still willing to help."

"Of course, I will. I told you, I love you, and that means helping you any way I can."

"In that case, there's something else you can help me with right now. Something that will require at least several hours of your time."

Her eyebrows rose. "And what might that be?"

He grinned. "Help me make up for neglecting my wife's needs. Do you think you could help me out?"

The flare of desire in her eyes was all the answer he needed. Bending to slip one arm beneath her knees, he swung her into his arms and started toward the porch.

"But, what about Chloe? She's in the house."

"No, she's not. She's right behind you."

Looking over her shoulder to find her sister standing a few feet away, Angelina's already flushed cheeks burned all the more.

"You'll have to excuse us, Chloe," Kit said, walking past his smiling sister-in-law. "Angel and I have some catching up to do."

"Y'all go right ahead and *catch up*, if that's what you want to call it. I'll put Sid in the barn, then I think I'll ride over to Jared's ranch."

A few minutes later, Kit had Angelina stripped to the skin and ensconced in their bed. His hands shaking in anticipation, he finally managed to get out of his own clothes, then climbed in beside her.

Propping himself up on one elbow, he leaned closer. His mouth just inches above hers, he whispered, "Forgive me for hurting you." He touched her upper lip with his tongue. "I never meant to." His tongue laved across her bottom lip. "I hope you believe that."

"Yes, I believe you. Now stop teasing and kiss me."

He chuckled. "Yes, ma'am." He lowered his head to do her bidding. After a long, mind-boggling kiss, he pulled away, his chest heaving. "Your kisses drive me wild, do you know that?"

She nodded. "Yours do the same to me."

When he started to move between her legs, she grabbed his shoulders. "Wait. Everything happened so fast that I didn't get a chance to use—"

His fingers pressed to her lips halted her words. "As long as it's all right with you, honey, I don't want you to be protected."

She stared up at him, the implication of his words clear. Tears of joy stinging the backs of her eyes, she whispered, "Yes, it's definitely all right."

Much later, after Kit had thoroughly taken care of his neglected wife's needs, as well as his own, he rolled away from her and sat up.

"What is it, Kit?"

"I just remembered, I have a letter to write."

"A letter!" Angelina watched with disbelief as her husband pulled on his trousers. "You'd rather write a letter than stay in bed with your wife?"

He glanced toward the bed, smiling at her languid pose, hair splayed across the pillow, skin flushed from both exertion and gratification.

"You know the answer to that, Angel. But this letter is long past due."

She stretched then rolled onto her side. "Don't be long."

Moving to the bed, he pressed a kiss on her forehead, then eased the door open and left the room.

Compared to his first attempt to write Blaine a month earlier, Kit's words flowed easily this time—the direct result of having come to terms with his past and the love of a whiskey-eyed woman. After apologizing for the tardiness of his letter, Kit said he was doing as Blaine suggested: letting go of his guilt and getting on with his life. Then he went on to explain the events of the past several months which led up to his making the decision to settle down with his new wife.

Folding the sheets of paper, Kit smiled. The look on Blaine's face when he read the letter would be priceless. Slipping the folded pages into an envelope, Kit reminded himself to talk to Angelina about the promise he'd made Blaine. If he and Angelina didn't visit San Angelo very soon, he had no doubt his friend would take matters into his own hands. The impatient Blaine Delaney would head for El Paso to see for himself if Kit had changed as much as his letter intimated.

Kit had just finished addressing the envelope when he heard a noise behind him. Turning toward the parlor, he found his wife standing in the archway, her hair a tousled mass around her shoulders. She had slipped into her dressing gown, but hadn't bothered to tie the belt securely. The tip of one pert breast, her sleek belly, and a creamy thigh were visible through the gaping fabric.

Pushing a strand of hair behind one ear, she gave him a pouty look, then said, "You're neglecting your wife's needs again."

A smile teasing his mouth, he shoved his chair away from the table and rose. Keeping his gaze linked to hers, he crossed the room and stopped in front of her. "Really? So soon?"

She nodded, a sultry smile curving her lips. "So, what are y'all going to do about it?"

Bending close, he whispered, "We're going back into our bedroom, then we'll get rid of this." He tugged on the belt of her dressing gown. "And then I'm going to make love to the woman who brought this man back from a lonely, miserable life."

"I love you, Kit." Her softly spoken words brought a lump to his throat.

He pressed a gentle kiss on her parted lips. "I know, and I love you. I'm a very lucky man. I found my own angel. Dancer's Angel."

Epilogue

Angelina bent to place the bouquet of poppies on her mother's grave, then lay another bunch of the golden flowers on her father's grave. "I'm so glad we had enough rain this spring for the poppies to bloom. Mama would have loved seeing how the meadow looks like a carpet of gold."

Straightening, she moved to stand beside her husband. "It doesn't seem possible Mama and Papa have been gone five years."

"I know," Kit replied. "It seems like only yesterday I first saw you come down the stairs of the Murray House. One look at you and my life suddenly turned upside down."

She looked up at him. "You don't regret going to the Murray House that night, do you?"

"Not in the least. If I hadn't, I might never have gotten over the notion no one should have to look at my scar, or come to terms with my guilt about Bethany and Thad, or found out it was okay for me to love again."

She smiled, lifting a hand to stroke the side of his face.

"What about you?" he said, kissing her palm. "Do you have any regrets?"

"Not a one. Getting over the stigma of having worked in a bawdy house was hard. But the folks in town were a little more forgiving after Elliot Wentworth was arrested and word got around about what he'd done. The members of the Ladies Aid Society have never mentioned my past since they asked me to join. And as for the people who can't forget where I worked, I decided a long time ago they aren't worth worrying about."

He nodded, then dropped his arm around her shoulder. "Do you want to go back to the house?"

"No, let's walk down to the stream."

Kit led them down the hillside, then along the banks of the stream swollen with the spring rains. "How things have changed since the first time we saw each other. We've enlarged the Diamond C twice and increased the size of our herd from two hundred head to nearly a thousand."

"That prize bull you bought from Blaine four years ago should get the credit for increasing the size of the herd rather than either of us."

Kit chuckled. "Yeah, guess he should. Does that mean I get the credit for increasing the size of our family?"

"Not necessarily. If it were up to me, I'd have been willing to have more than two babies in five years."

"Oh, no, you don't. Don't start on me again, Angel. Having babies is too hard on a woman, and I wasn't about to risk your health by getting you with child every year. You know that's why I insisted you continue using your protection."

She smiled up at him. "I know. I was just trying to get a rise out of you."

He grinned, the dimple she loved appearing in his left cheek. "That's easy, honey." He winked. "You know all you have to do is touch me, or kiss me, and I rise to the occasion."

She jabbed her elbow into his ribs, but couldn't prevent a laugh from slipping out. "You're terrible."

"Yes, but you love me anyway," he replied, stopping and turning so they faced each other.

"Yes, I love you," she murmured. "More and more every day."

"And, I love you." He lowered his face and captured her mouth in a heated kiss. When he pulled away a moment later, his breathing was slightly erratic. "You still drive me wild."

She gave him an impish grin. "I know."

He wrapped his arms around her waist and held her close.

His chin resting on top of her head, he said, "Do you think we should go over to the Rocking M and check on the kids? Chloe may be ready to tear her hair out by now."

Angelina smiled against his chest. Their three-year-old daughter Sarah, named for the child's grandmother, and their one-year-old son Kyle could be a handful. But Chloe had just returned from a trip back East to attend a seminar featuring one of the top veterinarians in the country and wanted to spend some time with her niece and nephew.

"No, they'll be fine. Jared will be there to help, so y'all don't have to worry."

"Since they won't be bringing Sarah and Kyle back until after supper, what would you like to do this afternoon?"

"It's an awfully warm day. I was thinking I'd like to take a long, relaxing bath." Soon after Kit conquered his inner demons and returned to the ranch to stay, he'd converted the storeroom in their house to a bathroom. Of all the improvements he'd made around the ranch, having a real bathtub was the one Angelina appreciated most.

"Umm, sounds like a good idea. Tell you what, how about we race back to the house, and the winner gets to use the bathtub first?"

She pushed away from his chest and took a step back. Her eyes twinkling with mischief, she said, "I have a better idea."

"Really?" One of his eyebrows arched. "And what might that be?"

"How about we forget the race, walk back to the house to save our energy, then share the tub?"

Kit gave a bark of laughter, then said, "You're right, Angel, that's a better idea. A whole lot better."

Dear Reader:

I hope you enjoyed reading about Angelina and Kit as much I enjoyed telling their story. If you're interested in learning more about the history of El Paso, I highly recommend the following books: *Pass of the North: Four Centuries on the Rio Grande* Volume I by C.L. Sonnichsen and *The Gentlemen's Club: The Story of Prostitution in El Paso* by H. Gordon Frost. Both books are wonderful reading as well as excellent narratives of El Paso's past.

My next release will be a novella in Zebra's 1996 Deck The Halls Anthology. My story, "The Christmas Portrait," takes place in Galveston just after the Civil War and is about a love so strong that nothing can destroy it—not even death. The anthology will be in stores in mid-November of this year.

I'm currently working on a trilogy called the Texas Healing Women. These books chronicle the progression of medicine in west Texas through three generations of women in one family during the last half of the nineteenth century. The first book, *Texas Silver*, is the story of Karina Valdez, a half-Mescalero Apache medicine woman also known as Silver Eagle, and Rafe Tucker, a veteran of the Mexican war looking for hidden treasure in mountains sacred to the Mescalero. I hope you'll watch for my Texas Healing Women trilogy, beginning with *Texas Silver*, an August '97 release, followed by *Texas Jade* and *Texas Indigo*.

I love to hear from readers, so please write and tell me what you think of *Dancer's Angel*. I promise to answer, and I'll also send you an autographed bookmark and my current newsletter.

Write to: P.O. Box 384 Paw Paw, MI 49079-0384

—Holly Harte